MW01688214

The Cast Key

To Marijke —

I sure do love Yvonne!

Donna Van Cleve

Books in the Taylor Family Saga

Grace Falling Like Rain
Mercy's Face
Torn Asunder
Anchor Point
The Last Key

The Last Key

Donna Van Cleve

Two Story Publishing House
Hutto, Texas

The Last Key
Published by
Two Story Publishing House
P.O. Box 482
Hutto, Texas 78634

www.donnavancleve.com
Email: donna@donnavancleve.com

Publisher's Cataloging-in-Publication Data

Van Cleve, Donna C.
The Last Key / Donna Van Cleve
320p. cm.
ISBN 978-1-936816-01-9 (pb)
1. Galveston – Texas – History – Fiction. 2. Hurricanes – Galveston – Texas – Fiction. 3. Romance – Fiction. 4. Prostitution – Galveston – Fiction. 5. Christian— Love Stories – Fiction.

2011920006

On the back cover: doorway background photo courtesy of Library of Congress Prints & Photographs Division.
Panoramic cover photo courtesy of the Galveston Historical Foundation & Eloise Howell

Acknowledgments

Thank you to the Author of Creation
for your guidance, inspiration,
& prompting me to finish these stories
for your purpose, honor & glory.
I trust you with all my heart
& attempt to lean not on my own understanding.
I try to acknowledge You in all my ways
& trust You to direct my paths.
Proverbs 3:5-6

Thank you, Vanessa, Jonathan, & Van
for your part in creating the cover

Thank you, Jeanne Sparlin, for the use of your
beautiful, turn-of-the-century home in Taylor, Texas
in the cover photos

My appreciation to Casey Greene & the
Galveston & Texas Historical Center
at the Rosenberg Library in
Galveston, Texas

Thank you, Denise Alexander with the
Galveston Historical Foundation, for your timely help
& part in the cover design

Thank you to Christy Anderson for sharing the story of
your husband's Galveston ancestor—a trolley driver who, along with his
family, spent the night of the storm on the roof of a streetcar

Thank you again, CJ, for making the blind spots visible.
Your hard work is so appreciated.

Thank you, Christy Roeder, for your valuable insight.

For my mother, Isla,
Whose eyes first saw this story;
My best and worst attempts at anything in life
Find safe harbor with you,
Along with my pieced and quilted heart.

I love your intelligence & humor & generosity;
You've taught me so much
By how you've lived your life,
More so than words;
Much more so than words.

I still see you vibrant & beautiful,
And that won't change,
Even when our roles reverse;
You've always been strong for us;
It's our turn now to be strong for you

I still hear you,
I've not forgotten your voice;
It lives in my memories
And there it will remain
Until it's perfectly restored on the other side.

I love hanging out with you,
Even in the storms.
No matter who gets there first,
Remember our date by the gate.
And until then, I'll walk side by side with you.

The Taylor Family – 1890

Matthew Taylor married to
Julia Taylor nee Stockton

Children:	Grandchildren:
Matt married to Catherine	Tres, William, Michael, Robert, & Timbo
Jenny married to Marcus Kimball	Josh, Luke, Maggie, & Clifford
Justin married to Allie nee Blake	Grace, Max, Bradley, & Mary J.
Jimmy married to Mercy nee Locke	Jack, Mae, & Biriney
Faith married to Ethan Murray	Caitlin/Katie (deceased), Ella Vae, Cele, & Sam

Chapter 1

June of 1890… Grace, Texas

Grace rolled her eyes and stifled a groan. Her cousin Maggie sighed as she and her two friends peeked around the door of the barn at the shirtless man working with the horse in one of the pens.

She couldn't believe this was the "surprise" her cousin Maggie wanted to show her. Grace stepped away from them and climbed the ladder to the hayloft where she could hide. She would not lower herself to participate in such silly girl frolics. Other than her two younger brothers, and they didn't count, she'd never seen a grown man without his shirt on—other than her father, though rarely, and that didn't count either. She'd never looked at a man the way Maggie ogled him.

Grace stepped quietly across the wood-plank floor to the loft opening that looked down on the big pen. From this vantage point she could watch silently, unseen. But not on purpose, she assured herself.

They said he was a college man, but she saw not one bit of softness about him like the educated men she knew. He looked like he was very familiar with hard work. His hair reflected an auburn tint and was a little long and unruly. His face was rugged and tanned down to a distinct V on his neck, the place where his shirts buttoned to. Her eyes traveled down to his chest and flat stomach, making her cheeks burn hot. She turned her head away, embarrassed, feeling like she was trespassing on his privacy.

What was Maggie thinking?!

The girls snickered below, and she looked down at the man again. He must have heard them because a scowl appeared on his face as he tied the horse's reins to a fence post and started walking towards the barn. Grace heard muffled screams and the sounds of the girls scurrying through the wide alley beneath her to the front of the barn and out the door.

She watched him grab his shirt off the fence and push his arms through the sleeves without breaking stride. He still frowned, and she realized then that she couldn't climb down from the loft without being seen, so she stayed put. Well, not exactly. She crept to the inside ledge of the hayloft so she could see what he was up to. She could still hear Maggie and the others laughing as they ran back towards town, but the sound stopped abruptly when he pulled the barn doors to with a slam and latched it from the inside.

He turned around and walked back across the barn. Grace tiptoed across the hayloft to watch him come back outside.

But he didn't.

She stepped back and held her breath, trying to hear what else he was doing. She dropped down on her knees and quietly brushed away the hay so she could peek between the boards, when the ladder creaked. She looked up to see his head at the top of the ladder.

Grace scooted backed into the shadows, hoping he wouldn't see her. He climbed the rest of the way and stepped off the ladder onto the loft floor—he hadn't even bothered to button his shirt.

Then he spoke. "I know you're up here."

She shut her eyes, willing herself to disappear, to drop through the cracks—anything but face him.

"Come on out." He put his hand up to shade his eyes from the bright glare of the loft opening.

Grace felt like she had rocks in her stomach. How could she explain what she was doing up here? She looked around for an escape, but the only way out was the hayloft opening. To the right of it, she saw a couple of ropes hanging on a hook and realized the ropes were attached to a beam mounted on the outside of the barn. A way out! She told herself she could do it; she and her brothers used to swing on the rope from the hayloft to the ground in their barn back at home in Dalton.

He spotted her and started across the loft.

Grace stood quickly to keep from losing her nerve and glanced at him.

He stopped in his tracks. "Katie?"

She turned and stepped towards the loft opening and reached for the ropes.

"What are you doing?" he yelled.

She grabbed them and swung out of the loft, but the momentum brought her back to hit the barn wall and then away again. She lost her grip on one of the ropes and began falling like a rock, and realized in a split moment that it was actually one rope sliding like lightning through a pulley. She grasped at the other half flying up as fast as she was falling down, but it just slid through her hand, burning it.

Something hit the ropes hard above her, which jerked everything to a stop. The jolt caused her to lose her grasp, and she fell the last few feet to the ground where she landed very unladylike on her backside.

Grace looked up and saw him working his way down the ropes towards her, so she hiked up her skirt and petticoat and jumped to her feet and ran like a mad bull was after her.

She climbed the fence and fell over the top of it, but that hardly slowed her down. She didn't know where she was going—she simply had to get away from there. She ran blindly towards the trees, hoping she could lose him and never have to face him again. She ran into the trees and undergrowth until she thought her lungs would burst. She hoped she was heading towards the river, which would eventually lead her back to her grandmother's house.

She fought her way through some prickly bushes and suddenly stepped off into nothing. She hit the ground hard and felt something pop in her right foot before pitching forward onto her stomach. She lay there trying to catch her breath for a moment, and then rolled over and found herself sprawled in the bottom of a dry creek bed. The steep bank stood taller than Grace.

She could hear him crashing through the brush above her, so she sat up and tried to stand. But when she put weight on her right foot, she collapsed in pain. She growled in frustration and started crawling away. Suddenly he was flying above her, yelling when he discovered the ground had dropped beneath him. He landed in the same spot she did, but somehow he rolled and stood to his feet in one graceful movement.

Grace turned over and sat there staring at him as he looked around wildly. His chest heaved in and out, and his eyes had a haunted look about them as he finally focused on her, seeming to recognize her for the briefest moment. Then the recognition faded as he squinted and frowned at her.

"What in the hell were you doing back there? Were you trying to kill yourself?"

Grace's answer was to drop her face in her hands and cry.

She always cried when she didn't know what else to do, and she had no idea what to do in this situation. She felt utterly embarrassed getting caught watching him with those other silly girls. And she wasn't a silly girl, but she was the one who got caught. Was that fair? And why hadn't he gotten around to buttoning his shirt?

"Ah, crud," he said under his breath. He knelt down in front of her. "Don't… don't cry. Are you all right?" he asked, his voice sounding more concerned now than mad.

Grace tried to breathe between the sobs and nodded her head as she wiped the tears away. But she couldn't look at his face so close to her own.

He touched her right hand. "You're bleeding."

She looked at the scratches on her hand and noticed her left hand was burning, too, as she turned it over to see a nasty rope burn.

"Why did you jump out of the loft? Didn't you realize how high up you were?"

"I didn't want to face you," she said just above a whisper.

"Am I that frightening?"

She shook her head, but she still couldn't look him in the face. "Maggie made us come, and I didn't want to spy on you."

He sighed like an old man. "Maggie's been pestering me for years, but who are you?"

"Grace."

"Justin's oldest daughter?"

She nodded, glancing up at him.

"You've grown since I saw you last. How old are you now?"

"Fourteen."

His face softened as he looked at her. He started to touch her hair, but pulled back.

"You remind me of someone I used to know. And you run fast like she did, too. I could hardly catch you."

"But you didn't catch me," she corrected him.

A look of awareness flashed across his face again, and his eyebrows rose in question like it was obvious he did, so she explained.

"I fell."

"Me, too, but you didn't keep going."

"I think I did something to my foot."

"You're hurt? Which one?" He looked at her shoes and reached for them.

She tucked them under her skirt.

"I'm sure it's better now." She started to roll over to push herself up, but he grasped her arm and waist and pulled her up as he stood.

Self-conscious at his touch, Grace murmured a thank you and tried to step away, but she cried out when she put her weight on her right foot. She would've fallen again if he hadn't held her upright. He paused only to button his shirt before he picked her up in spite of her protests and carried her all the way back to the barn. He sat her on a barrel, and she watched him saddle a different horse and mount it. He walked up beside the barrel and pulled her up effortlessly behind him to take her back to her grandparents' house.

He told her to hold him around his waist—that he didn't want her falling off and hurting something else.

She realized then that he saw her as a little girl—a helpless little girl.

Grace felt her cheeks turn even redder as she reached around him, only allowing her fingers to barely touch the front of his shirt. But when he spurred the horse forward, she had to grab his waist tightly to keep from falling off backwards.

He didn't say much on the way back, and try as she might, she couldn't think of a thing to start a conversation with him, not even a dull conversation.

When they rode by Kimball's Mercantile, Maggie and her friends stood on the front porch gawking, like they'd just now noticed Grace wasn't with them.

Grace couldn't help but take her hands off his waist to try to put some space between them, smiling apologetically to Maggie when he spurred his horse again. She grabbed him around his chest again to keep from falling off backwards.

She was convinced he did it on purpose this time when she saw a smirk stretched across the side of his face.

She turned around to smile apologetically at her cousin again, but Maggie looked fit to be tied. She knew she'd have some explaining to do later.

By the time they came up to the front of her grandmother's house, Grace finally thought of something to say.

"How'd you know I was up there?"

She could feel the chuckle with her hands rather than hear it.

"I didn't make a sound," she said defensively.

"I didn't hear you, but I saw dust and bits of hay falling through the cracks from the loft."

"Oh." She hadn't thought about that. "I'm sorry we bothered you."

"I'm sorry you 'bout killed yourself," was his response.

She couldn't help but snicker. Then she realized she hadn't thanked him for saving her life, but she couldn't word it like that. She'd owe him too much, then.

"Thanks for breakin' my fall," she said, deciding that was good enough.

"I can't believe you jumped out of that barn," he said, turning his head to the side. "But don't you ever go and do anything stupid like that again, Grace Taylor. You hear me?"

"Yes, sir," she whispered, feeling like a little girl again.

He rode around to the back and tied his horse to a hitching ring and insisted on carrying her into the house.

And by the time he stepped into the kitchen, Finn Samuel owned her heart.

The Cast Key

The Taylor Family – 1900

Matthew Taylor, 75, married to *Julia Taylor*, nee Stockton, 73

Children: / **Their Grandchildren:**

- Matt, 53, married to Catherine, 52
  - Tres, 31, William, 30, Michael, 29, Robert, 24, & Timbo, 20
- Jenny, 51, married to Marcus Kimball, 54
  - Josh, 32, Luke, 31, Maggie, 28, & Clifford, 24
- Justin, 49, married to Allie nee Blake, 44
  - Grace, 24, Max, 22, Bradley, 21, & Mary J., 19
- Jimmy, 43, married to Mercy nee Locke, 46
  - Jack, 22, Mae, 20, & Biriney, 17
- Faith, 43, married to Ethan Murray, 48
  - Caitlin/Katie (deceased 1884), Ella Vae, 21, Cele, 20, & Sam, 18

Chapter 2

Ten years later... September 1, 1900
Galveston Bay

Grace smiled at the memory of when she first fell in love with Finn Samuel. She was only fourteen at the time, and he was a grown man at twenty-one years of age. But she was patient and eventually caught up with him. Ten years of trying everything to win his heart did that, and now she was running as fast as she could away from what she finally realized was a lost cause. Finn's heart would open for no one. It sealed shut the day Caitlin Murray died sixteen years ago.

The air in the train suddenly felt like hot soup. She stood to try to lower the window a little further when she noticed the water. She looked out both sides of the train and all she could see was water. She knew then that she'd made a mistake... a huge mistake. Grace sat down as the tears began to flow again.

"That's usually not people's first reaction when they see the water," said a well-dressed woman sitting across the aisle and back a row.

Grace wiped the tears away with an already damp hanky. "I've never seen the ocean before."

"Honey, this isn't the ocean—it's Galveston Bay. The island is between us and the ocean."

Grace looked out the window again. "My mother will never come visit me here. She'd never get across this eternal bridge. How long is this thing?"

"A couple of miles, I think."

"My mother used to be terrified of bridges and water, and she's come to terms with small bridges, but this…this would overwhelm her." Her face scrunched up at the thought of not seeing her mother for a long time. She'd never felt more alone.

The woman stood up and moved to the seat next to Grace. "Is it a little overwhelming for you, too?" she asked, patting Grace's knee.

Grace nodded, dabbing her nose.

"My name is Marguerite, by the way."

"I'm Grace. Grace Taylor."

"Lovely name," the attractive woman said. "Well, Grace, I promise you'll be awestruck with the city of Galveston. Hands down, it's the most exciting place in the entire U.S. of A. I'll bet you've never seen anything like it."

"Is it always this hot and muggy?"

"Muggy, yes, but you're arriving at our hottest time of the year. November through April are the best months and Galveston's social season, but if you love the water, you can cool off until then at the beach. I hope you brought some light clothing and your bathing suit. And if you didn't, that's a good excuse to shop. You'll find the latest fashions here on the island." She stopped and took a breath. "Are you coming for pleasure or business?"

"I'm hoping to take a teaching job at the Rosenberg School. Are you familiar with it?"

The woman shook her head. "I don't know much about the serious side of Galveston. I come for the fun. So you're a teacher! Noble profession. If I recall, the school term doesn't start for several more weeks, right?"

Grace nodded. "I guess I should clarify my situation. I'm taking the place of a good friend of mine who was scheduled to interview for this position. But she received a marriage proposal a few days before she planned to head down here, so she convinced me to go in her place. I needed to… try something new, so here I am." She looked away from the woman's keen, brown eyes; afraid she would see that her reason for coming to Galveston wasn't the noble purpose of teaching. She had simply run away. "I still have to meet the headmaster's approval before I get the teaching position, but I do have two years' experience from my previous school in Waco."

"I've been through Waco a time or two. Nice town, but nothing like Galveston. Don't worry—I'm sure you'll get the job. If you need any references, you just let me know. I know some very influential people here." She paused for a moment. "But if you want my advice, don't take your tears and hanky to the interview."

Grace couldn't help but giggle at the woman's frankness. "I've been a blubbering fool this whole trip."

"Homesick already?"

"No, I'm not originally from Waco. My hometown is Dalton—south of San Antonio—too small and quiet for your tastes, I'm sure."

"I've learned to flourish wherever I am, and to be happy in any situation."

Grace looked at her wistfully. "I hope I can say that someday."

"Did you lose someone close to you?"

"In a way." The pain came again at the thought of losing Finn. But then she never truly had him in the first place.

"Then I guess you must be heartsick."

"Is it that obvious?"

"Honey, the stories I could tell you about my tragic love affairs! I'm an expert, but I think we're almost there."

The train began slowing down and blew the whistle as it approached Union Station.

"Oh, my," said Grace, pressing her face to the glass. "Look at all the ships and the big buildings!"

Marguerite laughed. "That's not the half of it, girl! Our conversation isn't finished, though. I'd love to meet you for tea soon. Where are you staying?"

"Temporarily at my friend's brother's house until I find my own place. Where are you staying?"

"At my cousin's on Broadway." She reached across the aisle for her handbag and pulled out a calling card and handed it to Grace.

"I'll be here for a month, but I'm sure we can get together soon. May I have one of yours?"

"I don't... have any," she said, feeling awkward.

"Then that's one of the first things you need to do while you're here. There's a nice stationery shop just off the Strand that will fix you up in no time at all. That's the first rule in Galveston: ladies go nowhere without their calling cards. But until then, write down your address where you're staying, and I'll send for you."

"Thank you, Marguerite... you are so kind."

The woman patted her hand again. "Honey, with your looks, men are going to flock around you like a bunch of hungry seagulls, and I think you're a little too vulnerable right now. I need to tell you a few things just so you won't be eaten alive around here."

Grace's eyes widened. "Alligators?"

"Yes, honey, the two-legged ones," Marguerite said, laughing. She stood up and grabbed Grace's arm. "Come on. Let's get you started on your new adventure. Will someone be here to meet you?"

"Yes, my friend's brother."

The two women disembarked amidst a throng of tourists and strode into the station building. Grace hoped she could spot her host in the crowd. She couldn't help but notice the intricate wood patterns in the paneled walls and the ornate columns supporting the ceiling high above the room. Passengers sat and stood around a number of long, oblong benches decorated with potted palms perched on the shelf running along the back of the benches.

"Everyone's taking advantage of these last few weeks of vacation before school starts. Galveston has its own opera house, a carnival, dances at the Garten Verein, and of course, its wonderful beach and bathhouses. And I'm sure my cousin will have at least one dance scheduled while I'm here."

Grace's face brightened at the thought.

They walked through the train station to claim their trunks.

"Oh, dear," said Marguerite, pulling Grace to one side.

"What is it?"

"Lesson number one, avoid that handsome devil walking this way."

"Where?"

"The one with black hair and those intoxicating blue eyes—Lucius Roderick, otherwise known as 'Luscious' on the island. He can charm the stockings off a nun."

Grace giggled at the thought.

"Grace!" A man's voice called out.

Marguerite's mouth dropped open to see Lucius Roderick walking up to them. He broke all rules of propriety by sweeping Grace up in his arms and swinging her around.

He set Grace down and held her at arm's length, looking her up and down. "Why, my little Grace is all grown up now. How long has it been?"

"Only four years, you cad, and I was grown up back then. You were too busy to notice."

"You know it was the other way around—you only had eyes for that fool—"

"I believe you know Marguerite…" she interrupted him, but then realized she didn't know her last name.

"St. John," Lucius finished it for her. He turned and reached for her hand and kissed it. "Of course I do. Meg and I go way back."

Grace raised her eyebrows.

"Hello, Lucius." Marguerite looked flushed, but pleased. "I tried to warn her about you."

He laughed.

Grace added, "He actually warned me about himself the first time I met him… goodness, was it actually eight years ago?"

"Did you ever get that first kiss?" he asked bluntly.

Grace acted shocked. "You are as impudent as ever, Lucius."

He turned to Marguerite. "It was supposed to be me, and it almost was, but we were rudely interrupted. Remember, Grace?"

Grace nodded, smiling. "Of course, I remember."

"Now I have to hear this story," said Marguerite.

"Are you going to your cousin's, Meg? Can we drop you off?"

"Yes, thank you. They're not expecting me until later."

"Give me your luggage receipts, ladies, and wait here until I get them loaded on the carriage. Then I'll be back for you."

Marguerite turned to Grace. "I can't believe you know Lucius. Don't tell me he's your friend's brother."

"The one and the same."

"And you're staying at his house?!"

"I've stayed at his parents' house in Waco—his sister is one of my best friends."

"This isn't his parents' house."

"Sissy told me he's going to stay at his office until I find a place, hopefully as soon as possible."

"Thank heavens," said Marguerite, leading her over to one of the highly polished wooden benches. "Your reputation would never recover around here. Look at that line—it'll take him a while to get our trunks loaded, so tell me about Lucius and your first kiss."

"Do you really want to hear that story?"

"Humor an old woman."

"You're far from old," said Grace, exhaling as she sat down. "Well, Lucius missed giving me my first kiss by mere seconds, but it was one of the most exciting nights of my life."

"Well, if Lucius didn't kiss you… who did?"

She leaned back and smiled as the memories came flooding back. "The reason I'm here in Galveston—Finn Samuel."

Chapter 3

Marguerite leaned forward. "So that's his name. Tell me every detail."

"Eight years ago, most of the other girls in Grace, Texas, the town I was named after, were in love with Finn Samuel, too. I'd heard he had other plans, though—plans that didn't include a female companion in his life.

"But that didn't stop me from entertaining fanciful thoughts. My family—my parents and my two younger brothers and sister came to Grace most every Christmas, and ever since I turned fourteen, I was allowed to go stay with my grandparents for a whole month during the summer."

"Your grandparents lived in Grace, then."

"They founded the town, but it's very small. Finn's actually from Brownwood, but he worked for my uncle Jimmy during the summers to help pay for his education. I was grateful that he had to work and stretch out four years of college into six because he was seven years older than I, and that meant he was still around the summer of my sixteenth year.

"I saw him at Sunday dinners and made myself available to run errands for my aunt Mercy or visit my younger cousins regularly. Sometimes I'd see him and sometimes I wouldn't. Mostly I just silently pined for him in my mind."

"Nobody knew how you felt about him?"

Grace shook her head. "My cousin Maggie was in love with him, too, and she had first dibs. Back then most every young lady of note in Waco and the surrounding communities attended the Cotillion, their coming of age ball. Maggie was the last Taylor grandchild to attend as a debutante, and that was two years before. The other Taylor granddaughters were still several years away from being old enough to attend, so Maggie insisted that I participate in the Cotillion that year."

"When was this?"

"In '92. Aunt Mercy was crowned the Cotillion Queen when she was eighteen, and afterwards she loved helping with the ball up until the year before she was married. That was around the same time her face was burned and scarred, and she had nothing to do with the Cotillion since then. She's still a beautiful woman—I don't even notice the scars anymore when I look at her."

"How did that happen?"

"That's another story for another time," said Grace. "Aunt Mercy's oldest daughter Mae turned twelve that year, and Mercy was already looking forward to her girls attending the ball a few years later. I figured that was why Aunt Mercy seemed so excited about me going to the Cotillion. She was practicing on me first.

"Maggie convinced Aunt Mercy that Finn should accompany her to the Cotillion as chaperones for me and some unsuspecting family friend from Waco. I was nervous about going to a dance with a complete stranger, but deep down I was thrilled about Finn accompanying us as a chaperone. I had to remind myself regularly that Maggie staked first claim on Finn. No one in Grace knew how I felt about him."

"That never stopped me, honey," said Marguerite.

Grace chuckled. "Well, I was convinced Finn still considered me a little girl, but I hoped he'd see me differently at the Cotillion, more like an eligible young lady. That's what *coming of age* means, isn't it?"

Marguerite nodded.

"I had brought one party dress from home, but my aunt told me it was entirely too sturdy and practical. Mercy took one of her old Cotillion gowns—a 'candlelight satin' she described it, and had her seamstress re-fit it for me. I had to wear a hoop skirt with it, and didn't even know how to sit down in it."

"You have to sit in the center of the hoop or you'd be showing your pantaloons to the world."

Grace giggled. "Exactly!"

"And you pick up the front when you walk up stairs."

"Aunt Mercy practiced with me beforehand, and she even made Uncle Jimmy dance with me so I'd get used to it on the dance floor." Grace took a deep breath and glanced at her bust. "I remember worrying that my chest was going to pop out the top of it. Daddy would have had a fit if he saw me in that low-cut gown! But I still felt like a fence post draped in satin."

Marguerite laughed. "I'm sure you were ravishing." She reached over and tucked a wayward curl under Grace's hat.

"I have my father's unruly hair. I'd never worn it any way but down or in braids, but that day my aunt piled it on top of my head and stabbed a couple of combs in it and stepped back to inspect her work. I remember that she seemed pleased as she pulled me to a standing position and led me to the mirror. I remember gasping when I saw myself. I didn't recognize the young lady staring back at me. I realized I wasn't a little girl anymore.

"I awoke before sunrise on the morning of the Cotillion. I'm not sure how long I lay there waiting for Maggie to wake up. We were staying at Mercy's parents' house, the Locke Mansion. My grandparents' house in Grace was three stories high and almost as big, but it was much homier than the Locke's house. I felt like I'd spent the night in a museum. But the grandeur of the house was definitely getting me in the right mindset to attend a ball.

"Aunt Mercy insisted we come into Waco the day before so we would have time to rest before the day's festivities, most of which had to do with primping. Rest? I could hardly sleep the night before. It still felt like a dream. We never had anything like this in Dalton. But the best part was to be in the company, no, the vicinity of Finn Samuel. I said no one in Grace knew how I felt about him, but I did talk to Vestal about him."

"Who's Vestal?"

"My grandmother's housekeeper and cook since forever. She's in her seventies now, and she's still in charge of the kitchen—at her insistence, but Meemaw and my aunt Catherine make sure that Vestal has some help doing even that now. Everyone considers her part of the family. She came to Texas with the Taylors and took care of Uncle Matt and Aunt Jenny—Maggie's mother—when my grandmother and my father were kidnapped by an Apache brave way back when my pa was only five years old."

"Oh, my goodness! You have to tell me that story, too!"

Grace smiled. "I've lived with these stories all of my life, so I haven't really thought about how amazing they are. My mother has been writing them down so we would never forget them, thank heavens. And when I was twenty-one she let me read her account of Uncle Jimmy taking her away from Grace and their abduction by the Apaches and meeting Jimmy's grandmother Nah-kay, a full blooded Apache woman. Nah-kay came to live at Grace when they rounded up most of the Apaches to live on reservations, but she passed away a few years ago. Momma loved her and said she was a remarkable woman, but I wasn't around her enough to feel comfortable talking to her. I love reading about her now, though, and wish I could've known her better in person. It's hard to believe all of that actually happened."

"My life seems absolutely dreary hearing about yours. Your own mother spent time with Apache Indians?"

Grace nodded. "They called themselves *Indeh*, and Momma was only eighteen when she was kidnapped. I shudder to think they almost lost their lives before I was even born. I guess I wouldn't have been born if that had happened. But she assured me that God had plans for them and brought them safely through the ordeal."

"How was she kidnapped?"

"Uncle Jimmy used to behave badly—Momma said he went through a tough time trying to figure out who he was and where he belonged. He was half Apache, but the Apaches almost killed him when he and Momma were kidnapped. My daddy never talks about the weeks he spent trying to find Momma and Uncle Jimmy, but he did mention that my mother had something to do with his brother's life changing for the good. Momma just says that God did it.

"I'm so glad she wrote down those stories. She says they'll be passed down to me some day, along with the house and the ranch, and it'll be up to me to continue recording the family history. I'm not sure we've done anything worth recording—my life so far would surely put someone to sleep reading about it. But that wasn't the case with my parents and grandparents. It's hard to believe all of that happened to them years ago. My grandmother's withered hand reminds me that it really did. No one talks about it, but Maggie told me that Meemaw's Apache captor crushed her hand to punish her when she tried to escape with my father not long after they were kidnapped. I can't imagine how terrifying that must have been. Nobody talks about that time, though, but Meemaw doesn't seem bitter about it."

"I can't keep this all straight in my head," said Marguerite.

"I know I'm rambling—I'll try to stay with Finn. I tried to think of a way to let him know how I felt about him, but not at the Cotillion. That was Maggie's night. I knew he didn't love her; otherwise they probably would've been married by then or at least engaged. Finn knew how she felt, too, but he'd made no effort to return her affection.

"I wondered if anything would change after he knew how I felt about him. I'd be devastated if he rejected me, but I don't think I'd have to worry about him flaunting it in front of everybody. Everyone knew how Maggie felt about him, but *she* was the reason everyone knew—Finn didn't flaunt her feelings. As for me and my feelings, no one else would know. But I was determined that before I went back to Dalton in July, Finn Samuel would know how I felt about him."

Chapter 4

Grace stood and stretched, and Marguerite stood with her. "My silly cousin. We spent half the day getting ready for the Cotillion in the same room downstairs that we slept in, but when Finn and my escort came to the door, she told Matilda, the Locke's housekeeper, to wait until she said to open the door. She grabbed my arm, whispering that I needed to come, too. She wanted us both to make an entrance from upstairs."

"I love to make an entrance," said Marguerite.

"I told her I'd definitely make an entrance falling down the stairs and landing at my date's feet—probably hoop side up."

Marguerite laughed.

"That's exactly the reaction Mercy and Jimmy had with my statement. They stood off to the side, laughing at us. I told her to go on, and I pushed her toward the stairs and said that I would stand on the first step and pretend I was just coming down, and then she could make her grand entrance. Maggie stopped pouting and picked up her skirt and hoop petticoat and ran very unladylike up the stairs to the second floor. I took my place on the first step. I was nervous about meeting my escort, but even more nervous about facing Finn. But picturing myself rolling down the stairs helped keep the smile on my face.

"Maggie whispered loudly from upstairs for Matilda to open the door. I remember Matilda grinning, too, as she bid the two men to come inside.

"Supposedly, Richard Roderick stepped in first and took off his top hat. I was pleasantly surprised at the rakishly handsome man—dark hair, blue eyes. I remember Matilda frowning for some reason, but my escort looked at me and smiled."

Grace sat down again, and Marguerite followed.

"I couldn't help but smile even bigger back at him. He walked over to me and bowed slightly."

Grace shut her eyes, lost in the memory…

"Hello, Miss Grace Taylor."

"How did you know it was me?"

He nodded his head towards the door. "Mr. Samuel prepared me, but he didn't do you justice."

I looked beyond him to see Finn standing just inside. He was staring at me like something was wrong with me. I looked down to see if my dress was on straight—it was, and started to reach up to feel if my hair comb was coming out, but Richard grabbed my gloved hand and kissed it.

Aunt Mercy walked up to us.

"You're supposed to wait until you're properly introduced, Mr. Roderick."

He gave her a heart-stopping grin. "Sorry, I just couldn't help myself. Samuel didn't tell me I'd be escorting the most beautiful belle of the ball tonight."

I thought that comment was a blatant exaggeration, but on the other hand, it was nice to know all this preening was paying off.

Mercy smiled politely, but her eyes weren't smiling. "Mr. Roderick, I'd like to introduce you to my niece, Grace Taylor. Grace, this is—"

"Excuse me, Mrs. Taylor," Matilda interrupted, "but this isn't Richard Roderick. This is his older brother Lucius."

Mercy frowned. "We were told that Richard would be accompanying my niece this evening."

Lucius waved his hand in the air as if to dispel the confusion. "I do apologize on behalf of my brother for the last minute change, but Eleanor Holmes, the love of his life, found herself without an escort—seems the love of *her* life, who unfortunately isn't my brother, was taken ill by a bee sting or something of the sort. So when Richard found out, he gallantly offered to escort her and asked me to take his place. I'm sorry if this inconveniences everyone, but I would hate for Miss Grace to come all this way and not get to attend the Cotillion, especially looking so beautiful in that dress."

That was even a little much for me, but I still didn't mind the compliment, especially in Finn's presence.

"Thank you, Mr. Roderick," I said, relieved I would still get to attend. "How kind of you to step in for your brother."

"My pleasure, Miss Taylor."

I chanced looking at Finn again. He still stared at me, but I couldn't tell if he was mad or glad of the situation.

Someone cleared her throat behind me.

Maggie! I had forgotten all about her; in fact, no one noticed that she had come down the stairs to make her grand entrance, and here I was still standing on the first step blocking her from view.

"Oh, I'm sorry!" I stepped down and moved to my left away from everyone so Finn could see her. Lucius followed to stand beside me. I turned to see Maggie smiling at Finn, waiting for him to say something. I looked back at Finn and saw that he was still watching me. I don't think he had even seen her yet. The silence was awkward. I glanced back at Maggie, and her smile faded.

I blurted out, "Doesn't Maggie look beautiful this evening, Finn?" The blue dress did bring out her blue eyes. Our hairstyles were the same—twisted and coiled buns piled high on our heads, but her straight hair lay more closely to her head—the latest style I was told, but my wavy hair refused to be tamed. I felt like I wore a big headdress on top of my head.

Finn followed my gaze and finally noticed her. He walked over to help her down the last couple of steps.

"Of course she's beautiful," he said, allowing a reserved smile to appear. "All the Taylor women are beautiful."

Aunt Mercy stepped up and hugged him. "Hello, Finn. I almost didn't recognize you. You look so handsome in your dress suit."

"Thanks for sending it ov—"

"Hush." She reached up with her fingers and kept him from finishing the sentence. "Tonight we're going to pretend you are the big business man you plan to be some day."

Jimmy reached across and shook Finn's hand. "You clean up nice, kid." He looked around at the group. "You wouldn't believe the dirt this boy was wearing yesterday."

Mercy reached up and shushed her husband, too. "Tonight we're going to focus on the beautiful and the unsoiled, not the ugly muck in the barnyard."

We all laughed.

"Now go and have a wonderful evening, my princes and princesses. Make it a night you'll never forget."

Matilda opened both of the front doors so our wide skirts could pass through easily, and Mercy waved us on like Titania, queen of the fairies.

Lucius and I walked out onto the gallery first. I glanced back to see Matilda put her hand on Finn's arm and tell him something before he and Maggie followed us outside. I turned back around and gasped when I saw the carriage waiting for us in front of the house.

The coach was white and wide open to the sky. Two tufted red leather seats faced each other, and Matilda's husband Rune, wearing a top hat and tails, sat in a separate coachman's seat.

I caught Lucius watching my reaction to it.

"Is this yours?" I asked him.

"No, your aunt rented it for the evening."

"She thought of everything." I turned around and waved at Mercy and Jimmy on the gallery before I paused to get in the carriage. I picked up the front of my dress and hoop petticoat and stepped up to the seat behind Rune, but almost panicked trying to figure out how to sit down gracefully. A carriage seat was quite different from a simple chair, especially when a man was supposed to sit beside me.

Where, do tell?

Lucius seemed to understand my hesitation and picked up the

back of the hoop and helped me to sit. He managed to squeeze under the edge of the hoop beside me.

"You've done this before," I said.

"A few times, yes."

"Thank you."

"My pleasure."

We watched Finn help Maggie up into the carriage, and Lucius stood to help her get seated, too. Finn hadn't a clue what to do with the hoop when he started to sit down. I noticed he waited and watched Lucius before he sat under the edge of Maggie's hoop, too.

I waved again at my aunt and uncle as the carriage rolled away from the Locke mansion. The setting sun added to the sensation that we actually were princesses in a fairy tale. Or maybe I was dreaming. Was this really happening?

People on the street stopped and stared as we passed by, and some even waved. I felt like we were in a parade. Everything felt so magical. And the pavilion where the Cotillion was held only made it more so.

Chapter 5

Wide stone columns held up the portico roof leading to the entrance. The style reminded me of the Greek ruins I'd seen in books, but in this case the building was pristine. We could see light shining from countless chandeliers through a wall of windows beyond the columns, giving us a peek at the lavishness of the ball.

Climbing out of the carriage proved easier than climbing in. Lucius disembarked first and I stood, my hooped skirt filling the space between the two seats. I paused, having no idea where my feet were, much less where the step on the side of the carriage was and pictured myself missing the step and landing on my face. Lucius reached up and grabbed me around the waist and pulled me and my huge satin skirt through the small carriage opening. The thought of a camel going through the eye of a needle came to mind, and then I was safely on the ground.

I giggled with relief.

Finn stepped out of the carriage and did the exact same thing with Maggie, like that was the proper way to get hooped ladies out of a coach. I realized then that he probably had never attended anything like this.

Maggie giggled, too, and whispered to me as we walked on ahead. "I think we just committed our first faux pas."

"Our what?"

"Social blunder, but Finn can pick me up anytime."

I glanced back at Finn and smiled. He didn't smile back.

"He doesn't seem too happy to be here."

"He doesn't care for social events. In fact, I think Aunt Mercy's paying him to escort me."

I glanced back at Lucius and smiled. He smiled back.

I leaned toward Maggie and said, "I wonder how much it cost her to rent Mr. Roderick."

Maggie snickered in a very unrefined manner. "I believe she got her money's worth. He seems very capable at this sort of thing."

I nodded my head. "I do believe I'm in good hands tonight."

"Shush—here they come."

We reached the bottom of the wide steps leading up to the entrance. Lucius held out his arm to me and Finn followed suit with Maggie.

I held up the front of my dress, and when I figured out the width and height of the steps as my feet stepped blindly under the satin tent, I chanced looking up at the pavilion. It loomed even larger before us, and I could hardly contain my excitement.

Music drifted out of the open doorway where a page checked a list. We paused to let several couples walk in ahead of us. Lucius spoke to one of the girls, but she acted like she didn't hear him. Her escort glared at Lucius.

"How rude," I said quietly.

He sighed. "I'm afraid it's my fault. She hasn't forgiven me for not choosing her."

"For the Cotillion?"

He shook his head. "For marriage."

"Oh."

"I have too much living to do before I get married."

"Me, too," I lied, trying to sound nonchalant. Why in the world did I say that? I wanted more than anything to get married and have children some day.

"We may have more in common than I thought," said Lucius, putting his hand at the small of my back to lead me forward.

He mentioned our names to the page and we entered the ball to stand in line for someone to announce our names.

"We'll see you on the dance floor," said Maggie, pulling Finn ahead of us since she was a chaperone instead of one of the debutantes.

I took a deep breath, trying to settle my nerves.

"You'll do fine."

I smiled at Lucius. He seemed to know exactly what I was thinking.

"Except that every woman here will be jealous."

"Because I'm with you?"

Lucius chuckled. "Thank you, my dear Grace, but they'll be jealous because standing next to you makes them look like old hags."

"You exaggerate entirely too much, Lucius."

"Watch and see if people avoid us, and then you'll realize I'm telling you the truth."

I was surprised and unnerved after they loudly announced our names when people stared at us and more than a few talked among themselves and turned away. And unlike the enthusiastic response for the others, very few people clapped for us. It seemed like everyone stopped and focused their attention on us, and not in a friendly way.

"This is awkward," I whispered under my breath as we walked across the room to find Maggie and Finn.

"Just smile and hold your head high, Grace. They're just spoiled, shallow people."

"Then why would my aunt even want me to come to something like this? Maybe we ought to go home." I felt close to tears.

Lucius sighed. "It's not you, Grace. They're angry at me."

"Why? Because of that girl back there?"

"And several more that also thought I should marry them."

I frowned at him. "And you tried to make me think it was my fault. Why, you buzzard!"

Lucius threw his handsome head back and laughed. "I've been called a number of derogatory names in my life, but that's the first time anyone's called me a buzzard. And you're probably right. But you *are* beautiful, Grace, and I'm honored to escort you here tonight."

I didn't say anything. I didn't know what to say. Maybe I should cut our evening short and ask Maggie and Finn to take me home. I spotted them across the room. She was smiling and hanging on Finn's arm and every word. No, I couldn't do that to her. This was more her night than mine, although I noticed Finn's eyes on me more than he looked at her. I was sure my time was coming, but I didn't want to lose my cousin in the process. I just had to be patient.

Lucius continued to defend himself. "I never led them on—they knew what they were getting into, but they all thought they could change my mind somehow. So this is fair warning, pretty lady. Women have a tendency to fall in love with me, so watch your heart."

I muffled a snort. An *arrogant* buzzard at that, I thought to myself. "Thank you for warning me, Lucius," I said sarcastically, "but you don't have to worry about capturing my heart. It belongs to someone else."

"Competition, eh? I like a good challenge."

"You're not even in the race."

Lucius laughed again, turning more heads.

"All right, I concede. I'm a buzzard, but I can be a fun buzzard. Come on, Grace. Don't be angry with me. I'm sorry I ruffled your feathers, and I promise I'll give you the best night of your life."

We had almost reached Finn and Maggie. He was staring at me again, and I felt a flutter in my chest. Maggie was talking to another lady, but stopped when she saw me—her face showed concern. I pasted a smile on my face just as Lucius swung me around and onto the dance floor.

"I love the waltz," he said. "And I am a good dancer, if I say so myself."

He was right. I had no trouble following him. And on a dance floor of dozens of hooped dresses, he maneuvered us expertly in and out without bumping into anyone. The men still frowned at him, though, and the women looked…envious. I lifted my chin a little higher after seeing that. And by the end of the dance, I couldn't help but smile.

"Am I forgiven?" he asked.

"No, but I've decided not to waste this beautiful evening and enjoy myself, in spite of you."

He laughed again and we danced through two more songs before joining Maggie and Finn.

"Is everything all right?" Maggie whispered to me.

I nodded my head and forced a smile.

She asked Finn and Lucius if they would bring us some punch, and when they walked off, she turned to me.

"What's the matter?"

"Did you hear when our names announced?" I asked.

"Of course—didn't you hear Finn and me clapping?"

"I think you were the only ones."

"I guess I was concentrating on your grand entrance—you and Lucius make a striking couple. I think everybody noticed."

"But not everybody's glad to see us. Some of his former lady friends are here, and they don't seem to be too forgiving. It makes me feel uncomfortable."

"But what do *you* think of him?

I shrugged. "I think he's arrogant. He even warned me not to fall in love with him."

Maggie giggled. "How conceited."

"He won't have to worry about that, but I am enjoying dancing with him. He's very good at that."

"I noticed. I'll do good to get Finn out on the dance floor at all tonight."

"I'll ask Lucius to ask you to dance."

"Would you? And ask him to dance a reel with me. I want Finn to see me spinning around in this dress."

"You do look beautiful tonight, Maggie. I'm sure he can't keep his eyes off of you."

"Have you notice him watching you tonight?"

My heart lurched in my chest. Did she know? "No, why would he be watching me?"

"You remind him of Caitlin."

My heart sunk like a rock. "Our cousin that died?"

Maggie nodded. "Do you remember her?"

"Faintly. I think I was eight years old when she passed away, but

I hadn't seen her for at least a year before that. I mostly remember how sad everyone was for so long."

"She was his first love."

"Oh, I didn't know that." And the evening was getting sadder by the moment. Finn wasn't staring at me because he was captivated by me. I reminded him of someone else he loved. "He called me 'Katie' in the barn…"

"The barn?"

"That day I broke my foot summer before last. I didn't understand why he called out that name until now."

"Her family called her Katie. They even use a heart with a KT in the middle of it as a brand on their cattle in memory of her. Finn even designed it for them. Well, Aunt Mercy said he had carved it for her in a piece of wood, and her father ended up using it for their brand. Can you imagine using a heart as a brand? Isn't that odd?"

"I think it's sweet." I barely got the words out.

Finn and Lucius walked up with dainty glass cups of punch in each hand.

"This is pretty good stuff," said Lucius. "We had several helpings there at the table before we brought these. I've already danced up a thirst."

The music began playing slower. Maggie took a sip and looked around to find a table. She spotted one several rows back and motioned for us to follow. I felt Finn's eyes on me again, but I couldn't meet them this time. It changed everything to know what he was thinking. I wanted him to see me—not Caitlin.

"Let's set our punch here and claim this table," she said, grasping Finn's arm. "This one's slow enough for you, Finn. Come on." She led him back to the dance floor.

Lucius looked at me and held out his hand. I grasped it and followed him.

He pulled me close. "Why the sad face? I thought you were determined to enjoy the evening in spite of me."

I leaned back a bit and looked at his handsome face. He was right. I should enjoy the moment and not dwell on the past or even future, for that matter. I might as well give Lucius my undivided attention tonight. Finn could reminisce all he wanted, and I hoped he and Maggie were very happy together.

I gave Lucius my best smile.

Chapter 6

We danced every dance until a reel was played.

"I need to catch my breath," I told him truthfully. "Please dance with Maggie—she's gathering cobwebs sitting there with Finn, and she loves to dance."

"If you say so, but my mind and heart will remain with you," he said as he led me back to the table.

"Oh, hush up. Is that the kind of words you used on your lady friends? And they fell for that?"

Lucius laughed and held out his hand to Maggie.

She lit up like a candle and accepted it. I watched them weave their way back to the dance floor.

Finn stood to help seat me next to Maggie's empty seat.

"You look like you're enjoying yourself," he said.

"I am, very much," I answered, chancing meeting his eyes. My stomach fluttered, darn it. His voice didn't help. I loved his husky voice.

"Be careful with Lucius, little girl."

"I'm not a little girl, Finn, and what exactly do you mean?"

"He has a reputation of being a womanizer."

I chuckled. "Don't worry; he's already warned me about that."

Finn looked surprised.

"He even told me that those women knew what they were getting into, but they thought they could change him anyway. I told him he didn't have to worry about me falling for him."

"How do you know that?"

"Because I'm interested in someone else."

"You're too young to have a beau."

"I'm sixteen, Finn. I'm plenty old enough to have a beau."

"Well, just be careful around Don Juan."

"Don Juan?"

Finn shook his head. "Never mind."

"I'll probably never see him again, but tonight I'm going to take advantage of him and his dancing. Why aren't you dancing with Maggie?"

"I'm better at other things—not this frilly stuff."

"Like what?"

"Horses, cattle, fixing things, growing things; come to think of it, I'm better at just about anything besides this."

"Climbing down ropes, rescuing a silly girl who hurt her foot running away from you."

Finn smiled. "You made quite an impression on me that day."

"I did?"

"I still can't believe you jumped out of that loft."

"I was mortified that you caught me up there. Did I thank you for saving my life?"

"I'm sure you did, although I remember you didn't talk much at all. I figured I scared you speechless, either that or you didn't give me a second thought."

"I could never forget you, Finn." Our eyes held for a moment. *Why can't you see how I feel about you?*

We didn't speak again until I saw Maggie and Lucius heading back to the table laughing.

"Would you please dance one dance with me before the night is over, Finn?" I quickly asked him.

He nodded his head. "A slow one."

I felt light-headed, but in a good way.

"Did you see us out there? If that had been a race we would've won! I've never turned so many circles in my life. Thank you, Lucius—that was exhilarating."

"Promise me another one, fair lady, and we'll show them up all over again," said Lucius, kissing her hand as he seated her.

"Of course! You're a wonderful dancer," Maggie said, flustered at his charming comment.

I couldn't help rolling my eyes at Finn, who grinned at me.

I loved his smile—minimal, not exaggerated, but so much more real than Lucius' smile. Lucius seemed to be very aware of himself at all times, like he was putting on a performance for everyone around. And everyone around could hardly take their eyes off of him. I looked at his pale blue eyes—such a contrast to the dark pupils. Tall, dark, and dangerously handsome—no wonder women seemed to have a hard time resisting his charms.

Maggie turned to Finn. "Did you see us? My head is still spinning."

Finn nodded, lying. "Grace and I noticed that you were enjoying yourself immensely." He glanced at me with a smirk, daring me to say otherwise.

Lucius addressed me. "Are you rested enough, ma belle?"

He held out his hand, and I grasped it and stood.

"You have a lot of endurance."

"I'm known for that," he said, escorting me back to the dance floor, "in more ways than one."

"Does your job require physical labor?"

"Oh, no, my dove," he said, smiling like I'd said something funny. "I'm not officially working yet, if you don't count interning in my father's law firm. I'm studying to be a lawyer."

"Really? The kind of lawyer that defends people before a judge or jury?"

"Good heavens, no. That's too emotional for my tastes."

"You have a dramatic flair about you. I think you could be very persuasive in a debate."

"That sounds suspiciously like a compliment. And how would an innocent young girl like you know about trials and lawyers?"

"We've had our share of crime in our small town; our sheriff was murdered a few years ago, and last year a man was tried for assaulting a woman. I didn't go to the trial, but that's all everyone talked about for weeks. What other kind of lawyer is there?"

"Rich ones, my dear."

"My mother says there's a lot more to life than money."

"I think she has it backwards. Money will get you a lot more life. And I know where I'm going to find both."

"And where is that?"

"Galveston. It's one of the wealthiest cities in the country, and it's all happening there—every kind of transportation—from wagons and railroads to commercial ships transporting raw materials everywhere. And the port receives every kind of goods imaginable from all over the world. And it all needs legal expertise. There's money to be made on every corner. Next summer I'll be interning with a law firm there, and hopefully, I won't be coming back."

We made our first pass around the dance floor by this time. I could see Finn watching us, frowning. Maggie was chatting with another woman at the next table. That seemed to be the standard position for us the next hour—Lucius and I dancing and Finn and Maggie sitting.

Lucius pulled me toward the large open doors that faced north. We walked along the deep portico overlooking the landscaped garden leading down to the river. Gas lamplights lit our way. It couldn't have been more romantic or perfect, other than I wasn't with Finn. But I enjoyed conversing with, or rather listening to Lucius and his dreams of Galveston. I didn't have any dreams other than to marry Finn and have his children.

We stopped by a bench and a statue of somebody barely clad in draped material. I made Lucius stand between us so he faced away from the temptress.

"This view is better anyway," he said, facing me. "Have you ever been kissed, Grace?"

That caught me off guard. I started to lie, but he was smiling like he saw right through me.

"I guess my daddy doesn't count."

He shook his head, still smiling. "I'm going to kiss you now, Miss Taylor."

"You know it won't mean anything to me," I warned him, although I'd wondered about this moment for years. "But I guess I could do worse."

He threw his head back and laughed. "Lucky me, then."

When he looked me straight in the face, I thought my heart would lurch out of my chest, and I know he could feel me shaking.

"It's not going to hurt one bit," he said. "In fact, I guarantee you're going to enjoy it." His voice lowered to a whisper. "Do you know how beautiful you are, ma cherie?" He tilted his head to one side and leaned toward me. I shut my eyes, waiting for the impact.

Someone shouted behind me, and I opened my eyes to see him looking over my shoulder.

He said an expletive under his breath, and then apologized.

"Hey, Roderick!"

I turned to see two young men charging toward us. They were dressed like dance attendees. Lucius pulled me behind him.

"Well, if it isn't Tweedledee and Tweedledum," he said quietly, then louder, "This isn't the time or the place, boys."

"You finally crawled out from underneath your rock, you snake," the shorter one said. His face looked red in the lamplight.

"Don't ruin this evening for Miss Taylor," said Lucius. "She's been looking forward to this night for months."

Not exactly true, but if it headed off trouble, I agreed.

"Well, Miss Taylor's welcome to leave right now. We'd be doing her a favor gettin' her away from you."

"Who are these brutes, Lucius?" I asked from behind.

"Allow me to introduce you to the Hitchcock brothers… the overly protective siblings of the lady who snubbed me earlier tonight."

"Don't you talk about our sister like that!" the taller one yelled.

I stepped around Lucius. "He said nothing to insult your sister, but for your information, she did snub us when we arrived."

"This isn't any of your concern, Miss," the short one said, putting his hand out. "Why don't you just head back to the dance while we have a little chat with Roderick."

"I won't go without him."

"Then have a seat and watch the show. This won't take long."

The taller one shoved me towards the bench, but he didn't know his own strength, and I saw Lucius lunge toward him as I fell backwards over the bench. My hoop skirt rose like a full moon followed by my ruffled pantaloons and slippers pointing to the sky.

I could hear the punches, grunts and scuffling of a fight while I wallowed around on the ground trying to get myself upright. I was on my hands and knees when I saw someone running by to join the fray.

I heard Finn's voice demand for them to stop fighting and looked up to see him throw the shorter brother down to the ground when he refused to quit. I finally pulled myself up to a standing position and was shocked to see Lucius' bloody face. He was leaning over, trying to catch his breath or trying to keep the blood from dripping on his clothes… or maybe both.

Finn threatened to report the assault to the authorities if the Hitchcock brothers didn't leave immediately, and they complied.

"Are you all right?" Finn asked. I noticed he was looking my way.

"Yeah," said Lucius, spitting blood out of his mouth.

"I wasn't asking you, Roderick."

"Oh, I'm sorry, Grace," he said, straightening up and taking a few steps toward me. "Are you all right?"

Finn stopped him. "That's far enough. You don't want to bleed all over her."

"Let me go get washed up and—"

"You're done for the night," Finn interrupted. "Your nose is probably broken, and you can't even see out of your left eye. Go on home, Lucius. I'll take the ladies back to the Taylors."

"You're not going to tell them about this, are you?"

"I'm sure they'll hear about it eventually, but it won't be from me."

"Thanks," said Lucius, holding his handkerchief to his nose. He turned to me and mumbled that he'd had a wonderful evening and would make it up to me some day, and then walked away.

I didn't realize I hadn't said a word since before Finn had arrived. The rudeness and gall of those brothers made me angry, but the violence of the fight terrified me at the same time. I couldn't stop shaking.

Finn walked over to me and tried to take hold of my hands clenched in fists in front of my chest. He gave up and grasped my shoulders.

"Do you want to sit down?" he asked.

I shook my head, no.

"You took quite a spill back there. Seems like you're always falling when I'm around you."

I didn't laugh at his joke, so he asked me, "Are you all right?"

I looked at his face and nodded.

"I'm sorry your evening's ruined."

I shook my head.

"It's not ruined?"

"No." I finally found my voice. "It's been one of the best evenings of my life."

This time Finn was at a loss for words.

I felt a breeze brush against my hot face. "I'll treasure everything up to the point Lucius almost kissed me, and I'll forget the rest."

"Lucius tried to kiss you?" Finn asked a little too loud. "You shouldn't have come outside with him in the first place, Grace. He has a history of breaking hearts around here—that's what got his face mangled tonight."

"He warned me earlier this evening that women have a tendency to fall in love with him."

"Oh, he did, did he?"

"And you don't have to worry about him breaking my heart. He's fun to be around, but he's not the type to settle down any time soon."

"Then why were you going to let him kiss you?"

"I've never been kissed…I just wondered what that was like."

"That should happen with someone you love."

"I wasn't getting married, Finn. I just wanted to know what it was like… that's all." I pulled away from him and stepped toward the path. "I'll find somebody else—"

He grabbed my arm and pulled me back to him and kissed me full on the lips. The moment I'd dreamed about for two years happened, and I didn't even have time to think about it. About the time I realized what was happening, he pushed me away.

"There. Now you've had your first kiss, so get that crazy notion out of your head."

"I wasn't ready! I can't even remember what happened!" I argued. "That one doesn't count."

He made a low grumbling noise, but he stood in front of me and reached up and placed his hands gently on each side of my face. I shut my eyes and waited, but his first kiss was placed softly on my forehead, then he brushed his lips across each cheek before he found my mouth. And then he took every bit of breath out of my body.

I could hardly remain upright when he asked me, "Will you remember that?"

Chapter 7

Marguerite sat there on the bench in the train station clutching her purse in front of her chest. She finally exhaled like she'd been holding her breath.

"I'll never forget that story myself," she said. "And the first time you met Lucius Roderick, he was beat up by some rascal brothers?"

"Shhh! Here he comes," said Grace. "Not one word about this, Marguerite."

They stood to meet Lucius. Marguerite was grinning like a cat with a bird in her mouth.

Lucius looked from one face to another. "What's going on?"

"I'm ready to see this amazing city," said Grace.

Lucius frowned. "Did you tell Meg about our first date?"

"I told her about my first kiss, and you brought that subject up, if you remember."

"Oh, right."

"And when you left that evening, you told me you'd make it up to me, but you never did, by the way."

"You told her about the fight, then?" Lucius whined. "Meg, that isn't for publication. I have a reputation to maintain here."

"Your reputation is already tainted… with the women anyway. A fight just adds to your mystique, Lucius," said Marguerite.

"Oh," he said, brightening. He stepped between them and offered his arms. "Then allow me to escort you beautiful ladies to your carriage. Then I can make it up to you, Grace, starting today."

"This looks familiar," Grace said when they approached the open-topped carriage, similar to the one on the night of the Cotillion, except this one was black.

"Coincidence," said Lucius. "It's easier to see everything this way, and we have a lot to show her, don't we, Meg. Or do you need to be somewhere soon?"

"They're not expecting me until later, so I have some time."

"Good—you know things about Galveston that I don't."

"Where are you from, Marguerite?" asked Grace. "Seems like I've told you everything about me, and I hardly let you get a word in edgewise."

"I enjoyed every bit of your stories, and I hope you'll tell me more about your family someday soon. But I'm from Houston. It's not as progressive as Galveston, but I would go to seed if I lived here—too much play and not enough work."

"What kind of work do you do?"

"Mostly charitable work—fundraising for good causes. That keeps me busy."

Lucius gave the coachman some instructions and sat down behind him, facing the women. The carriage turned around in the street and headed east.

"This is what we call *The Strand*, or Avenue B. You'll find a number of the streets here in Galveston have two names. But the streets are laid out in an easy-to-remember grid: the north-to-south streets are numbered, and the east-to-west streets are letters of the alphabet. But the Strand and the port are where it's all happening. Do you know why it's called the Strand, Meg?"

"I've heard two stories. The first is that it's named after London's Strand Street, but someone else told me that 'strand' means 'shore or riverbank'. Both sound logical to me."

Grace looked up at the stately buildings running along both sides of the street. "The architecture is beautiful. What is that building?" She pointed to a massive gray and pink granite building with huge arches over the windows.

"A bank," said Lucius.

"The Hutchings Sealy Bank," said Marguerite, "and it was

designed by the same architect who built my cousin's house."

"If you could call it that," said Lucius, giving Marguerite a wink.

"What do you mean?" asked Grace.

"You'll see when we get there. You're going to love the houses here on the island, honey—"

"Especially on Broadway," said Lucius. "Let me tell you a little about the Strand before we come to the end of it," said Lucius. "It only takes up about five blocks of Avenue B, but it's the lifeblood of the city. Some people call it the *Wall Street of the Southwest.* Did you know Galveston is one of the richest cities in the entire country?"

"I'm not surprised you know that fact, but I had no idea all of this was down here."

"Over a thousand ships come through here each year. If anything was shipped to Texas, it probably came through Galveston. And all of the shipping, trading, railroad and cotton moguls have offices here on the Strand. Some of the richest men in the state made their millions here."

"I remember how excited you were to get down here, Lucius."

"My brother-in-law came to Galveston with only five dollars in his pocket, but he turned things around rather quickly," said Marguerite.

"It's the land of opportunity," said Lucius, waving his hand dramatically through the air.

"I have to say, though, that you'll find most of these wealthy entrepreneurs are very generous towards worthy causes here—the orphanages, the churches, the schools, and they even have an opera house."

"You should know, Meg," said Lucius. He turned to Grace. "She's probably finagled more donations out of these men than anyone else I know."

"They gave willingly," said Marguerite, smiling proudly. "But did you know, Grace, that Galveston was the first city in the State to have electricity and the first telephones?"

"And one of the first breweries," said Lucius, "and a great course for a sport called golf and our own country club."

"She's not interested in that, Lucius. But she would be interested to know Galveston has the first ice cream manufacturer in Texas."

"That sounds wonderful," said Grace, "especially in this heat."

"Tom, swing by Stars." Lucius said to the coachman. "I'll treat you ladies to some ice cream."

Once there, Lucius sweet-talked the lady behind the counter to let them take the dishes with them so they could continue their tour of Galveston.

"Do you think she's ready for Broadway, Meg?"

Marguerite nodded with her spoon in her mouth.

"To Broadway, Tom!" Lucius hollered. "Let's start with the Landes House on E Street and then over to the Wallises on I Street and then go all the way down to 27th so we can make our way back east on Broadway."

"By the Willis mansion?" Tom asked.

"Yes! That's a good place to introduce Grace to Broadway," said Marguerite.

Grace was tempted to put the bowl up to her mouth and drink every bit of the melted ice cream from the bottom, but etiquette restrained her. Lucius had no qualms about doing it, but Marguerite was every bit the proper lady, so Grace followed her lead.

"Ohhhh! It looks like a church!" said Grace when she saw the first mansion. "That is the most unusual house I've ever seen. Are we on Broadway already?"

Marguerite laughed. "No, honey, but there are beautiful homes on every street in Galveston."

"That's the Landes House," said Lucius.

"The lacy ironwork on the galleries is a work of art," added Marguerite.

"And what does Mr. Landes do to be able to live in a house like this?" asked Grace.

"Cotton factors, shipping, wholesale grocers, liquor—like most of the wealthy on this island, they have their fingers in a little bit of everything."

"And here's the Darragh's house," said Lucius. "He's president of the Wharf Company."

"I've noticed the houses are so tall, and the galleries are high off the ground. Is that to catch the breezes from the Gulf?"

"Yes, but the main reason most all of the houses are built up is to allow for the overflows the island has every so often."

"Overflows?" Grace asked.

"Storm floods, higher than usual tides, heavy rains," explained Lucius. "The island's not much higher than the Gulf."

"Sounds terrifying to be at the mercy of the Gulf."

"You get used to it."

"The houses must be sturdy to survive all of that," said Grace. "And they're so different."

"Meg's an expert on that—what do you call all of this?"

"You'll see just about every kind of architectural style here on the island—most are Victorian or Victorian Gothic, but you'll also find Greek and Romanesque Revival, Italian, arabesque, Renaissance, and you'll see a lot of the houses with combinations of the different styles."

"There's that fancy ironwork again," Grace commented on a very tall house as they turned on Avenue I.

"The Wallis House—grocers and cotton factors," Lucius elaborated without prompting.

"I don't mean to sound dense, but I don't know what you mean by cotton factors, other than it has something to do with cotton."

"The cotton growers pay a cotton factor to sell their crops for them."

They passed in front of a massive, four-storied structure.

"Surely that's not a house," said Grace. "Does someone actually live in that fortress?"

"The Heidenheimers," said Lucius. "Grocers."

"Are they still working on it?" Grace said, noticing a roofless wall of arches to the side.

"I've had tea on that courtyard, and it's actually supposed to look that way," Marguerite explained, "—it's very fashionable to have Greek ruins attached to your house."

"What kind of stone is that? It's so smooth."

"It looks like some kind of poured cement or stucco—it's too uniform for stone," said Lucius.

"Look at that one!" said Grace. "The entrance points to the corner of the block. And I've never seen so many gables and odd angles on a roof before."

"Trube House—real estate and merchandising."

"Only the wealthiest can afford stone mansions and the stone carvers it takes to build them," said Marguerite, "but there are a lot of Gothic style houses made of wood in Galveston. This next house is one of the best examples of *carpenter Gothic*. The Sonnenthiels live here."

Grace turned and waited for Lucius to comment on this particular family's wealth-building trade.

He shrugged his shoulders. "Don't know 'em."

Marguerite continued, "I heard the carpenter spent years building all that intricate latticework."

"It's absolutely beautiful," said Grace.

By the time they turned onto Broadway with its wide esplanade of colorful oleanders and palm trees, Lucius was bored of the house tour. He instructed Tom to step up the pace as he stood and faced forward so he could see what was coming. He also took over the commentary.

"The first home on Broadway to see is Mrs. Richard Willis' home—her husband made his fortune in cotton factors, grocers, wholesale merchandising—probably the oldest in Galveston."

"It looks like a red fortress," said Grace, commenting on the red tile roof and red brick walls. "I like the white stone trim—otherwise all the detail would be lost against the red."

Lucius continued. "The next house is the Charles Fowler residence. He built this home through railroad and land development ventures. Now that I think about it, I heard he and his brother's trying to develop some land not too far from your hometown, Grace."

"Really? Near Dalton?"

"They're going to name it after themselves."

"Does Galveston have its own Statue of Liberty?" asked Grace, pointing towards to a very tall monument in the middle of the street.

"It honors the heroes of Texas—they erected it just this year.

Now the next house is one of my personal favorites on the island—the magnificent George Sealy mansion. He made his fortune in cotton, banking, and the railroad, among other things."

"Neo-Renaissance style," added Marguerite.

"And this next red brick house is the late J.M. Brown home—"

Marguerite whispered, "His wife calls it *Ashton Villa*, and it was the first brick house built on the island. We'll come visit her this week."

Lucius prattled on, "—hardware merchant, railroad and banking interests."

"You sure know a lot about these people," said Grace.

"It's going to pay off someday," he said. "And if it doesn't, I can always give guided tours."

The women laughed as he continued.

"Next door to the Browns is the Peter Willis home. He owns one of the largest mercantile businesses west of the Mississippi. And here comes the Frosh house—but I don't know how they made their money. And I don't know about the next one… or the houses on the next couple of blocks. I haven't gotten around to meeting everyone of note in Galveston… yet."

"These aren't houses, they're mansions," said Grace. "I thought our house in Dalton was large, but these would dwarf it. And all that keeps coming to my mind is how much time it would take to clean them."

"Oh, but that's the luxury of having hired help, honey."

"I guess I just revealed a bit too much about myself. Do you have servants?"

Marguerite nodded. "But I didn't always, and the same goes for my cousin. They started out very modestly, too, but you'll be surprised to see how far they've come."

"And here is Morris Lasker's house. Real estate, banking, and cattle built this beauty."

"They also had the same architect, Nicholas Clayton, as my cousin had for her house."

"Don't know who lives here… or there… but coming up is Captain Sawyer's house. Do you know anything about him, Meg?"

"No—maybe he was a captain in the Confederate army."

"Or a ship captain? I don't know, but that is one tall house."

Grace gasped at an imposing house towering above everything on the next block. "Now that one beats all—it's not a house, it's a castle!"

Lucius grinned at Marguerite. "And this, my dear Grace, is the humble abode of Walter Gresham, lawyer, railroad executive, legislator, and—"

"Thank heavens we're slowing down for this one—I can't take it all in!" said Grace.

"...my mentor—although he doesn't know it yet, and Meg's cousin-in-law."

The carriage pulled to a stop in front of the elaborate structure.

Grace looked at Lucius and then at Marguerite. "This is your cousin's house?"

She stared at the three-story conglomeration of granite and sandstone walls, towers and turrets and a multitude of chimneys rising stately from the multicolored tile roof. Leaded and stained glass windows, elaborate carvings, and Galveston ironwork on the galleries added to the palatial sense of the place.

"Goodness gracious," was the best she could respond.

"Kind of like your first view of the water, honey, it's a little overwhelming, isn't it," said Marguerite, patting Grace's hand as she stood to disembark from the carriage. "I'll give you a day or two to rest, and then we'll have you over for tea. Or we can wait until Josie goes calling and then I can give you the tour of it."

"I'd love to see every bit of it. It's... it's..."

"Decadent? Ostentatious? Grandiose? Yes, it's all of those things and more—much like this island. Welcome to Galveston, Grace Taylor."

Chapter 8

The next stop was two blocks closer to the beach and three blocks west on L Street to Lucius Roderick's more sensible home. Just 'a stepping stone house' he called it, but Grace thought it was lovely.

Painted the color of raw wool, the two-story Victorian house was trimmed in white with black storm shutters on the tall windows. A red stucco covered the basement wall between brick support pillars, and a five foot decorative iron fence surrounded the property with brick columns every ten feet or so. A number of rose bushes grew along the west fence.

Nine wide steps led up to the front gallery, which ran half the length of the front of the house. An identical gallery perched above it on the second floor.

Lucius helped her out of the carriage while Tom unloaded her trunk and satchel. Lucius grabbed her satchel.

"Tell me about the ambitious person who lives here," she said, smiling at him.

He grinned at her, but grew more serious as he looked at the house. "He puts in long hours at the firm. He studies his clients and the movers and shakers in this city to learn everything he can from them. He's going to make a name for himself someday, possibly build an empire that he can pass on to his children."

Grace raised her eyebrows. "So… you've allowed children in your future."

"Someday… when I find the right woman."

"That's good, Lucius. I'm glad you're not totally consumed with your empire-building. Your sister and I were afraid you'd die a rich, but lonely old man."

Lucius laughed as Grace allowed him to escort her up the steps to the front door. She noticed a stained glass transom window above the wood door that held a bevel-edged oval glass window.

He opened the door and allowed Grace to step inside first. She let her eyes get accustomed to the light and liked what she saw. A staircase led to a landing halfway up before turning and disappearing upstairs. The parlor opened to the right. A fireplace using the same brick as the pillars outside faced her. The room was sparse in furniture, but the pieces were tasteful.

"Very nice," she said. "Did you do this yourself?"

"Do I look like I'd be interested in decorating a house?"

"No, so it must've been your lady friends."

"Very few lady friends have seen this place. Actually, most of the furniture came with the house. The owner moved back to Dallas when her husband passed away."

Tom brought the trunk inside and Lucius directed him upstairs. "First door on your right." He turned back to Grace. "I think you'll enjoy your room. A door opens to the balcony and the windows pull in a good breeze."

"I'm so sorry to be putting you out of your house. I'm hoping to find a place very soon."

"I practically live at the office anyway—there's a comfortable sofa I'm quite familiar with."

He walked through the parlor and into the next room—a dining room, and pointed out the kitchen to the left. Then he hollered through a transparent door covered with a delicate wire mesh.

"Juju! I'm home! Come meet our guest." He told Grace that Juju did the laundry out on the porch close to the cistern.

Grace ran her hand over the wire mesh on the door. "I've heard of this material, but I've never seen it. The air passes through, but the insects can't."

"It's a screen door. I have screens on some of the windows, too.

The mosquitoes tend to be ruthless down here."

They stepped out on the back porch as an older woman draped some wet linens over a chair and shuffled towards them.

"Grace, this is my talented cook and housekeeper, Juju."

"Hello, Miss Grace!" said the older woman, speaking with a faint accent. "We were surprised to hear that Sissy wasn't coming after all. But that's all right. We're glad to have you, too!"

"Thank you." Grace immediately liked the woman.

"What are we having for supper?" asked Lucius.

"A quick clam chowder and biscuits. It's almost ready. Kitty's coming by to get me soon. She's draggin' me to the Garten Verein tonight—I guess to find me a husband."

"You'd make somebody a very lucky man, Juju."

She lit up like a lantern. "Oh, pshaw."

Grace smiled, watching Lucius charm the older woman. He knew how to make a woman—no matter what age—feel special.

"Kitty was wonderin' if you were comin'."

Lucius turned to Grace. "You feel up to a dance tonight?"

Grace shook her head. "I'm exhausted. Would you mind if I stayed in tonight?"

"I still have to make it up to you—you know, the Cotillion…"

"That debt was settled when you bought me ice cream."

"That was too easy—oh! I need to get Tom to take those dishes back to the drugstore. Let me try and catch him."

He ran back into the house. Juju started towards the kitchen.

"Can I help with anything?"

"No, ma'am!" she said firmly. "You're Mr. Roderick's guest."

"Well, I'm going to freshen up. Let me know if you need me to do anything."

"Thank you, but it's all taken care of."

Grace started to reach for the screen door when she saw a dark-haired young woman step around the corner of the house.

"There you are, Kitty! Come here and let me introduce you to Miss Taylor."

Kitty stopped in the yard and stared at Grace.

"Miss Taylor, this is my daughter, Kitty."

"Nice to meet you, Kitty."

She simply nodded once.

Grace figured she was a few years younger than she, but she saw little that resembled Juju. Kitty was pretty in an exotic way—gray, almond-shaped eyes, olive colored skin, shiny black hair twisted into a simple knot at the nape of her neck.

"Don't be rude, girl."

An almost imperceptible frown crossed Kitty's face, but then her demeanor changed when she said, "How do you do?"

Lucius pushed open the screen door. "I missed him, doggone it. I'll give him a few minutes to get back to the livery and then I'll give him a ring to ask him to drop them by Stars. Hi, Kitty!"

Her smile completely transformed her face. Grace thought she was stunning.

"Hey, Lucius! Are you… and Miss Taylor going to the dance tonight?"

"We're thinkin' about it."

"Please call me Grace, and if you don't mind, Lucius, I'm a bit road weary and I'd probably embarrass you—."

"I'm sorry, of course you'd be tired," said Lucius. "But you'd never embarrass me—I'd be the envy of the island with you on my arm."

Grace noticed that Kitty was frowning again. She glanced at Lucius to see if he noticed.

He didn't.

"Did Juju tell you that Kitty's attending medical school?"

That astonished her. Grace realized there must be much more to Kitty than a simple infatuation towards her mother's employer.

"Women can attend medical school here?"

"They graduated six this year," said Kitty. "I still have two more years to go."

"And she works at the Sealy Hospital, too."

"I'm learning more there than I am in the classes."

"That's amazing. I know your mother must be very proud of you."

"I am, and I'd better check those biscuits," said Juju. "Supper will be on the sideboard whenever you're ready to eat. We'll be leaving shortly."

"That's fine. I'll see you Monday… or maybe not. Miss Taylor will be here… I'm sure I'll get by sometime that day."

Grace felt another pang of guilt for displacing Lucius from his own home.

"Did you realize it's Labor Day?" Juju asked.

"I forgot about that—do you have plans?"

"I'd like to see the parade Monday afternoon."

"By all means, go to the parade."

"How 'bout I put a pot roast on in the morning and you can heat it up for supper?"

"Why don't you take the holiday, and we'll do pot roast on Wednesday. I'll take Miss Taylor to one of our fine eating establishments."

"Are you sure?"

"Of course, Juju—it's Labor Day. I just might take the afternoon off and go to the parade myself."

"We'll look for you then."

"And if you hear of any rooms for rent, I'd appreciate you letting me know," Grace said to Juju. "I'd like to start looking as soon as possible."

"I'll ask around. Now I'm sure those biscuits are burned," she said, hurrying past them through another screened door leading directly into the kitchen.

"Save a dance for me, Kit," said Lucius, holding the door open for Grace. "Let me show you your room, and then we can sit down to supper in about half an hour, if that's all right with you."

"That sounds nice," said Grace. "Nice meeting you, Kitty."

They walked upstairs together where he opened the first door on the right. A leaded glass transom window tilted out a few inches above the door. The bedroom was large and airy with pale green and blue wallpaper. A canopied, four-poster bed was tucked in a bay window on the west wall. An armoire stood on the north wall to the right of the door, and a table and chair sat by the tall window on the front wall of the house. A tall window opened to the balcony and extended all the way to the floor, but was covered with a hinged screen.

Grace walked over and looked at the porch.

"This is the coolest room in the house—it's situated to catch the gulf breeze."

"Is this a door or a window?" She opened the screen. "It's large enough to walk out of."

"Technically, it's a window—taxes are based on the number of doors in a house, but it's built to function as a pass-through, too. There's another one in my room across the hall. The official door to the gallery is in the hall. Hope this room will do."

"It's perfect. Thank you for everything, Lucius. I don't know what I would've done if you hadn't been here."

"My pleasure. And I can't tell you how fortunate you were to meet Marguerite St. John on the train today. She'll introduce you to people and get you in places the governor himself would have difficulty getting in."

"I'm not sure I have the right status after seeing the Gresham House."

"Meg came from humble beginnings, and unlike many around here, she hasn't forgotten that. And she's obviously quite taken with you. That's a good thing. Now rest a bit, and then we'll enjoy the best clam chowder on the island."

Chapter 9

Disorientation greeted Grace when she opened her eyes. Her head always felt like lead whenever she napped too long. For a moment she couldn't remember or recognize where she was. She looked around and saw the heavy bedposts, the sheer drapes gently lifted by a breeze, and the open door to the balcony.

Then it all came flooding back—leaving Finn, fleeing to Galveston, meeting Marguerite and Lucius, the beautiful houses, Lucius' home, Juju... clam chowder. She sat up in bed feeling ravenous. She ignored her shoes and stockings and hurried downstairs barefooted.

On the table were the remains of Lucius' meal and a note beside it. Grace picked it up and read:

You looked so peaceful sleeping, Grace, I didn't want to disturb you. It's almost 7:00 and I'm heading to the Garten Verein. If you change your mind, just go to the telephone on the kitchen wall, pick up the handset and turn the crank several times and when the operator answers, ask her to ring 245—it's the livery and they'll send a gig for you—just give them my name and they know where to come. I can't wait to show you off. But if you're still too tired, I'll see you tomorrow, ma belle. CR

Grace smiled at the familiar French term with which he ended the note. *Now that's the old Lucius I know to keep at arm's length,* Grace thought. *And what if I'm showing you off, Luscious?*

She giggled thinking about it.

"Finn, who?" she said boldly out loud, but the ache of the loss resurfaced.

The empty house reminded her how alone she was. She realized by the shadows in the house that it was much later than she realized.

"We need some light in here," she said, looking around for an oil lamp before remembering that Lucius had electricity. She found the light switch and pushed the top button and walked back to the parlor and found the switch for that room's fixture to turn it on as well. She came back and served herself a bowl of clam chowder, long grown cold, but still delicious tasting. She ate a second biscuit covered with honey for dessert. Then she gathered up the leftovers and dirty dishes on a tray and carried them to the kitchen, pausing to find the light switch.

Waco had telephones and electricity in the nicer homes and business establishments, and her grandparents had recently acquired electricity in their small community of Grace. The town also had six telephones—half of them belonged to Taylor households.

Grace's hometown of Dalton in South Texas had electricity and a few phones, but those services had yet to make their way to her family's house outside of town. Grace had lived away from home long enough to get used to such modern conveniences and was glad to see Galveston was so progressive—more so than any other place she'd visited.

She put the soup in the icebox and the remaining biscuits in a bread tin, and turned on the single faucet over a large bowl in the copper-lined sink. She picked up a large tea kettle on the gas stove to fill it, but then she wasn't sure how to light the stove and ended up washing the dishes in cold, soapy water.

Afterwards she turned off the light and walked back into the dining room, latched the screen door and closed the wood door behind it. At home, they never locked their doors, but she noticed this one locked with a key, so she looked around, noticing one hanging with a ribbon on a brass hook. It fit, so she walked to the parlor and tried it on the front door, which locked as well. She closed the windows downstairs, turned off the lights and made her way upstairs in the dim remaining light of the day.

She stepped into the bedroom, but didn't turn on the light, choosing to visit the balcony. She stepped through the window and sat down in a comfortable white wicker chair, taking in the sounds of the neighborhood. Several people walked by—their voices sounded young. She wondered if they were going to the dance. She could hear the murmur of another conversation in a house nearby and could smell onions cooking.

Two big trees anchored the front corners of the house, blocking her views down each direction of Avenue L, but the trees were beautiful.

A mockingbird sang through his repertoire on the highest point on the rooftop across the street. Suddenly, he fluttered up a few feet and came back down to continue to sing.

Grace smiled. "Show-off. You're trying so hard to get everyone to notice you. Maybe I should call you Lucius… no, Roderick. Roderick, the mockingbird. Well, I see you."

A scruffy little black dog started barking at her from the raised front gallery on the house across the street.

"Look at you," she said, leaning forward. "You look a little like my Obie from home."

A man opened the door and hollered at the dog, "Hush, Trixie!" He looked around and then leaned down to pet her before closing the door.

"So… Trixie's your name. I have a feeling we're going to be friends, little one."

She opened her hand, realizing she had brought the key upstairs with her. She remembered something Vestal told her years ago: *Don't be discouraged, Grace. It's usually the last key in the bunch that unlocks the door.*

Vestal explained that it meant to persevere—to keep trying. Grace was determined to persevere when so many others gave up, but she'd tried everything and had yet to find the right key to unlock Finn's heart. Maybe it could never be opened.

Suddenly the silence in the neighborhood was deafening. The birds and dogs were quiet; she heard no voices talking or the clomping of horses walking the streets. But then she became aware of a noise in the background—a steady cadence slowly inhaling and exhaling. It took her a moment to realize she could hear the ocean.

The ocean… does the ocean breathe?

Chapter 10

Grace stood on the second floor of the train station watching the crowd. Today she would try the last key. It worked for Sissy Roderick, whose beau had avoided a commitment for years. Sissy planned to move away and start another life elsewhere. When her beau saw she had gone so far as to schedule a teaching interview and buy a train ticket to Galveston, he had a change of heart and proposed to her. Now Grace stood there holding the same ticket to Galveston, confident she wouldn't have to use it.

She saw Sissy waving and pointing towards the west door. Her heart started racing when she saw Finn. He spied Sissy and walked towards her. She said something to him, and he looked up at Grace. She smiled and waved at him and began to hurry toward the stairs to meet him. The station was crowded, but she pushed through, ready to run into his arms. She had imagined this moment so many times, and now she was living it! She rushed around the last group of people and held out her arms to… no one.

Finn was gone.

Only Sissy remained, looking like she was about to cry. Grace turned around and around, and suddenly she was the only person in the empty train station. She ran outside, but could go nowhere, for as far as she could see was water.

She awoke with a start, and the tears came again. After a while, she berated herself for wasting time on the past.

"I gave you my heart for ten years, Finn," she said to herself. "You're not taking any more of my life."

She threw the sheet off and sat up in bed, glancing at the open balcony door. It was Sunday, but she could see it was still early. She decided she had time to go see the ocean before church. She had no idea how far Lucius' house was from the beach, but since she heard the waves last night, she assumed it wasn't too far. She tied her loose hair in a ponytail at the nape of her neck and dressed in her above-the-ankle split riding skirt, hoping to wade barefoot in the water.

She shut the yard gate and started walking south on 17th Street toward the gray horizon. The morning breeze cooled her face, defying the heat coming later. The walk proved further than she realized, but at about O Street she realized the hazy sky on the horizon was actually the ocean. The grays blurred into one and she couldn't see a distinct line between the water and the sky.

Ten blocks from Roderick's house she finally stepped onto the beach. A number of houses to her left were built on stilts. To the right a raised trolley track stood high over the surf. The electric lines to power the trolley were mounted on tall poles centered over the tracks every fifty yards or so.

Grace knelt and untied her shoes, stripped off her stockings down to her bare feet and walked toward the water. The sand felt soft under her feet and between her toes.

The bay water looked huge coming in on the train, but this ocean of water went on forever. It frightened her in a way to stand before such a powerful force. She hesitated before stepping into the foaming water that lapped at her toes. Then she took a deep breath and walked into the surf as she held up her split skirt, but the third wave soaked it to her knees. She gave up and let it drop, knowing she could dry it later.

The sun had yet to find its way from behind the morning clouds, casting a gray pall over everything. She could see a dark shadow way out on the horizon and realized it was a ship coming in. She'd never seen a ship before yesterday, much less an entire port of seaworthy vessels of all sizes. She hoped Lucius would take her down to the pier soon and tell her how all of that worked.

"Staggering, isn't it?" someone said behind her.

Grace turned around to see a tall, slender man standing just out of the water's reach and staring out to the sea. His face looked friendly enough.

"That's a good word for it," replied Grace. "Is this the first time you've seen it?"

"Oh, no. I grew up here, but the ocean never ceases to amaze me."

Grace looked back at the white-capped waves. "It seems… angry."

He chuckled at that comment. "Oh, this is normal for an overcast day. You wouldn't be standing anywhere near her when she's really angry."

Grace grinned at his referring to the ocean as a *she*. "So you've experienced her… temper?"

"Sure. My family's weathered some pretty good storms here, but the water always goes down, the sun always comes out, and things get back to normal. You need to come back later and see her when the sun is shining. She puts on a much different face then. My name's Walter."

"Nice to meet you. I'm Grace."

"Are you vacationing here?"

"No, I plan to teach at the Rosenberg School this term. Are you familiar with it?"

He smiled. "Went to school there. Good school, although I didn't appreciate it at the time. I know someone that teaches there… Daisy Thorne. She's probably about your age."

"I'd love to meet her."

"She lives at the Lucas Terrace Apartments near the beach on East Broadway."

"My interview with the principal is Tuesday morning. Maybe I could meet her before then?"

"Where are you staying?"

"The house on the northeast corner of L and 17th Streets—Lucius Roderick's home."

"Don't know him, but I'll probably see Daisy at church this morning. She's a good teacher, but this'll be her last year."

"Why's that?"

"She's engaged to a doctor from Austin. Sure hate to see her go. But I'll let her know you'd like to meet her."

"Thank you so much… Walter," said Grace, stepping out of the water. "Is this normal weather?"

He nodded. "For low tide."

"How high does it get otherwise?"

"At least halfway up the trestle pilings," he said, pointing to the trolley tracks to the west.

"Really? That high?"

"Twice a day."

"Do you like to get out in the water?"

"Sure, but I prefer the Bay side for boating—it's calmer. I do enjoy walking the beaches, though." He pulled out a pocket watch. "I'd best be getting along. Where do you go to church?"

"Is there a Baptist church on the island?"

"Sure! First Baptist is over on 22nd or 23rd—one of those and Sealy Street. Go west on Sealy and you can't miss it. And I'll tell Daisy to look you up."

"I appreciate your help, Walter."

"Maybe I'll see you around."

Grace smiled and nodded as she headed north, only stopping long enough to lean on a fence so she could don her stockings and shoes. Later at the house across the street from where she was staying, the little black dog started barking at her again. Grace squatted down and called her by name. 'Trixie' crept gingerly towards her and submissively rolled over on her back in front of her. Grace rewarded her by scratching her belly and her chin.

"You're such a sweet girl. I knew we could be friends."

By the time she opened the front door of Lucius' house, the sun had broken through the clouds. She wiped the sweat from her brow and walked through the house to the kitchen to grab a cold biscuit before getting ready for church.

She wasn't sure what time church started, and she forgot to ask Lucius to pick her up beforehand, so she figured she'd better leave early since she had to walk a ways.

She found a smaller room off the kitchen with a deep, copper-lined tub and a single faucet over it. She opted for a shallow cold bath since she still wasn't sure how to work the gas stove.

She ran upstairs draped in a tablecloth, and quickly dressed in a fitted, pale blue jacket and skirt with a lacy, white blouse. The straight skirt flared from the mid-thigh down for easy walking. By the time she reached the parlor, though, she changed her mind about wearing the jacket, so she removed it and draped it on the back of a chair.

With her Bible and a white parasol in hand, Grace walked out the door at 8:45 a.m. and headed north on 17th Street until she came to Sealy. She noticed a sign that said St. Mary's University pointing east as she turned the opposite direction.

She thought about her college days. Finn was responsible for that, too. She begged her parents to let her attend the Baylor Female College in Belton. She left out one little detail—Finn Samuel just happened to be living and working in nearby Temple. Finn still visited Jimmy and Mercy Taylor in Grace every so often, and he made it a point to take Grace along so she could see her kinfolks. She ended up with a college degree just so she could be close to Finn. Grace decided the principal didn't need to know that little detail during her interview on Tuesday.

Baylor Female College was also where she met Lucius' sister, Sissy Roderick. After the first year, they roomed together until graduation. Grace's college friends thought she was daffy for loving a man seven years her senior, but they got used to him being around since Grace always invited him to social gatherings.

During Grace's last year of college, Finn took a job in Waco, so she applied for a teaching position there. She was grateful now to have two years' teaching experience heading into this job interview in Galveston.

The yards and walkways along Sealy Street were awash in color with beautiful, blooming shrubs she wasn't familiar with. Some of them grew as tall as trees and shaded her walk in places. Grace couldn't help but ask a woman in one of the yards what kind of plant grew so abundantly on the island, and the lady told her they were 'oleanders.'

Grace loved looking at the houses, and Sealy Street had no shortage of beautiful homes. She had just passed a two-story Victorian home with first and second floor galleries running across the entire front of the house when she realized she'd found the church. The gleaming white stucco structure stood at least another story's height above the previous house, and the tops of the church's arched windows were at least twenty-five feet above the ground. When she walked around to the front, she noticed minaret-looking towers adorning the steep-pitched roof. A thirty-five or forty foot high, lacy flower-shaped window commanded the center front of the building. She couldn't recall seeing such an ornate Baptist church before.

A lone bicycle leaned against the wall beside the closest door, so she assumed the services started later. She closed her parasol and opened one of the heavy, arched doors and stepped inside, closing it behind her. The stained glass windows provided a rainbow of light leading her to a set of stairs. She paused at the base, running her fingers over a carved star symbol on the side of the banister's corner post.

"May I help you?" a voice asked from behind.

Grace started. She turned to see a short man dressed entirely too casually for a Sunday service.

"I guess this isn't the Baptist Church," she deduced.

The man smiled and nodded his head to the right. "It's a block further."

"I'm so sorry—I'm still trying to find my way around Galveston. Your church is beautiful, though; is it Catholic?"

"No," he laughed out loud. "I can't wait to tell Father Kirwin that one."

"Episcopalian, then?"

"No, this is the Congregation B'nai Israel Synagogue…"

Grace's expression must have registered no understanding, so the man elaborated.

"We're Jews, or to be more specific, a Reform Jew congregation."

"Jews?" Grace stared at him. "I've never met a Jew before."

The man chuckled. "Do we look so different from anyone else?"

Grace smiled apologetically. "Sorry, but you're one of the *chosen ones.*"

"And you don't believe you are?"

"Oh, yes. But I'm grafted onto the family tree."

"Ahhh… and you are?"

"Grace Taylor… I arrived here yesterday. I hope to teach school here."

"Wonderful! We can always use more good teachers around here. I'm Rabbi Cohen, and I like your first name."

"I was named after my grandparents' town."

"Your grandparents have a town?"

"They founded it, although it's very small. Originally it was named Taylor, but there's another larger town in Texas named Taylor, so they changed their town's name to 'Grace' after God brought my father and mother and uncle safely back home after a kidnapping and Apache Indian attack. This happened before I was born, and then they named me Grace," she said quickly, trying to make a long story short. "That probably made no sense at all."

"Sounds like a fascinating story."

"The Jews have some interesting stories, too."

"And you're familiar with them?"

"Of course! It's our history, too," she reminded him. "Adam and Eve, Noah and the Ark, and then Abraham, Isaac, and Jacob and the twelve tribes, and Joseph and his coat of many colors, and I love how God used him to save his people when the famine hit, and Queen Esther's story is one of my favorites, and then there's King David and all of the major and minor prophets. Then Jesus came and—"

"That's where we differ," he said. "But we respect your beliefs."

"But Jesus was a Jew."

"We believe he was a good man, even a rabbi—teacher."

"But not the Messiah."

"No, but we can agree to disagree." He took out his pocket watch.

"Are your services about to begin?"

"No, our Shabbat was yesterday, but I believe your services are about to start. I'm usually not here on Sundays; you just happened to catch me at the right time."

"I'm so sorry—I guess this means I'm trespassing."

"No, not at all," he said as he walked to the door, opening it for her. "And welcome to Galveston, Miss Taylor. If you ever need anything, I'm usually here six days out of the week, unless I'm traveling. Sunday is my day off."

"I'm honored to meet you, Rabbi Cohen." She stepped out into the bright sun and opened her parasol. "I hope I'll see you again soon. And I'll say a prayer for you."

"Thank you. And I, you. But remember to pray to the one true, El Elyon, on my behalf."

"Jesus will hear it, too," Grace said, grinning brightly. "Good day, Rabbi." She turned quickly before he could respond.

Chapter 11

The streets adjacent to the Baptist church were filled with carriages of every size. Some dropped off passengers, others secured their horses and one-horse gigs to the nearest trees or hitching posts, and still many others walked to church like Grace.

Someone came up beside her and took her by the arm.

"Meg and I have been looking everywhere for you!" Lucius said.

Grace smiled. "There you are! I'm sorry I didn't remember to make plans with you last night."

Marguerite walked up on the other side.

"Close that parasol before you put an eye out," she told Grace, who promptly obeyed. Marguerite took her other arm.

"Where have you been? We were so worried! Lucius saw your jacket in the parlor like you hadn't left the house—we've been up and down all the streets."

Grace felt terrible until Lucius whispered, "Only two."

"I'm sorry, Marguerite."

"I thought someone had kidnapped you, and before I'd heard all of your interesting stories!"

Lucius winked at Grace.

"Would you believe I accidentally walked into the Jewish synagogue a block back assuming it was the Baptist church?"

"You didn't!" Marguerite laughed loudly.

"Then I realized the church was much more elaborate than I was used to seeing in a Baptist church, and then I probably said more than I should have."

"You talked to the Rabbi?"

"Yes. He was very gracious and said he liked my name. Then I felt obligated to explain where my name came from and rambled on and on."

"Uh, oh."

"He was very kind, though, and he told me if there was anything he could do for me, to let him know," said Grace. She turned to Marguerite. "I didn't mean to worry you—how can I make it up to you?"

"Let's dine together after church, and you can tell me about the kidnappings in your family."

"Shouldn't you be with your cousin today? You've just arrived," Grace said as they walked into the church foyer.

"I found out from my youngest niece, bless her heart—she's my favorite and my personal snitch—that they've invited a widowed reverend from the Episcopal Church to try to spark some interest between the two of us. They're worried about my wandering soul, and Josephine thinks if I marry a preacher, I just might settle down. But I don't want to settle down. Oh, hello, Betty!"

She waved at a woman talking to a group of women across the foyer. The woman smiled and waved back.

"Who's that?"

"Betty Ballinger. She's probably shocked to see me here. You'll have to come with me to her house for tea on Wednesday. I'll introduce you then."

"You know your cousin is going to be upset with you," Grace whispered.

Marguerite picked up a couple of fans from a basket and handed one to Grace. "It won't be the first time, nor will it be the last. And Jesus and I do know each other personally, and He accepts me just the way I am."

Grace smiled. "I'm sure He does."

Later during lunch in the plush surroundings at the Tremont Hotel downtown, Grace told the story of her grandmother Julia Taylor and father Justin's kidnapping by the Apache warrior Nantan Lupan. Then she told the story of almost twenty years later when her uncle Jimmy took her mother Allie, their barely surviving an attack by the Apaches, and subsequent captivity with them.

"It took my father weeks to find them, and when he finally did, he was so angry he almost killed my uncle. I've heard these stories for years, but now that I'm telling you, it sounds so barbaric in such civilized surroundings."

"Are you going to eat the rest of your steak?" Lucius asked Grace.

She realized she'd been talking a lot more than she'd been eating. "No, I think I'll…"

"Good," he said, stabbing it and placing it on his plate. "I danced off that clam chowder by nine o'clock last night, and I only had a cup of coffee this morning."

"I think she was trying to say she was going to save it for later," said Marguerite.

Lucius stopped in mid-bite. "Oh!"

Grace laughed. "No, that's all right—eat up. I'll have another roll… and some more banana. I can count on one hand the times I've eaten a banana in my life."

"They ship everything imaginable through here," Lucius said with a full mouth. "You name it—you can find it here."

"Back to your family," said Marguerite. "Do your father and his brother get along now?"

"Oh, yes. Mother saw to that, and Uncle Jimmy's been a great friend and mentor towards Finn."

Lucius rolled his eyes. "What is wrong with that man? Who in their right mind would walk away from you?"

"Hush!" said Marguerite.

Grace's demeanor fell. "Sissy told you what happened?"

Lucius glanced at Marguerite, who was frowning fiercely at him. "She… uh…had to explain why you were coming in her place."

"Oh, right," said Grace. "It's just humiliating for everyone to know he rejected me."

"I have to agree with Lucius—the man isn't right in his head," said Marguerite. "Now tell me how your aunt's face was burned."

Grace told how Mercy had run off with a gambler, and Jimmy was hired by her father to find her and bring her back to Waco. She told how Mercy caused them to miss the stagecoach, and the next one wouldn't come through for two more days.

"Jimmy bought the only thing he could find to get them out of town—a funeral hearse. They crossed paths with some thieves who assumed that they were hauling a body, which kept them from getting robbed. But when Mercy was in Brownwood, the thieves showed up in town and one of them recognized her. He followed her to Finn's parents' house and attacked her in the barn, and in the process caught the barn on fire from his cigarette butt. Mercy crawled out, saving a five-year-old girl named Caitlin…"

Grace stopped talking when she said the name. She hadn't thought about Mercy's connection with Caitlin all those years before.

"Who's Caitlin?" asked Lucius.

Grace sat there, lost in her thoughts.

"The young girl who died years ago," whispered Marguerite. "The one Finn loved."

"He was in love with a five-year-old girl?" he whispered back.

"No, you dunce." Marguerite swatted his arm and said louder, "So that's when Mercy's face was burned?"

Grace nodded, looking up. "Can we finish this story later? I'm still tired, for some reason."

"Traveling across the state will do that—it takes me days to recuperate," said Marguerite. "And I can't miss my Sunday nap either."

Grace smiled. "Finn told me his mother took her naps very seriously. They had to be quiet around the house for an hour after lunch, and there were eleven children in that family."

"My word," said Marguerite, standing. "How did she do it?"

Grace gathered her Bible and parasol before standing. "The Samuels adopted all of them within a two-year period. I don't know what that woman was thinking, but those children couldn't have had a better mother than France Samuel."

Lucius walked ahead to pay for their meals as the women walked slowly towards the lobby.

"Someday I hope you can tell me what happened to Caitlin."

"Would you believe I was willing to *be* Caitlin for Finn? He told me several times through the years that I reminded him of her. I thought that might open his heart toward me, and for a while it seemed to do just that. But eventually I felt like I was losing myself, so I pulled away to try to figure out who I was and what I wanted in life. I decided he was going to have to accept me—Grace, just as I was. I actually focused on my studies and made good grades at college during that time, but when he moved back to Waco, I followed him like a trained pony. We picked up where we'd left off—comfortable companions, and I think he was content with that."

"Haven't you ever loved anyone else besides Finn, honey?"

Grace shook her head. "It's always been Finn."

"What about Lucius? He'd be quite a catch if you could ever get him to settle down."

Grace watched him walk towards them. "I'll definitely keep my eyes and heart open from now on."

Chapter 12

At mid-afternoon, Grace heard a knock at the front door. She opened it to find a petite young woman with reddish-gold hair.

"I'm looking for Grace?" she said tentatively.

"That's me. Are you Daisy?"

The woman nodded enthusiastically. "Walter Grover said you wanted to talk to me about the Rosenberg School."

Grace opened the door and let her in. "I'm so glad to meet you, Daisy! Come, sit down. May I get you some water? I'm sorry I don't have anything else to offer you—bachelor house, and he's rarely here, I'm told."

Daisy shook her head. "No thank you, I'm fine."

"Have a seat," said Grace, gesturing to the sofa. "On second thought, let's sit on the upstairs gallery. It's much cooler."

Daisy followed Grace up the stairs, and out onto the porch. They settled in the two wicker chairs.

Daisy looked around. "I love this house—not too big and not too small. And this gallery is wonderful."

"It's my favorite place in the house. Do you know Lucius Roderick?"

"I've never met him personally, but I do know him by sight and I definitely know who he is. Some of my friends have been trying to catch his eye." Her hand flew to her mouth like she'd said something wrong. "I'm sorry—are you and Lucius… close… like promised or anything?"

"Oh, no—we're just friends. His sister and I are best friends, though, and he's the only person I know in Galveston, so that's why I'm here. I'll be finding my own place soon, though. He's staying downtown, by the way."

"Whew! I thought I'd offended you."

"No, of course not," said Grace, smiling at the attractive young woman. "What about you? I'm sure he's noticed you—especially your hair. It's beautiful."

"Thank you," said Daisy. "But somebody's already caught my eye. We're to be married next year."

"Oh, that's right. Walter said you were engaged to somebody."

Daisy nodded and sighed. "Dr. Joe Gilbert. I can't wait to have my own house with him in Austin next summer. Right now I share a small apartment at the end of Broadway Street with my mother, sister, brother, aunt and a recent litter of kittens. It's getting quite crowded."

"Lucius' goal is to live on Broadway Street someday."

"Our apartment building is quite large, but it's nothing like the elaborate mansions down the street."

"I'd be content to live in a house like this, but Lucius calls it 'a stepping stone' house around here. He's very ambitious."

"And charming; he never lacked for dance partners last night. I don't recall seeing you there, though, and I would've remembered. My friends would've complained all night if you were with him."

Grace smiled. "I was too tired from the trip down here. So you were at the Garden…"

"Garten Verein—it's German for *Garden Club* or something of the sort. A beautiful place. There's another dance next Friday. Maybe you can come with Lucius."

"He *is* a good dancer... and it would be a good place to meet more people…"

"Good! I'll look for you."

"Your fiancé doesn't mind you going to dances?"

"No. He knows he has no competition in Galveston. And I just love to dance. I could introduce you to some of the staff from the Rosenberg School, too. Walter said you'd be teaching there this year."

"I hope so. My interview's Tuesday and I'm a bit nervous about it."

"Do you have any teaching experience?"

"Two years in Waco with older elementary students. I don't think I have the patience for the little ones."

"What did you teach?"

"My degree is in English, so I've taught reading, writing, spelling, history, and penmanship."

"I teach 7th grade history, English, and drawing. Where did you get your degree?"

"Baylor Female College in Belton. How about you?"

"Sam Houston Normal in Huntsville. This'll be my fourth year of teaching."

"You look so young!"

"I'm twenty-three, but I did three years of college coursework in one year."

Grace was impressed. "I'm twenty-four, and I took my sweet time at college." She left out the part about waiting for a marriage proposal.

"Normally, Galveston schools require a new teacher to work as a substitute the first year, but they made an exception for me."

"My record isn't nearly as stellar as yours. I was going to start looking for a place to live tomorrow, but maybe I ought to wait and see if I have a job first. I'm really worried now."

"That rule probably applies to teachers fresh out of college with no experience. Your two years should count for something. The thing to remember is that our schools have high expectations for the teachers and their students. If you're not challenging the students, they won't keep you. You'll find Galveston graduates going on to places like the University of Virginia, Harvard and Princeton."

Daisy told Grace about the principal, the daily schedule, and general school rules and procedures. Before she left, Grace felt much more confident about the interview. They agreed to meet at Murdoch's Bathhouse for a swim after the parade late Monday afternoon. Daisy shared one more tip as she opened the yard gate. "Avoid the water during the heat of the day. The sun will burn your skin before you even realize it. I'll see you tomorrow evening!"

Lucius came by early Sunday evening to introduce her to the trolley routes around town. He told her that his neighbor across the street worked for the trolley system.

"I've met his dog Trixie, but I haven't caught anyone else outside," said Grace.

They walked one block over on Broadway Street to catch the trolley. From there it turned on 25th Street and headed downtown.

"This is so much calmer than yesterday," said Grace, taking time to look at the details on the massive buildings.

"We're not all greedy reprobates," said Lucius. "Many of us actually do take Sundays off."

"And you attend church regularly? You didn't go just for me yesterday, did you?"

"Of course not! You'd be surprised at the number of good contacts I've made in church."

Grace looked shocked. "That's not the only reason you go, is it?"

"No—I'm just teasing you."

But Grace wasn't so sure. "There's more to life than getting rich, Lucius."

He grasped her hand. "But look how much good I could do if I did have money. Look around. Many of the men who built these empires built hospitals and orphanages and schools with their wealth."

"You do have a point," Grace admitted. "Just make sure you get there honorably so you won't have any regrets."

"Yes, ma'am. I need a good woman to keep me in line." He raised her hand and kissed it.

Grace's first instinct was to pull away, but she stopped herself and allowed him to. He seemed encouraged by her consent and looked around. She followed his eyes and noticed that the only other riders on the trolley sat near the front. She turned back to Lucius and the look in his eyes startled her.

He simply asked, "May I?"

She knew exactly what he was asking her, and casting Finn's memory aside, she nodded her head.

He put his arm around her and leaned in to kiss her, gingerly at first, but then more passionately. Her large hat provided some privacy from pedestrians on the street.

Grace realized that dancing wasn't the only thing Lucius was good at. When he finally pulled away, she grasped the seat in front of her to steady herself.

He smiled like he knew he'd made an impression on her.

"I've been waiting a long time to get to do that."

"You haven't either," she said. "I'm sure you haven't given me a second thought since the Cotillion."

He laughed. "Not so, although my empire-building has taken precedence over my family-building. But I'm close to a deal that's going to change all of that. And within another year, if all goes as planned, I'll be looking for a house on Broadway."

He leaned over to kiss her again, but this time she noticed the trolley driver watching in the mirror. Grace leaned away, ill at ease with Lucius' public displays of affection.

"Lucius," she cautioned him.

"It's different down here—'we live and let live.'"

She shook her head and turned toward the window to put her hat between her and Lucius' face. Her eyes caught a movement in a window on the second floor of a large house on the corner. A beautiful face… a familiar face. The woman caught Grace's eye and quickly disappeared from view. *Kitty?*

"Does Juju live around here?"

Lucius looked around. "On this street? No, she lives on the west side of town."

Grace turned around. "Then what's that big house back there on the corner?"

"Where are we?" Lucius turned around and snorted. "Oh. Well, you don't want to know."

"Why not?"

"Let's just say if Juju lived there, she'd be a little old for that line of work."

"What do you mean?"

"Ah, my innocent dove. How refreshing it is that you know little of the carnal side of life."

"Tell me, Lucius."

"Well, to put it mildly, it's a house of ill repute."

"Right here in downtown Galveston?"

"There's a lot more than one on that street."

"How do you know that?"

"Everyone knows about Postoffice Street, and nobody says much of anything."

"I don't believe that. Surely the law enforcement and city leaders are concerned about this—and especially the women of this town. How can they let it exist so close to their businesses and husbands?"

"It's a port town—prostitution and sailors go hand-in-hand. There's a joke going around town that the Heroes Monument they erected this year actually points the way to the brothels."

"Not funny."

"It's just the way it is, Grace."

"Do you know anybody that visits those places?"

Lucius paused. "Yes, and some of them are very highly regarded around here."

Grace was shocked. "But you've never visited them, right?"

"No, of course not, ma cherie. I've never stepped foot in those houses."

Chapter 13

Grace walked into the elegant ballroom on Lucius' arm. He wasted no time pulling her onto the dance floor and began turning her around and around. Chandeliers hung from the ceiling. Velvet drapes framed every tall window. Everyone enjoyed themselves, so she gave in to the moment and began laughing unreservedly. Suddenly, someone cut in and swung her away from Lucius. She could see him moving farther and farther away from her across the dance floor. The music finally stopped, and she walked through the crowd trying to find him. When the next song started up, she couldn't find her way off the dance floor.

Marguerite danced by. "Hi, Grace!"

Grace walked quickly alongside her as she danced.

"I can't find Lucius!" she yelled above the music.

"He's out on the gallery," she said, nodding her head toward a tall glass window.

Grace worked her way through the sea of satin and lace swishing all around her until she reached the door disguised as a window. She stepped through, but realized she must've misunderstood Marguerite. Grace wasn't on the gallery outside—she found herself standing in a long hall lined with doors. Scantily-dressed women stood beside many of them, wooing men inside—men with wedding rings on their fingers.

"No! Don't go in there," she begged them. "Please, think of your wives… your children!"

She turned around to go tell someone, but the glass window slammed shut. It wouldn't budge when she tried to lift it, so she pounded on the glass pane, but no one seemed to hear or notice her.

A familiar voice spoke behind her. "It's just the way it is, Grace."

She turned to see Lucius standing in a doorway entangled in Kitty's arms. "Care to join us, ma cherie?"

Grace opened her eyes in the darkened room, realizing it was a dream, a horrible dream. But then she realized the dream didn't include Finn for the first time in a long time. She wasn't sure which was worse, her unrealized past or her even more uncertain future. She climbed out of bed, grabbed a quilt, stepped out onto the gallery and curled up in one of the wicker chairs.

What am I doing here? Can I even trust Lucius?

Grace knew she should never become so dependent on Lucius that he would come to expect more than she was capable of giving. He kept making statements like she was part of his future. But she had just arrived on the island. She reminded herself that Lucius talked that way to every woman he was around. The image of his bloody and bruised face on the night of the Cotillion came to mind. That was branded on her brain for eternity, along with her first kiss that night.

She pulled the other chair close and propped her legs on it before leaning into the corner of the wide chair to relive the moment with Finn, like she'd done a hundred times before.

She fell asleep with thoughts of Finn wrapped around her, and woke to a gray dawn with the sound of the mockingbird sounding off like an alarm clock across the street.

"I hear you, Roderick," she said sleepily, stretching her stiff limbs. She looked for him on the rooftop across the street, and spotted him at the highest point again. "I named you well, didn't I?"

She took her time getting dressed, and ate the last biscuit, reminding herself to pay attention how Juju used the stove later. Lucius told her that Juju only came Mondays, Wednesdays, and Saturdays to clean, launder his clothes, and cook a supper meal for those three evenings. He ate the rest of his meals downtown.

He said he paid her generously to keep a house that was rarely lived in, but he didn't mind because he knew they needed the help with Kitty going to medical school.

Grace wondered how they could afford it. Maybe the hospital staff paid well. Kitty's mother did domestic work—hardly enough to live on, much less to help Kitty.

Surely her eyes deceived her last night, she thought. The woman in the window looked like Kitty…

She shook the thought out of her head. Any rumor of impropriety—whether true or untrue—could jeopardize Kitty's future.

A little later Grace headed downtown on the trolley to find a printing shop, at Marguerite's advice. Most of the retail businesses were closed for Labor Day, but a few that catered to the tourists were still open with signs saying they were closing at noon. She spotted a clothing store at the corner of 22nd and Avenue D, so she decided she'd better look for a bathing suit. She had accepted the invitation from Daisy Thorne to go bathing in the Gulf tonight, but she hadn't the proper attire. Daisy told her she could store her swimming suit at a bathhouse called Murdoch's.

A lady clerk showed her three styles to choose from: the first was a black, knee-length bathing dress with voluminous sleeves and skirt and a ribbon-trimmed navy collar; the second was another black, knee-length bathing dress with short sleeves and simpler skirt and a ribbon-trimmed navy collar, waist, and hem; and the third was still another black, knee-length bathing dress with ribbon-trimmed sleeves and a ribbon trimmed regular collar.

"Let me see, black, black, and black. You only have black?"

The lady nodded her head.

"It seems such a… stifling color to wear at the beach."

"These are the latest styles."

"Oh."

Grace's previously few experiences in the water meant stripping down to her light-weight underclothes to swim with family or female friends. Based on that knowledge, she chose the bathing suit with the least amount of material. She couldn't help but ask the store clerk if there had been reports of any drowning caused by women's bathing suits pulling them under. The clerk didn't think the comment was the least bit humorous, and her frown told her so.

Grace felt obligated to buy the matching voluminous swimming hat, black hose, and lace-up slippers.

As the lady wrote out her receipt, Grace asked where the nearest printing shop was and was given instructions to a stationery shop one block north next to the Galveston News building on 21st and Avenue C.

Grace thanked her and headed outside, walking north on 22nd Street. The Galveston News was in the middle of the next block, so she easily found the stationery shop. When she wrote down her name to order her calling cards, she realized she didn't have a permanent address yet. The proprietor suggested a blank line beneath her fancily-scrolled name where she could fill in her address—her temporary one now and her permanent address later. She liked that idea, so she purchased the minimum number so she could eventually have her permanent address engraved on her cards. He assured her they would be ready by the following day.

Grace walked out onto Avenue C and retraced her steps back to Avenue D. She looked east and west, north and south, and for as far as she could see, more tall buildings lined the streets—businesses selling jewelry, furniture, hats, shoes, clothing, liquor, and that wasn't even counting the saloons. She recognized the Tremont House, the grand hotel where she'd had lunch the day before looking west. It would take her weeks to visit many of the establishments here and realized she'd better watch her funds carefully in this town. There were too many enterprising businesses and entertainment venues enticing her to spend her money.

She watched an electric trolley pass by. She couldn't believe the ease in which people were able to move about the island. For trolley users, there were no horses to feed, catch, and harness to a wagon before traveling somewhere. Waco's streetcars were primarily powered by mules, with the exception of a few streets having electric-powered trolleys. She'd heard that all of their streetcars would be electric in the near future. But Galveston's system covered much more of the city.

Grace looked up at all the electric wires above her—for the trolleys and for providing electricity and telephone lines for the buildings. They crowded the sky in places, but she figured that was a small price to pay for such modern conveniences.

She continued walking another block to Avenue E, and remembered this was also Postoffice Street. On a whim, she caught a trolley heading west, wanting to see more of this indecent part of town. Back in Waco, she'd heard rumors of *Two Street* as its area of illicit behavior, but she'd never visited it.

She recognized the big house on the corner of 25th and looked up at the window where she saw the woman the evening before. The window was open, but no face appeared. She assumed this house was the beginning of the brothel area. She looked back down the street and could still see the towering Tremont House only two blocks away.

The following blocks of houses were of various sizes and most seemed unassuming. She never would've guessed they were anything but family homes or boarding houses, other than several had lattice panels on the porch like they were strategically placed there for visitors' privacy.

At one ordinary, white clapboard house two women with painted lips and eyes stepped out on the porch to light cigarettes. They noticed Grace staring at them.

Grace raised a hand at them, and shocked herself by smiling.

The smaller, younger woman waved back and returned her smile. Grace realized then that she wasn't a woman, but only a girl whose chest had yet to develop.

The older one shook her breasts at Grace in defiance, and both women laughed at her. The older woman started coughing—a deep ragged cough.

Grace turned to face forward then and stopped smiling.

What in the world am I doing?

"Lord, please help them," she said under her breath.

Chapter 14

Grace disembarked at 29th Street and caught another trolley going south. She lost count of the number of homes fronted by Greek columns and Victorian details and galleries on every floor. She had never seen a city where the citizens put as much effort into beautifying their property and even the public areas with flora and landscaping as Galveston. Her own hometown of Dalton seemed too hot and dusty to grow much of anything that bloomed. Waco made a little more effort, but nothing like Galveston. She felt like she'd found the Garden of Eden.

The trolley passed by a beautiful park, and through the trees Grace saw an unusual-shaped building in the midst of it. The trolley turned east on Avenue O and stopped to pick up several men. She was able to get a better look at the structure, which reminded her of a glass-paneled hat box with a smaller matching glass-paneled crown sitting on top.

"Is that round building where they have the dances?" she asked the trolley driver.

He nodded. "Garten Verein, and it's octagonal."

"Oh. Do you ever go there?"

"Sure. They serve dinner at the Club House on Wednesday nights—the wife and I don't miss 'em. Nice park, too… games… music," he said as he looked over his shoulder. "You were in church yesterday, right?"

"Yes, sir."

"Thought you looked familiar. You new in town?"

"Arrived on Saturday."

"Then welcome to Galveston. This is a great town."

"Thank you. Everyone's been so friendly here. I do feel very welcome." She remembered something. "I heard my neighbor works for the trolley system."

"What's his name?"

"I don't know, but he's right across the street from us—well, my host's house on the corner of 17th and Avenue L."

The man smiled when he heard that. "That'd be Robertson. He's on one of the downtown lines."

"I got a glimpse of him at his door Saturday night, but I don't know that I'd recognize him in uniform. I hardly even noticed the other trolley drivers this morning for looking at all the beautiful houses and extraordinary buildings—especially the churches. There's so much to see here—I can hardly take it all in."

The trolley turned back north on 25th Street.

"This street is as close as I'll be able to get you to 17th. You can catch a car coming up on Avenue N or even Broadway to get you within a couple of blocks."

"I don't mind walking. Just let me out on Avenue L, and I'll get to see some more houses."

She learned his name was Mr. Anderson, and he told her he'd introduce her to his wife at church on Sunday.

Grace was surprised to find Juju at the house by the time she came back. She'd brought a variety of groceries for Grace, "at Mr. Roderick's request," she said.

Grace could smell fresh bread baking, and her stomach reminded her how little it had been fed that day. She noticed something yellow in a bag and reached for it. Bananas!

She tore one from the bundle and then looked up at Juju. "May I have one?" she asked, remembering her manners.

"Of course you may, missy," she said, grinning. "Mr. Roderick said you loved bananas and to make sure I brought you some."

"You and Mr. Roderick are too kind." She quickly peeled it back and took a bite, closing her eyes and enjoying the flavor. "I didn't realize I was so hungry," she said with her mouth full.

"Have you had lunch?"

Grace shook her head. "But don't go to any trouble. I'll just have another banana."

"Pshaw—you need to eat something more substantial than that. We'll have roast beef for supper, but I can fry you an egg and some bacon if you'd like."

"That sounds so good, but this is supposed to be your day off. Can I help you with something?"

"No ma'am… on second thought, would you mind taking that basket and those clippers on the counter there and go out and cut some fresh roses for the table?"

"I'd love to." She grabbed the basket and started towards the back door.

"In that case, clip any dead or dying blooms off while you're at it."

"Thanks for letting me do something around here."

"You sound like Kitty."

Grace paused in the doorway. "Really?"

"That girl works harder than anybody I know. She's workin' double shifts at the hospital until classes start back up in October. She told me we'll be sittin' on easy street when she gets her doctor's degree, and I can start lettin' go some of my clients… but not Mr. Roderick. He needs us. Now shut that door before you let any more flies in," she fussed good-naturedly.

Grace quickly shut the screen door and lifted her skirt to walk down the steep steps to the backyard, thinking about what Juju said about Kitty. She was convinced now that it was some other woman's face in the window last night—not Kitty's.

The roses were planted all along the iron fence on the west side of the house. She went through and clipped all the dead blooms first, and then cut ten red and yellow roses, leaving about ten or twelve inches of stem. She felt good to be doing something useful around here.

Juju was slicing the end off of the bread loaf when she walked back inside the kitchen. A crystal vase half full of water sat on the counter waiting for the roses.

Grace started stripping the lower leaves off the stems.

"I'll finish that. Wash your hands, and I'll bring your plate to the table. I'll be leaving here soon. Do you like the crust or an inside slice?"

"Either's fine."

"You're entirely too easy to please. I'll save the crust for Mr. Roderick, then."

"I'm surprised he has a preference."

"He told me he likes a challenge—even with his food," she said, chuckling. She followed Grace to the dining room and sat a full plate in front of her. "You'd better watch yourself, missy. I think you're his next challenge."

After lunch Lucius sent Tom to pick up Grace and bring her downtown for the parade. The streets were already filling with crowds of people in anticipation of the event. Tom dropped her off at the south side steps of City Hall where Lucius waited. Grace closed her parasol and looked up at the grand building, which was built right in the middle of 20th Street. She almost lost her balance looking up at the belfry clock tower, the height of which dwarfed everything in sight. Statues stood at each corner of the belfry. The minaret-looking towers attached to each corner reminded her of the same style as the synagogue.

"Impressive, isn't it," said Lucius, taking her arm and leading her up the steps.

"It's a work of art," she said. "Don't they know how to do anything plain and simple in this town?"

Lucius laughed. "I've yet to find it."

He led her to the covered front gallery on the second floor where they could look out from the large archway down 20th Street. Half a dozen chairs were placed beside the balustrade. He led her to one and took another.

"How did you manage this? These are the best seats in town."

"I owe quite a few favors now."

"Lucius!" Grace looked concerned. "We can stand on the street—I don't mind."

He laughed again. "You're so easy to please. I have some friends at City Hall, and they invited me—us to join them. They'll be here soon."

Grace breathed a sigh of relief. Then she learned his *friends* just happened to be the mayor and his wife, who made a brief appearance at City Hall before heading over to the large, covered second floor gallery in the Mallory Building to view the parade with a number of other influential people in town.

"Next year, we'll view the parade from that vantage point."

"Well, I'm impressed with this point of view."

"You'll be even more impressed with that one, and I'll be there soon. But you made an impression on the Joneses, and I'd be willing to bet you get an invitation to call on our first lady soon." He reached for her hand and pulled it up to his lips.

Grace felt uneasy with Lucius' unconcealed ambition and the insinuation that she played a role in it. But shouts from the street level signaled the parade had started, and she pushed her misgivings aside and let the excitement of the moment wash over her.

From their vantage point, they could see Market Street running east and west as well as south on 20th Street. Crowds of people lined both streets, and she noticed some men and women had even climbed out of the second-floor windows onto the porch roofs of the businesses.

Grace couldn't help but stand and lean over the balustrade to see what was coming down Market Street. She had seen a number of parades, but nothing like this one. Businesses, local union groups, schools, churches and every other kind of organization created elaborate floats drawn by horses and mules. The float themes represented every kind of skilled labor as well as noble themes such as patriotism and charity. Musical bands and uniformed men marched, flags and hands waved, and Grace couldn't help but wave back.

After the parade, Lucius told Grace he would pick her up for dinner at 7:00. She told him she was meeting a new friend at the beach for a quick dip, but assured him she would be back at the house well before then.

Later that afternoon Grace stepped back from the mirror at Murdoch's Bathhouse and inspected her new swimming attire.

"I've never looked so ridiculous in my life," she told Daisy, dressed in a simpler, black bathing suit. "Where did you get yours?"

"I made it myself."

Grace grimaced. "And you don't wear hose and laced up shoes?"

"I can't feel the sand between my toes if I wear shoes."

Grace sat down and stripped off the shoes and stockings. "I'm returning these… and what about this monstrous hat?"

"It's not so bad," said Daisy, trying to keep a straight face.

"Well, that settles it." Grace pulled it off and placed it with her other clothes. "Did you make your bathing cap, too?"

Daisy nodded. "I can make you a smaller one if you'd like me to. It'll keep your hair from tangling so badly."

"I can handle the tangles this time—I'd much rather prefer tangles to being laughed off the beach."

"Oh, I'm sure you'll still cause some excitement."

Daisy looked down at her suit. "Is it that hideous?"

"No, Grace. You're going to turn heads in a good way. And your blonde hair will definitely cause you to stand out among the bathers."

"I don't want to stand out—maybe I should wait until you make that cap for me."

"Don't be silly. There won't be as many people out there this time of day."

"I saw plenty when we arrived."

"Here, I'll take off my cap, too. Now we'll both cause a stir." She shook out her long, reddish-blonde hair. "But you'll have to help me comb out the tangles afterwards."

"Agreed," Grace said, feeling less conspicuous.

They walked down the long hall to the pier outside. Grace noticed there were still quite a few men standing around, some even held binoculars.

"Come on," Daisy said, walking quickly down the steps to get to the beach. "Let's put some distance between us and the lurkers and leerers."

"Leerers? Is that even a word?"

"It's my word for them," said Daisy, glancing back at the pier. "Those men aren't bird watching with those spy glasses."

"They're watching the bathers?"

"The women bathers. It'll calm down around here once school starts and most of the vacationers leave."

Grace noticed long ropes stretched across the water in a grid pattern that bathers held onto. She followed Daisy to the farthest rope and out into the gently breaking surf.

"Is the water so rough that people can't stand up?"

"Sometimes, but mainly they're here for safety. You'd be surprised how many people can't swim. And thousands and thousands of people come to our beach every year. Sometimes there are undertows—waves that try to pull you back out with them, but they're beneath the surface and you don't always know they're there. Can you swim?"

Graced nodded. "It's not pretty, but I can keep my head above water and eventually get to where I want to go. The river at my grandparents' house is fairly swift at times." She gripped more tightly to the rope, feeling the pull of the receding wave on her legs. "But this is different, and I don't like not being able to see my feet."

"You get used to it, but I've heard that most people either love the ocean or hate it."

"And you love it."

Daisy nodded her head. "It's all I've known, and it's especially nice after a hot day's work."

Grace shut her eyes and faced the breeze. "It does feel good; although I'm sure I'll have barnacles growing on me in no time. The air is so thick down here."

Daisy laughed. "I don't even notice it. Oh! I forgot to tell you. One of our tenants is moving out this weekend, if you're interested."

"I'm interested."

"It's one of the apartments on the third floor, but they're smaller and less expensive."

"I'm definitely interested. Who do I talk to?"

"Our manager lives in the apartments—come by tomorrow and I'll introduce you."

"That's great news—I feel bad keeping Lucius out of his house."

"I'm sure he doesn't mind."

Grace noticed some huts on wheels—some were parked in the sand and others were rolled into the surf. "What are those contraptions over there?"

"The epitome of lavishness… or modesty," said Daisy. "If women don't want to deal with the sand in their surf-bathing, they can rent one of those changing rooms on wheels, climb in and change into their bathing suit. Then they'll get rolled out into the surf where they can step directly in and out of the water."

"Have you ever used one?"

"Good heavens, no. The sand doesn't bother me." Daisy looked around and said under her breath, "Oh, no."

"What?"

"Some of the men are drifting over here."

"What is it? Sailors?"

"Worse… they're bankers."

Grace laughed out loud. "You're kidding me."

"No, I'm serious. Not that all bankers are bad, but this bunch is obnoxious. They think they own everything and everyone."

"They probably do."

"Shush—they're heading this way. Ignore them."

"Miss Thorne!"

Daisy turned and faced west.

The young man dove underwater and came up beside Grace. He shook his wet head like a dog, splattering the women.

"Fancy meeting you here, Daffodil."

"I'm always here at this time and you know it, Chandler," said Daisy, not bothering to hide her disdain. "And you know my name, too."

"Daffodil, Daisy… I forget which one you are."

Two other men worked their way over to them.

"Who's your friend?"

They ogled the women openly, especially their wet swimsuits, which left little to the imagination. Grace started wading toward deeper water.

"Don't you have an orphan's home to repossess or something? We prefer to swim alone," said Daisy, following Grace.

The men followed.

"Well, you're being rude, Miss Thorne in my side. We'd just like to meet your friend."

"My *friend* doesn't want to meet you."

"It's not safe to swim alone," another one said.

Grace's foot stepped on something that moved. She screamed and lunged backwards into Chandler.

"Something's down there!" she yelled.

"It's probably a shark!" he said, steadying her.

"A shark?!" She panicked and tried to get around him to head toward the beach.

"Grace!" Daisy yelled. "Calm down!"

Chandler picked her up, and Grace let him, wrapping her arms around his head like a vise. He turned and started wading blindly back toward the beach.

"Grace! It's probably just a crab!"

Grace looked back over Chandler's shoulder to see the other men howling with laughter, but her only thought was to get out of the water.

They bumped into something.

"I'll take her from here," a familiar voice spoke sternly.

"I've got her," said Chandler in a possessive tone.

"Let go of his head, Grace."

Grace turned around to see Lucius' standing in the shallow surf, blocking their way. She let go and reached for him, but Chandler still held tight.

Lucius looked at Chandler and said threateningly, "You won't be able to block my fist from your face if you don't let her go."

Chandler handed her over and backed away.

"Don't you ever approach these ladies again. I know who you are, and I know where you work. Now get out of here," he said as he looked up at the others. "And take your friends with you."

Lucius turned around and carried her out of the water and set her down on the sand.

"Are you all right?" he asked. "You're shaking."

"All I heard was the word 'shark' and I panicked," she said, disgusted with herself.

Daisy ran up to them. "Those idiots. Are you all right, Grace? I'm sure it was just a crab. There are always crabs around."

"I'm sorry, Daisy. I feel like such an idiot, but crabs horrify me, too."

"I don't believe I've had the pleasure," said Lucius to Daisy.

"What's wrong with me? Daisy, this is Lucius Roderick, my hero," she said. "Lucius, this is Daisy Thorne, who works at the Rosenberg School that I hope to be teaching at this year."

"How do you do?"

"Much better since you ran those scoundrels off."

"I thought I was going to meet you at the house," said Grace.

"I decided to take the rest of the day off and join you since it was a holiday. It was easy to spot you from the pier. Your presence seemed to be the main topic of conversation up there."

"Daisy's going to make me a cap soon; then we won't stand out so much. And I think I'm going to wear shoes and stockings from now on so I won't have to worry about the crabs."

"And I won't have to worry about men ogling your legs."

Grace felt the heat creeping up her cheeks. She looked down. "Lucius, your shoes are wet!"

"I didn't have time to change before I noticed you were surrounded by sharks. Comc on—we can eat at one of the restaurants on the beach."

They started walking toward the bathhouse.

"Would you like to join us, Miss Thorne?"

"No, thank you. I need to get home."

"We have to go change," Grace said to Lucius. "Daisy said one of the apartments at Lucas Terrace will be vacant this weekend, so hopefully I'll be out of your hair soon."

"You know you can stay as long as you want, Grace."

"I know, but…"

"We've already discussed this."

"You need to come by as soon as you can," said Daisy. "It'll rent fast."

They walked up the steps to the bathhouse built out over the water. Lucius glared at the men standing on the pier gawking at the two women, and most of them looked away. He stopped at the entrance.

"I'll wait right here for you," he said, turning around and folding his arms across his chest, daring anyone to look their way.

Chapter 15

Grace stepped up on the trolley and turned around and waved at Daisy standing in the door marked #5 at the Lucas Terrace Apartments. She felt giddy since she'd just put money down to hold apartment #9 on the third floor. The manager said it would be available to move into on Saturday afternoon—after a good cleaning.

Her interview at the Rosenberg School that morning went very well, and she felt confident she had the teaching position, too. The principal told her he would let her know officially by Thursday, but she felt sure that was just a formality. During the interview she was pleasantly surprised to learn that along with her letter of service from her previous school in Waco, three additional people had contacted the principal to offer their unsolicited recommendation to hire her. She would have to do something special for Daisy, Lucius, and Marguerite St. John in the near future.

She rode the Avenue J trolley to 21st Street and waited to catch one going downtown to pick up her calling cards. Other than the embarrassing escapade in the Gulf yesterday, things couldn't be unfolding more smoothly in her new life. She decided she must be in the center of God's will. He had brought her into contact with Marguerite and Walter, who introduced her to Daisy. Within only a few days she had a job, a place to live, and an exciting social life ahead of her, thanks to Lucius and Marguerite, with whom she'd made a date to spend much of Wednesday. She couldn't wait to see the Gresham house, but was a little apprehensive about meeting the family. They seemed to live like royalty. And on Friday, she planned to attend her first dance in Galveston with Lucius, although he hadn't asked her yet.

Lucius. A month ago she never would've guessed she'd be on the verge of a relationship with one of the most eligible men in Galveston. He seemed to truly care for her, but she reminded herself that he'd gotten in trouble before when it came to leading women on and breaking their hearts. She'd have to tread carefully with him.

But it felt so good to have someone taking care of *her* every need for once. She hadn't experienced that before… not in this way. With Finn, the role was reversed. She was his caretaker, and the more she did for him, the more he let her. But he still wasn't willing to commit his whole heart, and even though he wanted more of her at times, she withheld that one part of herself she was determined to save for marriage.

"I hope you're missing me fiercely at this moment, Finn," she said angrily. "Who's taking care of you now?"

"Pardon me?" a woman asked.

Grace jumped. "Sorry! I didn't realize anyone else was around. I was just mumbling to myself."

She was thankful the trolley pulled up at that moment and allowed the woman to board in front of her. She sat towards the back, away from the other passengers, and berated herself for letting Finn ruin her otherwise perfect day. When she disembarked, she looked at the trolley driver's name tag… Truitt. Not her neighbor.

At the stationery shop, the clerk told her the cards would be ready after lunch, so she decided to tour some streets she hadn't seen yet. She walked one block over to Avenue D and caught the trolley heading east with the purpose of riding its entire route back to that point. This time she noticed the trolley driver's name… Robertson, and introduced herself to him and sat on the first seat to his right.

"Will I distract you too much if I talk to you?"

"Nah, I don't even have to steer this thing—it follows the tracks. I just start and stop it," he said, looking around at her. "I saw you yesterday, didn't I?"

"Was that your trolley? I'm sorry I didn't notice you at the time. Mr. Roderick told me that you worked for the streetcar system, but he didn't mention your name. Then I talked to one of your co-workers, a Mr. Anderson if I remember correctly, and he told me your name after I told him where you lived. And I've already met your dog."

Mr. Robertson smiled. "I was wondering who Trixie was barking at the other night. We hardly ever see Mr. Roderick during the day, but we've gotten to know Juju."

"Did you get to see the parade yesterday?"

"A little bit before it started. We still had to run our routes, but I saw a lot of the floats on their way to the parade."

"It was spectacular."

"Yeah, folks don't do anything halfway around here. There are a lot of hard-working people in this town, but we know how to have fun, too. So, where you headed?"

"Back to where you picked me up. I just moved here and I need to learn my way around."

"All right, and you can ask me about anything on my route. I'm a veritable encyclopedia when it comes to this town."

Grace thought for a moment, and waited while some passengers loaded before asking, "I thought of a question."

"Fire away."

"Why is it so important to have a house on Broadway Street?"

"Well, that depends on the person. It's one of the highest points on the island, so some folks like not having to deal with the overflows that come occasionally. But for many of the ones who've built their mansions there, Broadway represents status… prestige. Everybody's trying to outdo everybody."

"Do you want to have a house on Broadway someday?"

Robertson laughed. "Oh, no. I know my place."

"But this is America—you can determine your own place in society."

"I know that, but that's not what I meant. I don't want a high-fallutin' job and the anxiety it would take to maintain that kind of lifestyle and those huge mansions. I like where I live. I like my job, and I like the people I meet and work with. But don't get me wrong, I'd like to have more money and be able to buy my wife nicer things, but I don't need to live on Broadway. And I don't mean to sound like there are only high-rollers on Broadway. It has its share of modest houses, especially on the west end. And the rabbinage is right in the middle on the 1900 block."

"What's that?"

"That's what Rabbi Cohen calls his home. It's nice, but nothing extravagant."

"I actually met the rabbi on Sunday."

"Are you Jewish?"

"No, but I mistook the synagogue for the Baptist church."

Robertson chuckled. "I bet he thought that was funny."

"He seemed amused, and I'm sure he won't let me forget it if I ever see him again."

"I'm sure you'll see him again. He's involved in everything."

"That's unusual, isn't it?"

"I guess so. He's definitely changed my opinion of Jews because he isn't stand-offish like I first thought he'd be. In the hospital, he'll visit anyone and tell them 'There's no such thing as Episcopalian scarlet fever, Catholic arthritis, or Jewish mumps.'"

"He sounds like a remarkable man."

The streetcar turned north onto 9th Street and picked up several women in white uniforms and started back south.

"Is that the hospital?" she asked, pointing to a large red brick and granite building to her left.

"That's the medical college. The hospital's the big white building to your right. We're fortunate to have those facilities on the island."

"Do you know Juju's daughter Kitty?"

"Sure—she rides my line just about every day."

"I'm so impressed that she's studying to be a doctor."

"That gal has come a long way—did you know she was adopted?"

"No, I didn't."

"Kitty's mother died when she was a baby."

"You knew her mother?"

"No, but Kitty couldn't have gotten better parents than Juju and Harvey."

"What happened to Juju's husband?"

"Accident on the wharf a few years after they adopted Kitty. It's been a struggle for them ever since. But you'd never know it by being around them—they're two strong women."

The streetcar turned west on Avenue G.

Grace noticed a Victorian house that looked like it had ship wheels in the ornate wood trim on the porch.

"So... you're moving to Galveston," said Robertson. "What do you think about it so far?"

"I still can't get over these houses. I've never seen so many beautiful homes in one place. And the buildings are amazing, too. I'm in awe of this city—I had no idea it was so big and cosmopolitan."

"I've heard it described a lot of ways, but I think that's the first time I've heard it called 'cosmopolitan'."

"Compared to where I come from, it's very sophisticated. And it lacks for nothing."

"Oh, I can think of a few things we don't have."

"What's that?"

"Rolling hills, clear running streams, higher ground... like where I grew up in Virginia."

"That sounds like my grandparents' place."

"Where do they live?"

"Central Texas—west of Waco. They're on a river, and it's flooded at times, but the houses are on the high side. Are you used to the overflows here?"

"Yeah, but that doesn't mean I like 'em."

"What's the worst overflow that you remember?"

"There have been two bad ones since I've lived here—the first in '75 was caused by a tropical cyclone that hit about 100 miles south of here. We got a lot of rain and flooding, but Indianola got the worst of it—almost wiped 'em out. Then, let me think, back in the mid-80's another one hit the same place and Indianola never recovered. Hey, you said your name was Taylor?"

Grace nodded.

"There was a big trial going on in Indianola when that first storm hit, and one of the prisoners escaped because of it. The trial was connected with the Sutton-Taylor feud. Are you any kin to that bunch?"

Grace shook her head. "I remember my mother telling me a story about my Uncle Jimmy Taylor getting beat up in Brownwood because they thought he was the same Jim Taylor that ran with John Wesley Hardin. And I heard *that* particular Taylor was involved in the feud."

"A lot of people were killed on both sides. I think everybody breathed a sigh of relief when it ended."

The nurses got off on the corner of 21st Street, and the trolley turned north.

Robertson gestured to a red brick building on his left as they approached Avenue F. "That's our barn," he told Grace, "where the streetcars are parked after hours."

She noticed that tracks turned directly into the building. "I hadn't thought about where the cars go at night."

He waved at a man standing near the large bay hollering at some children across the street. "That's our electrician Payne. He and his family live right around here, which is handy since he's always working on these cars."

"You said you originally came from Virginia. What brought you down to Galveston?"

"My father was on the losing side of the Civil War. He didn't talk about it much, but my mother said there were too many hurt feelings—we had family on both sides. My father wanted to raise us away from that and heard about the opportunities in this beautiful city built on an island. He thought he was coming down here to get rich," said Robertson. "His first job was on the wharf, but the yellow fever got him in '67. We hadn't lived here two years before we lost him."

"I'm so sorry."

"My mother was convinced the yellow fever came from the immigrants arriving on the ships, so she made me promise to never work on the wharves."

"Do you think that's how the yellow fever got here?"

"I don't know… maybe. They started quarantining people for a period of time, and they found a lot more diseases than yellow fever."

The trolley turned west on Avenue E.

"So how long have you worked for the trolley system?"

"I started back in '69 when mules pulled the cars. I was only fourteen, but I've always been tall for my age and I told 'em I was older. Momma needed the help, and I'd been fascinated by the streetcars ever since the city started using them a couple of years before. I sure was happy to see them convert to electricity. I got tired of fooling with those hard-headed mules."

Grace watched the buildings for a while. She noticed she was looking at almost eye-level to the ground floor of some of the buildings.

"Do the overflows ever get in the buildings? They look like they're built up fairly high."

"The streets flood fairly easily, but I've only seen it get into the bottom floors of the businesses downtown a couple of times—those storms I told you about. Are you worried about the overflows?"

"A little. The Nueces River near my hometown would get on the rise every few years, and it washed out bridges occasionally, but it never flooded the town."

"Well, we have our own weather station here in Galveston run by two very competent brothers. It's in the Levy Building one street over on Avenue D. Remind me to point it out to you on the way back. If a storm's coming, they fly a red flag with a black square in the middle of it. If it's a cyclone, they'll put up two flags. Word gets around pretty fast—everybody's good at looking out for each other."

"Do you think what happened at Indianola could ever happen here?"

"Nah. Mr. Cline wrote an article for the newspaper about that very thing some years back. He said that the way the ocean floor is shallow leading up to the island would disperse any big waves that might come from a tropical cyclone. He has several degrees—including a medical degree, and he's studied weather for years, and he's been right so far."

"That makes me feel better," said Grace, smiling.

They passed by the big brothel on the corner of 25th Street.

Robertson glanced over at her. "You were on the line Sunday night, too, weren't you… with Mr. Roderick?"

Grace's cheeks grew hot. She was mortified that someone noticed Lucius' amorous behavior towards her.

"That was your trolley?"

"Yeah, but that wasn't my usual schedule. I was covering for a friend."

"I wonder why Lucius didn't introduce us."

"He didn't even notice me. I think he couldn't keep his eyes off of you," said Robertson, chuckling.

"Well, I apologize for our improper behavior."

"No apology necessary. Most folks don't notice us drivers. But I could tell you were uncomfortable, and that told me you weren't one of his usual lady friends."

"His usual lady friends?"

This time Robertson's cheeks turned ruddy. "Please forget I said that."

"So he's made it a habit to kiss women on the trolley?"

"I didn't say that."

She looked around at the brothels. "And does he make it a habit to visit this neighborhood?"

His face looked pained. "I can't say, Miss Taylor. That's between you and Mr. Roderick."

"Then I'm going to have to have a little talk with Mr. Roderick," she said curtly.

"Please reconsider, Miss Taylor. If he knows I spoke out of turn to you, it could cost me my job."

Grace frowned at him. "Why would they fire you over the truth?"

"Mr. Roderick's becoming a very powerful man in this town—he has a lot of influence."

"Lucius wouldn't dare—"

"Yes, he would, especially if this puts a strain on your relationship and he finds out I caused that, so please accept my apology for speaking out of turn."

Before she could respond, a girl came running out of one of the smaller houses on the street screaming for help. Grace recognized her as the young girl she had seen the day before.

"Stop the trolley!" Grace yelled.

"I can't stop in the middle of the block."

"Please, Robertson—she needs help!"

"This ain't no place for a lady, Miss Taylor!"

"Then I'll have to jump!" She stood up and braced herself in front of the open door.

Chapter 16

Mr. Robertson shut the power off and the trolley stopped with a lurch.

"Miss Taylor, you don't know what you're getting into."

Grace ignored him as she stepped off the trolley and ran back to the hysterical girl. She tried to find out what was wrong, but couldn't understand anything the girl was saying except the name 'Lilly.'

The girl grabbed Grace's hand and pulled her toward the house. She glanced back at the trolley and saw that Robertson was backing up, so she followed the young girl up the steps into the house.

The dark parlor was stifling and reeked of stale cigarette smoke and heavy perfume, but neither could mask a musty smell about the place. Grace caught a whiff of something else—alcohol? She didn't know enough about strong drink to be able to tell for sure. She followed the girl through a dining room cluttered with the remains of previous meals. They entered a dark hall to the left and the girl pulled Grace through an open door at the end. A small oil lamp cast a feeble light across the room.

A sick smell greeted her, and it took every bit of Grace's will power to keep from covering her face with her hands. She forced herself to look at the bed, but was surprised to see it empty. The girl pulled her towards it, and Grace couldn't help but hold back.

"Tell me what's wrong."

The young girl turned and looked at her. What was left of her lipstick stained a larger area around her mouth like a clown's face. Tears had made tracks down her cheeks caused by the black kohl shadowing her eyes.

"Lilly's… sick." She walked toward the far side of the bed and knelt down.

Grace followed her to see a crumpled form on the floor between the bed and the wall.

"Do you think she's… still alive?" the girl asked.

Grace knelt down and touched the woman's wrist. She felt a faint pulse.

"Let's get her on the bed. Lilly? Can you sit up?"

No response.

"We're going to have to lift her ourselves," said Grace. "I'll get her shoulders and you lift her feet. What's your name?"

"Anise, and I can take her shoulders. She doesn't weigh much."

"Should we call a doctor?" Grace caught a whiff of licorice.

They lifted her onto the bed. The woman groaned with the movement.

"Or has she had too much to—" Grace stopped in mid-sentence as she watched Anise push the dark hair away from the older woman's face, revealing a swollen, bloody face.

"She's been beaten! We need to tell the authorities." Grace pulled the tattered gown up to cover the woman's bare chest. Her arms and shoulders bore the marks of a violent struggle.

"Lilly told me no! She said we'd bring trouble on ourselves."

"When did she tell you that?"

Anise looked down.

Grace's heart fell. "This isn't the first time this has happened, is it."

Anise shook her head.

"Did he hurt you, too?"

"Not this time." The young girl's face skewed up as she started to cry again. "I hid from him this time."

"You can't let men do that to you, Anise. How old are you?

"Eighteen."

"I know that's a lie. What are you doing in a place like this?"

"Please, please don't tell anyone. Thank you for helping me get Lilly on the bed. I can take care of her now. I thought she was dead, and I didn't know what to do with a dead person, but since she's still alive, we'll be all right now."

"She needs to see a doctor. Go get a damp washcloth, Anise. A clean washcloth."

Anise hurried out of the room.

Grace walked over to the window and opened the heavy drapes, filling the sunbeams with a cloud of dust. She turned around and at first glance was tempted to draw the curtains shut on the filthy room.

Suddenly she heard a door slam and a man's voice. Anise answered and then cried out in pain. Grace ran out of the room, grabbing the first thing her hand touched.

She came out of the hallway and almost ran into a man holding Anise by the hair.

"Let her go!" yelled Grace, wielding her weapon.

The man leered at her. "And who's this beauty threatening me with a ladies corset?"

Grace glanced at the corset in her hands. "It has whale bones in it," she said, trying to sound fiercer than she felt.

The man laughed and jerked Anise's head back. "You and Lilly been holding out on me." He pushed her to the floor towards the hall door. "Find my wallet, runt. And if there's any money missing, I'll take it out of *your* hide this time."

Anise scrambled out of the room.

"You ought to be ashamed of yourself," said Grace.

"Me? They stole from me!"

"You attacked them, and one of them is just a child!"

"This is a whorehouse. You're the one who ought to be ashamed. You're a different cut, though. I bet you charge a pretty penny."

Grace threw the corset at him. "Get out of here!"

"Or what?" He stepped towards her.

She backed away, seeing the intent in his bloodshot eyes. "I'm not a prostitute. I'm a teacher!"

"A teacher? Is that your game? I bet you could teach me a few things."

She turned and ran towards the open front door, but he caught her and pulled her back. She slapped him across the face, and he slapped her back, knocking her down. Her hat fell forward across her face as she crawled towards the door.

"Mr. Robertson!" she screamed, pushing her hat off her head.

He pulled her back and slammed the door. "What you hollering for, teacher?" He glanced outside. "There's nobody out there."

She scooted back across the floor towards the parlor and rolled over on her hands and knees to get up.

"Now we can do this the easy way, or we can do it the hard way." He grabbed her around the waist and lifted her off the floor.

Grace's mind went blank with terror. She threw her head back as hard as she could and heard a crunch when it hit his face. He cursed, but he didn't let go. She saw a few stars herself.

"So I see you like it the rough way." He spit blood on the floor, and dragged her towards a closed door off the parlor, kicking it open.

"Did you take over Sadie's room?" He threw her on the bed. "Stop your screaming, woman! You oughta know this ain't good for your business."

He approached her on the bed, and Grace kicked him in the stomach. Her skirt kept it from doing much good, other than make him enraged. He towered over her, drawing his arm back to hit her.

Grace covered her head and clamped her eyes shut, waiting for the blow.

But it never came.

She could hear voices and a scuffle in the room. She rolled over on her side and pulled her knees up close, still covering her head and face and hoping this was a bad dream.

Grace wasn't sure how long she lay there—a few seconds or a few minutes, but the scuffling noise changed to a dragging sound, and the voices faded to silence.

"Miss Taylor? Are you all right?"

Grace opened her eyes and turned toward the voice. Mr. Robertson's tall frame filled her line of sight.

"Did he hurt you?" he asked gently.

She reached up and touched her cheek, still stinging from the slap earlier—was it only a moment ago? Her lip felt swollen, too, but she shook her head.

He took her arm, pulling her to a sitting position. She looked beyond him.

"He's gone."

She covered her mouth to try to hold the tears back. "I thought you'd left."

"I had left." He handed her a kerchief.

She looked up at him.

"I went down the road to Miss Russell's. I didn't know what the problem was in here, but by the way that young lady was acting, I figured it was bad. Miss Russell provides her own security, and I thought we might need 'em. And when I heard you hollerin' from down the street, I was glad they came along. You don't have to worry about him—they'll take care of him."

"Shouldn't we tell the police or the sheriff?"

Robertson shook his head. "They don't like to involve the police unless they absolutely have to."

"But the police know what's going on here?"

Robertson nodded his head. "They turn a blind eye because if they see any trouble, they'll have to do something about it, and then the public will hear about it, and then somebody will start a campaign to shut down this neighborhood."

"It should be shut down. That man beat Lilly and he's hurt Anise before." Grace's eyes widened. "Lilly's in the back bedroom. She needs to go to the hospital."

Robertson nodded his head. "The street will make sure they're taken care of."

"And Anise is too young to be in a place like this."

"That's not your concern," he said, offering his hand to help her stand. "Come on,"

Her legs felt like jelly. "We can't leave them here."

"They take care of their own, but right now we need to get out of here before your name gets caught in the rumor mill. Just your being here could jeopardize your teaching job."

"Oh," Grace said, mortified at the thought. She followed him into the parlor and stole a look toward the dark hall off the dining room. She could hear Anise talking to someone. Robertson picked up her hat and handed it to her.

"They'll be taken care of," he said as he opened the door and stepped out onto the porch.

"But you said everyone knows about Postoffice Street, so everyone condones it, right?"

"There are three attitudes about prostitution here on the island: the folks who know this is wrong and either pretend it doesn't exist, or they speak out against it which puts them in the minority; the second group is the hedonists who openly participate in carnal sin; and the third bunch is the self-righteous hypocrites who put on a pious face Sunday morning, and then visit the back alleys of Postoffice Street any other night of the week." He peeked around the latticework. "Come on—the coast is clear."

"And which group are you in?" Grace asked as they walked quickly to the streetcar.

"My route takes me down this street almost every day, but that's as close as I get. We've been told to be tolerant towards others' lifestyles. The Bible tells me that this is wrong, but if I speak out against it, I could lose my job."

Grace climbed the steps and sat in the seat behind Robertson this time so she could look in his mirror and attempt to straighten her hair and put her hat back on. But she froze when she saw the other passengers staring at her from the back of the streetcar.

Chapter 17

Grace sat quietly throughout the remainder of the route as she thought about what happened on Postoffice Street. She stood when she reached the place where she first boarded Robertson's streetcar on Avenue D downtown.

"It's been so nice to make your acquaintance, Mr. Robertson," she said loudly, and then more quietly, "Thank you… for coming back for me," her voice broke. "I don't know what I would've done… "

"Try not to dwell on that."

"I guess I didn't think before I jumped off your trolley."

"You have a compassionate heart, Miss Taylor. There's nothin' wrong with that."

"And I'm so sorry for the damage I may have inflicted on both of our reputations."

"Don't you worry about mine," he said. "By the way, my wife will be home from Houston tomorrow with our youngest two. I'm sure she'll want to invite you over for supper soon when I tell her about you."

"I'd like that. Goodbye, Mr. Robertson."

She stepped off the trolley and walked away, afraid to catch the eyes of the other passengers, some of whom must have witnessed the fiasco on Postoffice Street. How could the first half of her day be so perfect, and in no time at all turn into a nightmare. She shuddered again at the thought that she could've been in Lilly's condition if Robertson hadn't returned.

Another thought washed over her like a cold wave.

Lucius would never tolerate her actions today.

At the stationery shop Grace picked up her calling cards, staring at her beautifully engraved name on the bright white card. She realized her social life could end before it even got started due to the recent debacle on Postoffice Street. She had only wanted to help.

She caught the southbound trolley on 21st Street to head back to Lucius' house. She replayed over and over in her mind alternative ways to help the hysterical Anise, but she always came back to the fact that she would try to help her. Who could turn away from such a desperate cry?

The trolley stopped at the corner of Sealy Street, and on a whim, Grace disembarked. The sun beat down on her, but she only had to walk one block to her destination.

She looked up at the gleaming white walls of the synagogue, marveling again at the beautiful windows and ornate structure. She had no idea if Rabbi Cohen was even there, but found her answer when she walked around the corner to see a familiar bicycle leaning up against the wall.

"Thank you, Lord," she said under her breath as she opened the heavy entry door. "Brother Cohen? I mean… Rabbi Cohen?!" she called out. She stood in the foyer, afraid to go further. She heard him respond from somewhere.

"Yes… I'm coming!" He walked quickly into the foyer and across the room. "May I help you?"

"Hello, Rabbi." Grace offered her hand. "Do you remember me?"

"Ah, Miss Taylor—my wayward Baptist! Of course I remember you!" He took her hand and squeezed it firmly. "What can I do for you?"

Grace took a deep breath. "I'm not sure, but I got myself in a predicament today, and I'm not sure it will get resolved."

"Would you like to come to my office and tell me about it?"

"No, I don't want to take up too much of your time…"

"That's what I'm here for." He led her to a nearby bench. "Now, tell me what happened."

Grace wasn't sure how to broach the subject to a Rabbi. "You're familiar with what's happening on a certain stretch of Postoffice Street, right?"

The Rabbi looked concerned. "If you're referring to the prostitution district, then yes, I am aware of it."

"I was riding the streetcar along that stretch a little while ago, and a young girl ran screaming out of one of the smaller houses. I insisted that the trolley driver stop and I ran over to try to help her. She took me inside and showed me her friend, who was unconscious. She'd been beaten, and I think she was sick, too, by the way the room smelled. The young girl has been abused, too. While I was there, the man came back and... I didn't know what I'd gotten myself into." Grace wasn't sure how to explain the rest of it.

Rabbi Cohen looked away. "This is intolerable."

"The trolley driver solicited some help from a Miss Russell's house down the road. He said they would take care of things, but I'm not sure that's going to happen. I was told they try to keep things like that quiet."

"Would you like for me to visit the house?"

"Are you allowed to? Would it damage your reputation?"

"Where is a greater need for mercy than that street?" he said. "Can you imagine how lives could be changed if we placed more value on people than our reputations?"

Grace exhaled with relief. "So it wouldn't be too much trouble?"

The Rabbi shook his head. "You'll be shocked to know I visit the jail, too. If I recall, didn't your Jesus disregard his reputation and spend time with tax collectors and other sinners?"

Grace smiled. "You're right. And the woman needs a doctor's care—I'm hoping they took her to the hospital, but I doubt that happened. And the house was filthy."

"I'll be making my rounds at the hospital in a little while, and I'll check to see if she was brought in. Did you happen to get her name?"

"Lilly, and Anise is the young girl. She told me she was eighteen, but I don't think she's more than fourteen years old, if that much.

She doesn't belong there, and if they took Lilly away, she may be at that house by herself."

"And do you know the address?"

Grace shook her head. "It was on the north side of the street—I think in the 27th block. White one-story… lattice covered the front part of the porch…" she shut her eyes to try to picture it. "There were pink oleander bushes in the front."

"Pink oleanders… white house… Lilly and Anise. I'll definitely check on both of them."

"Thank you so much." Grace's eyes filled with tears. "I just didn't know who to talk to about this, and then I remembered what you told me on Sunday."

Rabbi Cohen smiled. "I'm honored that you felt comfortable enough to entrust me with your concern."

"I need to get going," she said, standing.

"Don't forget this," he said as he picked up a small package and handed it to her. He walked her to the door and opened it, squinting in the sunlight.

"Thank you again," she said, turning to shake his hand.

"My pleasure." His forehead creased as he looked at her face. "Are you sure there's nothing else you'd like to tell me?"

"No, other than I appreciate you taking the time to help."

"Well, be sure and put some ice on that cheek. Will I need to use my boxing skills when I visit this house?"

Grace's hand flew to her face. "No—he's… it's been taken care of," she said awkwardly, horrified that her face showed evidence of a fight. "Goodbye, Rabbi." She smiled and walked quickly away.

At the house later, Grace undressed to take a bath and was aghast to find blood splatters on the back of her blouse and skirt. She was surprised to feel a sense of satisfaction knowing that her attacker was probably nursing more painful wounds than she was at the moment. She filled a smaller tub in the kitchen to soak her clothes, and filled the larger tub in the adjacent room for her bath. She found several more bruises as she soaked the soreness away.

Afterwards she tried dabbing bath powder on her face to cover the bruise, but to no avail. As she dressed for supper, she practiced stories to account for the bruise, but felt bad about having to lie about it to Lucius.

The clock ticked closer to facing him, and Grace began to feel sick to her stomach on top of a dull headache that had been lingering all afternoon. She realized she hadn't eaten since breakfast.

She jumped when the phone rang loudly. She walked to the telephone in the kitchen and picked up the handset, leaning forward to speak into the transmitter.

"Hello?" she said tentatively.

"Grace?"

It was Lucius.

"Yes?"

"I'm running a little late—are you really hungry?"

"Uh, no… actually, I'm not feeling very well."

"Really? What's the matter?"

"Upset stomach, headache—I think I was out in the sun too long today."

"Then maybe I should come check on you right now."

"No, no, that won't be necessary—would you mind so much if I just went to bed early?"

"No, not at all—I do need to meet with a client—I could do that over supper now."

"Oh, good. I didn't want to spoil your evening."

"That could never happen, cherie. Oh, and Sissy said hello; I got another telegram from her today."

"Really? What'd she say?"

"She wanted to make sure you had arrived in good health and were adjusting well."

"I hope you replied that I was."

"I certainly did. And they're talking about visiting the island in a couple of months."

"That's great news! I miss her. Oh, and I'll be moving into my own place on Saturday."

"So soon? You know you can stay as long as you want."

"You're too kind."

"What are your plans for tomorrow?"

"Marguerite's invited me to spend the day with her. I hope I can keep up with her."

"Will you be visiting the Gresham house?"

"Yes—she's promised me a tour."

"I've seen the front rooms, but pay attention to the rest of the house. I want something similar for my own house."

"You mean castle."

Lucius laughed. "Something like that. If I build, I'm thinking about hiring Nicholas Clayton to design it for me… but I want your opinion, too, Grace."

"You ought to wait and let your future wife help you."

"I'm working on that."

"I don't want to impose."

"What if I want you to impose? I'd be the most envied man on the island with you on my arm."

Grace pictured Lucius escorting her around town with a black eye and shuddered. "Go meet with your client," she said, ending that line of discourse. "I'll see you tomorrow night."

"Rest up, and get to feeling better, darling. Are you sure I can't bring you something… hold your hand… kiss your lips?"

Grace couldn't help but roll her eyes. "I'm sure."

"Then dream about me… I'll be dreaming about you."

"You don't have to try quite so hard, Lucius. Goodnight."

She replaced the handset on the hook before he could respond, and shut her eyes with relief, grateful she didn't have to face him with the truth tonight.

"Thank you, Lord," she said aloud as she turned and looked around the kitchen for something to eat.

She jumped when the phone rang again.

She grabbed the handset and said, "I promise I don't need a thing, Lucius."

"Well, well, well," said a familiar voice. "Don't you sound like Miss Independent!"

Grace laughed. "Marguerite! It's so good to hear your voice. I've missed you these past two days."

"Are we ready for tomorrow?"

"We are! So much has happened—I can't wait to tell you."

"Your interview went well?"

"Yes, thanks to you and Lucius and Daisy, but I want to tell you about it in person."

"I'll send the carriage by at nine."

"You won't either—I'm only a few blocks away."

"All right then, and when you get here, come around to the back—I'll save the best for last."

"I get to see the whole house?"

"Yes—Josie and the girls will be out most of the day calling on friends."

"Don't you want to go with them?"

"That's all I've done the past two days, and there's only so much social conversing and discreet tête-à-tête I can take in one week—you'll see what I mean. You and I have been invited to lunch at Ashton Villa tomorrow."

Grace put her hand on her cheek, feeling sure another headache would make its appearance about noon tomorrow. "I'll have to talk to you about that, but are you sure she won't mind you showing me the house?"

"She'd be absolutely affronted if someone found out they live a normal life behind the facade, but what she doesn't know won't hurt her."

Grace laughed. "You are a devious woman, Marguerite. I can't wait to see you."

"I'll meet you at nine o'clock at the back of the house, sweetie. Are you going to dream about Lucius?"

"How did you know about that?"

"These lines aren't private, honey. I heard the last few sentences of your conversation, so be careful what you say on the phone… right, Lucretia?"

Grace heard a subtle click on the line.

"Oh, dear. Didn't we just discuss trespassing?"

Marguerite laughed. "That isn't nearly as dangerous as Lucius."

"Well, I have to say my dreams have consistently not involved Lucius—my unconscious mind still doesn't know he exists."

"You're going to have to let Finn go sometime, honey, and Lucius is as good a reason as any."

"I know. Goodnight, Marguerite."

Chapter 18

Grace arrived at the Gresham house a few minutes early, so she took her time gazing at the outside of the castle-looking structure. At first glance, the walls of the house looked light brown, but then Grace noticed rows of different types of stone in varying shades of pink and gray. She counted three floors, not counting the windows on the basement and attic levels. Large, cylindrical turrets anchored the front two corners of the house, rising up to their intricately tiled cone roofs, separate from the rest of the steep roof. Windows of every size and shape ruled each floor and gable, and numerous tall chimneys, each one a different design, lavishly crowned the roofline.

Every facet of the house was elaborate. Many of the windows were leaded and stained glass—some framed by columns or topped with beautifully carved reliefs. She noticed the black iron columns and lacy ironwork on two smaller stacked galleries on the west side as well as the large gallery to the right of the huge front door. She walked parallel to it as it wrapped around to the east side, and noticed an identical gallery of wrought iron sat above it on the second floor.

A glass-walled conservatory jutted out of the east side wall. Some kind of metal covered its roof rather than the colorful tiles. Grace could see ferns and palm fronds through the tall glass windows that formed the walls. She stopped and looked around at the landscaped yard, dwarfed by the size of the house sitting on it. She thought it would have been more fitting on a country estate rather than the middle of the city.

"It's a peacock sitting on a sparrow's nest," said Marguerite, standing in the alley with her hands on her hips.

"Exactly!" Grace laughed as she closed her parasol and hurried over to embrace her friend. "It does seem to overwhelm the space. But the house is breathtaking."

The smile on Marguerite's face disappeared as she held her at arm's length. "What happened to your cheek?"

"I was hoping it would fade overnight," said Grace. "I foolishly ran headlong into a predicament I almost didn't get out of."

"That sounds frightening! Come sit down and tell me all about it." Marguerite led her to the back of the house where a table was set with iced lemonade and tea cakes.

Grace recounted the events of yesterday—from meeting her neighbor, Mr. Robertson on the streetcar to soliciting Rabbi Cohen's help on behalf of Anise and Lilly.

"And how did Lucius handle the fact that you were assaulted? I bet he was livid."

"He doesn't know yet—I wasn't feeling well last night—"

"For good reason!"

"—and I'm hoping he doesn't find out."

"Oh, honey, he'll have to be blind and dumb to miss that bruise, and it isn't going away any time soon. He's probably going to be upset that you didn't go to him right after it happened."

"What more could he have done? Miss Russell's hired help took care of that brute, and Mr. Robertson said the *street* would take care of the girls—that they don't like for this kind of mishap to draw attention to their business. But I asked Rabbi Cohen to make sure the girls were all right. Anise shouldn't even be on that street."

"Why did you even get involved? That man could've killed you… or worse—taken your virginity!"

"Don't you have that backwards?"

"It'd be hard to survive the scandal of a…" she looked around before whispering, "rape."

"Well, I wasn't raped, and I'm fine, and I just may start a

campaign to close down Postoffice Street while I'm here."

"Sweetie, why don't you join something less volatile, like the suffrage or temperance movement?" she said sarcastically. "I think some men would think the island would sink into the ocean like Atlantis if the Line was closed down."

"So a man's reputation remains intact while he sows his wild oats, but a woman's reputation is ruined if she loses her virginity, even forcibly? Something's very wrong with that."

Marguerite sighed. "You're right, honey, but it's hard to change an attitude that's set in stone around here."

"Well I started our day off on a depressing note. Let's forget about my near-catastrophe and let me tell you the good news. As of Saturday night, I should be in my own apartment right down the road, and I'm almost positive I have the job at Rosenberg."

"That's great!"

"And I'm sure your reference made that happen. Thank you, Marguerite."

"You're very welcome. Did you remember to get your calling cards?"

Grace nodded and patted her small drawstring purse on her wrist.

"Let me show you the house, and then I want to hear some more stories about your family." She grabbed her glass and stood. "Bring your lemonade and follow me."

A set of high, wide stairs at the back of the house led to the first floor, but she took Grace to a door to the right of it that opened to the basement. The ceiling inside was the exposed floor joists and crossbeams supporting the house.

"It reminds me of the belly of a ship—those wood beams are massive."

"They hold a lot of weight above it."

Grace noticed murals on the wall—some well done and others looked more like a child's paintings. "Somebody's had fun with these walls."

"Josephine's the artist—you'll see a lot of her paintings upstairs, but she entertains casually down here. She calls it her *grotto,* and this is where my cousin lets her hair down. I think it's because she doesn't have to worry about appearances down here, or something getting scratched or ruined with these brick and stone walls. Did I tell you they raised six children in this house—including four rambunctious boys?"

Grace turned away from one of the murals and shook her head.

"Josephine gave birth to nine, but her oldest daughter married before the house was completed, and she lost two sons in infancy."

"How sad. Do you have any children?"

"Three of my own and four stepchildren from my last and late husband."

Grace's eyes grew wide. "How did you do it?"

"You marry a man whose children are grown," she said bluntly. "My own were enough of a handful for me when they were younger, but we're all very close now. One daughter's married, one's trying to get married, and my son is attending the University of Virginia, his Uncle Walter's alma mater."

"You don't look old enough to have married children."

"Bless you, girl. I started *very* young, and I wouldn't recommend it," she said. She pointed to a door at the right. "That's where the laundry is done. There's a large cistern hidden under the conservatory, although they have city water, too."

Marguerite walked through an arch into a room on their left and showed her a wine cellar in one corner before leading her into another room with two arched openings on one wall. Marguerite spoke to several women preparing food and told them to pay them no mind—that they were just passing through.

"We won't stay long down here since we'll get in their way. It's the busiest area in the house." She walked around a narrow floor to ceiling closet sitting in the middle of the room.

"That's the dumbwaiter waiter—they cook the food down here to keep from heating up the house and then send it up to a warming kitchen next to the dining room on the first floor. The dumbwaiter waiter is four stories high, so they use it to send everything else under the sun up and down, too."

They climbed the winding stairs behind the dumbwaiter waiter to the first floor, and Marguerite opened every door to reveal a servant's lavatory, a trunk room, and the warming kitchen where the windows looked to be ten feet high or more. A butler's pantry containing the china, silverware, and glassware separated the kitchen and the dining room, which Marguerite wasn't willing to show Grace just yet. She pointed to a call box on the wall where family members could summon the servants from almost anywhere in the house. A coat closet full of brass hooks for guests' wraps curved around the back of an interior fireplace.

Grace commented on the beautiful wood paneling on the walls and open stairs.

"Josephine would have a conniption if she knew I told you this, but it's long leaf pine—much cheaper than the other types of wood used in the front rooms. The pine is used extensively throughout all the service areas and family rooms of the house, but I agree with you—it's beautiful."

Grace ran her hand over the paneling.

"Are you finished with your lemonade?"

Grace nodded and handed her the glass. Marguerite set their glasses on a shelf in the dumbwaiter waiter and then started up the stairs to the right of it. A lower wainscot of long leaf pine accompanied the stairs. Halfway up the curving stairs, a beautiful stained glass window graced the wall.

"What an odd place to put a magnificent work of art—who would see it back here?"

"You're looking at the back side of it, honey, and you're seeing only a portion of it."

The stairs continued to curve to the left as they climbed to the second floor. Behind the doors in this L-shaped hall revealed another lavatory and a small office.

The next door Marguerite opened was the former nanny's bedroom.

She explained, "The children have outgrown the need for a nanny, so Josephine uses it as a guest room. I claim it as mine."

The next room was the Gresham's main bath room.

Grace noticed three faucets above the large tub. "What a luxury to have hot water piped to the bath, but what's the third faucet?"

"Rain water—Beulah told me it's better to wash your hair with rain water—fashionable, in fact."

"I guess I've been fashionable for years and just didn't know it," giggled Grace as she pushed back a stray lock. "Lucius has piped-in water *and* a big cistern at his house."

"For years here on the island, rain was the only source of water, but I've heard frightening stories of drought here when the cisterns went dry and hundreds of cattle died. The city figured out a way to pipe water from the mainland to prevent that from happening again, but something could always happen to that water source, too, so I think folks want to be prepared for any potential problems."

"I take so much of that for granted—water to drink and bathe in. When I was a young child, I faintly remember a bad drought back in the '80's. My aunt and uncle were right in the middle of the fence cutting war in Central Texas. Finn was involved, too, because he helped fence part of their ranch. One time he got caught in a wagon with a cattle rustler trying to escape from my dad and grandfather and uncles."

"Oh, my. What happened?"

"Finn took a shovel and knocked the rustler off the wagon, and my Aunt Faith held a gun on him until my uncles came. They took him to jail in Brownwood."

"How old was Finn at that time?"

"I think around fifteen."

"That was very brave for such a young man."

"He was defending Caitlin… she was in the wagon, too."

"Oh."

"It wasn't very long after that incident that Caitlin was accidentally killed falling from that very same wagon… and Finn saw it all. I think he blamed himself for a long time."

"How old is Finn now?"

"Thirty-one."

"Well, he should've gotten over it by now."

"That's exactly what I thought," said Grace as they walked out of the bath room. "But I guess some people never get over a lost love." She looked around. "Each floor's stairwell hall is getting smaller the higher we go. Are you ever going to let me see the rest of the house?"

"Yes, starting on the next floor."

They began walking up the stairs to the third floor when Marguerite pointed to a metal grid over another exposed section of the stained glass window. "Walter had to mount that over the pane not long after they built the house because the boys got in the habit of slapping it every time they ran past it—I guess for good luck."

"They sound pretty normal," said Grace, smiling at the thought.

When they reached the top of the stairs, the first thing Grace saw was an ordinary window on another inside wall. She walked over and peeked through it to see a large metal tank. A window to the outside situated above the tank provided the light to see by.

"This is one of the two copper rainwater cisterns on this floor. The second one is in this attic room," she opened a door to an unfinished, rafter-ceilinged room, "right above the bath we saw below."

"We've run out of stairs to climb, so please tell me we're going to see the rest of the house now."

Marguerite smiled. "Follow me."

She opened the door to a bright hall lit by sunlight. Transom windows opened up around an enclosed dome inside the house, protected by another cone-shaped ceiling above it with skylights forming the upper portion.

"What is this?"

"The top of the rotunda dome, which we'll see downstairs, but what most folks don't know is that it's a very elaborate way of lighting and cooling the house," said Marguerite. "Warm air is drawn upwards through these transom windows and out the attic. In the cold spells, these windows are closed, which traps the warm air, and the upper floors are the warmest rooms."

She opened the first door to the right. "If I'm not the only guest, I choose to sleep in this bedroom. I was one of the few that wasn't intimidated by the boys and their pranks."

Grace could see that the ceiling of the room followed the various rooflines.

"I don't know if it was because they were worried about fires, but they put stoves in the boys' bedrooms rather than fireplaces. Wise decision, I'd say."

She opened the next door, revealing a narrow hall. The first door was a cedar-lined room filled with clothes hanging from brass hooks all over the walls and ceiling.

"The cedar keeps the moths away," said Marguerite.

"They don't keep their clothes in their rooms?"

"No, they tell the servants what outfit they'd like to wear the following day, and the clothes are pressed and placed in their rooms by the next morning."

Grace sighed. "I could get used to that. I hate to iron."

"I need to re-train your thinking if Lucius is in your future. He won't allow you to lift an iron, honey."

"Oh, don't tempt me."

She followed Marguerite up a few stairs to a small, sun-lit circular room, surrounded by arched windows halfway up the wall. One large easel stood in the center, along with a stool, a chair, and a table cluttered with paints and brushes. Numerous canvases, painted and bare, leaned against the wall.

"Josephine's studio!"

Marguerite smiled and nodded. "It's built in the top of the southeast tower of the house. Go look at the view."

Grace stepped gingerly around the easel and looked out the nearest window. Then she stepped to the middle of the windows for a panoramic view of south and east Galveston.

"Look at all the rooftops! This city just goes on and on! But I can still see a sliver of ocean on the horizon. This is amazing." Grace looked around at some of the paintings, including the one on the easel. Most were portraits and landscapes. She turned to Marguerite. "I feel like we're intruding on Josephine's sanctuary, though."

"What she doesn't know…" Marguerite stepped back into the hall beside some stairs leading up.

"I'll never tell," said Grace, laughing. "What are the stairs for?"

"The attic… dark, dusty, crowded, and probably a few critters."

"This is high enough for me."

Marguerite showed her the two remaining bedrooms, and a large parlor she called the *winter parlor.* "On cold days, the family spends a lot of time up here because it's the warmest room in the house."

"Except for this dome up here, these rooms seem very similar to my home in Dalton—very comfortable."

"Remember that as we start going down."

They retraced their steps to the stairwell and headed down to the second floor. But this time, Marguerite took Grace back through the main bathroom to another door at the other end. It led into Josephine Gresham's bedroom, lavishly decorated compared to the more modest rooms upstairs.

Grace walked through the room, taking in the beautiful furniture, fabric, and rugs. The elaborate fireplace was a work of art, and almost every surface held a variety of accoutrements.

"This is definitely a contrast. But you said, 'Josephine's room.' Does that mean Walter has a separate bedroom?"

Marguerite led her to an adjoining room, less cluttered and more masculine, but every bit as opulent. The southeast corner opened up to the same circular-shaped room as Josephine's studio above, but with taller windows the visual effect was even more stunning.

"The gallery outside extends from Josephine's room, around Walter's room, to the sitting room out here," she said, gesturing around the east and south walls. She walked out of the bedroom. "And this is the family summer room where they like to spend time together."

Grace couldn't help but stare at three huge stained glass windows on the towering stairwell wall behind them.

"Let me show you the girls' bedrooms and then we'll walk down those stairs. This is my niece Josephine's room—I call her Josie to simplify matters." She opened the door directly across from Walter's room, revealing a bedroom equally as large as his.

"She's definitely her mother's daughter," said Grace, noting all the collectibles among the lavishly furnished room.

Marguerite stepped out of the room and to the left.

Grace noticed a window in the wall before they reached Beulah's door. "This house has more indoor windows. What's this one for?"

"That's in Josephine's closet, and there's a matching one in Walter's closet, too—for ventilation purposes."

She opened the door in front of them. "And this next bedroom is my Beulah's room. I think she takes after me."

"Oh, dear," teased Grace. "Can the world handle two Marguerites?"

"She enjoys life, but she's a pragmatist, too, like me. Her room is very tasteful, but less cluttered, don't you think?"

"It's lovely, and definitely less complicated."

"We both prefer simplicity over ostentation. This house amazes me, and I love to visit, but I couldn't be content here. My house in Houston is nice, but it's nothing like this. I can live in my house—my possessions don't own me, and if something breaks or gets damaged, I don't go all to pieces over it. Now the rest of this house is more like a piece of art, and it would be very tempting to let it own me if I lived here."

Grace followed her to the intricately carved banister overlooking a magnificent stairwell whose steps, she noticed, followed the circular pattern of the domed ceiling, an octagonal-shaped rotunda lit by a center skylight, also eight-sided. The borders on each section of the octagon were hand-painted to emphasize the shape of the dome, sitting atop heavy layers of crown molding and a wide strip of painted garlands, followed by more cornices bordering the painted border.

"Beautiful, isn't it?"

"Stunning."

The three towering stained-glass windows covered the wall facing her; each richly framed in wood and topped with separately framed round windows that gave the over-all appearance of giant key-holes in the wall. Two were built on an outside wall and backlit by sunlight; the third window was darker since it was the one that backed to the private stairwell. Ornate arches of a lighter hue bordered each window and continued down beside them in columns that stopped halfway down the wall for mere ornamentation rather than support. Carvings of children's faces and lions' heads trimmed the bottom of the columns.

"The rotunda is fifty-five feet high, and the detail is incredible. These stairs were hand-carved in Cincinnati."

Marguerite started down the stairs. "In the back of the house you saw long leaf pine paneling, but up here, you'll see oak, cherry, maple, and walnut on the walls and floors."

They reached the bottom of the stairs. A fireplace was tucked underneath in the curve of the stairwell, with no obvious chimney.

"Does this fireplace actually work?"

"With gas—a most ingenious idea. The servants love this one—no messy ashes to deal with."

Grace looked up at the landing hovering above it. A five-pointed star was carved in a solid portion of the banister.

"That looks like our state seal."

Marguerite nodded. "You're right. Walter was elected to the Texas House of Representatives while this house was being built."

She turned around to face the room. "This is the stair hall, which faces the entrance hall."

The openings to all of the rooms off the halls reminded Grace of the Arc de Triomphe in France, except these were framed in wood.

"My apartment would fit in this hall alone," said Grace.

"We'll start in the music room to our right and work our way around to all the rooms."

The music room opened to the parlor. Grace estimated that the ceilings on this floor had to be fifteen or twenty feet high, each adorned with a deep molded oval embossed design dropping from the center with linear patterns surrounding it. The windows covered at least ten or twelve feet of the height of the walls. Each was topped by stained glass transoms, and the lower windows were shaded by wood shutters rather than drapery. At first glance Grace thought the entire walls were paneled, but then realized that the wood on the walls was the generous framing surrounding the windows, which took up most of the wall space. Four massive wood columns supported the arch between the music room and the parlor.

"When Josephine has dances, she pushes the furniture to the walls and rolls up these beautiful rugs to expose the pine board flooring—the best for dancing." She walked towards an alcove at the front end of the parlor. "She hides the musicians over here—behind a small forest of her beautiful ferns."

Grace giggled.

"Every room was designed around its fireplace, and each one is unique. They ordered wood and stone from around the world. I think this room's paneling is mahogany."

Marguerite stepped into the entrance hall. "All of these rooms can be closed off to the hall by pocket doors. And the front doors are actually two sets of pocket doors."

Grace walked over to take a closer look at the massive doors, which resembled smaller versions of the stained glass windows behind the staircase. Above, an unusual, flower-shaped light fixture hung from the hall ceiling.

Marguerite followed her eyes. "Calla lilies are Josephine's favorite flower. Clayton included them throughout the house."

A carved wooden basket stood to the side of the front doors. Grace could see a number of calling cards piled inside of it.

"One day a week everyone has *home day* when they receive guests. Josephine's home day is Tuesdays. You'll have to come next week and meet the girls."

"Are you sure?"

"Of course! Put one of your cards in the basket, and we'll make it official."

Grace pulled a card out of her purse and placed it on the top of the stack. "Will all of these ladies be coming, too?"

"Heavens, no. They're very particular about who they invite into their house on home day."

Grace looked worried.

"They'll love you! Just don't mention cleaning or ironing," she teased. "Come on, we're almost done." Marguerite grabbed her arm and pulled her into the library. "These parquet floors and paneling are made of walnut—very expensive, especially when it's used so extensively throughout a room."

Glass encased bookshelves filled the corner walls on each side of the pocket door openings. Above the bookshelves were murals painted on the walls in between the wood columns adorning the walls and framing the windows.

"Josephine painted all of these murals, as well as most of the portraits and still-life paintings you see throughout the house."

"She's very talented."

"Did you notice that this room follows the identical layout of Walter's bedroom above it? That's fitting since he claims them both."

"I love these round rooms," said Grace, walking to the sitting area to the right. "But of all of them, I think I love Josephine's studio on the third floor best."

"This fireplace is made of pink marble brought all the way from Africa. She told me where all of this came from, but I've forgotten half of it."

Marguerite walked over to a closed pocket door and slid it into the wall, revealing the dining room. "All the pocket doors are paneled the same wood as the room is paneled in, so the wood is different on each side of the door."

Grace followed her into the dining room. Wood panels and columns covered the entire walls. Like the other rooms, the windows were also shuttered except for the stained glass transoms above them.

"I do know that this room is in oak, and its theme has to do with the ocean. See the shell design in the stained glass windows? And Poseidon's face is carved in the corbels at the tops of the columns."

She walked to the fireplace wall and opened the shutters to the window on the right side, which opened to the conservatory.

"I wondered how you'd get to this room!"

They stepped into the sunlit room filled with ferns and a variety of palms and other exotic-looking plants. The air was warm and thick with moisture.

"This is Josephine's other passion, and she's good at it. Personally, I can't even grow cactus. But I do have a beautiful yard and garden—I have the best landscaper in Houston."

The tall windows that made up the entire walls added to the exotic feel of the room with the onion dome pattern in each of the top panes.

"This is one of the few floors that has tiles, for obvious reasons."

"It's wonderful. I feel like I've stepped in another world in this house. Lucius told me to remember all of this—he has big plans for his own house on Broadway soon."

Marguerite raised her eyebrows in question. "Sounds like his plans include you, too."

"We have such a short history; we don't really know each other. This is all so exciting, though, and I have to keep reminding myself to not get caught up in all of this. It's definitely taken my mind off of Finn, at least until my head hits the pillow at night. But Lucius is moving way too fast for me, and it's getting harder and harder not to let him."

"Then let him."

Grace shook her head. "And what happens when the gold leaf wears off and we finally see our real selves, faults and all? I want to build our relationship first, then we can build a house, and although this house is breathtaking, I feel like you do. I don't want to live in a museum where you can't touch anything. I want a house we can live in—all of it, not just the part few people ever see. My mother doesn't mind anyone seeing any room of our house. And my parents are the same people at home as the people you see at church. They're unpretentious and transparent—what you see is what they actually are. That's important to me. But I think Lucius wants a showplace like this where appearances are paramount."

"It's hard not to be that in this town—especially where Lucius is heading financially."

"See? That's why we need to take our time."

"Are you sure? You know he'll put the world at your feet, honey. How can you pass that up? Most women on this island would give anything to be in your shoes."

Grace felt torn, but she tried not to show it.

"But you're not most women, and that's probably why he has his sights set on you. I have to warn you, though… when Lucius wants something, he can be very persuasive."

"I'm not saying I'm not interested in Lucius. I just don't want to play the role of a professional hostess and curator of his empire."

Chapter 19

Mathilda Sweeney, youngest daughter of Rebecca Brown, greeted Marguerite with a hug in the foyer of Ashton Villa. Grace thought the two women looked to be around the same age.

"Your home is lovely," said Grace.

"Thank you! Did Marguerite tell you that Mother named it for one of our ancestors in the Revolutionary War?"

"She mentioned Ashton Villa on the day we arrived, but I didn't know where the name came from."

"The exterior of this house looks like we're in New Orleans," said Marguerite.

"It's the ornamental iron gallery that does it—will you come back for Mardi Gras, Marguerite? Didn't we have fun at the last one?" She turned to Grace. "I came home to live a few years ago after Daddy died," she said, and then lowered her voice, "and my divorce."

"Meet your first fallen woman, Grace," teased Marguerite. "Get over it, Mathilda! Life goes on, and I'm sure you've been a great help to your Momma."

"She's already told me that Bettie's getting the house, but I know my sweet sister won't kick me out."

"There's certainly room for you both," said Marguerite, glancing towards the parlor to their left. "Where is everybody?"

"We're having lunch in the drawing room upstairs where we can catch a breeze," said Mathilda, leading the way. "Mother says it's too stuffy in the gold room, but I think she just doesn't feel like coming downstairs some days."

"So if Mohammed won't come to the mountain, the mountain will come to Mohammed," said Marguerite, laughing.

Mathilda led them into a large room with white walls and white chiffon curtains and half a dozen white dresses and hats around a table near an open window.

Grace caught herself before she raised her hand to shield her eyes, but she couldn't help squint at the brightness of the room. Like the parlor downstairs, every edge seemed to have a tinge of gold.

"What's so funny, girls?"

Grace followed the voice to an older woman sitting at the head of the table.

"You know Marguerite, Mother—the life of the party has arrived."

"Marguerite! I heard you were in town. Come over here and sit by me. Scoot over Coar, make some room for my friend. You know I can't see beyond the end of this table."

"Well, if you'd wear your spectacles, Rebecca, you could see clear across the island," said Marguerite, leaning down to kiss the matriarch. "How are you, dear friend?"

"I'm just fine, but those horrid things—they make me look old."

"Your age makes you look old, Mother, but you're still beautiful. The eyeglasses won't change that."

"I do wear them for the parades," she admitted. "I love the parades." She noticed Grace standing beside Marguerite. "And who's this exquisite being you've brought with you?" She waved her hand at the left side of the table. "Scoot down another seat, girls."

"This is Grace Taylor from Waco. She's brand new to Galveston, so I hope you all will make her feel welcome. In other words, don't scare her off."

"Grace… what a sweet name," said Rebecca, holding out her hand.

Grace leaned forward and took the offered hand. "I'm pleased to meet you, Mrs. Brown." She looked around the table. "I'm pleased to meet all of you."

They took their seats, and a servant placed an iced drink in front of them.

"Gracious sakes, what happened to your face?" said the older woman squinting at her.

Grace paused, trying to decide between running into a door frame or bedpost.

Marguerite spoke up. "It's a bruise, Rebecca, nothing more."

"What happened?"

"Didn't it have something to do with a streetcar, Grace?"

Grace nodded, hoping Marguerite's story would suffice.

"You poor girl," said Rebecca.

"Speaking of poor girls," said Cora, "did you hear what happened on Postoffice Street yesterday?"

Grace stiffened in shock. Marguerite reassuringly patted her leg underneath the table.

"We've already heard this, Hattie," said Mathilda.

"But these ladies haven't." She turned to Grace. "We heard a thirteen year-old girl was forced into prostitution, and Rabbi Cohen bicycled down to Postoffice Street and marched right into this house of ill repute. She was barely dressed, so he wrapped a blanket around her and marched downtown with his bicycle on one hand and the girl on the other. They walked into a clothes store where he ordered the saleslady to 'fit her out from head to foot,' and then took her home. Can you believe that?"

Grace visibly relaxed.

"Postoffice Street—my pastor wouldn't be caught dead down there!" a woman said across the table.

Grace couldn't be silent. "How fortunate for that young girl that the Rabbi had the courage to rescue her from that lifestyle."

The room was uncomfortably quiet.

"But how will her life change?" another woman said. "What boy would want to court her now that she's… soiled?"

"If you remember the Scriptures, Gertrude, Jesus rescued harlots, too," said Rebecca, "and crooked tax collectors, and smelly fishermen, and demon-possessed lunatics. He gravitated toward the people who needed Him the most. And many of these undesirables became His most faithful followers."

"Well, He's Jesus," said Gertrude flippantly. "That's what He's supposed to do."

"Did you know that a harlot is in Jesus' lineage?" added Marguerite.

Grace looked at her in surprise.

Marguerite smirked. "Are you shocked about the harlot or the revelation that Marguerite St. John knows the Scriptures?"

Grace grinned. "Maybe a little of both. I sure don't remember that lesson in Sunday School."

"The Son of God is descended from a harlot? I don't believe that," said Gertrude.

"Her name was Rahab, the prostitute who hid the Israelite spies in the wall of Jericho. She was the mother of Boaz."

"Whose wife was Ruth—you're right!" said Mathilda. "I never made that connection."

"You could argue that it was Joseph's ancestors," said Cora. "Remember, Joseph isn't Jesus' real father."

"Rahab isn't mentioned in Mary's lineage, but Boaz was," said Marguerite, "and we know who his mother was. God saw fit to mention her in Jesus' lineage, and if Rahab was so soiled and unusable, don't you think He would've left her out of the genealogy altogether?"

"And if we claim to be Christians, we're supposed to reach out to the undesirables, too," said Rebecca, squinting at Grace. "I agree with you, young lady. We're very fortunate to have someone that has the audacity to fight the flagrant vices on this island when the rest of us are content to turn a blind eye. Henry Cohen always puts the welfare of people first—no matter who they are or where they're from, and we all can learn from that. And that's my last sermon for today." She raised her hand. "Leo, we're ready."

Mathilda announced to the table. "Mother has something extra special for you today—she had it shipped in from New York."

Leo set a tray of small white bowls in the center of the table. Each held a quivering mass of translucent red and yellow substance.

"I was only able to get strawberry and lemon, and I want you to taste both."

"And what, pray tell, is this stuff?" asked Marguerite, poking it with her spoon.

"Jelly? Gelatin? No, that's not right," said Rebecca. "What do they call this, Leo?"

"The package said *JELL-O*, ma'am."

"Is it a food or garnish?" asked Cora, making it jiggle.

"Food, silly," said Mathilda. "It's supposed to be our dessert, but Mother couldn't wait to let you try it."

"I've never heard of such," said Grace, taking a bite of the red. "It does taste like strawberry!" She tried the lemon. "Is this made from strawberries and lemons?"

Mathilda said, "No, I think they concoct those flavors artificially somehow."

"I love it, although it's kind of springy when I try to chew it."

"What fun!" said Marguerite. "You never fail to surprise me when I come here, Rebecca."

"I'm so glad you are enjoying it."

"You realize Mother is testing you, don't you? She wants to see your reactions before she serves it at our next dinner party."

At three o'clock, Marguerite took Grace for tea at the Oaks, Betty Ballinger's home on the corner of Avenue O and 29th. Grace was surprised to learn that it was also a short meeting of the Galveston Chapter of the DRT.

"I'm not familiar with this DRT club," whispered Grace.

"Daughters of the Republic of Texas."

"Are you a member?"

Marguerite nodded. "We have a Houston Chapter, but I like to keep in touch if I'm in town. Betty and her cousin Hally started the organization to keep alive the memories of those who helped bring about Texas' independence. Josephine's and my grandfather fought with Sam Houston at the Battle of San Jacinto."

"Is she coming to the meeting?"

"No, she had a prior commitment. Do you mind me sharing a little about your family?"

"I guess not."

Marguerite stood and introduced Grace to the group, saying her family came to Texas right after it became a state, and that her grandparents founded a town near Waco which they renamed Grace after her grandmother and father Justin were rescued from the Apaches after being kidnapped for six years.

That caused a murmuring among the group. Grace suddenly felt uncomfortable with everyone focusing on her.

"Twenty years later, Grace's mother found herself in a similar situation with the Apache Indians. Justin Taylor found her and brought her home and married her, and Grace here was their firstborn. In fact, Grace was named after her grandparents' town, so she has a lot of history connected with early Texas."

Betty spoke up. "We'd love to hear more, Grace. Would you be willing to share your family stories at one of our future meetings?"

"Uh… sure."

"Wonderful! We'll put you on the agenda."

Afterwards, a number of them came up to introduce themselves and ask Grace for a calling card.

One particular woman standing there told her friend, "This is the woman I was telling you about." She turned to Grace. "I'm so glad you're all right, other than your cheek, I see."

Grace's hand went to her cheek. "What do you mean?"

"You were the one who helped that poor girl at that brothel," she continued. "My husband and I imagined the absolute worst scenario after hearing all the screaming in the house, but I couldn't get Howard off the streetcar to help you, and I was scared to death. He said it was none of our business. I'm still upset with him. I'm so sorry we didn't help you."

Grace smiled with relief. "Everything worked out fine, thanks to Mr. Robertson."

"And Rabbi Cohen, too, we hear. It's an honor to finally learn your name, Grace."

"Thank you, and likewise, I'm sure."

Marguerite waited until the women walked away before she spoke. "If you want to change things for the better, this is the group you'll want to know. They do more than preserve our history; I think they're shaping our future."

Chapter 20

Try as she might, Grace couldn't talk her way out of seeing Lucius Wednesday night. He told her he'd come by the Oaks at six o'clock to take her to supper across the street at the Garten Verein. The meeting ended well before five so Marguerite kept Grace company on the gallery as she waited for him.

Grace leaned back in the rocking chair and closed her eyes for a moment, letting the sea breeze caress her face. "This has been one of the most enjoyable days of my life, Marguerite. Thank you."

"My pleasure. I've thoroughly enjoyed seeing old and familiar things again through new eyes."

Grace turned and looked at her. "Do you pick up strangers regularly and immerse them in this culture?"

Marguerite laughed. "Only the ones I feel drawn to, and I couldn't help but notice how sad you were on the train."

Grace reached over and squeezed her hand. "I'm so glad you were forward enough to approach me."

"You wouldn't have done the same if the situation was reversed?"

Grace shook her head. "Other than Finn, every friendship I've had was instigated by the other person."

"Really? I never would've guessed that about you."

"I guess it's safer that way, but I'm determined to do better down here."

"Why was it different with Finn?"

"Years ago I received some advice from my grandmother's friend, Vestal."

"I remember you mentioning her the other day."

" I guess she was like another grandmother to us. I told her about this boy I liked—Finn, although I didn't say his name. I told her that someone I loved like a sister liked him, too, so I didn't feel free to let him know how I felt. She told me what perseverance meant and that I'd better not make the same mistake she did. Years before, she and her best friend loved the same man, too, so Vestal pulled back and let him choose. Her friend pursued him relentlessly, and the man eventually gave in and married her. Vestal learned later that the man actually loved *her* best, but he assumed her silence and apparent lack of interest meant she didn't feel the same way. She was devastated that she missed her chance with the man she loved, so that's why she followed the Taylors to Texas.

"She told me I shouldn't wait for this boy to pursue me, that if I really loved him, I should let him know how I feel. And if he didn't feel the same way, at least I'd know one way or the other. She didn't want me to make the same mistake she'd made and regretted for the rest of her life.

"I asked her why she didn't find someone else. She said she still loved that man and was afraid no one else could measure up to him. She didn't think it would be fair to marry someone else and not love him like she should.

"I guess she was right, but I wondered if she ever regretted not having children of her own. I know I wanted to have children some time in my life. I eventually asked her about that, and she said that the Lord knew what he was doing sending her down to Texas with the Taylors. She loved their children and grandchildren as if they were her own. And she took care of my grandparents' older two children during those six years my grandmother Julia and my father were with the Apaches. My grandfather 'bout went out of his mind searching for them. But he knew Matt and Jenny were fine with Vestal so he could leave for long periods of time.

"Vestal told me that it's not always the most talented or most beautiful that wins in life. It's the one that perseveres, and that I needed perseverance to be successful at most anything. Then she said something I've never forgotten."

"What was that?" asked Marguerite.

"She told me not to be discouraged, that it's often the last key that unlocks the door. I didn't know what that meant at first, but then I realized that she was telling me to not give up. I tried every key I could think of to unlock Finn's heart, to no avail. And then I thought for sure that the dramatic stunt I pulled at the train station would work. But he literally ran away from me."

"He's damaged goods."

"And even though I came on down here, I felt sure he'd follow me."

"One spoke short of a wheel."

"I can't believe these years have meant so little to him."

"A donkey's ass."

"Isn't that the same thing?"

"It's doubly worse."

Grace laughed. "You're not going to let me wallow in misery, are you."

"No, not when you have a delectable alternative."

"I need to slow that train down. I feel like it's going to derail if I don't."

"What are you going to tell him about your cheek?"

She glanced back at the house. "The truth didn't seem so bad in there earlier."

"That woman thought you were some kind of hero, but Lucius won't respond that way."

"I hate to lie."

"Well, you'd better make up your mind soon because here he comes."

Grace grabbed her arm. "How did you word it earlier about the streetcar? It wasn't actually a lie."

Marguerite whispered, "Follow my lead."

Lucius took the steps two at a time.

"Hello, Lucius."

"Marguerite." He tipped his hat towards her.

Grace kept the left side of her face angled toward Marguerite.

"And how are my two favorite ladies on the island?"

"We're wonderful, and now I must bid you adieu—I promised Josephine I'd go with her to her Bible study and prayer meeting." She hugged Grace. "Goodbye, my clumsy friend! You watch your step on those streetcars from now on. I'll see you tomorrow, honey."

Lucius looked confused until Grace turned to face him, and then his eyes widened. His hand reached for her chin.

"Good Lord!"

"I'm fine, Lucius. I got off the streetcar yesterday when I shouldn't have."

"Did you run into a post?"

"No, but if you'd rather not be seen in public with me, I could go home." She felt a slight pang of guilt at turning the tables.

"Don't be silly! You'll still be the most beautiful woman in the park. Come on, we're going to enjoy this evening."

This time Lucius drove a smaller carriage to the park, tying up the horse near the walkway closest to the Club House.

Grace enjoyed the beautifully landscaped gardens. She could hear music playing from a nearby bandstand and saw families playing croquet together.

"This is a beautiful place."

"Wait 'til you taste the food."

The menu for this week's fare at the club included sliced ham, plum sauce, baked yams, cabbage salad, and afterwards, to Grace's delight, ice cream with preserved peaches. They chose to eat on the outside patio so they could watch the goings on in the park.

"That was wonderful," Grace said, taking a deep breath and leaning back in the chair. "Do you do this every Wednesday night?"

Lucius nodded. "Unless I'm working late."

A couple of young girls ran by, giggling and looking over their shoulders at some boys running after them.

Grace smiled, remembering the giddy feeling of the chase. Her smile faded when she remembered her chasing Finn was all for naught. She could feel Lucius' eyes on her.

"Are you all right?"

She nodded and smiled. "It's been a long day. Marguerite's hard to keep up with, but the more I get to know her, the more I like her."

"She's a remarkable woman. And what did you think of the Gresham House?"

Grace's face lit up. "I've never seen anything like it. And when she showed it to me, she started in the basement and the private areas of the house that few people see before she showed me the impressive front rooms."

"Why'd she do that?"

"I think she wanted me to see that the Greshams were real people and to not be so intimidated when I meet them formally next week. Have you seen the entire house?"

Lucius shook his head. "No, only the front rooms. Did you get some good ideas for my house?"

"Don't you want a house that you can live in?"

"Of course, but I want it to reflect my abilities and accomplishments."

"A showplace."

"A man should be proud of his home… and his wife." He raised her hand to his lips.

"So you want a show wife, too."

"If you mean do I want to be able to show off my wife, too, then yes, especially if she looks like you."

Grace pulled her hand back.

Lucius looked surprised. "What's wrong with that?"

"Nothing. I just feel like we need to slow down a bit. You need to slow down. I feel like you're making plans that involve me, and you don't even know me, Lucius. I haven't been here a week—"

He looked at his pocket watch. "Would you like some coffee? They'll stop serving in a few minutes."

"No, thank you… did you hear a word I said?"

He leaned over and kissed her cheek. "Every word; and we'll talk about it some more… right after I get my coffee."

Grace looked away in frustration. A few seconds passed before she realized she was staring at someone several tables over, and to her surprise, he was staring back. She blinked several times before familiarity set in. Mr. Robertson smiled and waved his hand and leaned over to say something to a woman sitting with him.

Grace looked around and then stood up and walked over to him.

"Mr. Robertson, how nice to see you! A co-worker of yours told me he came here regularly, but I didn't know you did, too."

"How are you, Miss Taylor?" he asked as he stood up to greet her. She noticed his eyes flinch when he saw her cheek.

"I'm just fine," she assured him, "thank you."

He turned to the woman beside him. "Maeve, I'd like you to meet Miss Taylor, who's currently staying at Mr. Roderick's house."

Maeve's face lit up. "Oh! How nice to meet you! I'm sorry I haven't been here this week to welcome you."

"She and Trixie are already friends."

Maeve smiled broadly. "That's something! Trixie doesn't cotton to just anybody. She even snapped at the preacher a couple of weeks ago."

"I grew up with a lot of dogs." Grace looked behind her. "I need to get back to our table—I'm here with Mr. Roderick, and he's… uh… not familiar with how I acquired this bruise. I told him I got it getting off the streetcar."

Mr. Robertson smiled. "That's an unusual way to put it."

"How about joining us for dinner Saturday?" Maeve asked.

"I'll be moving over to Lucas Terrace apartments on Saturday afternoon."

"Then what about a quick lunch then? Guilmet won't be home from work by then, but that'll give us time to get to know each other better. We'll be sorry to see you leave the neighborhood."

"I'd love to join you for lunch."

"Grace!" someone called out.

Grace turned to see the woman from the DRT meeting walking towards her, dragging a reluctant partner.

"Mr. Robertson! If this isn't a dandy reunion here! Grace, I wanted to show Howard that you were just fine, other than your poor cheek." She turned to Mr. Robertson. "We thought the worst hearing all that screaming going on in there—we thought somebody was dying, but then you and those brawny men charged the house and dragged that beast out of there. You should be proud of your husband, Maeve—he rescued Grace, unlike Howard here."

"I'm very proud of my husband," said Maeve, smiling apologetically at Grace. "Why, hello, Mr. Roderick."

Grace's heart sunk in her chest. She took a deep breath before turning around. "Look who's here, Lucius—your neighbors!"

Lucius forced a smile and offered his hand. "Good to see you, Guilmet… Maeve."

"And this is… Howard and… I'm sorry, I've forgotten your name," said Grace.

"Adele Mayer."

Lucius nodded. "So you all were present on the streetcar when Grace was injured?"

"Yes," said Adele. "She is such a brave woman—and Mr. Robertson, too. Right, Howard?"

"Are they still serving coffee?" Howard asked Lucius.

"Yes," he said, setting down his cup and grasping Grace's arm. "Would you excuse us, please? I'd like to show Grace this beautiful park before it gets too dark."

He didn't wait to hear their responses, escorting Grace away from the patio and club house. He didn't speak for a full minute, finally stopping at a bench by a statue of a man.

Grace wasn't sure how much he heard, but she knew he was angry.

"So… this… bruise was not caused by falling out of Guilmet's streetcar."

"I didn't exactly say that."

"Right, you just assumed I would think it."

"I didn't want to worry you."

"And so I have to overhear secondhand that you were attacked by some beast, which I assume is a man. Would you like to explain exactly what happened and why you didn't want to tell me? Where did this happen?"

Grace looked down. "On Postoffice Street."

"Downtown—at a business?"

"Sort of..." Grace said, swallowing hard.

"Do I have to coax every detail out of you?"

"It happened at a house... a brothel."

"You were attacked at a brothel?" He turned around. "Grace! I don't even know where to begin asking you to explain yourself! Or maybe I do... what were you doing at a brothel?!"

"I was killing some time until my calling cards were printed, and I just happened to find Mr. Robertson's streetcar, and I rode along his route while he told me a lot about the city and—"

"Get on with it."

"This very young girl—I'd seen her the day before on that route—anyway, she came screaming out of the house—screaming for help. I couldn't ignore that—she didn't look any older than my students. Mr. Robertson stopped the streetcar and I went to see what was wrong."

"You had no idea what you were walking into."

"True, but she took me inside to the back bedroom where another woman she... worked with was on the floor. She'd been beaten and was unconscious. Anise thought she was dead."

"So, you're on a first name basis with a whore now."

"She's just a young girl, Lucius! She shouldn't even be there."

"Well, how'd you hurt your cheek?"

Grace took a deep breath before answering. "The man came back, claiming they'd stolen his wallet. I think he was drunk, and he assumed I worked there."

Lucius looked ill... angry and ill.

"And he attacked you," he said, trying to maintain control. "He hit you."

Grace nodded. "I bloodied his nose, if that makes you feel any better."

Lucius was quiet for a moment. "Is that why you didn't want to see me last night?"

She nodded again.

"Did he... "

"No... no! Mr. Robertson got some help and they came and took him away. I wanted to tell you, but I was afraid you'd be angry at me… like you are right now."

"I get angry when I get scared, and what you did scares the hell out of me. What were you thinking, Grace? You could've been raped or even killed!"

"I'm sorry—I just reacted without thinking. Next time…"

He grasped her by the shoulders. "Next time? There won't be a next time, Grace. Don't you *ever* do anything like that again."

"But—"

"You should've gone to the authorities and let them handle it—or better, come to me and let me take care of it. I can't believe Guilmet let you off that streetcar."

"He didn't want to, but I threatened to jump."

Lucius groaned. "Promise me that from now on you'll think before you act."

"I just wanted to help her."

"I know," he said, pulling her to himself. "Was this the young lady that Rabbi Cohen rescued yesterday?"

"How'd you hear about that?"

He leaned back and looked in her face. "The story spread like a fire downtown—especially after he marched her into that store and demanded they clothe her decently. He found out about her from you, didn't he?"

She nodded. "I didn't know who else to go to."

"I can't stand the thought that you put yourself in such danger," he said, touching her face, "or that a man dared to raise a hand to you."

"I'm fine, Lucius."

"I also heard that Rabbi Cohen conducted a graveside service for a prostitute today."

Grace's heart stopped. "What?"

"They said she died last night of unknown causes, but I know better now."

Lucius caught her before she sank to the ground.

Chapter 21

A movement in the office doorway caught Lucius' eye, but he didn't bother to look up from his desk until he realized somebody continued to stand there. The man's clothes were disheveled; it looked like he hadn't shaved in a week. He held a smudged Stetson in his hand, and his eyes looked weary. Weary and worried.

He knew those eyes.

"Finn Samuel?" Lucius pushed back his chair and stood.

Finn walked over and extended his hand. "How you doin', Lucius?"

"Very well," he replied, gripping his hand. "I thought you'd get here before now."

Finn gave him a half smile. "I would've, but I thought she went home to Dalton. I beat her letter to her parents' house—they didn't even know she'd left Waco or where she was heading. That wasn't a good moment; I thought her father was going to tear my head off. But her letter arrived the next day, so I headed this way."

"Sissy knew."

"I took off half-cocked and didn't talk to anybody—I didn't even pack a bag." He ran his hand through his hair. "How is she?"

"She's doing very well; at least she seems to be enjoying herself immensely."

"She is?"

"Well, I haven't noticed her pining away if that's what you're wondering. Look around, Finn. We have everything here—wealth, opportunity, status, education, the arts, every pleasurable activity imaginable."

"I've come to take her home."

"You may be too late."

"What do you mean?"

"She's already making a life for herself, Finn. She has a job; she put money down on an apartment; she's made new friends… and very affluent friends, I might add."

"She hasn't even been here a week," Finn said tetchily.

"Life moves fast down here, and I think she likes it."

"I'll be the judge of that. Where can I find her?"

"What do you have to offer her? I heard about your brother's business venture going bust, and you were his biggest investor. Do you even have enough money to get her home?"

Finn looked shocked. Lucius knew he'd hit his mark.

"That's none of your business."

"Why don't you think of Grace for once and turn around and go home? You had your chance and you lost it."

Lucius saw a flash of anger in Finn's eyes.

"So you're already circling. I see you haven't wasted any time, Roderick."

"I think it's only fair that you know. You saved my hide once, and I owe you for that. I'd be happy to pay your train fare home."

"You gonna tell me where she is?"

"I don't know where she is at the moment, but she spends the nights at my house," he said smugly.

When Lucius saw him clench his fist and start towards him, he raised his hand and quickly added, "But I stay here, Finn."

He stopped and glared at him, and then turned to leave.

"She's very happy here, Finn. If you don't believe me, come to the dance at the Garten Verein tomorrow night and watch her from a distance. You'll see for yourself she's moving on with her life. And you might want to clean yourself up a bit. You wouldn't want to embarrass her around here."

Finn stormed out of the building, afraid if he stayed one more second he would lose control of his temper. He'd already lost control of his finances, and he hated to admit it, but Lucius wasn't too far off the mark. He barely had enough money to get Grace and himself back to Waco. He wasn't even sure if he wanted to go back there.

How did Roderick already know about his financial losses? He'd just learned of it himself only a week ago.

Joseph had lost almost everything. Finn was angry at himself for not keeping a closer eye on his brother's business, but he had his own job. And since he'd missed almost a week of work now, even that was in jeopardy. His brother was brilliant when it came to inventive ideas, but he proved again that his timing was terrible. And he tended to focus on the creative end of the business rather than the financial. He was destined to work for a salary under someone else's supervision rather than himself.

Joseph swore he would pay Finn every cent, but Finn knew better. His brother's good intentions rarely turned into deeds, and besides, he had a wife and six children to feed.

After several disdainful looks by folks dressed nice enough for church, which made him stop and question what day it was… Thursday, a familiar reflection in a store window stopped him in his tracks. He looked on either side of him before he realized the man he saw was himself—and a rugged depiction at that by Galveston's standards. He took off his hat and swatted it against his pants, raising a cloud of dust. He felt pinpricks of fear on the back of his neck when he realized what he was up against with Lucius—power, wealth, and the confidence of success. And Lucius seemed determined to win.

He stared at his reflection again, realizing that he had very little to offer Grace in comparison. For years she was there… everywhere he turned. He thought she would always be there for him, and he took that for granted. In the deepest part of his heart, he knew she belonged to him, but still he couldn't help but keep her at arm's length for fear of losing her like he lost Caitlin.

A painful moan rose at the back of his throat at the thought that death wasn't the only way to lose somebody. And this was his fault.

She deserved better.

Finn looked down the street towards the train station, wondering if he should walk down there and check the schedule for the next train out of here. But something rose up in him, and he knew he couldn't walk away without finding out for himself if Grace still wanted him or not.

A man in a bowler and spiffy suit frowned at him, but the woman glanced at him with interest in her eyes.

He wiped the sweat off his brow and looked up at the store sign—a clothing store. He stepped onto the boardwalk and entered the store.

A short, well-dressed man approached him, looking him up and down. "May I assist you, sir?"

"I need a change of clothes."

The man looked him up and down again over his wire-rimmed glasses and nodded a bit too enthusiastically, Finn thought.

"Follow me," he said, taking Finn to a table of black woolen suit coats and pants. "This is what every well-dressed gentleman on the Strand is wearing."

Finn felt the material and frowned. "In this heat?"

"You get used to it. And we definitely need to get rid of that," the clerk said as he handed Finn a bowler hat and reached for his Stetson.

Finn backed up. "Don't touch my hat," he said, thrusting the bowler between them. "It stays with me."

The clerk looked shocked. "This isn't the wild west down here, sir. We're civilized."

Finn looked at the price on the suit. "Maybe too civilized for me. I think I just need a shirt, preferably white."

The clerk sighed loudly and walked to another table and turned around and looked intently at Finn from his neck to his arms to his midsection. He picked up a white cotton dress shirt and handed it to him.

"This should do."

Finn unfolded it and held it up against his chest. The sleeves seemed long enough. He unbuttoned it and tried the neck size, and it fit as well.

"You know your stuff," he said approvingly.

The clerk smiled at the compliment. "I've had years of practice. Is there anything else you'd like?"

Finn looked around. "I think this will do for now. On second thought, do you happen to know Lucius Roderick?"

"He's one of our best customers—works across the street. Is he a friend of yours?"

"We go way back—we're both from Waco."

"He has excellent tastes in clothing. Do you plan to see him while you're here?"

"I don't want to bother him at work—I'd like to surprise him at home. Do you know his address?"

The clerk nodded. "We've made quite a few deliveries there—his house is on the corner of 17th and L Streets."

"17th and L—I appreciate it."

Finn followed the clerk to a counter near the door and watched him record the purchase on a ledger. He could see his funds dwindling before his eyes.

"Do you know where someone could pick up some temporary work around here? What about the docks?"

The clerk shook his head. "It's all pretty much closed shop."

"What do you mean?"

"They hire only union members, although there have been some rumblings about forcing them to open it up to nonmembers, too, but I haven't seen that happen in years. I'm sure Mr. Roderick knows of something."

Finn forced a smile. "You're right. I'll ask him when I see him."

The clerk wrapped the new shirt in paper. "Are you familiar with the streets?"

Finn shook his head. "First time here."

"Numbered streets go north and south; letter streets are east and west, although the first ten letters go by other names, too."

"That'll help," said Finn. "And do you know where I can get a bath around here?"

The man looked at him over his glasses again. "Just a bath?"

Finn looked down at his dusty clothes. "Well, it's obvious that a bath isn't the only thing I need."

The clerk smiled knowingly and said, "If you're anything like Mr. Roderick, I know exactly what you mean." He reached under the counter and handed Finn a card.

"Just go to the back of the establishment and tell them…" he looked cautiously from left to right before continuing, "tell them La Longue Carabine sent you."

"The long rifle?" asked Finn, "like Natty Bumppo's nickname?"

"Ah, so you're a reader."

"*The Last of the Mohicans* is one of my favorite books."

"Mine, too." The clerk tapped the card in his hand. "Their services are the top of the Line, but if you tell them *I* sent you, that'll get you the best rates," he said, winking at him.

"Oh," said Finn, a little disconcerted about the wink. "I'm all for saving money." He looked down at the card. "And where is this... Mollie Walters place?"

"Three blocks south," the clerk pointed with his thumb, "And four blocks west. You can't miss it—it takes up half the block."

"They must do a booming business."

The clerk chuckled and handed him his package. "That's one way of putting it. Take the trolley so you won't be so tired by the time you get there."

Finn nodded, hoping the man wouldn't wink at him again. "I appreciate your help, Long Rifle."

He walked outside and headed south. After three blocks, he turned west and took note of the name on the hanging street sign. As he walked down the street looking at the buildings, he vaguely wondered which one was the post office.

Chapter 22

Finn stopped and looked around the intersection of 26th and Postoffice Street. He saw no signs on any of the buildings—most of which looked like residences or boarding houses, but based on what the clerk said, Mollie Walters was one of the biggest ones.

A movement above caught his eye, and he saw a woman looking at him from the second story window. He tipped his hat and made his way around to the back alley to find a tall, wiry black woman hanging sheets and towels on multiple rows of clotheslines strung across the back of the building.

He knew he had found the right place.

He took off his hat as he approached her. "Hello, ma'am," he said. "Are you Miss Walters?"

The woman grinned widely, showing a big gap between her two front teeth. "I been called a lot of things, but I never been mistaken for Miss Walters. I'm Delilah, but Miss Walter's out. Go on in, though, somebody will be around."

She put a couple of clothespins in her mouth and grabbed several towels.

"Could I ask you a question?"

"Shore!"

"How much do you, I mean, Miss Walters charge for both me and my clothes?"

"Well, since you come to the back, it won't be more than fifteen. You don't mind an older woman, do you?"

"Not if she does a good job."

"Oh, they do a good job all right, maybe even better than the younger ones."

"Experience should count for something," said Finn, thinking fifteen cents was very reasonable for a bath and his clothes laundered, but then he remembered what the clerk said. "And if La Longue Carabine sent me, how much would it be then?"

Delilah laughed. "So you seen the little pistol, huh. Miz Mollie will take five off the top for his referral."

Ten cents! Finn decided he just might tip them the extra nickel.

"Go on in the house. They'll take good care of you."

"Thank you, ma'am."

Finn walked up the steps onto the porch, opened the door and stepped inside. "Hello?" he said into the shadowed hall. "I'm here for a bath?"

His eyes adjusted, and he saw bare feet coming down a staircase on the right side of the hall. Then bare legs appeared in front of a swath of sheer material trailing behind them. He cleared his throat uncomfortably when an ample cleavage came into sight followed by the face of the woman he saw in the window upstairs a few minutes earlier.

She was smiling at him like he was her next meal.

What kind of laundry business is this? He thought to himself, and then it dawned on him where he was. He stepped back.

"I think there's been a misunderstanding."

The woman raised her eyebrows. "You don't like what you see?"

He noticed her eyes then—a pale blue, no, gray. He figured she was in her forties—maybe even old enough to be his mother. Aged, but still beautiful.

He almost stumbled as he backed away from her. "No, no, it's not that. I just thought I could get a bath here—I've been traveling for days, and my clothes need washing—"

"I can bathe you." She walked up to him. "And Delilah could wash your clothes."

Finn caught a whiff of her perfume and grabbed for the door behind him. "No, thank you, ma'am. I can bathe myself. I didn't realize this was a.. a…"

"Female boarding house?"

Finn knew she was toying with him. "You must be Miss Walters."

She laughed—even her laughter was inviting. "No, Mollie's out for the moment. But I'm sure I could help you."

"No, thank you. I don't need your services. Do you know where I can get a bath and get my clothes washed? I've come to Galveston to fetch someone, and I don't want her to see me like this."

"You must be fetching your sweetheart." The woman's face softened. She sighed as she closed the front of her robe and tied it in place. "Come on, darlin'." She walked over to a door and opened it.

"I can't."

She shook her head. "There's a tub in here—you can use it. Leave your clothes outside the door and I'll get Delilah to wash them for you."

When Finn hesitated, she added, "I promise no one will bother you."

"I… I don't know. How much do you charge?"

"It's on the house."

Finn shook his head. "You have to eat, too. What would Miss Walters charge?"

The woman smiled ruefully. "Her lowest price is ten dollars… whether you use the services or not."

He almost choked on that. "I can't pay that."

"Do you know how to handle a hammer and a saw?" She stepped into the room.

"I do." He followed her into the room.

"It'll take a little while for your clothes to dry." She flipped a rug over to reveal some rotted boards. "Some of our guests tend to get a little careless with the water. If I bring you the tools and some boards, could you replace these damaged ones?"

"I could."

She held out her hand. "Then we have an agreement."

Finn grasped her soft hand. "I appreciate it, ma'am."

She walked over and turned on the single faucet over the tub. "Towels are in the cupboard. Soap and razor are on the shelf below the mirror if you want to shave. Someone will bring hot water in a few minutes."

"What's your name?" Finn asked as she walked away from him.

She stopped without turning around. "Other than Mollie, nobody uses their real names around here, but you can call me Pearl."

"Thank you, Pearl."

She turned and looked wistfully back at him.

"What?" he felt compelled to ask.

"You remind me of what I missed out on years ago." She smiled sadly. "Wish somebody had come for me."

She turned and closed the door behind her.

Finn looked around the room and felt a heaviness as the thought of what went on under this roof settled on his shoulders.

He tried to push the thought out of his head. "Lord, help 'em," he said quietly to himself.

He walked over to the table and poured some water in a bowl, and took off his shirt and dropped it on the floor. He picked up a straight razor and tested the edge—it was plenty sharp, so he splashed water on his face and reached for a shaving mug on a shelf. He removed the brush and wet it, then swirled it vigorously on a well-worn piece of soap in the bottom of the mug working up a good lather.

He just started to slather his face when another woman—younger and blonde and just as scantily dressed as Pearl came in with hot water. She walked over and poured a little in the bowl.

"Would you like for me to shave you?" she asked.

"No!" he replied quickly. "Thank you."

She emptied the rest of the hot water in the tub.

In the mirror Finn saw her watching him while he began to shave. He nicked himself twice before he gave up and set the razor down.

"Sure you don't need my help?" the woman smiled a little too smugly.

"Nah, I think I'll just let it grow."

"Looks good on you," she said as she sauntered out of the room.

He washed off the lather and used a towel to wipe his whiskers dry, thinking he might as well leave it be until he got back to Waco.

Delilah and another woman walked in with a stack of boards and a box of tools and nails. Delilah left immediately, but the other woman started slowly unpacking the tools, casting glances his way.

"That's fine," he said, feeling like he was on display for the whole house. "I'll do that."

After she left, he walked over by the door and undressed. He gathered his clothes and opened the door to find two more women loitering in the hall. He quickly dropped the bundle and shut the door to the sound of giggling. He looked for a lock, and when he didn't find one, he propped a chair under the knob so he could take his bath in peace.

Even then he wasted little time washing the remnants of days of travel from his body so he could get to working on the floor. He wanted no more interruptions either, especially since he had nothing to wear until his clothes were laundered and dried. He planned to save his new shirt for seeing Grace later.

The floor took the better part of an hour to cut out the rotten boards, then to measure and cut the replacement boards. He liked to work with his hands and especially when it came to handling tools and the power they held.

After he replaced the boards, he gathered up the tools and remaining scraps, wiped the sawdust into a pile, and then replaced the rug over the now paler patch in the floor. He noticed the settee, then, and grabbed several towels to spread over it before he sat down and leaned his head against the back of it. Maybe he had time to shut his eyes for a few moments before he set out to find Grace.

He was tired… so tired.

Chapter 23

The room was almost dark when Finn opened his eyes. He looked around trying to figure out where he was and noticed he was stretched out on a couch naked as the day he was born. He could hear music coming from somewhere nearby, along with voices and occasional laughter.

He sat up with a start and saw his clothes folded neatly on a table nearby. He thought it must be just after sunset, but then he realized the light came from a low-burning lamp on the table. He saw the bathtub and remembered where he was and then glanced at the door to see the chair had been moved away from it.

Grace! He needed to see Grace.

He walked over to the table and picked up his pants when someone knocked quietly on the door.

"Just a minute," he said, trying to step in the pants leg.

The door opened and Pearl walked in and shut the door behind her.

"Wait!" He stumbled around to put the table between them.

She sighed impatiently and turned away from him. "You don't have a thing I haven't seen before."

He couldn't help but notice she'd changed into a red gown. She looked good in red.

"Well, I don't make it a habit to be seen by women I don't know." He ripped at the paper wrapped around his new white shirt.

"Too late for that, sweetheart." She turned around and saw him struggling to get his new shirt unbuttoned.

"Let me help with that." She started towards him, reaching for the shirt.

"I can do it." He shook his head and pulled away from her. "How did you get in here anyway?"

"Lacy got the ladder and crawled through the window. And then Carmen gathered up the tools, and Victoria drained and wiped down the tub, and Delilah brought your clothes in."

"Gosh, does anyone else in the house want to see the sideshow?" He held his arms away from him to expose his chest. "Don't they get to see enough skin around here?"

Pearl was quiet for a moment. "It's not the fact that you were naked that grabbed their attention. They're fascinated with the idea that an ethical man walked through the door—a man who's not interested in using them to satisfy their lust. They never see that in this place."

"What?"

"You have scruples. You treat us with respect without expecting something in return. And it looks like you're not afraid of hard work. Those are very attractive qualities in a man."

Finn didn't know what to say to that.

"You're blushing again," said Pearl. "That's very appealing, too."

"I'm no saint," he mumbled. "What time is it?"

"After nine."

"Nine o'clock? Why didn't anyone wake me?"

"You didn't ask to be wakened. We all had a nice nap. Did you want to see your girl tonight?"

"Yes." He put one arm through the sleeve.

"It's a little late for that; she probably goes to sleep with the chickens. Why don't you wait until morning?"

"I may not see her all day…"

"How do you know that?"

"Lucius told me she met a bunch of people here and her days are busy with… social stuff, I guess."

The smile left Pearl's face. "Lucius who?"

"Roderick."

"You know Lucius Roderick?"

"Unfortunately. Do you?"

"We go way back."

Finn frowned. "He's a customer here?"

"I didn't say that."

"Oh, yeah. You have to be discreet in your business."

"Lucius is a good man…"

Finn snorted.

"He's very ambitious, and he knows what he wants in life. What's wrong with that?"

"And he wants Grace."

"Your girl?"

Finn nodded.

"How does she feel about him?"

"I don't know, but she's staying at his house."

Pearl raised her eyebrows.

"His sister is one of Grace's best friends, but he's staying downtown." He finished buttoning the shirt and turned around so he could tuck it in. "I think I'll go ahead and head over to the house."

"You know where he lives?"

Finn nodded.

"I hope you realize you have some stiff competition with Lucius. He's one of the most sought after men on the island."

Finn frowned at her. "Thank you, Pearl. That makes me feel so much better. Lucius told me I should just turn around and go home, too."

"Does she love you?"

"As of last week, she did."

"And what happened to change that?"

"She proposed to me in a very public place…"

"*She* asked you to marry her?"

"I guess she got tired of waiting for me to do that…"

"How long have you two been together?"

"Off and on for years—Grace was always around, and I guess I thought she'd always be around." He grabbed his boots and socks and sat down on the couch to put them on.

"So you took her for granted."

"I told you I wasn't a saint."

"Well, what was the last straw that made her come to Galveston?"

The image or Grace waving at him from across the train station flashed through his mind. The knife went through his heart again when he thought of how he'd humiliated her.

"When I saw her at the train station, Sissy—that's Lucius' sister—was there to watch the meeting. She congratulated me on our engagement, and when I asked her to explain, she said that my showing up there meant I'd agreed to marry Grace. I just turned tail and ran out of there."

"Ouch."

"It felt like an ambush," he explained. "I'd just gotten some bad news about losing all my investments in a business, and I couldn't handle the thought of marriage. Grace had sent me a letter explaining the situation, but I never saw it. I was just told I was supposed to meet her at the train station at a certain time, but I didn't know why. I don't think she really intended to move to Galveston, but pride kept her from staying after what I did to her."

"You want to be able to take care of her."

Finn realized she understood. "Yeah."

"Then what's changed? You obviously didn't get a windfall since you last saw her. You have little more than the clothes on your back."

Finn looked away. "Nothing's changed, other than I know now that I can't live without her. But I'm afraid I may have already lost her."

"Then fight for her." She picked up his hat and handed it to him. "You've got some making up to do."

"I know. " Finn grabbed his folded shirt and stood up.

"Do you plan to stay with her tonight?"

"We're not married."

"That doesn't stop most of the people I know."

"We follow different rules."

"The girls are going to love that about you, too," she grinned.

"Then please don't tell the girls."

"So where do you plan to stay the night?"

"I don't know yet." He started towards the door. "Thanks for letting me clean up. Did Miss Walters ever get back?"

"Yes. She came in and inspected the floor while you were sleeping. She said you did good work."

Finn looked at the ceiling and sighed in frustration. "Don't you know the meaning of propriety, woman? My sense of it is still intact."

"We have some front steps that need fixin,' too," she said, ignoring his comment. "Mollie said you could stay here if you could do some more work for her."

"Could I have some actual privacy, or will you allow everyone parade through my room again?"

Pearl smiled apologetically. "Sorry… uh… what name would you like for me to call you?"

"Finn Samuel, and that's my real name."

"All right, Finn. We'll put you in a room that actually has a lock on the door."

"Tell me exactly where it is so I don't walk in on something I don't want to see."

They stepped out in the hall. Delilah sat knitting in an over-stuffed chair at the foot of the stairs. Finn nodded at her.

"Hello, sir," she said, smiling widely.

Finn looked away uncomfortably.

"It's the second door over there. I'll put your other shirt in it for you," she said, taking it out of his hands. "Delilah stays in the first one." She turned to Delilah. "You make sure nobody bothers him or they'll have to answer to me, understand?"

"Yes, ma'am." Her wide smile faded.

Pearl turned back to Finn. "It's Mollie's guest room, so it hasn't been used for business purposes if you're worried about that."

"I just want a clean bed and a roof over my head."

"The door will be unlocked. Just come on in and go to bed."

He nodded, cringing inwardly at the thought of Grace's reaction if she found out he was staying in a bordello. But at the same time, he was grateful that he had a place to stay for the night that wouldn't cost him anything but a little time and sweat. He paused on the back porch.

"Thanks, Pearl," he said looking back over his shoulder.

"Anytime, cowboy," she said.

He turned and almost ran into a soldier coming up the steps.

"Pardon me," he said, stepping around him.

The young man grabbed his arm to stop him.

"Hey, was she good?" He nodded toward Pearl still standing in the doorway.

Finn's fist knocked him clean off the tall steps.

Without losing stride or a backward glance, he stepped into the dark night.

Chapter 24

Finn guessed it was close to ten o'clock by the time he found Lucius Roderick's house. He would've made it sooner if he hadn't lost count of the streets, not all of which had street signs. The moon was almost full, though, and along with occasional gaslights on some streets, he was able to find his way.

When he finally reached the corner of 17th and L Streets, he wasn't sure which of the four houses at that intersection belonged to Roderick. He stood in the middle of the street and looked around at each one. He quickly ruled out the house on the southeast corner when he heard a dog barking. Lucius wasn't the pet-owning kind. He walked closer to the house on the southwest corner and could see that it was too modest and homey-looking for Lucius, so he eliminated that one. He walked between the two remaining houses which looked similar, but then he noticed a child's swing in the tree at the northwest house, so he approached the house on the northeast corner of the intersection, feeling quite confident in his skill of deduction.

A light burned in the upstairs room on the left. He could hear two voices—women's voices. He walked around to the front of the house and listened. A lump appeared in his throat when he recognized Grace's laughter. How he'd missed that sound.

She sounded happy.

He saw someone pass in front of the open window. It wasn't

Grace, though; the hair was darker.

Finn pushed the gate open to get closer and cringed when it squeaked loudly. The voices hushed upstairs, and almost immediately he saw a movement in the window again. The dog from across the street started barking again, but this time a light came on behind him. He turned to see a very tall man at the door, shielding his eyes from a light on the porch. Finn was shocked to see that he held a shotgun in his right hand. When the man dropped his left hand to lift the gun barrel leveling it towards him, Finn knew he'd been spotted. He stepped back from the gate.

"Hey!" the man yelled, heading down the steps of his house. "I shoot first and then ask questions later. Get away from that house!"

Finn thought he sounded very convincing, so he did the first thing that came to mind.

He ran.

He wasn't sure if it was the second or third block that he finally slowed down to catch his breath. *What kind of place is this?* he thought to himself. Up until this point, everyone had been so courteous and helpful here… except for Lucius.

Lucius! That had to be it. He must've hired the neighbor to watch the house for him—to keep him away from Grace. He growled loudly in frustration, which started the dogs in the neighborhood to barking, too. He turned and walked north until he found a street sign to get his bearings.

He had no idea of the time when he came back to the alley behind Miss Walter's house, only that it was late. Most of the city was asleep on the streets he'd walked, but Postoffice Street was wide awake. The eighteen-or-so-block walk had allowed him time to do plenty of thinking that night. On the way to see Grace, he'd gone over and over in his mind how he would apologize to her. He imagined her forgiving him and throwing herself in his arms. His heart raced when he thought about kissing those innocent lips and marrying her as soon as possible so he could explore every part of that beautiful body. She could've been his years ago, but he wasn't willing to surrender his own heart.

What was wrong with him? Where had his head been all these

years? In his work? Tied up with Caitlin's memory? Running from the fear of commitment?

Grace was his, and he didn't know how much he wanted her until she was gone. He didn't realize how much he loved her until he lost her.

Lord, is it too late for us? He prayed fearfully. *Please don't let me mess this up, too. I won't take her for granted anymore.*

On the way back, common sense reared its level head and told him he'd better slow down and focus on earning some money before he approached her. It only took a few years of teaching to realize *that* vocation wouldn't build up his bank account, and that he didn't have the patience for it. He loved researching and experimenting with new methods of raising livestock or farming. He loved working with his hands and improving equipment. There was a lot of manufacturing and commerce here. Maybe Galveston was the place he could make his mark in the world.

But at the moment, he couldn't even afford to buy Grace a good meal in one of these nice restaurants in town, much less marry her and take her where? He laughed ruefully at the thought of having to spend their honeymoon night in a brothel. He could survive with little on his own—he'd done that for years. But taking care of Grace, too? And now she'd been introduced to an exciting, more extravagant lifestyle than she'd ever experienced with Finn. Could he ever fit in with this lifestyle? Much less compete with it?

His thoughts drifted to Dalton, Grace's hometown. Finn had asked Justin Taylor for his daughter's hand, and Mr. Taylor offered him a job to come work for him in Dalton. He told Finn that's how he and his wife Allie had started out—working for his uncle on the ranch that he would inherit one day. Justin told Finn that the ranch would be Grace's after they were gone.

That was one tempting solution, but his pride told him he couldn't go into their marriage empty-handed. That is, if Grace wanted anything to do with him now.

Finn waited in the shadows of some oleanders in the alley until a group of sailors passed, and started to step out when he saw Pearl come out onto the porch with a man. She put something in his hand

and kissed him on the cheek. He was surprised to see little evidence of passion between them. It looked like a friend kissing a friend.

When the man turned, Finn was shocked to recognize Lucius. His temper flared again and he almost stepped out to confront him, but something told him to keep quiet. He slipped further back into the hedge until Lucius passed by. When he was out of sight, Finn crossed the alley and entered the house.

Delilah's chair was empty; he could hear her talking upstairs. It sounded like somebody had stayed past his time and she was demanding payment for it. He walked up to the foot of the stairs, hoping to catch Pearl before she went back to her room, but the stairwell was empty. He noticed the basket beside the chair contained towels, not yarn.

He walked over to the guest room and stepped inside, letting his eyes adjust to the darkness. The moon cast enough light through the window for him to see a table and lantern to the left, so he walked over and lit it. A double bed sat longwise against the window. A chamber pot sat beside a commode with a pitcher and washbowl atop it. A few flowery prints decorated the walls, and he noticed a light switch beside the door. He walked over and turned it on, but just as quickly turned it off for fear of being seen through the window. He blew out the lamp, preferring to undress in the dark.

He sat down and took off his boots and socks, followed by his shirt, which he draped over the back of a chair. He laid his pants on the seat and turned back the bedding. He stretched out on top of it to try to cool off. The breeze felt like it had a texture to it. He could even taste salt on his lips after several hours on the streets.

He stared at the ceiling above, grateful for somebody's piano playing masking any sound of visitors upstairs. But he found it hard to keep his mind from wandering up those stairs, wondering what was going on. He shook his head to try to clear it, but the thoughts kept creeping in around the edges, eating away at his resolve.

The September heat wasn't the only thing causing him discomfort that night. He decided he needed to find another place to stay… and soon.

Finn woke up early, rummaging around for the bag of tools to start working on the porch. When he couldn't find them, he knocked on Delilah's door. When she didn't answer, he knocked again and almost jumped back when she threw the door open.

"What in Hades do you want?" she said irritably, squinting at him. "Don't you know it's the middle of the night?"

Her hair looked like she'd been wrestling with the devil and lost.

Finn was confused. "The sun's already up, Delilah, and I need to start on that porch. Could you tell me where the tool box is?"

"My day don't start 'til after lunch around here—I'll get you your tools at that time, honey buns, and not before. And unless you wanna see the dog ugly side of Miz Walters, you'd best not be hammerin' on anything around here 'til she says so."

She slammed the door in his face.

Finn stood there for a moment staring at the door, completely at a loss how to react to that. Then he turned around and headed outside. He decided he wasn't going to waste any time sitting around waiting for them to get out of bed. Surely he could find some paying work for a few hours.

He came back around two o'clock with five dollars and two bits in his pocket. He earned three dollars after rigging a block and tackle to unload two wagons of granite slabs for the son of an undertaker. His father had paid the boy six dollars to do it, thinking he'd have to hire at least three or four workers to carry the heavy stones. The boy was so pleased with Finn's help that he split the money fifty-fifty and headed to the beach early.

The remaining $2.25 was earned cleaning, waxing, and polishing three streetcars—six bits per trolley. He could've earned seventy-five cents more on another streetcar, but he had to get back and work on the porch so he'd have a place to sleep tonight.

Finn's arms and shoulders ached from the trolley work. He tried to think of a way to make it faster and easier, but nothing came to mind other than good old manual labor.

He picked up the tools from the back of the house and walked around to the front porch. The new boards were stored underneath. Everywhere he'd worked today, he'd taken off his shirt to keep from soiling it, but he was hesitant to do so here. He used a crowbar to pry up the old steps and was pulling off the sixth one when a well-dressed, older woman stepped out on the porch.

Finn wiped the sweat from his eyes and looked up at her.

"So you're the reason my girls are all in a tizzy."

"You must be Miss Walters."

"In the flesh. I'm sorry I missed meeting you last night, but I liked what I saw of your work."

"Thank you, ma'am."

"And you were sleeping quite soundly. Will you have this finished soon? Fridays are one of our busiest nights."

"It'll probably take about four hours."

"If you get it done in three, I'll give you two dollars for your effort."

"Make it five, and I'll get it done in two and a half, Miss Mathilde."

Mollie Walters laughed. "You're good, Mr. Samuel. And I see you've learned my given name."

"You've gained quite a reputation around town."

"Glad to hear it."

Finn hadn't meant it as a compliment, but he kept quiet.

"So you've just wrangled five dollars and overnight lodging out of me for replacin' these porch steps. Wouldn't you rather spend ten minutes with one of my girls, and we call it even?"

Finn shook his head. "I need the money."

"That's a very generous amount for a common day laborer."

"Now I'd say that's a matter of opinion; I'm not common, ma'am, and we both know you can afford it."

"Then don't let me slow you down," she said, still smiling.

Finn was relieved she agreed to his offer.

Mollie turned and spoke to the blonde loitering by the door. "Go get Mr. Samuel a glass of water, Lacy, and bring him an undershirt to work in this heat."

Finn finished replacing the porch steps with ten minutes to spare, but his aching muscles paid dearly for it. Along with the two previous jobs that day, he hadn't seen that much physical labor since his college days working with Grace's uncle, Jimmy.

He gathered up the tools and scraps and trudged around to the back, grateful that the *customers* hadn't started arriving yet. He couldn't guarantee that he wouldn't run them off. Pearl must've failed to mention to Mollie his response to the young man last night. But Finn felt no remorse for his actions.

Delilah was outside gathering towels and sheets.

"Do you know what time the dance is tonight?"

"What dance you talkin' 'bout? This is a big town."

Finn thought for a moment. "A garden place, I think."

"That German place? Garten Verein?"

"Yeah, I think that's it."

"Well, I hear the kids get to start dancing at seven, and then the grown-ups take to the floor at 8:30. You dance?"

Finn snorted. "Not very well, and I'm not even sure I can get up these steps right now much less walk across town to a dance."

Delilah chuckled. "Looks like you put in some honest work today. Just set those tools by my door and I'll put 'em up."

"Thanks, Dee."

"Goodness, gracious, you must be tired if you can't even say my whole name!"

He nodded, plodding slowly up the steps. Inside he set the tool box beside her door and removed his hat so he could peel off the wet undershirt and drop it on the floor.

He entered his room and stepped out of his damp pants and hung them over a chair to dry. He dampened a towel and washed off before he stretched out on the bed, taking pleasure in the breeze on his damp skin. He couldn't remember when a bed felt so good in spite of his aching muscles. He smiled as he thought about the money he made today—really good money. Things were looking up.

Thank you, Lord.

He heard the tools rattle in the box outside.

"Delilah?!" he called out.

"Yeah, hon?"

"You going to be sitting in your chair tonight?"

"Yes, sir."

"If I'm not out of my room by eight o'clock, could you knock on my door?"

"You got a liaison?"

"Sort of."

"Then I'll wake you up, if need be."

"I appreciate it."

"Anything for you, sugar."

Unless it involves knocking on your door before noon, Finn smiled as he thought to himself. That was one scary woman before noon.

Chapter 25

Grace stood before the full length mirror in Lucius' bedroom, feeling an odd sense of familiarity with the scene. She was wearing a dress Lucius had sent as a gift for the dance tonight. Daisy stood behind her looking over her shoulder.

"It's absolutely gorgeous!" she said. "How did he know it would fit you?"

"I have no idea," she said, turning to the right and then to the left. "I don't ever remember wearing a red dress before—blue was always my color because of my eyes."

"The red makes your eyes look even bluer."

"Really? But do you think red is appropriate for the dance?"

"You'll definitely get everyone's attention."

Grace frowned. "That's what I'm afraid Lucius is wanting, but I'd much rather fade into the background."

"That doesn't seem to be Lucius' style."

"I'm afraid I'm becoming much too beholden to him. He's let me inconvenience him by staying here. He's treated me to some really nice restaurants; that's definitely a luxury for me."

"It's not like you've been taking advantage of him forever. You've barely arrived."

"Seems like it's been ages. So much has happened this past week." She turned to Daisy. "I really appreciate you staying the past two nights with me. I'm fine when the sun is shining, but after learning what happened to that woman, I seem to have lost my nerve when it gets dark."

"I'm flattered that you felt comfortable enough to ask me. Thank heavens for Mr. Robertson last night. I wonder who that was loitering at the front gate?"

"Probably an innocent passerby. At least we know it wasn't that horrible man at the brothel," said Grace. "They said his ship left Wednesday."

"He should be in jail for what he did." She looked at the clock on the dresser. "We have plenty of time before the dance to go to the beach. You feel up to it?"

"The walk, yes. A swim, no."

Daisy helped Grace out of the red dress and laid it carefully on the bed.

They left the house, but it wasn't until they stepped away from it and crossed the street that they noticed a brisk breeze was coming from behind them.

"That's odd," said Daisy, looking behind her as they continued to walk. "The wind almost always keeps my hair out of my face while I walk to the beach."

"Maybe a norther's coming in." Grace held her hair back from her face. "I would welcome some relief from this heat—especially for the dance tonight. I'd rather not perspire all over that beautiful dress."

"I'm sure they'll have all the windows opened at the Garten Verein to pull in a breeze. You'll have a great time."

"I can't believe your fiancé isn't jealous about you going to the dances."

"If you met Joe, you'd know why he doesn't have a thing to worry about. I'm the luckiest girl in the world."

"How'd you meet?"

"Very clumsily on my part. We were at a sailing party, and I fell into his arms stepping into a boat. He seemed to feel obligated to take on the role of my protector from then on."

"I'm sure obligation had little to do with it—you're beautiful, Daisy," said Grace, smiling at her. "But did you fall into his arms on purpose?"

Daisy snickered. "I didn't have the sense at that time to think up something as brilliant as that. But I am convinced God brought us together."

"I always thought God was steering me towards Finn, but maybe it was because I had hold of the rudder and wanted him so badly. How did you know Joe was the one?"

Daisy looked toward the ocean, smiling as she thought. "I felt safe with him—not only physically, but my heart was safe with him, too. He was so easy to talk to—I could tell him anything." She looked at Grace. "He's much more educated and well read than I, but he's never made me feel beneath him in any way. He sends me books—even romantic ones."

"And you two have been together how long?"

"Four years now."

"And you're willing to wait until next summer to get married?"

"Actually I've been ready to marry him since the first year, but Joe was in medical school, and he wanted to get his practice going before we settled down. I keep telling myself we'll have a lifetime together."

Grace looked ahead, unseeing. "I've loved Finn for ten years; but seriously for the past five."

"I'm sorry it didn't work out for you."

"I've been fighting the feeling that I'm behind now—that I should've already married and started my family. But now that I've met you, I realize I need to step back and not rush into anything with Lucius or anyone else for that matter. We don't even know each other well, and he's already hinting around like we have a future together."

"He's about as charming as they come. I don't know him well enough to discern his sincerity towards you."

"When Lucius lived in Waco some years back, he had a reputation of getting any girl he courted to believe they were getting married. No telling what they gave up before they realized he wasn't as serious about them as they thought."

"Oh, really? Then you do need to keep reminding yourself of that, friend." Daisy put a reassuring arm around Grace. "You're not ready to be in a courtship with anybody right now, and Lucius seems to be pushing you pretty hard. Don't let him take advantage of you."

Grace nodded. "I'm already the jilted woman. I just don't want to be a desperate one. Please don't let me do anything stupid, Daisy."

"Do you want me to stay with you tonight, too?"

"No, I'll be fine. I've kept you away from your mother long enough," said Grace, but her face said otherwise.

Daisy chuckled. "She's seen me every day and hasn't missed me a bit. I'll stay with you again tonight, and then I'll help you get moved in tomorrow afternoon."

Grace felt relieved.

"Whoa." Daisy said, staring ahead. "I think things are a little too rough to wade in the water this evening."

Grace followed her eyes. She watched a big wave break against the piers of one of the bathhouses, sending spray high into the air. She didn't like that one bit.

"The swells are even bigger than usual," said Daisy. "Hey, there's Walter." She yelled at him over the roar as he walked ahead of them.

He turned around and waved, and then trotted back towards them.

"Hey, ladies!" He tipped his hat, and then pushed it firmly down on his forehead to keep it from blowing off his head. "Hello, Miss Taylor. Hope you've been enjoying our fair island so far."

"I have, thanks in part to you putting me in touch with Daisy. She's been a huge help."

"I told you so," he said, looking very pleased with himself. "I don't think you're going to get your swim today, Daisy."

"Looks rough."

"I'll bet there's a mean riptide under all that, too," he said, turning to Grace. "Didn't you tell me when we first met that you thought the ocean looked angry?"

Grace nodded, looking wide-eyed at the turbulent water.

"Well, this isn't her angriest face, but something sure has her dander up. The wind's out of the north, and that usually means you can walk halfway to Cuba, but the tide's still rising in spite of it. I don't recall seeing that before." He looked towards the gulf. "Heard talk downtown that a storm's coming."

Grace looked up. The sky was overcast, but the lumpy clouds didn't look threatening. "It must be a norther—the wind's coming from the north," she said again.

"Hope it doesn't spoil the dance tonight," said Daisy. "You going, Walter?"

"I don't know. I have to work tomorrow."

"Most everybody has to work tomorrow. You don't have to stay late. At least come for a little while—I need somebody to dance with."

Walter looked at Grace. "That's all I'm good for—keeping Daisy entertained in lieu of her fiancé."

Grace laughed.

Daisy punched his arm. "No, you're a good dancer, Walter. I wouldn't pester you if you weren't."

"Well, how can I refuse that?"

A particularly large wave sent spray their way. The girls jumped back.

"We'd better get back and start getting ready," said Daisy, grabbing Grace's arm. "We'll see you later, Walter."

Grace paced back and forth across the parlor. The red dress rustled dramatically with every turn.

"Why don't you sit down—you're going to be worn out before we even get to the dance," said Daisy, sitting on the one-armed settee as she glanced out the window every so often.

"I don't want to wrinkle this dress before Lucius sees it." She glanced at the clock on the mantle. Eight-fifteen. "It seems so late—hasn't the dance already started?"

"For the children. The adults aren't allowed on the dance floor until eight-thirty."

"But he left for the dance at seven last Friday."

"You'd be surprised at how much business takes place among the men before the dance. And the women get to visit."

"Everything seems to have a financial purpose to Lucius—even the entertainment." Grace stopped and faced her. "Can you see the bruise?"

Daisy turned and squinted her eyes in the soft light of the lamp. "Nope. That stuff Marguerite gave you hid it well. You said she'd be there, right?"

Grace nodded as she started pacing again.

"I can't believe you're already acquainted with her and the Greshams."

"I haven't met the Greshams yet. I'll be visiting them on Tuesday—their home day. Marguerite said Beulah might make an appearance tonight, though, if she's able to get away from her euchre game."

"You sound like you'd be comfortable around them."

"If they're anything like Marguerite, I would. She's a treasure. I'm so thankful we met on the train coming down here."

"But the Gresham house is so… so… grand—like something royalty would live in."

"You should see the rooms the family lives in… I mean really lives in—the higher you go in that house, the more normal they become. Mr. and Mrs. Gresham's bedrooms—"

"They have separate bedrooms?"

Grace nodded. "They were extravagant, and the girls' bedrooms were very nice, but the third floor rooms were very ordinary… and comfortable-looking."

"I could never sleep in a separate bedroom from Joe."

"Maybe Mr. Gresham snores like a freight train."

"Or maybe it's Mrs. Gresham!" said Daisy, throwing her head back laughing.

"Shame on you," said Grace, giggling. "But what if your Joe snores?"

"Then I'd plug my ears, and we'd still sleep together," she said, peeking through the curtains. "He's here! Are you sure Lucius won't mind me coming along?"

"At this moment, I really don't care if he does or not," Grace said with a lowered voice. "You're staying with me tonight, and I can't abandon you, right? And it was his idea anyway for someone to stay with me after…" she didn't finish the sentence, remembering what happened to that woman on Postoffice Street.

"I know," said Daisy, standing. "But put that out of your head now. We're going to enjoy the evening."

A knock at the door made Grace jump.

"Let me get it," said Daisy, hurrying to open it. "Step back a little so the light will hit you just right."

Grace sighed impatiently and stepped back. A stronger sense that this moment had happened before washed over her again.

Daisy opened the door, and Lucius stepped inside.

Grace remembered then.

She was back in Waco on the night of the Cotillion. She smiled at Lucius and couldn't help but look beyond him for Finn to walk through the door.

Chapter 26

Finn woke with a start when someone touched his arm. The room was dark; he was facing the window. The breeze felt good on his face. He'd fallen asleep again, but he hadn't slept long enough to make his head fuzzy. He knew exactly where he was this time.

"Thanks, Delilah," he said without turning around.

"You're welcome, sugar."

He smiled at Pearl's pitiful job at imitating Delilah's voice.

Then he reached for the sheet and was relieved to feel he was covered to his waist. He rolled over to see that Pearl had pulled up a chair beside the bed. He watched her light the lamp.

"Hey, Pearl," he said in a raspy voice. He rolled his neck and stretched his stiff arms.

"Hello, Finn. Delilah said you needed to wake up at eight so you could go to the dance. I hadn't seen you in a while, though."

"I've been working."

"That's what I hear." She smiled at him. "I haven't had the chance to thank you for defending my honor the other night. That's only happened one other time in my life. I forgot what that felt like."

"What?"

"When you knocked that sailor off the steps, but Mollie would throw a shoe if she knew."

"You didn't tell her?"

Pearl shook her head.

"Who else stood up for you?"

"Nobody you'd know, but it's nice to take the memory out every so often and run it through my mind. And I'll enjoy doing the same with what you did the other night."

She looked tired.

"You all right?" he asked.

She nodded. "I've made it a rule to be discreet about what goes on around here…but I think I need to tell you something."

"I've been wanting to talk to you, too, but you first."

"Something happened this week on Postoffice Street, and I put two and two together and figured out it had something to do with your girl."

Finn sat up. "Grace? On Postoffice Street? Is she all right?"

"She's fine, and she did something very brave, but it could've been bad for her. She—"

"What happened?" he couldn't help but interrupt.

"If you would just hush and let me finish—just remember she's fine."

Finn swallowed the fear and nodded.

"One of the girls over in the next block came screaming out of the house about the time a streetcar passed, and Grace happened to be on it. She made the streetcar driver stop so she could run over to help the girl—a very young girl who shouldn't have even been on the Line, but her mother was inside—"

"Her mother let her daughter prostitute herself?"

"Unfortunately, and I'm sure it wasn't her daughter's choice. Her mother had a habit—an addiction, I should clarify, that destroyed her sense of moral decency years ago. I guess you could say we've all lost that along the way. But there are worse vices on the street, and what Lilly did to her daughter was one of them. Everyone turned a blind eye when it came to Anise living in the house with her, but Lilly wasn't well physically or mentally and no one wanted to take responsibility for her or her daughter.

"On Tuesday of this week, one of Lilly's customers beat her up, and that's what Anise was screaming for help about. Grace followed her back into the house, and the man returned, accusing them of stealing his wallet. If the streetcar driver hadn't gone to Madam Russell's house for help, no telling what would've happened to Grace. Mollie used to have bouncers on the payroll when we had a full house of girls, but—"

Finn felt the blood drain from his face. "What happened to Grace?"

"The man roughed her up a bit, assuming she was one of the house girls, but Russell's enforcers arrived and took care of him."

He pulled the sheet around him and stood. "I need to see her."

"You didn't get to see her last night?"

"Some man across the street ran me off with a shotgun—probably someone Lucius hired to keep me away from her."

"That doesn't sound like Lucius."

"And that's what I wanted to talk to you about. I saw him here last night after I came back," he said crossly.

Pearl grabbed his arm. "Sit down. He's not a customer of mine, well, not anymore. We're just friends."

"So he was here to visit as a friend, and Mollie doesn't make him pay?"

Pearl looked uncomfortable. "He pays, but he prefers the younger girls now," she said. "Lucius has his good side, Finn. He's helped me for years with… legal matters."

"Legal matters? I saw you give him something. Are you paying him to protect this place?"

"No!"

"Then is it opium?"

Pearl's eyes widened. "No! I don't mess with that stuff, and he doesn't either." She paused, looking like she was trying to choose her words carefully. "I'm helping somebody out that I don't want them to know about me or what I'm doing for them."

Finn frowned at her. "That makes no sense. Why would you want to help someone anonymously? I would think it would be good business relations for the community to know that prostitutes are doing good deeds," he said sarcastically.

"Now that's just mean."

"Mean? It's the truth. Who are you hiding from?"

"Nobody."

"Then who are you trying to protect?"

Pearl looked away, anguish written across her face. "I don't want her to know that her mo—" she stopped.

Finn stared at her. "You have a child—a daughter?" he whispered.

Pearl began to cry. "See what happened to Anise? I could never let my child be exposed to this… horrible excuse for a life."

"Who is she?"

Pearl's expression turned defensive. "She doesn't know about me, and that's how I want it. She's grown up in a good home and has a good future ahead of her, and I'm grateful for that."

"How does Lucius fit in?"

"After her step-father died suddenly, I asked Lucius to help find her mother a job, which he did, and now he pays for her tuition with the money I give him."

"She's in college?"

Pearl nodded. "So it won't be hard for you to figure out who she is, but swear to me you won't share this with anyone."

Finn saw the fear in her eyes. "I won't tell anybody, Pearl."

She looked visibly relieved.

"Does anyone else know?"

"Mollie does, of course. She knows everything about me."

"Why don't you leave this place and establish a relationship with your daughter?"

Pearl laughed ruefully. "I didn't know when I got on this streetcar I could only go where it took me."

"Have you ever tried getting off?"

"How would I ever escape a whore's reputation?" She looked away. "For the first few years, I told myself I would save my money and walk away from this life, but then I didn't know where to go that my past wouldn't catch up with me. Mollie's talking about retiring in a few years, and I think she wants me to take over the business."

"Do you want to?"

"Mollie always told me that I've made my bed, and now I have to lie in it. She hit the nail on the head with that one. Besides, I don't know what else to do."

"Well, I'm thirty-one and starting over, but I'm not even entertaining the thought of doing something illegal or something that's going to hurt people."

That ruffled her feathers.

"Maybe you haven't been desperate enough and saw no other way out. How's what I'm doing hurting anyone? We're providing a service to the community."

"Last time I checked, adultery and fornication outside of marriage is a sin, not some charitable service to the community."

"Well, if women would take care of their husbands' needs, we wouldn't have a market for this business."

"Oh! So it's the wives' fault now. Don't you blame them for their husbands' unfaithfulness."

"You'd be surprised how many self-righteous, *church-going* men come through these doors."

"King David was a man after God's own heart, but his lust for Bathsheba caused him to commit adultery and murder, and caused the death of his infant son. God forgave him, but he had to live with the consequences of his actions for the rest of his unhappy life. Those *church-going* men are risking their families and futures, too, and they'll have to answer to their Maker someday, but in the meantime, Pearl, the fact that Christians sin still doesn't make it right either for you *or* them. You just called this business *a horrible excuse for a life* a moment ago. Why are you defending it now?"

"Don't you preach to me, Finn Samuel. You just live your own life, and I'll live mine." She stood up and stormed out of the room and then came back in again. "And if you come back tonight, cowboy, you pay like any other customer!"

Chapter 27

Lucius stared at Grace through the open door. He was right. The red dress looked stunning on her. She smiled at him, and he was lost in those striking blue eyes for a moment, but then he saw her looking beyond him… almost like she expected someone else to walk through the door.

Finn! Had he found her? Had she seen him somewhere in town? He wheeled around, almost expecting him to be standing there.

The porch was empty.

He looked back at Grace, whose face registered confusion.

"I thought you saw someone behind me."

She smiled and shook her head. "Seeing you walk in here reminded me of the first time I met you."

He walked over to her and reached for her hand, lifting it to his lips. "Your beauty swept me away that night, but I think you're even more beautiful tonight."

He leaned in to kiss her lips, but Grace turned her head away and looked over his shoulder and smiled, so he whirled around again. This time he saw that they weren't alone.

Her school teacher friend stood by the door.

"Miss Thorne!"

"Hello, Mr. Roderick."

"Please call me Lucius. I didn't realize you were standing there. I'm sorry!"

Grace explained. "Daisy's staying with me again tonight—I hope you don't mind that I invited her to come with us. She loves to dance."

"Not at all!" he said convincingly, he hoped. Damn.

"I feel like I'm intruding," said Daisy.

"You are not intruding," he lied again. "I appreciate you staying with Grace at night. I know I slept better knowing she wasn't alone."

"I'll be helping her move into her apartment tomorrow."

"You'll be getting your house back, Lucius."

"Oh, that's right. I'll be working tomorrow, but call me when you're ready to go, and I'll send a carriage for you."

"And thank you for this beautiful dress, but you shouldn't have gone to the expense."

"This moment was worth every dollar."

"I hope I'm not too dressed up."

"You're perfect," he said. "And be sure to bring your parasol—it may rain on us. A storm's coming."

They stepped out on the porch, and Lucius held out his arm to escort Grace down the steep steps, but she didn't notice because she was looking up. He followed her gaze and saw a full moon shining like a streetlight through a break in the clouds.

"And then, maybe not."

Grace took hold of his arm and lifted her skirt to descend down the steps, now easily visible in the moonlight.

Lucius spoke over his shoulder. "I'd be glad to help you down the steps, Miss Thorne, if you'd wait a second."

"I'm fine, Lucius—don't you worry about me. In fact, pretend I'm not even here."

He laughed. "And miss the opportunity to escort the two most beautiful women on the island into the Garten Verein? I'll be the envy of every man there."

He didn't miss Daisy elbowing Grace at that comment. He helped them into the carriage and sat down beside Grace.

"What is that delicious fragrance you're wearing?" he asked, leaning closer and inhaling.

"Soap," she said, giggling. "Lavender soap."

He wasn't sure, but he thought Daisy muffled a snort.

Maybe he ought to tone down the charm around these two. They weren't as predictable as the usual caliber of women with which he socialized on the island—beautiful and empty-headed, experts on social etiquette and fashion and insipid about the rest of the world. But oh, so easy to manipulate. The game was getting old, though. He wanted more from life—a beautiful, intelligent wife, children to carry on the legacy he was creating.

And he thought Grace might just be the one.

He was pleased with his encounter with Finn, casting doubt in his ability to take care of her. He would've made a good trial lawyer—the juries would be putty in his hands. He was sure Finn would come to the dance, and he was sure Finn wouldn't pass the dress code to enter. But there were plenty of windows all around the octagonal building. And he wouldn't miss seeing Grace in this red dress, especially if every other woman was wearing white. She would be the talk of Galveston after tonight, and if Finn had any shred of consideration for Grace, he'd walk away and let her live the life she deserves.

"Lucius?"

"I'm sorry. What did you say?"

"Shouldn't we be concerned about the storm that's coming? Or preparing for this possible flooding somehow?"

"Overflows, dear; flooding sounds so threatening. But if you've noticed, most of the structures on the island are built higher to accommodate the storm tides, and many of the streets have gutters to help drain the water afterwards."

"I grew up playing in the overflows," added Daisy. "Most of the kids on the island have."

"That ocean is so big—doesn't it make you feel small living next to it?"

"I guess I'm used to it."

"See there, Grace—there's nothing to worry about. It's not like we're living on Atlantis here… about to sink into the ocean."

"That's the second time I've heard the word Atlantis this week—was it a real place? Didn't the ocean literally swallow it?"

"Plato described it as if it were," said Daisy, "but then he also discussed Poseidon like he was real and that Atlantis was his home, so that settles it in my mind."

"So you're familiar with mythology."

"I like to introduce some of the stories to my students during the year. I prefer Greek mythology over Roman."

"How refreshing to converse with educated women." Lucius hoped he sounded sincere.

"That doesn't intimidate you?" asked Grace, squeezing his arm.

"Not in the least."

"Good. Well, I'm looking forward to this dance, and especially dancing with you, Lucius," said Grace. She leaned forward. "He's a good dancer, Daisy, or have you two danced together before?"

"I've seen Miss Thorne at the dances, but I haven't had the pleasure. Would you save a dance or two for me?"

"Of course, and please call me Daisy."

The carriage slowed to a stop, and Lucius spoke to Tom through a small window, instructing him to come back at 11:00 p.m.

"Early day tomorrow," he explained to the women.

"Eleven is fine with me. We have a busy day tomorrow, too."

"Don't you want to wait until Sunday to move when I could help?"

"I only have a trunk and a satchel. We can handle them just fine."

Lucius stepped out of the carriage and helped the ladies disembark. He watched Grace's face as she took in the surroundings, lit by gaslights throughout the park.

"It's magical!" she said. "And look at the pavilion—all lit up like a birthday cake! It's beautiful."

They could hear the band playing and could see through the windows the adults taking to the dance floor. Lucius grasped Grace's arm and started escorting her. Daisy walked on the other side of Grace.

"Did you know the Greeks started the birthday candle tradition?" said Daisy. "So much in literature alludes to mythology and even biblical references. Most of my students are well-versed in the Bible, but they haven't a clue about mythology. Shakespeare used a lot of allusion, too, and if students aren't well-read, they miss the point."

Lucius stepped up the pace, hoping to get Grace inside before Finn showed up.

"Are we boring you?" teased Grace.

"Not at all—I'm just anxious to start dancing."

"Me, too!" said Daisy, striding past them. "I'm going to find Walter."

Lucius nodded to the attendant at the door, and gracefully guided Grace right onto the dance floor. She was looking at the high raftered ceiling, and missed seeing all the heads turning towards them. Lucius nodded his head, acknowledging the faces he recognized. All eyes were on Grace, and he couldn't help but revel inwardly at the impression they were making. He knew they were by far the most handsome couple here, and the old cronies on the Strand would insist that their wives invite Grace into their homes and social activities. She was in, and that meant even more open doors and business contacts for him.

He looked at Grace, who seemed uncomfortable all of a sudden.

"What's the matter?"

"I feel like this is the Cotillion all over again," she said and then leaned in close to his ear. "Everybody's staring at us. Is there somebody's brother waiting in the wings to beat you up tonight?"

Lucius threw his head back and laughed as he whirled her around. "I've matured a bit since then, my beauty, and have learned to not make enemies if I can help it. Everyone's staring because you're ravishing."

"Everyone's staring because I'm the only one here not wearing a white dress. Did you know I'd be the only one in a bold color tonight? I don't like to call undue attention to myself, Lucius."

"You can't help it, Grace, so why don't you embrace it. I thought you were the type to set the fashion trends, not follow them."

Grace smiled begrudgingly. "I don't have time to think up fashion trends, much less have the courage to set them."

"But most of these women are obsequious minions, not leaders. Mark my word; you'll see a room full of red dresses at the next dance. You follow your heart, Grace. And in spite of the dangerous stunt you pulled the other day, I love that about you."

Grace's face lit up.

Lucius thought he must be making progress with her feelings toward him. Maybe a political career like Walter Gresham's was in his future. And his future never looked brighter. He glanced at the windows, wondering if Finn was out there watching… hoping he was.

He couldn't help but smile to himself.

The song ended, and they made their way to the tables that lined the dance floor.

"There's Daisy and Walter," said Grace, pointing across the room.

She started to walk that way when Lucius pulled her around to lead her in the opposite direction.

"First, I'd like to introduce you to some of my colleagues and customers," he said, looking around for familiar faces.

He managed to introduce her to at least eight men that his firm had worked with on the Strand or attempted to gain their business. Most of them enjoyed a dance with Grace, and for those who brought their wives, Lucius reciprocated.

Lucius felt like that simple gesture would guarantee continued or new business with these contacts. Grace's skills were proving to be more profitable than he realized. Her beauty was merely the tip of the iceberg, and he relished the thought of uncovering the rest of that asset.

As Lucius and Grace were catching their breath after a polka, he noticed a commotion at the door. He leaned over to Grace and said, "I think you'll be happy to see this."

He guided her around a particularly wide fellow and faced her towards the door. Grace clapped her hands together and laughed in delight.

The uproar was Marguerite St. John making an entrance in the midst of a sea of white… in an emerald green dress.

Chapter 28

Several hundred well-dressed people filled the Garten Verein dancing pavilion, but Finn saw only one through the window. He'd never seen Grace more beautiful, and he felt a tug of disappointment that she looked so happy. He realized he was hoping she was as miserable as he was, but Lucius was right. She looked like she *had* moved on. Finn had taken her for granted all these years. He assumed she'd always be by his side. His heart ached for her more deeply than he'd ever felt, and now that he was so close to her, this window pane might as well be a deep chasm separating them.

Earlier he tried to enter the dance through the pavilion's front doors but was told the Club had rules concerning dress. He wore his new white shirt, but that wasn't enough. He needed a coat and tie as well. He still had the suit Grace's Aunt Mercy had bought for him eight years ago, which he wore to church and funerals, but he left town so fast in his pursuit of Grace that he failed to pack anything. He simply thought he'd pick her up in Dalton and bring her back to Waco. But this situation wasn't simple at all. He realized that Grace had a lot more options now, and his competition was fierce.

He looked down at his clothes and reminded himself that Delilah told him as he walked out of his room that he looked 'devilishly handsome.' And he turned a few women's heads on the streetcar coming over here. But standing on a bench at the window of the dance pavilion, he felt more like a hobo on the outside looking in at a lifestyle in which he was no longer entitled to participate.

He studied Grace more closely, looking for signs of her ordeal on Postoffice Street earlier in the week, but she looked fine. Pearl's information was correct; Grace was fine.

They made a handsome couple, he thought irritably. Lucius moved smoothly on the dance floor. Finn danced, but barely. Grace succeeded in dragging him to a few dances each year, but mostly he avoided them. And now he watched her follow Lucius' lead effortlessly, moving as one across the floor.

Finn realized he would probably just embarrass her if he *had* made it inside. Why hadn't he attempted to improve in the things she was interested in? Was he that self-centered? He knew he couldn't blame his lack of commitment on Caitlyn either.

He tasted failure in his mouth. He'd had his chance with Grace, but he lost it. If he'd married her years ago, they would be working through this financial calamity together. But how could he approach her empty-handed now?

Her choice would be crystal clear—Lucius and a life of affluence and privilege versus Finn starting over with an uncertain future. And as much as he hated to admit it, Lucius couldn't be a complete cur if he'd been watching out for Pearl's daughter for years.

He leaned his forehead against the glass, fighting the urge to break through the doors and drag Grace out of there.

Think of her for once, you selfish mongrel, he thought to himself. He took a deep breath and looked at her one more time.

"Goodbye, Grace," he said quietly, groaning at the pain of what he was giving up.

He saw her turn toward the window. Finn quickly jerked his head back, but she stopped in the middle of the dance floor staring at the window. Several couples bumped into each other trying to avoid running over them. Lucius followed her gaze, but Finn didn't wait to see what happened next.

He jumped off the bench he was standing on and turned and ran towards the shadows of the trees in the park.

He didn't remember how he made it back to Mollie Walter's. He only remembered the gnawing sense of emptiness that suddenly defined his life. How could this be happening to him… again?

He stopped to catch his breath at the back porch steps before walking inside and grabbing a towel from Delilah's basket.

"What you doing?" She snapped at him as she grabbed it back. "This ain't the laundry pile, huckleberry."

He pulled out a ten dollar bill and dropped it in her lap.

"Send me the blonde," he told her. "Lacy, is it? I'll be waiting for her in my room."

Delilah was shocked into silence for a moment. Then she asked in a quiet voice, "Are you sure, honey?"

He nodded his head, refusing to look her in the eyes, but he could hear the disappointment in her voice. He pushed that out of his head, too, as he stepped into his room and shut the door, none too quietly.

He ripped off his new shirt, losing several buttons in the process, and then wrestled with the still-buttoned cuffs now turned inside out. When he finally freed his hands, he threw the shirt across the room and fell back on the bed, covering his eyes with his left arm like he was shielding them from the light.

But the room was dark.

After a few minutes, the door opened and in his peripheral vision he could see the silhouette of a woman against the light in the hall. She shut the door behind her and walked over to the bed.

He braced himself, not sure what was going to happen next.

"What do you think you're doing, boy?"

He let out a long breath, not realizing he'd been holding it. "I'm not a boy, Pearl."

"You're acting like one. I thought you were different."

"Well, this *boy* is expecting Lacy any minute, so you might ought to mosey on out of here."

"You don't want to do this, Finn."

"Yes, I do," he said. "Why are you trying to dampen my mood? You all have been after me to sample your services ever since I got here, so you ought to be happy I'm finally taking you up on it. And I paid my ten dollars, in case you're worried about me mooching."

Finn felt her hand on his as she placed a folded bill in it.

"You're not sleeping with Lacy tonight."

"Then are you available?"

He heard her exhale in frustration.

"Yeah, move over," she said resignedly.

He could hear her gown rustling and the bed springs squeak.

Finn sat up and backed against the wall. "I didn't mean that, Pearl."

She lit the lamp by the bed, and he could see that she was still fully clothed, and in a dress instead of a nightgown.

"I know you didn't. You're just frustrated." She pulled the chair up to the bed. "What happened tonight?"

Finn paused to figure out how to answer that. "I guess I let her go."

"You talked to her?"

"No… I saw her through the window, and Lucius was right. She looked happy, and she looked like she'd moved on. And she deserves a lot more than I can give her right now."

"Why didn't you talk to her and find out how *she* feels?"

"I couldn't even get in the damn door—they had a dress code, I was told. I guess I wasted my money on a new shirt for nothing."

"So you think she'll be happier with Lucius?"

"He'll give her everything she ever wanted, and it looks like he'll do a better job of taking care of her than I ever did."

"You act like you're never going to change; that this financial situation you're in will always be this way."

"Well, you could tell the mirror the same thing—you act like this is the only life you could ever have."

Pearl glared at him. "Good or bad, I made my choices, and I've lived my life. But you have so much life ahead of you."

"You sound like you have one foot in the grave. You have a lot of life ahead of you, too, Pearl."

"We're not talking about me. We're talking about you and Grace."

"But it's my fault for losing her and losing my money, and I don't know how long it's going to take for me to turn that around. She waited long enough for me to wake up; I can't expect her to wait until I'm back on my feet." He ran his hand across his forehead and through his hair. "It's too late, Pearl. I've lost her, and I can't blame anybody but myself."

"I wish you could see you through my eyes," she said softly.

Finn looked up, questioning her with his look.

"You're a cut above the rest, Finn, and I include Lucius when I say that. You work hard, and you have principles and live by them—those are such appealing qualities in a man. You're smart; I have no doubt you'll get back on your feet in no time. There's a clarity about you—I see no scheming, underhanded motives like I do with so many other men I'm around."

"I think you're making too much of my character. I almost made another huge mistake."

"I think you would've backed off with Lacy, too."

Finn nodded. "And I'm sorry I spoke out of turn to you earlier, Pearl. I had no count to be rude—you've done nothing but help me since I arrived on your doorstep."

"I'm sorry I yelled at you, too."

"I deserved it."

"Yes, you did." Pearl agreed. "What are you going to do now?"

"I'm going to try to get some sleep tonight, and then I'll head back to Waco on the first train out of here."

"Didn't you hear a word I said? Why are you so quick to give up on her?"

"I'm doing this *for* her!"

Pearl stood. "Then for her sake, don't leave town without asking her what *she* wants."

Finn looked away, fighting the urge to let hope take root.

Chapter 29

Grace ran towards the door, but Lucius caught her and pulled her aside.

"Grace, you look like you've seen a ghost. What's the matter?"

"I saw Finn."

Lucius looked around. "Where?"

"Through the window—if you'll excuse me…" She started toward the door.

"I'll go with you."

He followed her outside and watched her run down the steps and around the building. She stopped and stared at an empty bench next to the wall where Finn must've stood to look inside.

She turned around and shielded her eyes from the gas lights in the park. "Where did he go? If he came for me, why did he run away again?"

"I didn't want to have to tell you this, but I heard some news about him from home."

"What are you talking about?"

"Sissy told me that she heard that Finn lost all of his investments with his brother. He's flat broke."

"When did this happen?"

"I think right before you came down here."

Grace sat down, stunned at the news. After a moment, her face looked hopeful. "That must be why he ran away from me in Waco! It wasn't because he didn't love me."

She jumped up. "I need to find him."

"Grace…"

"I know this is unfair to you, Lucius, and I'm sorry, but Finn needs me right now."

"He just ran away from you again!"

"I need to talk to him." She started pacing. "I know we can work this out—it's… it's just his pride standing in the way. He didn't want to have to tell me this, not when I forced him to face my ultimatum." She stopped and looked at the pavilion wall. "Maybe Daisy and Walter can go with me to the hotels—there aren't that many in the city, are there?"

"It'd take half the night to visit every hotel, but you won't need to do that."

Grace turned and looked at Lucius. "Why not?"

"I hoped… you would never have to find out," he said as he led her away from the windows, most of which were open, "but I know where he's staying, and it's not in a hotel—"

"You knew Finn was in town and didn't tell me? How dare you keep that from me!"

"Grace, listen to me! He's staying at a brothel on Postoffice Street."

"What?"

"A whorehouse."

"I don't believe you."

"Why would I lie to you about that? Do you want me to take you there and show you? I'll take you right now if you don't believe me." He grabbed her arm and started down the walkway.

"No, stop, let me think for a moment. There has to be a good explanation."

Lucius shook his head in frustration. "He could be partnering with the devil himself and you'd still think he was innocent."

"I know Finn; that's just not like him to go to… one of those places."

"You must not know him as well as you think you do, otherwise, why did he abandon you and then show up here, just to run away again? He sounds unstable."

"I don't know." She stepped back and sat down on the bench, covering her face with her hands.

"He's not as wonderful as you think he is."

Grace looked up. "And how did you find out where he was? Did you visit the brothel yourself?"

"As a matter of fact, yes, but not for the reason you think."

Grace couldn't imagine what other reason he would visit a brothel. "I'm listening," she said in a challenging tone.

Lucius sat down beside her. "Remember the day you saw the woman in the window in that brothel—that day we were riding the streetcar together?"

Grace nodded. "She looked familiar to me."

"For good reason. She's a prostitute, and almost twenty years ago she had a baby girl that she couldn't take care of, so she gave her up for someone else to raise."

She sat up straighter. "Juju!" whispered Grace. "Kitty and Juju."

Lucius nodded. "Pearl is Kitty's birth mother, and from a distance she's watched out for her daughter. When Juju's husband died, Pearl asked me to help find her a job. I ended up hiring her myself, which is one of the smartest things I've done since I moved down here. Kitty has no idea who her mother is—she lives in a whole other world away from Postoffice Street, and Pearl wants to keep it that way. She gives me the money to pay for Kitty's medical school, and Kitty thinks she's receiving a scholarship. I know I can count on your discretion about this, right?"

"Of course, Lucius." Grace reached for his hand. "I'm so sorry I assumed the worst of you."

"Do you want me to go talk to Finn for you or ask him to meet you somewhere? I really don't want you to have to step foot in that place."

"You'd do that for me?"

Lucius lifted her hand to his lips. "I'd do anything for you, Grace. I hope you realize that."

"I need to know why he came down here just to turn around and run away again. Something's not right."

"I'll get to the bottom of this. But then can you do something for me?"

"I'll try."

"If Finn refuses to see you—if he abandons you again, will you open your eyes to the truth about him—that he's not the man you think he is?"

Grace looked down and nodded.

"He's not in any position to take care of you. You don't want to strap yourself to a man like that."

"Finn is very capable of…" she stopped herself. "Please tell him I need to… I want to see him before he goes."

"Well, he won't be going anywhere tonight. I'll find him in the morning for you." Lucius stood. "I smell rain. Maybe we ought to call it an evening."

Grace felt relieved. "Do you mind?"

"No, I have a busy day tomorrow. I think we danced enough, wouldn't you say?"

"I have to say you were hands down the best dancing partner I had all night. Some of your friends couldn't stay off my feet."

Lucius chuckled. "I'm sure your beauty flustered them a bit, but I appreciate you making an effort with them."

"I do need to improve my social skills."

"You were wonderful."

A light rain began to fall.

Grace jumped up. "Oh! Your dress!"

"My dress?" He grabbed her upper arm and led her quickly to the entrance foyer. "Well, that dress never looked as good on me! I guess you're going to have to keep it."

"You've been too generous, Lucius. I don't want you to get in the habit of giving me gifts like this."

He touched her face. "It makes me happy to see you happy."

Grace looked away. "I need to find Daisy and tell Marguerite goodbye."

"There's Marguerite," he said, directing her to the left side of the octagonal room. "You go talk to her and I'll go find Daisy."

Grace came up beside Marguerite and excusing herself, she pulled her aside. "Finn was here," she spoke close to her friend's ear.

"What?!" Marguerite said loudly. "Here at the dance?" She looked around the pavilion.

"He's gone now."

Marguerite grabbed her arm and walked her to the ladies' toilet room.

"Where did he go?"

"He was looking through one of the windows."

"From outside?"

Grace nodded.

"Did you get to talk to him?"

Grace shook her head. "When I saw him, he left. We ran outside, but he was gone. Lucius is going to find him for me and ask him to meet me tomorrow. I'm so afraid he's going to leave town."

Marguerite smirked. "Lucius offered to find him for you? Honey, that's letting the fox guard the hen house. He's not going to do anything to make it easier for you and Finn to get back together."

"But he said—"

"He wants to please you, Grace, but even more so… he wants *you*, so don't count on him helping Finn."

Grace's face fell. "He told me that Finn's staying at a brothel on Postoffice Street. Do you think he was telling the truth?"

"I don't know."

"He told me he'd even take me over there tonight if I didn't believe him."

Marguerite's eyebrows rose. "I don't think Lucius would've offered to do that if Finn wasn't there."

"What time does the first train leave in the morning?"

"Let me see—tomorrow's Saturday. I think the first one leaves at nine forty-five—no that's leaving from Houston. Going back home, it leaves at nine o'clock."

"Should I go find him tonight?"

"On Postoffice Street at night? Good heavens, no! Remember what happened to you the last time you were there? And that was broad daylight. It's no place for a lady."

"Well, then, I'm going to get up early and find him."

"Do you want me to go with you?" she asked tentatively.

Grace smiled. "You're sweet to offer, Marguerite, but I know you're not an early riser."

Marguerite looked relieved. "Well, it shouldn't be as risky for you in the morning—I imagine the whole street will be sound asleep by then. But go to the train station first—if he's not there, you'll know he's still on the island and you'll have more time to find him."

"Good idea," said Grace, hugging her friend.

"Let me know what happens," said Marguerite, touching Grace's head. "Your hair is damp—is it raining?" She walked over to a window and pulled back the drape.

"Just a light shower, I guess the storm's coming in."

Marguerite waved her hand. "Looks like it's already stopped. Some of the men said the storm probably blew itself out before it got here."

Chapter 30

Grace realized her tossing around was keeping Daisy awake, so she slipped out of bed and looked in the two extra bedrooms for a place to sleep. They were empty of furniture. The only other room upstairs besides a storage closet was Lucius' bedroom, so she ended up crawling into his bed to keep from disturbing her friend. The last clock chime she remembered heralded three a.m.

Ante meridiem—before noon. And Finn told her she would have little use for her Latin in real life. She chuckled out loud at the thought of seeing him again in the morning.

"Carpe diem, Finn. We can get through anything so long as I know you love me."

Then she wept at the thought of losing him all over again.

It was still dark when she opened her eyes again.

Someone else was in the room... Lucius' room. She sat up in bed.

"I didn't mean to wake you—" a voice said quietly.

Grace exhaled as Daisy turned on the light.

"The sky's looking stormy, so I need to get home. Mom will be worried. It's been raining off and on for the past several hours, and it's stopped for the moment, but I imagine we'll have an overflow before long. Our apartment's only three blocks from the beach."

"What time is it?"

"Almost eight."

"I'm late!" She threw her legs off the bed and ran across the hall to the other bedroom to get dressed, pulling off her nightgown on the way.

Daisy followed her. "Do you mind me going now?"

"No, Daisy, of course not." She stopped long enough to hug her friend goodbye. "I appreciate you staying with me these past three nights. I would've gone out of my mind with fear if I'd been by myself. Please tell your mother thank you for me—for letting you stay with me."

"Sure—I'll see you later when you move in?" She walked over to the stairs.

"If it's still raining, I may have to postpone bringing my trunk over until tomorrow, but I'm definitely going to spend my first night there tonight—rain or no rain." She stepped into her skirt, pulled it up and buttoned it.

"I can't wait! We're going to have so much fun together this year," Daisy said, heading down the stairs. She stopped on the landing to add, "I hope everything goes well with Finn!"

"If I can get across town to find him!" shouted Grace. She finished dressing and pulled her hair back in a hairclip, letting it drape down her back since she didn't have time to put it up. She hoped she wouldn't see anyone she knew.

She stepped out on the porch and looked up. The clouds hung heavy with rain but were restraining themselves for the moment, so Grace took off running for the streetcar tracks on Broadway two blocks over. She hoped she wouldn't have to wait for long. Her fashionable parasol was more for protecting her from sunlight rather than raindrops.

She made it to Broadway and looked east, hoping to see a streetcar coming west. The Union Station was a good fifteen or twenty blocks away, but the streetcar made numerous stops which took time. She prayed she wouldn't miss the train's departure before she found out if Finn was on it. She decided to start walking west towards 21st Street where a north-south track ran.

At 18th Street she saw a woman and a young boy standing in the middle of the street looking south. Grace spoke a greeting as she walked by, but they were so mesmerized by something they didn't even respond. She followed their gazes and couldn't help but stop and stare herself. The beach was at least a mile away, but huge waves were hitting a railroad trestle and shooting up into the sky—higher than even the telephone poles.

Grace shuddered and hurried on. When she was about a half block away from 21st Street, a southbound streetcar turned west onto Broadway and stopped at the intersection. She shouted and waved and began running. The driver waved back at her and waited until she embarked before continuing.

"Thank you, sir," she said, sitting on the first seat trying to catch her breath.

The driver grinned. "Not the best day for walkin', is it, ma'am."

"No, sir."

After a few minutes, the rain began again. Grace stood and raised her window to keep the rain from blowing in.

"Do you think this is a norther?" she asked the driver.

"Nah, I think we're getting a tropical storm."

"Coming from the north?"

"It's the way the winds blow off of it—I know it sounds confusing, but that's the way I've seen it happen. If it's a tropical cyclone, the wind will switch directions on the back half."

"Aren't you worried?"

"Nah, it'll blow over and we'll dry out like we always do."

"How long have you lived here?"

"Thirty years."

"I've been here a week, but so much has happened, it feels more like a month."

The older man chuckled. "Yes, ma'am. There's a lot going on in Galveston."

"Do you know Mr. Robertson?"

"Guilmet? Sure. We've worked together for years."

"I'm supposed to have lunch with his wife today."

"Good family. Tell Maeve hello for me."

"What's your name?"

"Gilmore."

"Sure will, Mr. Gilmore. Could you tell me the time?"

He took out his pocket watch. "Eight-twenty-four."

"Does this trolley go by the Union Passenger Station?"

"Within one block of it, ma'am."

"Will we make it before the nine o'clock train leaves?"

"With ten minutes to spare, if there are no delays."

Grace took a deep breath and tried to calm down. What if Finn was already on the train? Would they let her board to find him? And what if she didn't have time to search every car?

She cringed at the thought of her last encounter with Finn at a train station. The plan that worked beautifully for Sissy ended up disastrous for her. She wouldn't make that prideful mistake again.

By the time the trolley slowed, Grace was standing at the door. Gilmore had barely pulled to a stop before she jumped and ran the block to the station. She didn't even slow down when she went through the doors of passenger station and then onto the platform. She could feel the train engine rumble in her chest as she weaved in and out of people saying goodbye and waving to folks already in the cars.

She stopped at the first passenger car and told the porter that she needed to see if someone was on board. He told her the train was about to leave. She begged him to let her just step inside and look—assuring him she would only take seconds to do so.

"Please, sir, my future depends on it," she said with conviction.

He set the footstool back down and let her step aboard.

The car was full, but a quick sweep of faces told her he wasn't there. She stepped down, thanked the porter and hurried to the next car and was able to scan their faces, which told her Finn wasn't on this one either. The train had two more passenger cars, and the third car's porter stood in the door and refused to let her pass after she told him she wasn't a passenger.

"But my future depends on it," she tried that line again.

The train whistle blew loudly, signaling the departure.

"You should've arrived earlier or bought a ticket to be able to board this late. Everyone else has said their goodbyes."

"But I'm not saying goodbye," Grace tried to explain.

"Sorry, ma'am." He shut the door.

Grace ran along the side of the train car trying to see in. She could clearly see the faces of the people next to the windows on this side, but she couldn't see beyond that.

"Finn!" she yelled every few steps. "Finn Samuel!"

The train started moving.

She stopped at the end of the platform and watched as each car passed through a curtain of rain and finally disappeared from sight. She wiped a stray tear from her cheek and told herself that he wasn't on the train—that if he was, he would've heard her cries and found her. She reminded herself that if he came this far, he wouldn't run away again. He couldn't.

Dear Lord, please don't let him be on that train.

She turned around and walked back into the station, ignoring the stares of the people loitering about waiting for the rain to let up.

She passed right by them and walked out into the rain.

On the corner of 25th and Mechanic Streets she stood on the raised boardwalk under a store's awning and waited a good twenty minutes for the next streetcar before she remembered that Postoffice and 25th was the intersection the brothel was located at. She had to be close. The downpour slowed to a light rain so she dashed across the street and tried to stay under the business awnings as much as possible as she walked south.

The water seemed to be collecting in the street rather than draining—maybe this was the start of the overflow everyone kept talking about. She looked around—people were scurrying to get out of the rain, but they didn't seem to be too concerned. It looked like business as usual. She glanced at a big clock in a drugstore window—nine-twenty-nine—as she passed. She noticed men drinking coffee at the counter.

Ten minutes later, she found herself standing at the front door of the brothel where Finn was supposedly staying. The big house looked unassuming—few outsiders would realize that debauchery resided on the other side. She took a deep breath and rapped on the door.

No response.

She knocked again, louder this time, and after a moment heard footsteps shuffling inside.

A young woman with tousled blonde hair opened the door and looked her over with sleepy eyes.

"What?" she said curtly.

"Uh… good morning," Grace began politely.

"If you're trying to sell, save, or sample something, you're at the wrong house." She started to shut the door.

"Wait!" Grace put out her hand. "I'm looking for someone… his name is Finn."

The blonde's eyes opened completely. "What do you want with Finn?"

Grace thought she sounded almost jealous. "So you know him?"

"The whole house knows him, but we call him Cowboy… what do you want with him?"

Grace wasn't sure if anger or disappointment took the upper hand. "I need to talk to him," she said sharply.

The blonde sighed impatiently. "Let me see if he's here."

The door shut in Grace's face. It started raining again, and the northeast wind whipped a spray under the porch. She stepped to the far left side of the porch, closer to the wall.

After a minute, the door opened again.

"Well, where'd she go?" The blonde stuck her head out the door.

"I'm right here," said Grace stepping up. She started to feel a chill all of a sudden, but she wasn't sure if it was from the dampness or the fact that she was talking to a prostitute. She felt brave with young Anise, but facing a woman that was in this business by choice was another matter.

"He's gone."

"Do you know where?"

"No. But a train ticket was delivered to him last night."

Grace's heart fell in her chest. "He left town?"

"I don't think he'd keep a train ticket for a souvenir, and it's not in his room. His room's empty."

"Lacy?! What are you doing?" another voice spoke from behind the blonde.

Another woman appeared at the door—the woman with gray eyes. Grace was staring at Kitty's mother.

The woman took one look at Grace and reached for her, pulling her inside.

"Come inside! Good heavens, Lacy—you have the manners of a goat. The poor girl's soaked to the bone."

Lacy glared at her. "She's looking for Cowboy."

"Finn," Grace couldn't help but correct her.

"Pearl's the one who started calling him Cowboy," Lacy said snidely, "but we all know he doesn't wear his spurs when he sleeps." She flashed a knowing grin and turned around and sauntered off.

"Finn doesn't wear spurs," Grace couldn't help but say, "except when he's working cattle."

"Ignore her," said Pearl. "She always wakes up in a sour mood. So… you must be Grace."

Grace was shocked that the woman knew her name. "How do you know that?"

Pearl smiled. "Finn, of course. You're the reason he's here… on the island, I mean."

Tears flooded Grace's eyes. "Did he leave already? I just came from the train station, but I didn't have time to check all the cars before they left."

"I don't know—he was talking about doing just that last night, but I told him he'd better not leave until he talked to you."

"So he might still be here?" said Grace as she sat down on a velvet settee, and then remembering where she was, quickly stood back up.

"I don't know," said Pearl, stifling a laugh as she sat in a fancy wing chair. "Sit down—all the *business* takes place elsewhere."

Grace sat down gingerly, her cheeks burning with embarrassment. "I'm sorry—I just don't know what… or how I'm supposed to… uh… Could you tell me why Finn was staying… here?"

"Your innocent fellow thought this was a laundry and bath house."

Grace couldn't help but smile. "You're kidding!"

Pearl shook her head.

Grace laughed out loud. "That sounds like Finn. I told Lucius there must be a good explanation for him being here."

"Lucius told you he was staying here?"

"Yes, and I assumed the worst." Grace's smile faded. "But why did he stay here after he learned his mistake?"

"He needed a place to stay, and we had some work that needed to be done, so we traded out—his carpentry skills for room and board. He rebuilt those steps you walked up out front. I don't know if you heard about his investments…"

"Lucius told me about that, too."

"Well, Lucius is doing his best to make Finn sound like a bum, isn't he. But I know why, and I'm sure you've gathered that by now."

Grace nodded. "Lucius has made his intentions known, and he's met every need since I arrived, and he's very considerate… and handsome…"

"He's the best catch in town."

"Yes, but I really don't know him that well… and…"

"And?"

"I love Finn. I've always loved Finn."

"I can see why."

"Really? Have you gotten to know him?"

Pearl nodded. "A little, but if nothing else, this business has taught me to be a good judge of the male character, and your man is about as good as they come."

Grace smiled. "I think so, too."

"If he's still here, he's probably looking for you, too."

"Then I don't want to take anymore of your time," said Grace, standing. "If you see him, could you tell him where I'm staying?"

"He knows where you're staying."

"Then why hasn't he…" Grace stopped. "My neighbor ran someone off from the front yard Thursday night—that must've been him!"

"He's been trying to find you ever since he arrived."

"Then why did he run away at the dance last night?"

"He got the idiotic idea that you'd be better off without him."

Grace groaned in frustration. "What is wrong with him?"

"Stubborn pride. He wants more for you than he can give you right now. Don't let that boy go—he loves you, Grace, but after he got down here and saw what Lucius could do for you last night, he was thinking about doing you a big favor by leaving town."

"I can't imagine my life without him." Grace stood. "He came this far, so I know he cares about me. But if he's left the island again, I'm going after him. Is there another train leaving today?"

"This afternoon." Pearl walked her to the door. "I'm so glad to have met you in person, Grace. I want to thank you for helping Anise, too."

"You heard about that?"

"Everybody on the street heard about that. I had no idea you were the young lady everyone was talking about until Lucius told me."

"I just did what anybody else would've done."

Pearl reached for her hand and squeezed it. "No, few would bother to get involved."

"Well, I appreciate you taking care of Finn. I'd better go now." She looked up at the clouds. "Oh, it's stopped raining—maybe the worst of it is over. She hiked up her skirt and hurried down the steps to catch the next streetcar.

"Avoid the gutters on the sides of the roads—some of them are waist deep, and you can't tell since they're full of water!" Pearl shouted after her.

"I will—thank you, Pearl!" Grace said over her shoulder.

Chapter 31

Grace looked east and west on Postoffice Street—no streetcars in sight, and the dark clouds looked like they were ready to dump their cache again. She walked one block south and looked both directions on Church Street. People were hurrying around before the rain started again. She could see a lot of activity at the Tremont Hotel two blocks east and figured the rain put a damper on a lot of tourists' plans at the beaches. Looking west, she saw a little boy floating a boat in the flooded gutter and recalled Daisy saying how they all grew up playing in the overflows.

A streetcar crossed the intersection a block back on Postoffice Street behind her. She shouted and waved, but it was too far away.

Grace dropped her hand in frustration. Then she noticed something strange toward the north. The town was quickly disappearing behind a gray curtain swallowing up buildings and streets in its path. It took only a moment before she realized it was a heavy line of rain coming towards her, so she turned and started running south on 25th Street. She laughed aloud at the eerie feeling that the curtain was alive and chasing her, but then a sudden fear at the thought of it made her run even faster.

The torrent of rain overtook her less than two blocks away from where she started running. She had turned east, hoping she could make it to the Baptist Church on 23rd Street, but the rain forced her to stop and seek cover under the nearest house's front gallery.

She splashed through the puddles in the yard and ran up the tall steps, but was soaked to the skin again in a matter of seconds. The gallery faced south so it offered protection from the deluge, but it couldn't stop the chill she felt from the sopping clothes.

Grace jumped when she noticed a short, older woman standing beside her. The noise of the rain had covered the sound of the front door opening.

"Hello!" the woman said loudly. "Can I help you?"

"Hello!" Grace responded, still trying to catch her breath from running. "I'm sorry I'm intruding on your gallery—I got caught out in the storm."

"That's quite all right!" The woman smiled. "Come inside and dry off!"

Grace shook her head. "I'll ruin your floors—I'm dripping wet!"

"I already have towels and blankets by the door." She grasped Grace's arm and pulled her into the house.

Grace was surprised at the strength in the small woman's grip, and followed like an obedient puppy. The woman handed her a towel for her hair, and then wrapped her in a blanket and led her to a chair in the parlor. A uniformed maid appeared with a tea service tray and poured hot tea for them.

Grace held the warm cup with both hands as she blew the top of the tea, letting the steam hit her cold face. "You're certainly a shelter from the storm, Mrs.?"

"Mahaffey. Dorothy Mahaffey."

"Nice to meet you Mrs. Mahaffey. I'm Grace Taylor."

"How did you get caught afoot in this rain?"

"I've been chasing the streetcars and keep missing the few that I've seen from a distance."

"The rain slows down the routes."

"Does it usually rain this much on the island? You seem so prepared for this kind of thing." Grace wrapped the blanket even tighter around her.

The woman chuckled. "No, it's just that I'm planning a little soirée at noon, and I'm sure my friends are going to get thoroughly soaked before they walk through that door."

"You're not worried about an overflow?"

"Not here—we're near the highest elevation in town. I heard the streets close to the beach are flooding, but it won't get this far. Where do you live?"

"I've been staying at 17th and Avenue L."

"With this heavy rain, the streets will probably catch water, but it shouldn't be bad that far from the beach."

"It's hard to believe it was so hot this week—the rain out there felt like ice water."

"We're not finished with the heat yet. It'll warm up again in no time."

Grace drank the tea, enjoying the warm sensation spreading down her throat. She looked around the high-ceilinged room.

"Your home is beautiful."

"Thank you," Mrs. Mahaffey beamed. "We finally built it about a year before all of our children started leaving home. It took us a long time to get here, and now it's just me and Jacob left. The house is really too big for us by ourselves now, but it's wonderful around the holidays when everyone comes home."

"I can imagine," said Grace. She glanced at the nearest window. "Listen—I don't hear the rain anymore. It's like it's coming in waves. I guess I should get out there and try to find a streetcar again." She stood and pulled the blanket from her shoulders and started folding it.

"Here, I'll take that—you're more than welcome to stay for the soirée; surely the storm will have blown over by then."

Grace gave her long, wavy ponytail one more squeeze with the towel and handed it back to Mrs. Mahaffey. "I appreciate the offer, but I have to get back to the house."

"Well, I hope we get to meet again under more favorable conditions some day, Grace."

"Me, too, Mrs. Mahaffey." On impulse, Grace offered her hand and the woman grasped it with both hands. "I appreciate your hospitality, in spite of me barging in on you."

"You get home and get out of these wet clothes, all right?"

Mrs. Mahaffey walked Grace to the front gallery and they both looked at the sky, still filled with heavy, dark clouds. They could hear a brisk wind whistling through the space between the Mahaffey house and the neighbor's.

"Good luck, dearie."

Grace sighed and smiled at the woman, pulled up her skirts and walked down the steps into the puddles standing in the yard. When she reached the street, she turned and waved at Mrs. Mahaffey, and looked more closely at the big, two-storied Victorian home she had just walked out of.

"Love your house!" She shouted before she splashed on down the street.

Then she remembered she was heading east and could see no streetcar tracks or overhead cables on this street. She did notice a number of wagons crossing the next intersection heading north—wagons loaded with more than just adults and children. She could see trunks and bedding and household belongings piled haphazardly—like people had quickly left home.

She felt a sudden prick of worry at the back of her mind, but then quelled it at the thought that Lucius would know what to do if the overflow came as far as Avenue L and 17th Street. He would take care of matters. He was used to such things.

She found herself torn between the desire to see Finn and the hope that he had left Galveston before any danger of an overflow hit. At a house on the southwest corner of the intersection she noticed a man nailing down the storm shutters.

"Is the storm going to get worse?" she yelled towards him.

The man turned and held onto his hat as he faced her and the wind. He trotted down the steps and hurried over towards the picket fence bordering his yard.

"Yes, ma'am," he said. "They raised the second flag at the Levy Building downtown."

"That means a bad storm's coming, right?"

The man nodded his head, still holding onto his hat.

"From the north?"

"Yeah, and then I heard it could also come from the south."

"Have you been through one of these before?"

"No, ma'am, and it scares the heck out of me. This pile of sand isn't near high enough for my liking. Some of my colleagues laughed at me when I left work early and came home to try to batten down the hatches, as they say."

"People that have lived here a long time have told me it'll just blow over and the water will drain off like it always does."

"Well, I'd rather be safe than sorry. You might ought to get on home—it's looking bad."

She looked up at the darkening sky, and then looked back and wished him well. She quickly gathered up her damp skirt so she could see where she was stepping and turned south on 24th Street. Gusts of wind coming from the north felt like hands pushing her roughly along.

Chapter 32

Finn threw the train ticket on the desk.

"I won't be needing this," he said to Lucius.

Lucius raised his eyebrows as he picked up the ticket. "Are you sure about that?"

"I'm sure. Now where is she?"

"She's at home… my house," he corrected himself.

"I was there, and she's not at your house. Juju and Kitty came while I was waiting for Grace—they said the west end of town is already flooded. Juju told me she might've gone to the apartment she was moving into today, but her trunk was still upstairs."

"Making yourself at home already? She was going to wait and let me help her with her trunk tomorrow—after the rain's past. She's probably with Daisy getting the apartment ready."

Finn shook his head. "This isn't just a normal rainstorm, Lucius. Water's already surrounded Lucas Terrace on the east end of town. I couldn't even get that far, but I did talk to some folks in a police hack that they'd evacuated from those apartments, and they said they didn't see a yellow-haired woman at the Thornes' flat when they asked if any of them wanted to go to higher ground. They said the Thornes and a number of others decided to ride out the storm there."

"Maybe she's visiting her friend Marguerite—she only lives a few blocks over on Broadway."

Finn shook his head. "I've already checked. Mrs. St. John hasn't seen her either."

Lucius looked surprised. "How do you know about Marguerite?"

"Your housekeeper told me Grace was friends with her." Finn glanced at the clock on the wall… eleven thirty-five. He watched Lucius walk over to the telephone on the wall and pick up the earpiece. He turned the crank several times and then spoke into the mouthpiece.

"How are you doing, Sue?" He paused for her answer. "I'm sure they'll let you go home if it gets any worse. Could you connect me to my house?"

He put his hand over the speaker and turned to Finn. "The telephones are still working, so the storm can't be too bad." He turned back to the mouthpiece. "Juju, is Grace there?"

"Good. Can I speak to her?"

"All right… no, don't disturb her… let her take her hot bath. Well, I'm going to send Tom to pick you up… no, I don't think it's going to be as bad as you think, but I'd feel better if you all were with me downtown… I'll tell Tom to take his tallest hack… I don't know if Kitty will be able to get to the Infirmary… the overflow's getting pretty deep on that side of town, too. Trust me… it'll run off before you know it… see you soon."

Lucius turned the crank again. "Sue, ring 245 and tell Tom to take his tallest hack to my house to pick up my guests and bring them back here to my office… thanks… and if Tom's not available, tell them to send someone else as soon as possible. And if there's a waiting list, you tell them I'll make it very worth their while to move Lucius Roderick to the top of the list… thanks, beautiful. I owe you."

He replaced the earpiece and turned to face Finn.

"Grace is at home now, and I'll bring them here, if it makes you feel better."

"It does… thank you." Finn took a deep breath and let it out.

Lucius ignored the question. "You look like you've been swimming."

"The rain's heavy out there, and I had to wade through knee-deep water much of the way over here. I had to empty my boots before I entered the building."

"You're still dripping." Lucius walked to the door and called for someone named Julius to come mop up the floor. The man brought an armful of towels and handed several to Finn.

Finn wiped the excess water from his hat and clothes the best he could.

Lucius walked back to his desk. "Now, this is still a regular workday for me, so if you don't mind…"

"I'll wait for her downstairs."

"There's coffee down the hall." Lucius nodded to the right.

Finn looked at him in surprise.

"We can at least be civil," Lucius said.

Finn nodded before stepping out of the room to find the coffee. He poured himself a cup and gingerly took a swallow, breathing a sigh of relief afterwards. He came in here ready to fight for Grace, if need be, but Lucius couldn't have been more helpful.

Maybe he knows he's lost. He couldn't help but smile at the thought. *Or maybe he knows he's won.* He frowned.

Dang.

Lucius seemed to know Grace was already at home while he'd been running all over town trying to find her. He had the means and the clout to rescue the women while Finn stood around like a wet, starving dog waiting for someone to throw him a bone.

Why did things get complicated when Lucius was around?

Finn's stomach growled loudly. He realized he hadn't eaten anything since yesterday. He picked up a dish cover and found a few cold pastries, probably left over from breakfast.

They tasted pretty darn good with the coffee.

He poured himself a second cup and headed downstairs to wait for Grace. He'd know within the hour if Grace was going to be a part of his life again… or if he'd lost her for good.

Maybe he should've hung onto that train ticket.

* * *

"What are you doing?" Grace asked as she descended the stairs dressed in dry clothing for the first time since she left that morning.

"We're rolling up the rugs and taking them upstairs," said Juju.

"Oh, my gosh—is the overflow going to get this high?"

"It might; it's already filled the streets and into the yard, and it's not just from the rain. That's Gulf water out there. The tide gets high fairly often on our side of town, but I don't ever remember the Gulf getting this close to Broadway before."

Grace pulled a chair out of the way for the women as they carried the parlor rug toward the stairs. She ran to the library across the foyer and started dragging the furniture off that rug.

The lights blinked and the house went dark.

"Don't be frightened, Grace!" hollered Juju from the other room. "We always lose power in a storm! I'm surprised we had lights this long."

Juju brought a lit oil lamp into the room. "We don't have much time before Tom gets here. I'll light the other lamps."

Kitty came into the room. "Momma thinks our house is under water by now."

"I'm so sorry! What about your valuables?"

"We brought our photographs and jewelry… and Momma's wedding silver, and extra clothes, of course. We set everything up as high as possible before we left, but I'm sure a lot of it will get soaked."

They each took a short side of the desk and tried to pick it up, but it was too heavy. They moved around to one of the long sides and pushed it off the rug against the wall. They rolled up the rug and with Juju leading the way carrying another lamp, hauled it up the stairs to stack with the ever-growing pile of Lucius' belongings in the center of the hall.

They came back to the parlor

"Will the books be all right in the cabinets?"

"Move them to the top two shelves."

"Will that be high enough?"

"It should be. I can't fathom the water getting into this house, but I can't bear the thought of losing those books because we didn't take the time to move them higher."

Kitty put the desk chair and a smaller ladder-back chair on top of the heavy desk while Grace finished moving the books higher in the shelves. When that was finished, they went back to the parlor, and moved the upholstered chairs upstairs, along with the dining table chairs. They set the sofa on top of the dining table.

"I've already moved everything in the kitchen to the tops of the counters and work table. And I've drawn water in the bath tub and every empty container I could find so we'll have clean water when we come back. The cistern's full, but sometimes the overflows knock them over."

"I closed all the shutters I could reach except for the windows along the lower front gallery since they're protected from the wind and giving us a little light, but we'll secure them before we leave the house."

Something hit the side of the house hard. They all jumped at the noise.

"What was that?" asked Grace.

"Probably slate shingles off the neighbor's roof. It's going to be dangerous heading back to town with those wind gusts. Maybe we ought to put pots over our heads when we go outside."

Something else hit the house.

"I think that's an excellent idea, Momma." She ran to the kitchen and brought back two big pots.

"We need three, honey," said Juju.

"No, we don't." Kitty said, looking at Grace.

"I'm not going with you, Juju," she explained.

"What?!"

"I'll wait here for Finn, and then we'll come if we think it's safe enough."

"It's probably not safe to travel right now."

"Grace, you have to come with us."

"I can't miss him again. You said he was waiting here for me when you got here. And then you told him I might be with Daisy or Marguerite, so he should know by now that I'm not with them. He's probably on his way back right now."

"We can't leave you here by yourself."

Grace just shook her head. "Finn's come all this way for me, and we've played hopscotch ever since he arrived. Neither one of us is going to run away from each other anymore. I'm staying right here until he gets here."

"Lucius isn't going to be happy about this."

"It's my decision, not his. Could you tell him I'm sorry?"

Juju frowned, but then nodded her head. "Do you know where the extra lamp oil is?"

"In the buffet?"

Juju nodded. "And there's more in the kitchen. And there's canned food in the pantry for supper."

"I see Tom!" Kitty said excitedly. She opened the front door and waved at him.

Grace followed her to the door. Tom looked like he was hanging on for dear life trying to stay on the driver's seat. The horse was skittish standing in the knee-deep water. The wind sounded something like a constant roar, broken only by gusts that raised or lowered the volume.

Tom signaled urgently for them to come on.

"Get your slicker on, girl," said Juju, "and try to keep those bags dry." She turned back to Grace. "We should be back in time to fix Sunday dinner in the morning." She pulled the strap of a bag over her head before Grace helped her get into her slicker and belt it tight.

They walked out onto the front gallery, protected against the torrential rain and driving wind.

Kitty insisted on carrying her load first to the wagon and then came back to help her mother.

"Be safe, and I'll see you soon," said Grace.

"God protect and keep you, honey," said Juju, giving her an awkward hug.

Kitty came back, saying that Tom had heard that the big waves had destroyed the bathhouses on the beach, and that some of the houses had already been knocked off their foundations.

"Are you sure you won't come with us?" Juju asked Grace.

"I'm sure, and don't worry; I'll be fine… especially when Finn gets here."

Juju pulled the pot over her head and held it with one hand, and latched onto Kitty before they stepped gingerly down the stairs into ankle deep water.

Halfway across the yard, Kitty turned around and yelled, "I forgot to tell you—your neighbor called earlier and said she needed to postpone your lunch date! She went downtown and her husband wouldn't let her come back to the house by herself!"

Grace nodded that she understood and waved them on. She watched them climb into the carriage and Tom reached through the window behind him to retrieve something. She smiled when she saw him put the pot on his head and tie the handles underneath his chin with his kerchief.

Tom struggled trying to get the horse to turn around in the flooded street. She could see debris in the water making the animal skittish.

Debris? Almost a mile from the beach?

Tom finally got the horse turned around and Grace waved, trying to keep the panic at bay at the realization that she might be the only one left on the street.

Lord, help them get to Lucius safely. Please keep Finn safe. Please protect me and give me courage to get through this storm, Father.

She stood there until they passed around the corner out of her sight, and then turned to go back inside when she heard something crying on the wind.

Chapter 33

Grace listened intently for a few minutes, and then heard the sound again. She realized it wasn't a human voice; it was a dog yelping.

Trixie?

She looked across the street, but the rain was so heavy at the moment, she could barely see the roofline. The porch was just a dark shadow in the midst of the gray.

Maybe if she called her, the little dog would swim across the street.

"Trixie!" she shouted into the storm. "Trixie! Come here!"

She heard a howl in response, but saw no head bobbing in the water towards her.

Maybe she's tied up, Grace thought with a groan. She looked up, expecting a torrent of roof tiles to come down at the very thought of her heading across the street.

The house shuddered in response to a particularly strong gust, as if it was daring her to step off the porch.

She ran inside and slipped out of her dry dress and underclothes, and shivered as she donned the still damp skirt and blouse she'd worn earlier that day. She kicked off her shoes, refusing to ruin another pair, and ran upstairs to see if Lucius had a rain slicker—anything to help block the blow from something wind-driven.

She found a canvas overcoat and grabbed it, then ran downstairs to the kitchen to find a pot to protect her head. It was full of water, so she dumped it in the tub in the adjoining room, and then headed to the porch with her gear.

Her heart pounded as she stood there fumbling with the overcoat. She could hardly button the buttons. She picked up the pot and held it with both hands as she started down the steps. Two steps from the bottom, she tripped on the edge of the long coat and pitched forward into the muddy water.

No one heard her scream on the way down, nor did they hear her scream in frustration again when she struggled to stand, horrified that Lucius' tan canvas coat was now a dirty brown color.

She was proud of the fact that she didn't let go of the pot the whole time she was wallowing around in the flooded yard. She hurried to the gate, held open by the force of the wind and paused as she watched the water in the street. There was a current of sorts bringing debris from the direction of the beach. Another current seemed to be traveling from the east as well as running into what looked like swells from the waves—how could that happen so far from the beach? The road in front of the house was flooded as far as she could see both directions.

She took a deep breath and stepped into the street, and almost fell again when her foot didn't touch the ground immediately. The sullied brown water came to just above her knees; she didn't realize the street level was that much lower than the yard.

The wind helped push her across the road faster than she realized, and she stubbed her toe when she kicked the raised grade on the other side. She stepped up into the yard, and splashed across to the Robertson's front gallery and gathered up the drenched coat and skirt to hurry up the steps.

There was no place to hide from the wind on this porch. The overcoat flapped all around her as she tried to find Trixie. She could hear her whining, but she couldn't see her. She realized she must look like some monstrosity with the pot on her head, so she removed it and squatted down and called out the dog's name again.

A black streak bolted from underneath an overblown wicker chair in the corner and almost knocked Grace on her backside. Trixie was sopping wet and shivering from fright and smelled like a dog, but Grace was so happy to find her, she didn't care… at least for the moment.

She petted her and talked to her soothingly before standing with the dog in her arms. She wasn't sure how she was going to carry the dog and hold the pot on her head, but she decided to not waste time thinking about it. She picked up the pot with one hand and placed it on her head. The dog tried to jump out of her arms until her voice calmed her down again. The pot completely blocked her sight when she wrestled with the dog, and the wind kept trying to blow it off her head. She held the dog with her stronger right arm and used her left to keep the pot in place as she worked her way down the steps.

The water seemed deeper in the Robertson's yard—about mid-calf, and when she reached the edge, she felt around with her bare foot before she stepped into the deeper water in the street. She waded through debris piles of wooden planks that the wind kept pushing into her legs. She kept her head down, feeling the jab of smaller objects hitting her body, but the heavy canvas protected her. She noticed one of the planks had lettering painted on it that said, *Swim at your own risk*. She groaned at the irony of it, and then realized with a shock that the debris must be from the bathhouses on the beach.

It took her twice as long to get back across the street struggling against the wind. She never was so happy to stub her toe again when she reached the edge of the yard and stepped up out of the river that used to be a street.

On the front gallery she shucked the dog, the pot, and the soiled coat in that order and hurried into the house with Trixie right on her heels. Storm or no storm, she decided she and the dog both would get a cold, soapy bath, using a small laundry tub.

Grace had to use one hand to hold onto the dog and the other hand to bathe her. Trixie didn't like that one bit and kept trying to climb out of the tub.

"You act like you've never had a bath, Miss Prissy."

Trixie snapped at her when she tried to soap her face.

"I just risked life and limb to rescue you, and that's the thanks I get?"

She settled for dousing her with soapy water, and declared that she was clean enough. She used several towels to dry her off before she was willing to let the dog loose in the rest of the house.

When she opened the door to the washroom, Trixie bolted out into the kitchen, sliding around the door to the dining room. She could hear her toenails tapping through the house.

"I probably won't see you for a while, little dog," she said smiling.

She turned around and started to strip her damp clothes from her body when she heard the frantic tapping of Trixie running again. Grace stepped back in the kitchen to see the wet ball of fur come tearing around the corner of the dining room into the kitchen. She stopped with her rear end up in the air when she saw Grace. Her mouth was open, her eyes daring Grace to move.

"You're not mad at me?"

Grace stepped forward and Trixie jumped up and ran around the table in the kitchen, slipping and sliding when she couldn't keep her feet under her. She stopped at the door, frozen in position, waiting for Grace to move again.

"You're playing with me, aren't you?"

Grace took the bait and the chase started. She ran after the dog through the dining room and into the parlor, and by the time Grace made it to the stairs, Trixie had already run into the library and under the desk and circled around to meet her in front of the stairwell. She flashed on by, taking the same route through the house, so Grace shot up the stairs to hide from her.

She hid behind an upholstered chair on the landing and waited. She could hear the tap, tap, tapping through the house as the dog came back from the kitchen, into the library again and back, stopping where Grace had been standing in front of the stairs. She heard her take off through the house again and then coming back to stop at the stairs.

Grace couldn't help but snicker, convinced she had her fooled.

But then she heard the tapping coming up the stairs, so she froze, hoping Trixie wouldn't see her.

The dog's nose led her right to her, and Grace screamed with delight. The dog jumped up on her, thrilled to have found her, and the chase began all over again. Grace even climbed on top of the big desk to hide, thinking Trixie wouldn't figure that out, but the little dog always found her.

Trixie's tongue was hanging out, and Grace's chest was heaving by the time she called it quits. She lay on the floor in the entrance hall laughing while the dog climbed all over her trying to lick her on the face.

"I don't need my face washed… on second thought, I do, but not by you."

Grace's laughter suddenly turned into wails.

Where are you, Finn? She looked questioningly at the ceiling. "Lord, why has this been so hard? All these obstacles… does this mean Finn and I aren't supposed to be together?"

She wept even harder at the thought of life without him.

Vestal's words whispered in the back of her mind, *Often it's the last key that unlocks the door.*

She rolled over and looked at the front door, expecting to see him standing there.

But he wasn't.

She wiped the tears from her eyes, and then stood up and headed back to the washroom to finish cleaning up.

Trixie shadowed her every step.

She reached down and stroked her head. "I'm so glad you're here with me." She whispered to herself. "Thank you, Lord."

Another gust shook the house, and Grace heard the wind and rain again. She realized that for a short while, the little dog made her forget about the storm raging outside… and that she may be riding it out on her own.

The tears came again. "I can't do this by myself, Father. I've never seen a storm like this before—it terrifies me. But I know that You're here with me—help me remember that."

Chapter 34

Through the lobby window, Finn saw a horse struggling to pull a buggy down the Strand. The water in the street was already over the axles and probably sloshing into the carriage. He pulled his damp hat low on his forehead and ran outside, staying close to the building. As soon as the driver was able to get to the north side of the street, somewhat protected from the gale blowing out of the northeast, Finn planned to step out to help the women unload.

Windows shattered in the upper floors of the buildings across the street; the wind carried shards like bullets. Finn saw how vulnerable the driver was sitting atop the front of the carriage. As it got closer, he was relieved to see that the man had some kind of metal pot on his head.

He shouted and waved him over to the closest building. It wasn't in front of Lucius' office building, but it would get them off the street sooner and let the driver get to safety. They would be protected by the south-facing buildings and overhangs.

"Are you Tom?" he shouted when the man pulled the buggy beside the boardwalk.

The man nodded and Finn breathed a sigh of relief. The driver looked almost as exhausted as the horse.

Finn leaned out into the deluge to reach for the door and open it, and placed one foot on the carriage frame, which was several inches under water. He grabbed Juju in a bear hug and lifted her over the water and onto the boardwalk.

"Am I glad to see you!" he said over the roar of the wind.

The woman looked shocked and then upset.

You're welcome, he thought to himself as he turned around and grabbed her daughter.

"I'm so sorry, Finn!" he heard her yell behind him.

She's apologizing now? He set Kitty beside her mother, who still stood there. "Go on!" he said, shooing them with his hand. "Get inside!"

"She didn't come!!"

He wiped the rain off his face and turned back to the carriage, reaching for Grace, but no one was at the door. He pulled himself inside and found the hack empty. His heart dropped in his chest.

He jumped back out and led the two women further under the overhang.

"Where's Grace?!"

"She wouldn't come!" yelled Kitty. "She didn't want to take the chance of missing you again!"

Finn closed his eyes, feeling sick to his stomach. "She's at the house by herself?"

Tom shouted at the horse, trying to get it to go forward in the flooded street.

"Wait!" Finn shouted, stepping to the edge of the boardwalk. "I have to go back."

Tom shook his head fiercely, almost dislodging the pot. "I've got to get home! I have family, too, and I don't think Sleepy's gonna make it!"

"Which way you heading?!"

"To the livery four blocks south to leave the rig, then I'll walk the rest of the way."

"Can I ride with you that far?"

Tom nodded, causing the pot to fall over his eyes.

Juju grabbed his arm. "Finn, it's too dangerous! You can't go back!"

Finn pushed them toward Lucius' building. "Get inside."

Kitty pointed to the carriage. "There's another pot in there! Cover your head!"

He nodded and waved them on as he climbed in the carriage. He could hear Tom shout and the carriage rocked with his movements, but the horse didn't take a step.

Finn forced the stew pot over his sopping felt hat and tied it with his kerchief like Tom had done. He climbed out of the hack, stepping into water up to his thighs, and waded to the front of the wild-eyed horse. The heaving chest was the only thing moving on the animal. He seemed frozen in place.

"Come on, Sleepy," he spoke loud, but calmly near the horse's ear. He patted the horse's quivering neck. "Not too much farther, old boy. We can do this together."

The horse's nostrils flared and he tried to throw his head back, but Finn kept a firm hold on the bit.

"Come on now."

He rubbed the horse's neck, noticing a nasty cut across his withers from flying debris.

"I know this is scary as hell, but Tom has a dry stall and hay waiting for you." He patted him again, wondering if he'd just spoken a lie. Was there a dry place left on the island?

The horse gave in and took a step, but then shied away from some floating wooden blocks that had paved the street only a few hours before. Finn pushed them away and pulled the horse forward.

Sleepy followed willingly this time.

"Good boy," he said, rewarding him with another rub on the neck. "Let's go home."

The horse started walking. As they passed in front of the law firm building, Finn noticed JuJu and Kitty watching him from the open door. Their expressions looked like they were viewing a funeral procession. Lucius stood rooted to the floor behind them.

Finn looked away, focusing on wading alongside the horse until they made the turn south onto 22nd Street. Then he patted the horse forward and waited until the carriage was beside him and jumped in.

He pulled off the pot and his wet, misshaped felt hat and leaned his head back to catch his breath.

Lord, keep her safe. Please let me get to her. Let me have the chance to tell her how much I love her and ask her forgiveness. She wouldn't be down here in this mess if it weren't for me. I know she's scared right now—give her courage, give her Your peace. Please let me reach her.

He shut his eyes, trying to calm himself and rest, knowing the difficulty ahead trying to get back to her. The water had risen over a foot during the time he'd been waiting for Grace at Lucius' office. An old-timer in the lobby called this storm a cyclone and said that they hadn't seen the worst of it yet. He said the wind was going to change directions after a while and blow even fiercer from the south. The wind sounded and felt ferocious right now.

Finn wondered if anything would be left standing on the island.

It took thirty minutes for the hack to travel four blocks through the flooded streets. But when Sleepy came to the ramp into the livery, which raised it higher than the street, the horse somehow found the energy to trot up it. The water hadn't made it inside at that point.

Finn followed Tom's lead and removed the awkward pot from his head before helping him unhitch the horse and roll the carriage to the side near several others.

Tom led Sleepy into a stall and latched the gate.

"Will the water get much higher?" asked Finn.

"I don't know, but this is looking as bad as I've seen it."

Finn looked around the large barn that held about a dozen horses. "What's going to happen to these horses if the storm gets any worse?"

"The Weathers will take care of them," said Tom, walking toward the door. "I've got to get home."

"You're abandoning them to the weather?" Finn followed him.

Tom said over his shoulder. "No! Duard and Martha Weathers live upstairs—they'll take care of 'em."

"Oh!" said Finn, relieved he had misunderstood. "Where do you live?"

"Denver Resurvey—west side of town. It's going to take a while for me to get there. Where you headed?"

"Seventeenth and Avenue L."

"We can walk south together for a few blocks."

"I'd appreciate the company."

Tom walked to a door facing south and stepped outside, protected from the northeast wind. He looked up at the debris carried by the wind. It sounded like hail hitting the buildings.

"After a bad fire some years back, the city required buildings to use slate tiles on the roof to try to keep fire from spreading. But now the slate's causing a different kind of danger." He placed the pot over his head and tied the kerchief securely under his chin again.

Finn followed suit. "We look like a couple of drunken idiots."

Tom looked at him. "But maybe this'll let us get home with our heads still attached to our shoulders."

Finn nodded. "You're right. Let's go."

They kept to the protected south-facing side of the building until they came to the intersection where they needed to turn and walk south. But they paused when a piece of slate suddenly sheered a finial off the top off a lamp post.

"Maybe we ought to wait until the wind dies down a bit," Tom yelled over the wind.

"You think that's going to happen?" asked Finn.

Tom looked around and swallowed hard. "No."

Finn took a deep breath and exhaled a prayer. "Please protect us, Lord. Help us get to our families."

Tom stared at him. "She's your family?"

"If we survive this, she's going to be."

Tom put out his calloused hand and said loudly, "Congratulations, Mr. Samuel. I thought for sure Mr. Roderick had his dibs on her."

"Not anymore," Finn said with conviction.

"I noticed he didn't make the effort to come for her, but you did."

"I think his priority was inside." Finn grabbed Tom's arm. "We're wasting time—let's go." They stepped down into the water and wind and started across the street.

Chapter 35

Grace spread the fifth quilt on the landing where she decided to ride out the storm. Most every room in the house had one or two exterior walls and windows. The wind driving the debris into the house sounded like a battle was taking place outside, and the cannons were winning. She heard a window shatter upstairs in one of the north bedrooms, but was too scared to check on it.

The front windows remained un-shuttered, still protected from the north wind. She stepped out on the gallery several times to check the water level, which continued to rise. The water was well up into the yard, almost level with the first step. The wind blew the rain horizontally, but she could still see debris flowing up the street opposite of the wind. That didn't seem right—the elements seemed to be fighting against each other.

The oval glass in the front door worried her, but she hoped the front gallery would shield it. The door and parlor windows provided what little light the storm hadn't completely snuffed out, but Grace also placed a lamp on the second step up from the landing.

She wrapped the top quilt around her and let Trixie burrow in beside her. She leaned back against several feather pillows and reached for the two books she grabbed to read during the storm—her Bible and *Adventures of Huckleberry Finn*, not necessarily because she wanted to read that one. She heard the book was banned from a number of libraries due to some parts were deemed too coarse for intelligent and respectable people. But that wasn't the reason she picked it up when she packed up Roderick's books. She brought it to the landing simply because the title included the name *Finn.*

She noticed the dog's eyes were closed by the time she opened the book and read a warning on one of the first pages:

Persons attempting to find a motive in this narrative will be prosecuted; persons attempting to find a moral in it will be banished; persons attempting to find a plot in it will be shot.

She laughed out loud, startling Trixie. Grace reached down and rubbed the scruffy head.

She wondered why there was such a fuss over the book if Twain himself had written such a warning to not read more into the story than there actually was. Then she wondered if Twain meant that was Huck Finn speaking the notice. She would read this book someday, but not today. She smiled as she set the book aside, running her finger over the title before she picked up her Bible.

She opened it where the satin ribbon marked chapter three in Proverbs. She knew verses five and six by heart: *Trust in the Lord with all thine heart and lean not unto thine own understanding. In all thy ways acknowledge him, and he will direct thy paths.*

"Lord," she said aloud, "I don't know what's happening right now. I'm terrified of this storm raging outside, but I know You can give me a peace in the midst of it, and I ask for it, Father. I don't know what's happening in my life right now either. I thought You made it clear that my path was to come to Galveston after Finn rejected me. Finding a job and a place to live and meeting some wonderful people in this amazing city seemed to confirm that. All of those things gave me hope that I just might be able to survive losing Finn. And then he showed up here just to run away from me again. But if he made the effort to follow me down here, I believe he truly loves me.

"I thought we would find each other by now, and I refuse to think he left the island without talking to me, but I'm not sure what's happened to him. I pray that wherever he is, that he's safe, Father. Please keep him safe. And please help me to be brave since I'm here by myself… well, I know You're with me so I'm not really alone. I just don't like storms... and high water... and this wind is so frightening. I've never heard wind like this before. Please let the house hold up against it.

"Thank you for letting me hear Trixie in the storm and that she's safe beside me. And please keep the Robertsons safe wherever they are... and Daisy and her family safe... and Marguerite and the Greshams... and Walter Grover and Rabbi Cohen and everyone else I've met safe... oh, and Juju and Kitty and... Lucius, of course... and Pearl. Lord, please help her get away from Postoffice Street and that lifestyle."

The windows rattled with a particularly strong gust, and Grace burrowed down into the pillows and pulled the quilt over her head and started quoting scripture.

"*God is my refuge and strength, a very present help in times of trouble.*" She said it over and over again because it was the only one she could think of at the moment. Mrs. Neagle always quoted it in church every Sunday when the preacher asked for folks' favorite verses. Another one finally came to mind, so she said that one aloud, too: "*Perfect love casts out fear.*"

She pulled the cover back and opened her Bible and thumbed through the Psalms, finally stopping at chapter 91. She stood and read it aloud, shouting it at the top of her lungs at the storm raging outside.

"*I who dwelleth in the shelter of the Most High shall abide in the shadow of the Almighty. I will say of the Lord, He is my refuge and my fortress, my God, in him will I trust. He shall cover me with his feathers and under his wings I will find refuge; his truth will be my shield and rampart. I will not fear the terror of the night!*"

She skipped down to verse fourteen and continued as if the verses were written specifically for her, "*'Because she loves me,' says the Lord, 'I will rescue her; I will protect her, for she acknowledges my name. She will call upon me, and I will answer her; I will be with her in trouble, I will deliver her and honor her. With long life will I satisfy her and show her my salvation.'* Thank you, Father. I believe Your words. And I know whether my body survives this day or not, my soul is in your hands."

Grace leaned over and placed the Bible on the step beside the lamp, crawled under the blanket, laid her head on the pillow, and shut her eyes. The weariness of the harrowing trip across town to find Finn that morning as well as the worry of the last several days faded to the edges of her mind. One of her last thoughts was the hope that the wind would be calm by the time she awoke.

So in the midst of the furious storm, Grace Taylor fell asleep.

Chapter 36

Finn stood with Tom on the south side steps of the Texas Heroes Monument in the middle of Broadway and 25th. The water was only knee deep in the street, but Finn noticed that Tom seemed more frightened by that than anything else he'd seen that day.

Finn watched him reach down and put his fingers in the water and lift it to his lips.

"Salty!" he shouted over the wind. He looked south and then back at Finn. "I've never seen this before!"

"Everything's so dark I can hardly see; what do you mean you've never seen this before?!"

"The bay and Gulf—they've come together! There isn't a square foot of dry land on the island now, even with this north wind pushing back the Gulf!" He looked back toward the Gulf. "God help us when the wind shifts to the south! Nothing will hold it back then."

Finn swallowed hard. He couldn't believe the storm could get any worse.

Tom leaned toward him. "You'd better get your lady to higher ground!"

Finn looked around at the dark, churning water that surrounded them. "And where is that exactly?"

"Go to the Greshams—their house is a fortress!"

"That's the house where Mrs. St. John is?"

Tom nodded and then offered his hand. "You take care! I've gotta get to my family now!"

Finn grasped it hard, hesitant to let it go. "The Gresham house is down this street, right?"

Tom nodded, gesturing east. "14th Street!"

He pulled away from his grasp, and Finn watched him splash across the street and out of sight.

Lord, help him, he said to himself as he stepped into the water and headed east on Broadway. After two blocks he turned south, staying to the east side of 23rd Street, holding onto the wrought iron fencing where he could to stay upright. He almost ran into a man doubled over walking north into the wind, also pulling himself along using the fence rails.

"Turn around!" the man yelled, holding a pair of leather boots tied together and draped over his head. "You can't go south! It's too dangerous—people are dying back there!"

"What?!"

"The houses are falling like cards—the waves are too strong. I saw debris drag two people under, and they drowned before my very eyes—I couldn't even help 'em!"

"I have to get to 17th and Avenue L!" Finn shouted.

"I'll go with you—I'm heading to Winnie." The man turned around and led the way to the corner and turned east.

Finn had no idea where Winnie was, but he was glad to keep company with someone who seemed to know his way around here.

"The pot's a good idea!" the man yelled over his shoulder.

"Juju gave it to me."

The man looked over his shoulder again. "You're going to Lucius Roderick's house?"

"Yeah, you know him?"

"He's there?"

"No, he's downtown; I'm trying to reach a friend!"

"That wouldn't be Grace, would it?"

"Yes! You know her?"

He nodded. "She's there by herself?"

Finn nodded. "She's waiting for me!"

"The house will probably flood! It may not even survive the storm!"

"I'm going to try to get us to the Gresham's on Broadway!"

"Good idea!"

They stopped at the next intersection, watching wreckage from houses pass by on a river of water.

"I'm Finn Samuel!"

"Walter Grover!"

They introduced each other without taking their eyes off the challenge before them.

"We have to cross it!" said Walter. "Wait until there's not so much debris to crush us."

"You don't have to come—why don't you head north where it's shallower! Here's a break coming up!" Finn stepped in the street and fell into water up to his neck. The cooking pot and what was left of his felt hat floated away as he floundered to get his footing.

Walter grabbed his wrist before Finn completely disappeared under the water. He pulled him a few yards away where the water was up to Finn's waist when he finally was able to stand. Walter stepped into the water beside him.

"The water's carved deep holes in some of the gutters! Don't fall," he shouted to Finn, "or you might not be able to get up!"

They held onto each other, pushing away floating planks and bits of people's lives as they crossed the street. They stepped up off the street level on the other side into more shallow water. They grabbed onto another iron fence to keep the wind from blowing them away as they caught their breath.

"Thanks…for… saving my hide!" said Finn, leaning close to Walter's ear.

Walter brushed it off like rescuing people was a common occurrence for him.

"We have to keep going!" shouted Walter. "We're in just as much danger from wind-driven debris, and your head's uncovered!"

Finn nodded, even though he felt like he couldn't take another step. He couldn't remember his muscles feeling so weak. The screaming wind refused to let up, causing the rain to pelt him like buckshot hitting the side of his face. The two men stumbled on, pulling themselves along the iron fence rails hand over hand as if traversing a horizontal ladder. Walter led the way, and Finn stumbled into him occasionally when the driving rain blinded him. The trees took on the appearance of ghostly apparitions, frantically waving their limbs in warning.

They crossed the next two debris-filled rivers that used to be streets before taking shelter on a south-facing front gallery of a large house. Finn laid flat on his back after crawling up the steps—sitting seemed to take too much effort at the moment. He shut his eyes for a moment, trying to remember how peaceful it was to sit on a gallery at the end of the day, but the groaning and trembling of the gallery on which he'd taken refuge pushed the calming memories away. He opened his eyes, trying to find anything familiar to latch onto in this nightmare. He stared at the knot holes that had bled through the white wash on the porch ceiling and noticed an abandoned web in the corner. Even the spider knew when to get out of the storm.

Walter knocked on the door. No one answered.

"Hopefully they're in a safer place." He sat down in a chair in the corner of the gallery. "We can't stay long," said Walter. "The water's rising every minute."

"Aren't you tired?"

"I walk miles every day."

"I work with my hands, but I ride more than I walk."

"It's only a few more blocks for you, but I have a good mile yet to go."

Finn sat up and pulled off his boots to empty the water from them. "I can't believe how hot it was yesterday, and today I can't stop shaking—the rain feels like ice!"

"That water's nasty, too. No telling how many privies it's turned over."

"Grace may not let me in the house. You want to come to the Gresham's with us?"

He shook his head. "I'm sure my family's worried about me."

"What are you doing out in the storm anyway?"

"I wanted to see it."

Finn stared at him. "You risked your life just to see the storm?"

"I've seen lots of storms... I didn't know it was going to be this bad. I'm not sure I'll make it home in this one, though."

"What if we can't get to the Gresham's? I don't know if Grace will have the strength to do what we've been doing."

"If you can't leave, cut several holes in the floor to let the water in to settle the house. Otherwise it may float off the foundation!"

"You think it'll get that high?"

Walter looked around and nodded. "When the wind shifts."

"Tom said it's really going to get bad then."

"That's exactly what I've been thinking. The water's halfway up these steps, and the north wind's been holding the Gulf back. A south wind will push it over this island when the back side of this storm hits."

Finn pulled his boots back on. "Tom said the bay and Gulf have already met."

"That's why the wreckage is going south on some of these roads—the wind and the bay are sweeping back towards the Gulf. It's going to all come back when the wind shifts, though. Let's get going—we may not have much time. Three more blocks, and you're there."

"Why don't you go ahead and turn north at the next corner? The water wasn't nearly this high on Broadway."

Walter smiled wearily. "That's mighty kind of you, Finn, but it'd be safer for both of us to travel together as far as we can."

Finn breathed a sigh of relief, knowing his chances of reaching Grace just rose considerably. He noticed Walter seemed almost calm. "Aren't you afraid?" he couldn't help but ask.

"I'd be stupid not to be, but I can't lose my wits about me either." He looked around the porch and grabbed a seat cushion that had blown into the corner and handed it Finn.

"Shield your head with it. I saw a piece of slate take off the top of a man's head not twenty feet from me a little while ago." Walter draped his leather boots over his head again. "That's when I put my waders on my head. You could do the same."

"I'll take my chances with the pillow," Finn replied, noticing the cuts on Walter's feet. He looked around the porch and then reached for the door. It was unlocked so he stepped inside and found a braided rope with gold tassels on the ends from a window drape. He came back outside and folded the limp cushion over his head and tied it tightly under his chin with the rope.

"Lovely," Walter said wryly.

Finn couldn't help but snicker. It felt odd to share humor in the midst of a dangerous situation, but it also gave him courage.

"Let's go get Grace."

Chapter 37

A loud crash startled Grace awake. She lay there trying to hang onto the remnants of a peaceful dream when she realized where she was. The constant roar told her the storm still raged.

The lamp cast a warm light on the landing where she sought refuge, but the rest of the shuttered house was dark. She leaned over and peeked down the stairs and could still see gray light through the oval window of the front door. Grace knew she needed to check the house and the water level outside, but was afraid to leave her cocoon, afraid of what she would see outside.

The house shuddered and creaked at the constant barrage of the wind. She yelled and jumped involuntarily when something moved under the quilt. A fuzzy head appeared, yawning widely, and Grace laughed as she remembered she had a pallet mate.

"Trixie! You scared the daylights out of me!" She picked up the dog and held her close.

"Let's go see what's going on out there," she said, feeling much braver with the dog around.

She set Trixie down and stood to walk gingerly down the stairs toward the front door. She peeked through the oval glass to see outside. The rain looked like it was blowing sideways, but it wasn't that heavy. She could still see the Robertson's roofline.

Grace took a deep breath and unlocked the door and opened it, stepping onto the gallery. It looked like the neighborhood sat in the middle of a river. The water lapped against the second step, but the current in the street was still running strong. The iron fence acted like a sieve preventing debris from entering the yard. A number of tree limbs lay in the water in the yard.

Grace saw part of a roof floating south down 17th Street—the opposite direction from earlier.

"I think the water's receding, Trixie!" she said. "The water's flowing back to the Gulf! Thank you, Lord! Now could You please do something about this wind? It's going to flatten everything on the island if it doesn't let up."

She stood there a moment longer, half-expecting Jesus to calm the winds right then and there, but it seemed to blow even stronger.

"We'd better get back inside," she said to Trixie, locking the door behind them. "Are you hungry? I'm famished. Let's see what Juju left for us."

Grace walked through the house into the dining room and lit another lamp in the dining room. She heard something bumping on the back porch, but was hesitant to open the door to see what it was, afraid that she might not be able to shut it with the wind blowing against it. She opened the door into the kitchen and saw that a large tree limb had fallen into the north window, breaking the glass. But it had wedged against the shutters, so very little rain had come through. The counter top was wet, though, so Grace moved what she could to the higher shelves above it.

Something bellowed loudly on the back gallery.

Grace went to the kitchen door that also led to the porch and chanced opening it. The door almost struck her head as it flew open, and she let it go. But there on the other side of the screen was the face of a cow… a Holstein milk cow.

"How in the world did you get up here?"

Grace tried to push open the screen door, but the cow wouldn't budge. She latched it back and struggled to close the wooden door, and finally got it shut and locked. She ran around to the door in the dining room, unlocked it and stood to the side before she turned the knob. The wind blew it open and it slammed against the wall, and the rain blew in this time, but it wasn't heavy.

Grace found she could push the screen door open against the wind and she reached out and touched the side of the cow. As if on cue, the cow turned and almost ran over her getting into the house. Grace tried to pull the screen door shut, but it slipped out of her grasp and the wind slammed it against the wall. She stepped onto the porch to grab it and noticed the water seemed deeper in the backyard. She held the screen door firmly and pulled it around to where the wind helped shut it, so she was able to latch it. But it took every bit of strength she had to close the wood door against the wind. After she closed and locked it, she dragged and pushed the heavy buffet across the room against the door, hoping that would be enough to keep it shut.

She turned around and noticed the cow had disappeared, but she could hear Trixie barking in the front of the house. She found the cow had walked into the library on the farthest side of the house away from the wind.

"How rude, Trixie," she told the little dog. "You were in the same situation not too long ago! We can't let her stay out there in this storm—it's still too dangerous. I know Roderick is going to be angry at me for doing this, but we'll put the house back in order before he comes home. Come on, let's find some food and put the coffee on—I'm feeling chilled with these damp clothes."

She pulled the pocket doors shut to keep the cow penned in one place, then headed to the kitchen again. The little dog followed her and watched Grace load the potbelly stove with kindling stacked in a bucket beside it to get a fire started. Roderick had a modern gas cooking stove, but Grace was afraid to use it during the storm. She was thankful the stovepipe was on the west wall away from the wind.

After the wood started burning good, Grace closed the cast iron door. She filled the coffee pot with water from one of the containers Juju filled before she left, and set it on the old stove. She rummaged around the ice box and found a small pot of soup from the day before and biscuits and crackers in a tin.

"We're going to have a feast," she said to the little dog as she set the soup pot on top of the stove.

She stood there stirring the soup, savoring the smell and soaking up warmth of the stove when something started banging in the front of the house.

"If that darn cow broke any of Roderick's bookcases…"

Grace set the soup pan to the side and ran out of the kitchen through the dining room and parlor. She stopped when she noticed the room seemed darker and realized the front windows were shuttered. A few minutes ago they were the only windows in the house that weren't covered.

A silhouette stood in front of the door, and the door knob shook and rattled.

Trixie started barking, and Grace couldn't help but scream.

"Grace!"

She heard her name called.

"Finn?!"

"Grace, open up!"

Finn's frame filled the oval pane.

She ran to the door and jerked on the knob.

The door didn't budge.

She stared at his rugged face as she kept yanking on the knob. His hair stuck straight out, it looked like he hadn't shaved in a week, and his shirt was a mess, but Grace thought he'd never looked more handsome than at that moment.

"It's locked!" he said, almost smiling.

Grace looked down at the ornate key sitting in the keyhole, and remembered Vestal's words… *often it's the last key that unlocks the door.*

She stopped struggling and looked up at him. "Are you going to run away again?"

"What?!"

She repeated the question louder. "Are you going to leave me again?!"

"Never!" he shouted. "Now let me in!"

She turned the key in the lock, and Finn almost knocked her down opening the door. He grabbed her and pulled her to himself and kissed her hard on the lips.

"I'm so sorry for ever leaving you," he said, kissing her cheeks, her hair, and back to her mouth.

"Twice," she managed to say before he took her breath away again.

He kicked the door shut. "Forgive me twice, then, no—I need a lot more forgiveness than that. I've been a stubborn, stupid fool all these years…"

"Your teeth are chattering," Grace noticed, interrupting his apology. "You're freezing! Come on," she said, pulling him through the house toward the kitchen. "Hush, Trixie!"

"You already have a dog? I'm trying to apologize."

"She's not mine, and apology accepted. Now where have you been all this time? I've been worried sick, thinking the worst had happened to you."

"I've been on the streets for hours trying to reach you."

"You could've been killed!"

"But I wasn't."

In the kitchen she pulled a chair close to the stove and made him sit down. She reached for a cup and poured him some coffee.

"Careful, the cup's hot."

He grabbed it without hesitation and held it close to his face, breathing in the warm steam. "It feels good to me."

She knelt down and pulled off his wet boots and socks and set them aside.

"Take off those wet clothes," she insisted. "And there's soap and water in the washroom.

"I don't have anything to change into."

"Lucius should have something upstairs you could wear," she said, hurrying out of the kitchen. Then she ran back and kissed him full on the mouth.

With tears in her eyes, she said, "I love you, Finn Samuel. I've always loved you. I hoped you'd come for me, but then that became my worst fear. I thought I'd lost you again."

She didn't wait for his response, turning around and running through the house and upstairs, thanking the Lord every step of the way for protecting Finn during the storm.

Another tree limb crashed into the house, but Grace barely noticed it as she rummaged through Lucius' chiffarobe. Grace found some dungarees and a white cotton shirt. In a drawer she found a soft cotton undershirt and thick socks, which she pressed to her face to wipe the tears streaming down her cheeks.

Finn had come for her.

Chapter 38

Grace found Finn shirtless leaning over the front of the potbelly stove, eating soup right out of the pot. Trixie waited expectantly at his feet.

"Sorry," he said apologetically, "but I haven't eaten much since I got to town."

"Eat all you want," she said, smiling.

He dropped a piece of biscuit for the dog; she caught it mid-air.

"I wouldn't have thought Roderick was the little dog type."

"He's not. Trixie belongs to the neighbors across the street; they're waiting out the storm downtown and weren't able to get back to her. She's been good company for me."

Grace put the clothes on the table and held up the undershirt. "You do have to put the biscuit and the spoon down, though, so we can get some dry clothes on you."

She noticed cuts on his shoulder and left hand and insisted on doctoring them before he donned the clothes.

Lucius' shirt was too small in the shoulders, so he just wore the undershirt. He stepped into the wash room to change his pants.

After a moment he spoke loudly through the door. "I can't get the three top buttons buttoned—do you have some string I could use?"

Grace looked around the kitchen and found a small burlap bag with the open end cinched with twine. She pulled it out and handed it to him through the door. In a moment, he stepped into the kitchen.

"Listen!" Grace said. "The wind sounds like it's letting up a bit."

Finn paused for a moment and then shook his head. "The wind's shifting, and it's going to get worse than ever. We don't have much time. Do you know where a hammer and nails are around here? I need to cover the glass in that front door."

Grace found a tin bucket of nails and a hammer in the pantry shelves in the washroom. Finn grabbed the hammer and a dinner knife and used them to pry up the pins from the washroom door hinges.

"What are you doing?"

"I'm going to nail this across the front door." He dropped the hammer and knife in the can and pushed the door off the hinges. "Bring the can and follow me."

He carried the wood door through the house and leaned it against the wall next to the front door. "Where's another interior door from a room that doesn't have windows?"

"Upstairs… we put a bunch of stuff in a storage closet."

Finn took the stairs two at a time.

"Watch the lamp by the landing," she said as she started up after him.

Finn picked it up on the way. "Come hold it for me so I can see what I'm doing."

Grace followed him and pointed towards the closet door.

Finn had it off the hinges in less than a minute, handed her the tools and picked up the door.

"Lead the way."

Downstairs Grace held the hammer and can while Finn carried the doors out on the gallery. He unlatched the shutters on the nearest window and told her to go open it and then to come back outside and help him hold the doors in place so he could nail them.

Grace looked at the water in the yard—it was almost halfway up the steps to the gallery now, and she knew the porch was at least six feet off the ground. The street level was almost two feet lower than the yard, so the water in the street was five feet deep. Across the street it was almost to the neighbors' front porch. She trembled at the thought of it rising even higher, but she could feel the wind blowing from the east now and that meant it would push even more of the Gulf over the island.

The interior doors were narrower than the front door, so Finn angled them so they would reach across both sides. The top door left an exposed corner of the transom window, so Grace brought a small cushion to wedge into the gap.

Finn told her to climb back into the house through the window, and then he nailed three of the four window shutters down, leaving the fourth to crawl through, and then tied it as best he could from the inside before closing the window.

"Let's hope that keeps the storm out." He turned to face her. "Do you know where an ax is?"

"I think there's one in the washroom—that seems to be a catch-all for Juju. What do you need an ax for?"

"Walter said if the water gets high enough, we'll need to cut holes in the floor to let the water in to settle the house; otherwise, it may float off the foundation piers."

"Walter?"

"Walter Glover or Gloves or—"

"Grover? You know Walter Grover?"

"Met him on the street; I couldn't get him to stay. He said to give you his regards, but he had to get home. I wanted to take you to the Greshams' house, but I barely made it here myself."

Grace jumped at the sound of objects hitting the east side of the house. The wind began to howl again. Finn grabbed her and pulled her toward the center of the house.

"It's started again; bring some food and water to the landing—it could be a long night."

Grace was in the kitchen when she heard him holler. She ran through the house to find him standing in front of the closed pocket doors. She forgot to tell him about the…

"Did you know there's a…" he began, "of course you know there's a milk cow in the library; so I guess the question is: why?"

"She was on the back porch, and I was afraid she would get hurt out in that terrible wind."

"Roderick's going to love that." Finn seemed entirely too pleased about that.

"I'm going to clean up after her," Grace said defensively.

"Are there any other surprises I should know about in this house?"

Grace shook her head, trying to grasp the truth that Finn was actually standing there before her—she wasn't asleep. This was real.

His face softened as he looked at her. He walked over and put his arms around her.

"Are you really here?" she whispered into his neck.

"I am."

"You're squashing the biscuits."

"I happen to like squashed biscuits."

"There's so much I want to say to you."

"And I have a lot of explaining to do, but we have all night." His lips found hers again, and for a moment, the storm was ignored.

He finally pulled away, telling Grace they needed to get on the landing; he said he would fetch the ax.

She made several trips to and from the kitchen and set their provisions on the steps. She gathered the lamps from around the house, leaving only one lit on the stairwell. Finn removed the chair from the landing and replaced it with the table from the kitchen.

"In case the roof falls in on us," he explained. "If the house starts to go, we'll have to get outside somehow, though."

He held out his hand for her, and they crawled under the table. Trixie burrowed under the quilt next to Grace as she unlaced her shoes.

"I'm so glad you're here," she said.

"The dog or me?" Finn teased.

"Well, if you hadn't cleaned up, I would've said Trixie," she teased him, watching his face. She loved that face—strong, rough around the edges—not smooth and perfectly handsome like Lucius. She reached out and touched his face.

"What's this?" she ran her fingers through the bristles.

"I didn't pack a razor. I started to borrow one a couple of days ago, but I changed my mind. I must look like a bear."

She leaned over and kissed him. "You look wonderful."

"Now you're shaking," he said, pulling her close. "Are you cold?"

She shook her head as she laid her head against his chest. "What if I'd lost you out there?"

"You didn't."

"What if the house falls?"

"We'll deal with that if it happens. Have you been praying about it?"

Grace nodded her head.

The house shuddered with a particularly strong gust.

She wrapped her arms around his midriff.

"Then let's trust God in this." He kissed the top of her head. "I think this is as good a time as any for me to tell you why I ran away from you back in Waco."

"I know why."

Finn leaned back and looked at her face. "You know? Since when?"

"Since Pearl told me this morning."

"You talked to Pearl?"

"I was trying to find you. I went to the train station first—I thought you might be leaving town again."

"I came looking for you, too, but I found Juju and Kitty here. They told me you might be at the Greshams' or at Daisy's, but I couldn't even get to her apartment, the water was so deep on that end of town. After that I went to Roderick's office to return the train ticket and ask—"

"He bought you the train ticket?!"

Finn nodded. "He wanted me out of the way."

"Why, that buzzard."

"I might've done the same thing if the situation was reversed."

"He knew how I felt about you."

"Well, he's in a much better position to take care of you."

"I can take care of myself—why did you think I wouldn't understand about what happened with your brother? We can work through that."

"I know that now, and it wasn't a matter of you not understanding… I guess it was because of my pride. I was ashamed to face you—I wanted better for you than that."

"You oaf… I just wanted you." She reached up and pulled his face down to meet hers.

After a moment, Finn asked, "What did you think of Pearl?"

"She's beautiful and gracious, but I sensed a sadness about her, too. I was so nervous to be there—thinking about what went on in that place…"

"And you know about that?"

"Not really, other than I know they do things that only married people are supposed to do with each other."

Finn chuckled. "That's a good way to put it."

"But she knew how uncomfortable I was and put me at ease."

"I hope you know nothing happened—"

"Pearl told me that, too. And she told me that the reason you showed up there was that you thought they were a laundry and bath business."

Finn's face flushed. "That was an awkward moment, but it ended up being a blessing."

"Staying at a brothel?"

"They let me earn my keep." Finn was quiet for a moment. "I hadn't thought about it before, but I think my mother…"

"France?"

He shook his head. "Before Momma—France… I think my… first mother might've done this… too."

"What do you mean?"

He seemed uncomfortable.

Grace spoke gently. "Your mother was a prostitute?"

He frowned. "That sounds awful to hear it spoken out loud. I don't remember too much about her, but I don't think she started off that way. I certainly didn't realize what was going on at the time—I was too young, but I do remember different men coming to the house quite often. She didn't know the Lord; she didn't know He could help her get out of that situation. I'm sure she was just trying to keep us fed, and she wasn't always able to do that."

"I'm so sorry, Finn."

"My mother got sick, though, and some people from the church came and got us. I think they tried to help her get well, but it was too late. Then we were sent to the Samuels, and that was the best thing that has ever happened to us."

"I know you have ten brothers and sisters in the Samuel family, but I didn't know there were any birth siblings of yours."

"Zane and Jenna—one older, one younger."

"I can't believe I haven't learned that about you before now."

"I don't think about it much—I don't have too many memories of the years before the Samuels, and the ones I do have aren't good ones. I know what it's like to go without, and I don't want you to resent me later if it takes a while for me to get back on my feet."

"I wouldn't."

"How do you know that, Grace? I don't say this to be mean, but you've never been without. I ended up staying at the brothel because they let me do odd jobs in exchange for a place to sleep. I didn't have the money to stay anywhere else—I just have enough money to get us home."

"I still have some money, Finn. You can use that."

He shook his head. "If Roderick doesn't mind you staying here a few more days, I should be able to pick up some money helping folks clean up and do some repairs after this storm."

"You and your pride. From this point on what's mine is yours and what's yours is mine. Oh, wait. We have to be married to say that. Are you ever going to ask me to marry you?"

"Didn't I ask you that already?"

"No, and I'm sure I would've remembered."

"You want me to get on my knee?"

"No. I just want you to ask me."

"Lean over in the light so I can see your face."

Grace complied.

"Did you know your cheek is blue and green and yellow?"

She poked him. "How'd you find out about that?"

"Pearl." He leaned over and kissed her cheek. "I can't stand the thought that someone hit you, and I wasn't there to protect you. Please don't ever put yourself in that kind of situation again."

"All right, now weren't you going to ask me something?"

"Have I told you how beautiful you are?"

"No, but thank you."

"I haven't?"

"No, now get on with it."

"Grace Taylor, would you do me the honor of becoming my wife?" he said quickly.

Grace shut her eyes.

"What are you doing?"

"I'm burning into my memory this moment I've been waiting for… for so long."

"Well?"

Grace opened her eyes. "Yes, Finn… finally, my love… yes."

Chapter 39

Finn pulled back from kissing his fiancée.

"What's the matter?" asked Grace.

"We'd better slow down or I'm going to start acting like we're married already. Did you know I never got your letter?"

"I gave it to Sadie—she promised she'd give it to you."

"She accidentally set a damp stew pot on it and it stuck to the bottom. She kept smelling something burning on the stove and finally discovered the charred remnants of your letter."

"Then how'd you know to meet me?"

"You made her promise to get the letter to me on time because we were supposed to meet at the train station at one o'clock—that's all she knew to tell me. And then Sissy shocked me when she congratulated me on our pending marriage. I was still reeling from my brother's bad news, and I just couldn't face you."

"I never should have pulled that stunt."

"Well, when I finally woke up to the fact that I'd probably lost you for good, I caught the next train to Dalton. I had no idea you'd gone to Galveston."

"Sissy knew."

"I didn't tell anybody except my boss, and I left word for my brother that I was going after you, so he thinks I'm in Dalton, too. And I beat your letter to your parents' house, and your father was about ready to shoot me himself not knowing what had happened to you."

Grace giggled. "That's my daddy."

"After your letter came, he calmed down and eventually agreed when I asked for your hand in marriage."

"You had the courage to ask him that?"

"He wants me to bring you home; he wants us to eventually take over the ranching operations."

"Would you want to do that?" she asked hopefully.

"I wouldn't be in my right mind if I said no—that sounds like a dream come true, but I can't go to your family's place empty-handed. Your parents don't know about my financial woes, and I'm ashamed for them to find out I have nothing to offer you."

"I told you, Finn—"

He put his fingers on her lips. "I love you for that, Grace, but this is something I have to do for me just as much as for you. I have to earn the right to be there. I don't want your father to think I'm taking advantage of you or them."

Grace felt tears stinging her eyes. "Does this mean we have to wait until your darn pride is satisfied before we get married?"

"No, honey," he said, pulling her close again. "I'll marry you tomorrow if you can find a preacher."

"You will?"

"I will."

The cow bellowed from the library. Grace jumped.

"I forgot she was in there, poor thing."

"She probably needs milking. Do you know how to milk a cow?"

"I used to."

Something massive hit the front of the house hard enough to jolt them. Grace yelled in fright as Finn pushed her aside and climbed out from underneath the table and ran down the stairs.

"What is it, Finn!?"

"I think that was a wave! Bring the lamp!"

He grabbed the ax and started chopping through the floor at the side of the stairs. Grace carried the lamp down to the third step and held it over the stair rail where he was working.

The wind screamed continuously.

"Oh, dear Lord, it's seeping under the door! The water's up on the porch!"

"I should've already done this!" he said, finally breaking through the wood floor.

The dark water gurgled up through the hole. He swung the ax several more times to make it larger, and then ran to the dining room, yelling for Grace to follow with the lamp.

She quickly pulled off her stockings and pulled up her skirt and stepped into the cold water. Finn shoved the dining table aside and started hacking away at the floor.

She watched the dark water spreading across the floor like a malevolent shadow. It took every bit of willpower for her to keep from running back up the stairs.

"What can I do?!" she shouted, feeling completely helpless.

"Just what you're doing!" He finished that hole and hurried to the kitchen.

She followed him and held the lamp as he hewed another hole in the floor where the kitchen table normally sat.

By the time they came back to the stairs, the water was above Grace's ankles and still pouring in through the holes in the floor.

"It's seeping around the window sill. How high do you think it'll get?" she asked, trying to keep from panicking.

"I don't know—that ocean is pretty big out there."

"What if it fills up the house?" Grace started crying. "Dear Lord, please help us!"

Finn grabbed her arm and pulled her up the stairs. "We're all right—the water just has to reach the same level as outside. We can watch it from here, and we can keep going up the steps if we need to."

"Do you think the house will float away?"

"I noticed it has a heavy cistern on one side, and big trees around it might help anchor it. And I counted three brick fireplaces that ought to help hold it in place. And the foundation piers are brick…"

A loud crash on the east side of the house interrupted him. The house shuddered. Finn took the lamp and crept down the stairs and peeked around the corner.

"What is it, Finn?"

"I can see a cloud of soot—I think the chimney fell, but the fireplace is still standing—that's a good thing—the foundation's still intact."

Grace could see that the water was even with the first step. She leaned over to see where Finn had cut through the floor, and a visible mound told her the water was still pouring in.

The cow bellowed again.

Finn turned around. "How 'bout some warm milk? I could get a bucket and—"

"Don't you dare leave me! Get back up here with that lamp!"

The wind was screaming so loud, Grace wrapped a pillow around her head to quell the relentless fury. Finn set the lamp on the step and crawled under the table. He pulled a quilt over them and pulled her close.

Something wet dripped on her face. Grace reached up and touched the bottom of the table.

"It's from me," he said loudly. "The roof started leaking, but not right over us. I felt it about halfway down the stairs. If the plaster falls, the table will protect us."

Grace burrowed her head into Finn's neck. "Just hold me! If the house goes, please don't let me go."

"I won't!"

Grace drew comfort in the feel of his body entwined around hers, even though the storm's fury threatened to take their sanity as well as their very lives. She didn't know how much time had passed before chunks of plaster from the wet ceiling began to fall from the ceiling. She tried to be brave, but the storm's relentless battering wore her down. She couldn't help but cry again.

Finn remained stoic.

After a while, he sat up and said, "Maybe I should check the water level!"

Grace shook her head and pulled him back to her. "Please don't let me go! That'll be the moment the house falls, and I'll never see you again."

He wrapped his arms around her and held her tight.

"I'm sorry I'm such a coward!" she said close to his ear.

Finn laughed out loud.

Grace thought he must have gone mad.

"You, a coward?!" he shouted over the wind. "I seem to recall a fourteen-year-old girl jumping out of the hayloft twenty feet above the ground. I don't know any man who would've done that, much less a young girl. And here you came down to Galveston by yourself to start a new life with no guarantee of employment or a place to stay. No, Grace, you're one of the bravest people I've ever met!"

"I wasn't brave! I was just running away trying to avoid the humiliation of facing you—both times!"

"And you could run like a rabbit! I don't know if I could've caught you that day if you hadn't fallen and hurt your foot!"

"Did you know I fell in love with you that day?" she said. The tears continued to stream down her face, but it wasn't from fear now.

"I think it was just infatuation!"

Grace shook her head. "I've loved you ever since then!"

"You should've given up on me years ago!"

The house trembled violently before something crashed at the front of the house.

She shook her head again. "No! But I'm afraid we're going to miss our chance to be together!"

"No, we won't!" he shouted over the roar outside. "I Finn Samuel, take thee, Grace Taylor, to be my lawfully wedded wife from this moment forward 'til death us do part, as God is our witness!"

"Short, and to the point!" Grace said, laughing through her tears. "I, Grace Taylor, take thee, Finn Samuel, to be my lawfully wedded husband from this moment forward 'til death us do part, and I ask God to bless this union in Jesus' name!"

"And now I pronounce us husband and wife! Kiss me, Mrs. Samuel!"

Water dripping from the ceiling doused the lamp's flame, plunging the house into darkness.

"The matches are around here somewhere!" screamed Grace, feeling around the collection of lamps sitting in the corner of the landing.

She felt Finn's strong hands pulling her back to him.

"If these are our last moments together in this life, we won't need a light…" he shouted just before his lips found hers.

Chapter 40

Grace opened her eyes, blinking the mist away. She sat up and hit her head on the bottom of the table.

"Ow!" She slouched down, rubbing her head, forgetting she had slept under a table.

Something stirred beside her. A cold nose nudged her left hand.

"Trixie?"

She rubbed the furry head, earning some enthusiastic licks in the process.

Downstairs was still dark … and quiet! She couldn't hear the scream of the wind anymore.

"Oh, dear Lord, we're still alive. Thank You, Jesus, for protecting us!" she whispered quietly.

The air felt damp and thick, and her nose crinkled at a foul-smelling odor. She could hear Finn sleeping soundly beside her, lying protectively between her and the stairs going up and down. She scooted to the end of the table and carefully crawled over his legs to stand on the going down steps.

She stretched and leaned her head back and could see light from the hall above. She climbed over the rail to reach the other steps and tip-toed upstairs to see where the light was coming from.

Wood slats were exposed in the ceiling in a number of places where the plaster had fallen. She stepped gingerly over the damp clumps and opened the door to her bedroom. The screen door to the balcony stood open, and the tall window behind it was shattered. Most everything in the room was soaked. Juju had stripped the bedding and pulled the mattress against the interior wall away from the windows. It was damp, but possibly salvageable.

Grace walked out of the bedroom to get to the gallery outside from the hall door. It took several firm jerks on the door to get it open, and she gasped at the sight in front of her. The railing was gone, so the view was unobstructed of a large house tipped over in the road directly in front of her. She stepped gingerly onto the gallery and could see debris piled everywhere. Water still stood in the yard, but it was shallow, and everything that was exposed was covered in a dark mud.

She covered her nose when she got another whiff of that awful smell and stepped back inside to check the remaining rooms upstairs. She could see the sky in the southeast corner of Lucius' bedroom, but the other rooms, although wet, were structurally intact. She went from window to window opening them and the shutters. She found only three that had broken panes, and some of them were jammed; she would need Finn's help to open them. She was relieved to find the closet where they had stored much of Lucius' belongings was relatively dry. The rugs rolled up in the middle of the hall floor felt damp, though, so she thought she'd better get them rolled out and drying soon so they wouldn't mildew.

She noticed the tree limbs outside the windows, which were full of leaves and branches the day before, were now stripped bare. She hoped everyone survived the harrowing storm.

She stepped back into the hall and a burst of joy shot through her chest at the thought that Finn was sleeping not twenty feet from her. They were alive, and they were married! They didn't have a legal certificate that said so, but she felt married in every other way. Aren't the vows before God the most important part of the process?

A little nag of doubt tugged at the back of her mind. She grabbed a broom from the closet and had a talk with her Maker as she swept up the glass in the bedroom.

Lord, forgive my lack of faith last night when I thought we were going to die. I don't know if Momma and Daddy are going to understand why we didn't wait to get married in Dalton. I don't know if I can explain adequately enough to anyone how terrifying last night was. Please help us find someone who can make this legal, too, as soon as we can.

Her sweeping took on a new vigor—surely it wouldn't take too long to clean the house and put everything back in place, she thought. Then she was determined to find a preacher with a marriage certificate.

Strong hands slipped around her waist and she yelped in surprise. Finn buried his head in her thick curls, and she leaned her head against his. It felt so good to be in his arms.

"Good morning, Mrs. Samuel."

"Good morning, Mr. Samuel," she said, smiling.

"We made it, didn't we."

"Yes, thank the Lord."

He turned her in his arms and kissed her good morning.

Grace pulled back, trying to catch her breath. "We have lots to do today before we can leave."

"What's the big hurry?" he tried to kiss her again.

"The house needs to be cleaned top to bottom, and the roof and some windows and the front gallery railing needs to be repaired, and we need to find a preacher and—"

"Whoa, whoa—a preacher?"

"I know we said our vows last night, but my parents won't accept it if we don't have a legal certificate. In fact, I'm pretty sure my dad will hurt you."

Finn threw his head back and laughed.

Grace frowned at him.

The grin left his face when he looked back at her. "Oh, you were serious?"

She nodded.

He looked around. "Then what can I do?"

"Some of the windows are jammed, and we need to air everything out and get as much of it in the sun as possible."

He kissed her quickly and hurried over to the first jammed window beside the gallery door.

"Watch for broken glass," she warned him as she continued to sweep up the fallen plaster.

He stopped in front of the open gallery door. "There's a tilted house in the middle of the street!" He stepped outside to get a better look.

"Dear, Lord," he said, "it's wedged in a sea of debris!" He looked down the road to the right and then to his left. "This looks bad, Grace. It goes on for as far as I can see! How many hundreds of houses were splintered to create this amount of wreckage? I've never seen anything like this."

Grace stepped out on the gallery beside him and grasped his hand. "Those poor people. I hope they weren't in their homes when they broke up."

Finn turned around and led her back inside. "We have a lot more work than I realized."

"I know," said Grace. "Help me drag these rugs where they can get some sun. I think it's too muddy outside to find a place to hang them out there. You can hardly see the iron fence for the debris caught in it."

They heard the cow bellow downstairs.

"I forgot about her! We need to get her outside."

"She needs to be milked first—I'll take care of that, and then I'll put her in the yard." Finn started down the stairs.

"Can you take Trixie, too? No, wait, I'll take her outside while you milk the cow since she's probably about to burst. Poor girl."

"Trixie or the cow?"

"Both!"

Grace picked up the dog and Finn picked up the table on the landing and took it downstairs.

"Ugh!" he said when he reached the bottom step. "Watch your step—there's mud everywhere."

Grace picked up her skirt with her free hand and shivered in disgust when she stepped into several inches of cold, slimy ooze coating the floor. Trixie started barking.

"So this is where that smell is coming from! It's horrible! Hush, Trixie!"

"Get back on the steps, Grace—I saw something move on the

floor. We need some light in here."

Finn set the table down and ran up to get one of the lamps on the landing. He lit it and brought it downstairs, tracking mud on every step.

Trixie continued to growl, so Grace backed up several more steps. "What is it, girl?"

Finn held up the light and stepped into the parlor. The cow bellowed again.

"I know, Miss Clara!" he said.

"Who's Miss Clara?"

"Our old milk cow in Brownwood. Seems like I had to milk her for years before I got to pass the chore down to someone else in the family.

"Is that when you started working for the Murrays?"

"Yeah. How did you know that?"

He set the lamp on the fireplace mantel and opened one of the east windows. The light flooded the room.

"My cousin Maggie was an authority on the life of Finn Samuel. Ugh! Lucius' beautiful wood floors are buried under this muck. It's going to take a lot longer to clean than I thought."

Finn opened a second window.

"Is it all right to step down now?"

"Let me get this snake out of the house first."

"A snake?!"

Grace screamed at the top of her lungs when she saw it slithering across the mud away from Finn and toward her. She ran up to the landing.

"It's just as scared of you as you are of it!"

"That's what Daddy always told me, but I still don't like 'em!"

"It's gone now."

"Where?"

"Probably the same place it came in—the hole in the floor. Let me get the windows open and check the rest of the house before you come down. That was a harmless one, but I'm sure they've got rattlesnakes on this island, too."

Grace quivered at the thought that a rattlesnake might be in the house.

Finn's voice faded as he walked toward the back of the house, but the last thing she heard was, "I'm surprised we didn't get any snakes in bed with us."

Grace made a garbled sound as she jumped over the quilts on the landing and ran halfway up the next set of steps. She put Trixie down and carefully shook out the quilts and folded them while she waited. She carried them and the feather pillows upstairs and stacked them in the closet.

After a few minutes, Finn was back at the foot of the stairs.

"All clear! I'm going to take care of Miss Clara now!"

"Are you sure?"

"Yeah!"

It took every ounce of courage for Grace to come back down the stairs. She groaned when she saw their muddy tracks on the stairs—more work they'd created for themselves.

She decided to finish sweeping and mopping up the puddles on the upstairs floors before starting on the filthy lower floor. She rolled up the skirt into her waistband to try to keep it clean before tackling the mud downstairs.

They were thrilled to find that the cistern still stood, but the water inside tasted salty, so they used buckets of it to wash out the mud in the house, sweeping it down the three holes Finn had chopped through the floors.

It was almost noon when someone hollered at the back porch.

"Hallo to the house! Miss Taylor, are you there?!"

Trixie bolted through the house ahead of Grace as she hurried to see who came to check on her. She found Mr. Robertson standing on the bottom step holding Trixie who was trying her best to lick his face. He was laughing, but it looked like he'd been through a night of hell. His shoes and clothes were muddy; his pants were tattered.

"Mr. Robertson! You're all right! Please come in and sit down!"

He shook his head. "I'm too dirty."

"We're all dirty." She walked down the steps and took his arm.

"I wouldn't mind sitting on your porch for a little while."

He looked weary to the bone.

"Finn! Could you bring some chairs!?"

Finn came out with two chairs, and Grace introduced them. He fetched another one, so they all had a seat.

"I hope I'm not intruding," he said, looking from Grace to Finn.

"Of course not!" said Finn. "I'm glad to take a break here. Grace is about to run me ragged putting this house back in order."

She pushed his arm playfully.

"Are you kin?" he asked them.

Grace looked at Finn and said, "We're… married… uh, I mean engaged to be married."

"Congratulations," said Mr. Robertson, with little expression.

"Thank you."

The man sat there for a moment, looking at Trixie as he petted her. "We thought we'd lost her—Maeve and the kids were heartbroken and so angry with me, but I couldn't let 'em come back."

"Is your house all right? We couldn't see across the street for the house that's blocking the view."

Mr. Robertson looked up wearily. "That *is* our house."

"Oh, I'm so sorry!"

"Maybe Maeve won't be so upset with me when she sees we might've died if we'd stayed here."

"Well, I'm sure Lucius won't mind you and family staying here. There are plenty of rooms, although we're short on beds."

"At this point, a pallet on the floor would be much appreciated. When I saw our house, I didn't know what to do or where to take my family." He looked around. "Bless you and this sturdy house. I'll go get Maeve when they clear the streets, and she can help you."

"Hopefully we'll have the mud off the floors by then, but the walls and furniture still need to be washed."

Mr. Robertson reached over and touched the water line on the wall, about two feet from the floor. "It's hard to believe the water got this high. They're saying the water was six or seven feet deep at the highest point of the island. That means the water at sea level was over fifteen feet. I just can't fathom that."

"Where did you and your family ride out the storm?" asked Finn.

"At the trolley barn a few blocks from downtown—several other families were there with us. We started out sitting in the trolley, but the water got so high, we ended up on the roof of the streetcar. But we're alive, thank the good Lord."

"Have you eaten anything today?"

He shook his head.

"Let me fix you something to eat, and how 'bout a glass of milk?"

"That sounds wonderful, Miss Taylor. Do you have any clean water? Most of the cisterns are overturned or tainted. I'm mighty thirsty. I left the barn before eight this morning, and it took me all this time to get through the streets. So many houses and buildings are damaged or destroyed, and the streets are almost impassable with all the debris and…" he paused, "and other things."

"I'll be right back." Grace stood and stepped through the open door to the kitchen, but she could still hear the men speak.

Mr. Robertson lowered his voice. "There are bodies everywhere, Finn—animals and humans alike. I saw dozens on the way over here. And there's a terrible wall of debris stretching for miles—we're right on the edge of it. Thank God you two are alive."

Grace brought him a glass of water and went back inside.

Mr. Robertson downed it in one breath. "That never tasted so good. Don't leave it unattended—that's a rare commodity on the island at the moment."

"Juju filled everything that would hold water, including the big tub before the storm hit—the water level came within six inches of the top of it."

"She's a wise one, that lady."

"We thought the house was going a number of times," said Finn. "Someone told me to chop holes in the floor to let the water help settle it."

"That probably saved it."

"We've swept and shoveled a ton of mud through those holes this morning—that's saved us miles of hauling it outside. I still have to patch them, though."

Grace brought him a plate of crackers, potted meat, a wedge of hard cheese, and a full glass of milk. He drank it down and handed her the empty glass.

"Thank you, Miss Taylor."

"Please call me Grace. You and I are way past formalities."

"That we are," he said nodding, "And you're welcome to call me Guilmet." He dug hungrily into the food.

Finn spoke up. "You wouldn't happen to be the trolley driver that helped Grace on Postoffice Street this week, would you?"

He looked up at Grace to see how he should answer that.

"I already know what happened," Finn added.

The man looked back at Finn. "Grace was on my trolley that day."

"I appreciate you helping her."

"I tried to stop her, but she's stubborn."

Finn laughed. "Yes, sir."

"Well, she's a gutsy young lady, I'll tell you that, and she probably saved that young girl's life."

"Would you two hush—I'm standing right here," said Grace, feeling her cheeks getting hot. "And Rabbi Cohen was the one who got her out of there."

"I wonder how he found out about that?" said Guilmet, almost smiling. He handed her the empty plate.

"I'm glad he had the courage to do something about it."

Trixie jumped in Guilmet's lap again. He petted her for a moment and then stood up, unfolding his tall frame and still holding the little dog. "I'd better get back to the Missus—she's probably worried about me."

"Wait," said Grace. "I'll pack up something for them to eat."

She disappeared in the kitchen and came back out with a small burlap bag of food.

"You need the drawstring back?" asked Finn.

She couldn't help but giggle.

Guilmet stood there with a blank look on his face.

"His pants would fall down if he..." she started to explain. "Oh, never mind. Here," she handed him the food, "and there's a mason jar of water in there, so don't let it break. Bring your family back to stay here tonight."

"Much obliged, Miss... Grace. Again, I'm so thankful you're all right. Maeve will be so relieved to hear that, and that Trixie's still alive." He looked at the dog and then back at Grace. "Would it be too much of an inconvenience if she stayed with you a while longer?"

Grace reached for the dog. "Not at all. I've enjoyed her company. And there will be more room in the house after Finn and I leave tomorrow."

Guilmet stared at her. "Nobody can leave the island, Grace. The storm destroyed all the bridges to the mainland."

"What about a boat?" asked Finn.

"There's not a seaworthy vessel left. They're sunk or overturned or run aground. And I heard there's just as much damage on the mainland as here. Don't know when you'll be able to leave."

Grace's heart sunk. She looked at Finn, who spoke up.

"Well, that'll give me more time to make the repairs on the house."

"I can help you with that."

"Good," Finn said, patting him on the back. "Be careful going back."

Guilmet walked down the steps. "You be careful, too. I heard there's already looting going on, and food and clean water are hard to come by. You might ought to stay here until we get back so the house isn't left unattended, or it may be stripped clean."

"I was hoping to check on my friends Marguerite St. John at the Greshams' house and Daisy Thorne at the Lucas Terrace Apartments. I was supposed to be moving in yesterday, but I need to let them know my plans have changed." She smiled at Finn.

"The Gresham house is still standing," said Guilmet, "but there's nothing left of Lucas Terrace."

"What?! You must be mistaken. That building is three stories high and made of brick. It's massive!"

Guilmet shook his head. "I'm sorry, Grace, but it's gone. They said nothing's left but a small pile of rubble."

Chapter 41

Tom escorted Juju to the house about mid-afternoon. Kitty was needed at the hospital; they were overwhelmed with the injured. Tom told Finn he never made it home yesterday—the water was too deep. He spent the night standing on the counter up to his shoulders in water along with a group of people at a grocery store.

As soon as it was light, he tried to find his home, but he could find no familiar landmarks to tell him where it was. The west end of the island was swept clean for as far as he could see—"thousands of houses just… gone," he told them. He didn't know what happened to his family other than they were gone, too. He said he stopped and buried several people along the way, hoping that if someone else found his loved ones, they would show the same kindness towards them.

Tom didn't cry a tear; he showed very little emotion telling his story. Juju tried to get him to eat something and then led him upstairs to rest. He hadn't slept all night.

It wasn't until Tom was settled that they learned that Juju's house had washed away, too, but she was thankful that she and Kitty were alive.

"We brought our most treasured keepsakes with us, so we're fine, unlike poor Tom. Mr. Roderick said if the house was still standing, we could stay here—we're much more fortunate than so many other folks. He said he'd try to send someone to check on us later, but he plans to stay downtown."

Grace was relieved Finn and Lucius wouldn't have to stay under the same roof tonight, but she was worried sick about Daisy and her family. Finn had offered to go ask around about her after Guilmet left at noon, but she was afraid to stay at the house by herself.

After Juju and Tom had arrived, Grace was happy to hand over the household reins to Juju, knowing the Robertsons would also be arriving soon.

Grace changed into her split skirt she normally wore for horseback riding. She donned her boots after hearing about the broken glass, exposed nails, and splintered wood in the debris piles they would have to climb over.

They left by the backyard—the yard gate in the front of the house was still blocked by the debris. They passed Juju sloshing through the mud and water where her fall garden used to be.

She stood there shaking her head as they approached her. "The salt water will probably kill everything."

"I'm so sorry, Juju."

"Such is life," she said, shrugging her shoulders. "We'll plant 'em again. And I'm fixin' ham and beans for supper."

"I'll be back to help you as soon as I can," said Grace.

"You've already done enough, young lady. I'll finish the floors and get started on those walls, too." She walked over to the cow and patted her. "I'm not sure what we can feed this ol' girl, though."

"We'll see you after a while."

"I'm not going anywhere."

Finn whispered, "I can't wait to get off this sandbar, and leaving hasn't even entered her head."

"Resilient woman."

They squeezed through the debris-filled gate and stopped outside the yard on 17th Street. The battered houses still standing were the only clues that a street lay between them. Tons of lumber was piled every which direction, barrels and empty cisterns lay overturned or crushed, useless for collecting water. Parts of roofs and whole sections of walls were strewn about as far as they could see. A closer look revealed the more personal items of people's lives—furniture, trunks, muddy clothes and household objects wedged throughout the wreckage. The south view was blocked by debris stacked twenty-five feet high.

"This is devastating—it's even worse than I thought."

"It's going to be difficult to make our way to Broadway. Why don't you stay here—I can go check on your friends."

Grace shook her head. "It's not that far to the Gresham house; and I was hoping we might run into a preacher, too."

"I imagine they're going to be very busy the next few days." He stepped onto a pile of lumber and held out his hand to Grace.

Grace lost count of the times they repeated that same action—Finn going first and pulling her along. It took forty-five minutes of working their way over and through massive amounts of debris to get to the Gresham house only five blocks away at 14th and Broadway.

Debris and the ever-present residual mud filled the mansion's manicured yard, painting what was green the day before a dreary shade of muck today. They could see that some of the windows were broken, but overall, the mansion looked like it had sustained minimal damage. On the grand steps in front of the house a dark water line stopped about six feet up. The first floor above the basement was a good eight or nine feet off the ground level, so the flood didn't reach the main floor.

Grace led Finn around to the back and walked up the stairs, avoiding the basement where they could see people cleaning out the foul-smelling mud and debris. A maid walked up behind them and took them inside. They stood near the dumbwaiter at the back stairwell while she ran upstairs to fetch Marguerite.

When Marguerite appeared at the top of the curved stairs, Grace met her halfway and the two women wept and hugged each other tightly.

"I assumed you were lost, dear child!" She looked down at Finn. "I was afraid you both were gone."

"Turns out she was looking for me, too."

"Well, I'm glad you two found each other. Did you hear about your apartment building?"

Grace nodded. "I can't believe that huge building is gone. I'm so worried about Daisy and her family, though. Have you heard anything them?"

"Yes, they survived, but barely. We got word that over twenty people clung to each other behind the door in what was left of Daisy's bedroom. Most of the walls and ceiling were gone and during the height of the storm, the waves were actually washing over them. It's a miracle they're still alive."

"Thank God."

"There's nothing but a pile of bricks there now, and I heard the Thornes are staying with friends or family. I imagine every house and building in the city is damaged, though. "I'm so glad you hadn't moved into those apartments yet—you would've been in that building otherwise. And they're finding bodies everywhere. We were told quite a few people are buried in the rubble of the church just east of us. And they can still hear people trapped in that gruesome debris pile, but no one can get to them."

"It's so much worse than we realized. We saw several bodies on the way over here, but we didn't know what to do about them. Is there someone we should tell? I saw them with my own eyes, but it didn't seem real. I've never seen a corpse before. Do you think a lot of people died last night?"

Marguerite nodded her head sadly. "After what I've heard this morning, yes—more than we can imagine. I want to show you something." Marguerite took Grace by the hand and led her up the stairs. "You too, Finn."

"The house held up well," Grace noticed.

"Yes, thank heavens. People criticized Clayton for over-building this house, but we're so thankful he did. About two hundred people took shelter with us yesterday—most of us sat in this stairwell until well after midnight, and then we moved to various parts of the house to try to get some sleep. The water was six feet deep in the basement—they're still trying to shovel the mud out of there. We lost some windows and some of the parquet flooring was damaged by the rain, but that's minimal compared to so many others."

They followed her up to the third floor and into Josephine's art studio.

"Will Mrs. Gresham mind us being here?"

"No, Josephine's helping to organize a relief committee," said Marguerite. "You've seen just a few blocks of the damage this storm has caused, but this view will give you a better idea what happened yesterday."

She stepped aside so Grace and Finn could look out the windows that wrapped around the walls of the turret-shaped room.

Grace gasped. For as far as she could see from east to west, the line of debris piled up like a dam behind the row of houses across the street. Beyond that, there was nothing all the way to the Gulf. She finally understood what Tom meant when he said the land was swept clean of any houses or structures. The day before, tall houses densely covered this same area—block after block all the way to the beach.

"It's all gone! How can that be?"

Finn leaned out of the window to look. "That debris pile looks like the boundary line of total destruction, and we were right on the other side of it."

"That's probably what saved your house—it ended up sheltering you in a way."

"But those poor, poor people on the other side," said Grace, overwhelmed by the magnitude of loss.

Someone called for Marguerite and she stepped out of the room.

Finn put his arm around Grace and leaned his head into hers. "I came so close to losing you these past few days—in more ways than just this storm."

He pulled her close.

Marguerite came back. "Grace, Rabbi Cohen is downstairs in the meeting—he even asked about you."

"What's he doing here?"

"He's helping with the relief effort."

Grace looked at Finn. "I wonder…"

"What?" asked Marguerite.

"Finn and I said our vows to each other during the worst of the storm last night when we didn't think we were going to make it…"

"You mean wedding vows?"

Grace nodded her head, "And we're committed to each other, but we really need a ceremony with a pastor and a certificate, if possible …"

"So her father doesn't shoot me," added Finn.

Marguerite laughed, and then stopped. "You're not thinking of asking Rabbi Cohen to do it, are you?"

"I don't know any other clergyman at the moment," said Grace. "Is he even considered clergy?"

"I don't know."

"I'm sure they're all extremely busy right now. I know our request seems selfish, but it wouldn't have to take long. "

"Come on," said Marguerite, motioning her toward the door. "It never hurts to ask, and I'm especially anxious to see the expression on his face when you do."

Grace paused. "Well, I don't want to bother him now…"

"Which do you want to face—your parents or Rabbi Cohen?"

Finn pushed her out the door. "I'd prefer the rabbi myself."

Chapter 42

Marguerite cornered Rabbi Cohen in the library and introduced Finn just before Grace posed the question.

Henry Cohen was quiet for a moment before he answered. "You want me, a Jewish rabbi, to marry you, a Gentile couple? Have you thought this through?"

Grace smiled. "No, not entirely, but I believe we worship the same God, and I know He'll honor this. And we would be honored, too, Rabbi, if you would witness and confirm our vows to each other."

"What about a marriage license?"

"We need one of those, too, but I don't know if we'll be able to get one before we leave."

"You're leaving Galveston?"

Grace nodded and looked at Finn. "We're going home as soon as we can."

"So when do you want to do this? I don't know if I'll be available for some time; the needs in our city are overwhelming at the moment."

"What about right now? A few minutes of your time is all we ask."

"Oh…well, you've caught me off guard, Miss Taylor. I'm not prepared."

"You don't have to say anything if you don't want—just witness our words to each other."

He laughed. "Me not say anything? Oh, no. If I'm officiating, I definitely have to say something. Mrs. St. John, will you be standing up for Miss Taylor?"

"I wouldn't miss this for the world," she said, smiling like she was witnessing something historical.

"Let me back up, though," Rabbi Cohen said, looking around. He walked over and pulled the pocket doors closed to the foyer and the dining room. "If I do this, it goes no further than this room."

Grace looked at Marguerite. "That's fine with us; right, Marguerite?"

She looked disappointed, but agreed.

Rabbi Cohen looked at Finn. "Do you have someone to stand up for you?"

Finn shook his head, no.

"It's not necessary for the marriage license. Why don't we stand over in the library's little rotunda here—Josephine's plants make a nice backdrop."

They walked over to the rounded corner of the library—identical to Josephine's studio on the third floor. Rabbi Cohen stood with his back to the windows, but Grace couldn't help but stare at the devastating ruins of the huge church across the street.

The rabbi noticed their faces and asked them to switch places, putting their backs to the window. He reached over and grasped each of their hands, placing Grace's hand in Finn's. Then he took a deep breath and smiled.

"What comes to mind after a quick plea to Yahweh for help is a favorite story of mine from the Tenakh—you might be familiar with it. And the words I quote from it aren't words between a man and a woman, but rather the words of a Moabite to her mother-in-law. But they are so fitting for a lifetime commitment between two people. It says, *Entreat me not to leave thee, or to return from following after thee: for whither thou goest, I will go; and where thou lodgest, I will lodge: thy people shall be my people, and thy God my God.* Marriage is a covenant between a man and a woman—to commit their lives to each other. It is not to be taken lightly or without forethought. Do you understand this?"

Grace and Finn both answered, yes.

"Would you like to say something to each other at this point?"

Grace turned to Finn as her eyes filled with tears. "Those verses sound like me in my relentless pursuit of you all these years. You always kept something of yourself back from me, like there was a part of you I could never reach, but I don't feel that between us anymore. Thank you for coming after me and trusting that with God's help, our love and hard work will get us though the coming months. I have no doubt of that, my love. My life is yours." She turned to Rabbi Cohen. "And I think that's all."

"Finn?" the rabbi prompted.

Finn took a deep breath. "I didn't realize we were going to do this so soon, but I'm ready. I suffered a loss years ago that hurt worse than anything I'd ever experienced, and I guess I put up a wall at that point, thinking it would keep me from getting hurt again. But I felt that same pain when I thought I'd lost you, Grace, even after I'd kept you at arm's length. I'm sorry it took you leaving Waco for me to realize how many years I've wasted, but no more. I love you, Grace, with *all* of my heart now. And I will for the rest of my life. I thank God that He gave me the chance to tell you that and for us to survive this storm and start our life together today. I wish I could've said that better, but—"

"I couldn't have said it better myself," said Rabbi Cohen, "and time is of the essence. You are no longer two individuals, but one. Do you have a ring?"

Finn's eyes widened. "No, I didn't think about that."

"In our wedding ceremonies, the vows are sealed when you place a ring on your bride's finger."

Marguerite pulled off one of her rings and handed it to Finn. "It's only a loan," she whispered.

"As you place the ring on her finger, say *You are consecrated to me with this ring.*"

Finn repeated the phrase and slipped the ring on Grace's finger.

"Grace, if you would repeat to Finn, *I am my beloved's and my beloved is mine.*"

Grace repeated the words.

"And now I pronounce you husband and wife. Mazel tov!" He shook Finn's hand and kissed Grace on each cheek. "And now I must go." He turned and started walking away.

"Aren't you forgetting something?" asked Marguerite.

"Oh!" said Finn, reaching into his pocket.

"Oh!" said the rabbi as he turned around. "You may now kiss your bride!" He smiled and opened the pocket doors just enough to step through them.

Finn pulled out a couple of bills and quickly kissed Grace before following Rabbi Cohen into the foyer.

"What were you talking about?" Grace asked Marguerite.

"The kiss, of course! What's Finn doing?"

"Paying the preacher."

Finn came back after a moment. "Rabbi Cohen wouldn't take the money, but he accepted my help with some repairs on his house. I told him I can start tomorrow, but what about Roderick's house?"

"Let Lucius take care of his own repairs," said Marguerite.

"He was gracious enough to let me stay there this week, I feel like I owe him something," said Grace.

"Well, we scraped most of the mud out of his house, and I guess Guilmet and Tom will be there to help with the repairs."

"You're right, and Maeve and Juju and eventually Kitty can help when she gets there—we'll get it cleaned and back in order in no time. You go help Rabbi Cohen tomorrow."

"Well, let me be the first to congratulate you." Marguerite hugged Grace.

"Thank you, my friend. I don't know what I would've done without you this week."

"When do you think you'll be able to leave?"

"I don't know. It could take weeks to rebuild the bridges. And how do we get word to our families that we're all right? I wonder when they'll hear the news about the storm."

"A disaster of this magnitude will no doubt travel fast. I need to get back to Houston and check on my own house. And I could do more good raising funds from there than getting in the way down here. If I figure out a way off the island before the bridges are rebuilt, I'll send word to you."

"Oh, Marguerite, would that be possible?"

"With my circle of friends? Absolutely."

Grace and Finn returned to the house on L Street just before dark. The dining table sat strategically over the hole in the floor, temporarily covered by two pieces of lumber. Finn assured Juju he would patch the floors as soon as possible.

The older woman slapped a mosquito on her arm and stood over the remains of the ham and beans, waiting for them to fill their plates. Everyone else—the Robertsons and Tom had eaten about an hour earlier and had retired for the evening.

Juju picked up the bean pot and scraped out the last of the beans on their plates and went to the kitchen. They forked slices of ham onto their plates and Finn quickly blessed the food.

Juju came back in and said impatiently, "Now eat so I can get this cleaned up."

Grace reached for a cracker.

"And where did you get that?"

"What?"

"On your hand?"

Grace held up her hand to show her the emerald ring on her wedding finger.

"Finn and I are married."

Juju frowned like she didn't believe them, but she didn't say it out loud.

"Well, that solves one sleeping arrangement—you can stay where you've been staying. I told the Robertsons to take Mr. Roderick's room, but they insisted on taking the northeast bedroom. Tom wouldn't stay in any of the rooms upstairs, so I fixed a pallet for him in the library. Kitty and I will take the other room, and Mr. Roderick will have his own room when he comes home."

"Is Kitty back?"

"No, she'll probably stay at the hospital for a few days. I'm afraid it won't be safe on the streets for a while. We heard people are cutting fingers and ears off the dead to get the jewelry. The neighbors behind us told us they heard shooting—probably looters. They'd better get this city under control or we might not recover from this." She slapped at another mosquito. She picked up the platter of ham. "You'd better use the mosquito netting tonight. You'd think the storm would've given us some relief from these blood-sucking gnats." She turned and walked into the kitchen.

"Is she always this way?" whispered Finn.

Grace shook her head. She pushed her chair back and followed her into the kitchen.

Juju was kneeling in front of the ice box with her head leaning on the door.

"Juju?"

The older woman turned away from her and wiped her eyes. "Yes, ma'am?"

"Are you all right?"

Juju turned and looked at her. "I'm fine." She shut the ice box door and ran her hand over the front of it. "I'm so glad Mr. Robertson thought to bring us some ice. I'll make us some butter tomorrow, and we'll be in good shape." She was quiet for a moment before she spoke again. "It was nothing fancy. I had my own garden, too, and chickens. I really enjoyed having chickens. I'd just put up new curtains in the parlor… but it's all gone now."

Grace walked over to her and kneeled beside her. "I'm so sorry, Juju."

"We'll be all right. I'm just tired, that's all."

Grace nodded her head. "Why don't you go on to bed? I can finish cleaning up."

The older woman took a deep breath and tried to stand. Grace stood so she could help her up.

"You're an angel." She started to walk away, but stopped. "You're really married now?"

Grace nodded her head.

"I like him. And I'm glad for you, girl."

"Thank you." She watched the older woman shuffle out of the kitchen.

Finn brought their plates into the kitchen and set them on the table. "Let's finish our supper in here. I'm kind of partial to this old table anyway," he said, grinning at her.

Grace smiled, but felt her cheeks growing hot.

"You want to sleep under the table again?"

"No, and don't talk so loud," she whispered and pointed up. "The Robertsons."

He reached over and pulled her into his lap. "Then we'll just have to talk closer together." He kissed her before she wriggled out of his arms and picked up the plates.

"We're married, Grace," he whispered.

She stacked one plate on top of the other and put them in the ice box. Then she turned around and walked over and took Finn by the hand and led him out of the kitchen and through the darkening house.

"I wasn't finished," he said, looking back.

At the foot of the stairs, she leaned over and kissed him and then finally spoke. "We can finish supper later."

Finn beat her up the stairs.

Chapter 43

Monday was a productive day. Everyone took turns after dinner sharing what all they had accomplished.

Maeve Robertson and her children were able to salvage some of their belongings that were still trapped in the slanted house. They even took the straw out of a mattress to feed the cow, which nobody had claimed yet.

Tom cleared the debris from the yard and fence and along with some neighbors' help, they started making a trail through the debris in the middle of the road so people could pass through more easily. He had gathered enough lumber to start repairing the front galleries and roof.

Guilmet had attempted to clear their lot across the street, but it didn't take long for him to realize he needed bigger tools and horsepower to remove much of the mangled mass, as well as to move their house from the middle of the road. He said the smells from the debris wall nearby was almost more than he could stomach. He said he planned to go to the trolley barn the following morning to see if he still had a job.

"We won't be able to put the streetcars in operation until we get the tracks uncovered and the lines up and running; I imagine that'll take weeks."

Grace cleaned out the library shelves and put all the books back in their places. Then she helped Juju pull the ruined wallpaper from the lower part of the walls and gave them a good washing with soapy, salty water from the cistern, removing the flood water stains.

Finn shared that he was able to patch Rabbi Cohen's roof with materials he picked up in the street—lumber, slate tiles. "It's all right there for the taking."

Juju had taken over the job of milking Miss Clara, and everyone enjoyed the fruits of her labor: butter, milk gravy, and pudding, as well as fresh milk to drink and cream in their coffee. She reported that they still had plenty of drinking water if everyone was careful with it. She even shared some water with the neighbors and heard more news about the storm. The death count was in the thousands now.

"There are so many, they're putting the bodies on barges and hauling them out to sea," said Guilmet.

Finn added, "Before I made it to the Cohens' house this morning, a man leveled a gun on me and said I had to help gather up the dead. But after he rounded up about half a dozen more men, I was able to slip away from them."

"Don't you go out there again!" said Grace.

"I have to—I'm not finished with the job, but I know now to keep out of sight." He glanced at Guilmet and Tom. "Be careful if you go downtown tomorrow. Some of those men looked like they'd shoot first and ask questions later—especially the one that tried to conscript me."

"We all need to help where we can," said Tom, standing. "There are a lot of hurting people out there." He walked out the back door.

Finn grimaced. "Why didn't somebody shut me up? I forgot about his family," he whispered.

"Well, I was the one that brought it up," said Juju.

"And I mentioned the body barges—we all needed a good kick under the table," said Guilmet. "I'll go talk to him."

Tuesday evening's conversation covered the progress and setbacks of the day, but this time everyone avoided the subject of death, for Tom's sake. When he was out of earshot, Guilmet told the others that the bodies that were buried at sea the day before had started washing up on the beaches, so the decision had been made to start burning them where they found them, animal carcasses included. They all had noticed the smell of smoke in the air that day.

Juju was pouring coffee after dinner when a familiar voice spoke through the back screen door.

"Grace?"

"Daisy?!" yelled Grace, jumping up from the table. "Is it really you?"

The door opened, and Daisy stepped inside with her arms outstretched.

Grace couldn't help but laugh and cry at the same time. "We thought you were lost when we heard the apartments collapsed. Then Marguerite told us you were all right, but we didn't know where you were staying."

Grace finally noticed the tall, young man standing behind Daisy.

She moved aside and introduced him. "This is my fiancé Joe Gilbert… I mean, *Doctor* Joe Gilbert."

He smiled and gave a short wave to the room. "Hello."

Grace looked at Daisy and then back at the doctor. "When did you… how did you get here?"

"I got here last night—train, boat, and foot—anyway I could travel."

"So people are able to come and go?" She glanced at Finn.

"No—it took some serious negotiating—"

"He means bribing," added Daisy.

"And a few threats, but my medical degree was the biggest reason that got me here. A lot of people are trying to get to the island, but the officials are really strict about it because of the lack of food and water."

"Are you hungry?" Juju asked. "Do you have clean water?"

"We're fine—we're staying at my uncle's house. He's a grocer so we have a lot canned goods. We have no idea what we're opening each meal—the labels were washed off, but nobody's complaining. We were wondering, though, if that was your milk cow out there."

"Nobody's claimed her. Would you like to take some milk back with you?"

Daisy looked at Joe. "That would be heavenly. But can you spare any?"

"Miss Clara's been very generous, in spite of her limited diet."

"Daisy's family hasn't had anything fresh since the storm."

"I'll pack up some butter for you, too," Juju said happily.

"I never thought I'd take things like that for granted, but we've really missed that with Mother's biscuits. She'll be overjoyed."

Grace noticed the oversized dress she was wearing. "What about you, Daisy, were you able to salvage anything?"

She shook her head, no. "Except for one of my kittens, and she's going to Austin with us."

Grace took her by the arm. "Excuse us for a moment; we'll be right back." She led her upstairs and into her bedroom where she opened her trunk. "I'm a little taller, but we're about the same size, I think. Take what you need."

"Oh, Grace, I can't take your clothes."

"Of course you can. I have plenty to spare, and if we get the chance to leave this week, I'll probably have to leave the trunk. We have no way of getting it across town."

Daisy pulled the baggy dress away from her petite frame. "I really hate to get married in my aunt's dress."

Grace picked up a white shirtwaist trimmed with lace around the collar and cuffs. "What about this?"

Daisy sighed. "It's so white and clean—I didn't think there was anything in town still white and clean. I did find a black skirt downtown, although it was soaked in the overflow."

"That was a flood we experienced, Daisy, not a simple overflow. I'd be out of my head if I'd gone through what you went through." Grace reached into the trunk and pulled out a chemise, bloomers, stockings, and handed them to her friend. "I'm sorry I don't have any extra shoes—I've ruined several pairs in the last few days."

"This is too much."

"Juju and Maeve can't wear these things, so they'll end up going to somebody. It would make me feel better knowing you had them."

"Well, when you say it that way, how can I refuse?"

"Good, and oh!" She dug around and found a white, felt hat.

"You're welcome to use this, too, if you can get the pink stain off of it. It must've sat next to something damp."

"It'll do just fine. Momma's going to help me put my hair up."

"When are you getting married?"

"Day after tomorrow at the Episcopal Church—they're saying we'll be the first wedding after the storm. Can you believe that?"

Grace smiled. "I'm really happy for you."

"Do you think you can come?"

"If we're still here, we'll definitely be there."

"We?"

"Finn came for me… in the middle of the storm on Saturday."

"Finn's here? He's downstairs?"

Grace nodded.

"Then why didn't you introduce me?"

"I've told Finn so much about you, I forgot you hadn't met him. Here, let me wrap these things in a towel so you can keep them clean. Then I'll take you to meet my… fiancé."

Daisy hugged her. "I'm so happy he came for you, and he proposed, too?! Hey! Would you like to make it a double wedding?"

Grace shook her head. "No, that's *your* special day. We'll probably have a ceremony in Dalton or Grace so my parents can be there."

"I guess we'll both be sending our resignations to Rosenberg."

Grace nodded. "I'm sure it'll take some time for the schools to be repaired." She couldn't bring herself to say Galveston wouldn't need as many teachers either. She figured Daisy lost a number of her students.

"I want to give you our address in Austin before I leave. You'll come see us sometime, won't you?"

"I promise we will. Now let's go downstairs and drink some watered-down coffee and visit a spell."

"With cream?"

Grace laughed. "With sugar and cream if you want."

On Wednesday morning, Finn started working on the upstairs gallery at Lucius' house. He had finished as much as he could of the repairs on the Cohen house up to the point where new materials were needed to complete them.

Grace stood by to assist Finn on the porch—handing him nails or boards or occasionally rubbing his neck or arms. She noticed he seemed to like that part best. She kept reminding herself that this wasn't a dream—that he really was here. Outside of the yard, the magnitude of suffering caused by the storm was almost too much to bear, but inside this small compound, Grace couldn't remember feeling happier. Gratefulness and guilt sparred inside her head.

Around mid-morning she went to the kitchen to get Finn a glass of water, and Juju handed her an envelope that had just been delivered to the back door. The front said, *Mr. and Mrs. Finn Samuel.* Grace tore it open to read the brief note:

Come to the house at 11 a.m. if you can leave today.

~Marguerite

"She did it!"

"Who did what?" asked Juju.

"Marguerite's found us a way off the island."

"So soon?" She heard Juju say as she ran upstairs to read the note to Finn.

"What time is it?" he asked.

"Almost ten."

"We'd better hurry." He wasted no time gathering up the tools. "Go pack your satchel and tell everyone goodbye."

Grace packed the few items of jewelry she owned, a small book of family photos, a handful of keepsakes, and a couple of changes of clothes. She told Juju that she and Kitty were welcome to keep the trunk and remaining items in it. She hung the red dress on a brass hook in Lucius' wardrobe, and wrote a quick note thanking him for the most memorable week of her life. She placed it on the table beside his bed, wondering when he would come home and find it.

Had it only been twelve days since she arrived in Galveston? It seemed like a lifetime ago.

She didn't get to say goodbye to Guilmet and Tom, who were downtown, or Maeve either, who was helping a neighbor down the street, so she wrote them a quick note, which seemed so inadequate.

As much as she wanted to leave the island, she found saying goodbye much harder than she realized. She started crying when she picked up Trixie, and when she hugged Juju goodbye, neither of the women could get any words out.

She bawled uncontrollably as she and Finn made their way through the debris to Broadway where a path had been cleared wide enough for a wagon to get through.

Grace held a perfumed hanky to her face to quell the stench as well as her tears.

Finn stopped about half a block before they reached the Greshams' house, set down the satchel and just held Grace until she quit sobbing.

"What more can we do here?" he said, rubbing the back of her head.

"I don't know."

"We were staying in a house we didn't own; we have very little money, and I'm not sure anyone's in the position to pay wages around here. I'm afraid we'll be worse off if we stay. I'm surprised Roderick hadn't kicked us out earlier."

"You're right. There's not much we can do… and yet I feel so guilty for leaving, but at the same time I feel so relieved to be escaping this nightmare."

"We need to let your family know we're all right. I'm sure they're worried sick about you."

Grace took a deep breath and nodded. "And yours, too."

"They don't even know I'm down here."

"I haven't given them much thought, but you're right. I need to be focusing on them… and us right now."

"It's almost eleven."

"Let's go home."

Finn picked up the satchel, and they started walking.

"I'm not even sure where home is," said Finn.

Grace linked her arm through his. "Home is with you," she said without hesitating.

They approached the imposing house and stopped in front of it. Grace noticed the water mark on the steps had been scrubbed clean.

"You could've had a house like this, Grace."

"Whatever gave you the idea that I wanted a house like this?"

"You looked so happy at the dance."

"I was trying to get over you." She looked up at the house. "I can admire the workmanship in this mansion, but I couldn't live here. Can you imagine how quiet and empty it would be when the children leave?"

"The children?" Finn smiled. "Sounds like you've put some thought into this."

"Most girls do. And I'd like at least four, please."

Finn laughed. "Four sounds good to me. Now are we front door or back door guests?"

"Definitely back door. I still haven't met the Greshams."

They passed through the front gate and followed the walkway to the left. The yard was still muddy, but clear of debris.

"Lucius plans to live in a house like this someday; he calls his house on Avenue L a 'stepping stone' house. But I felt comfortable there."

"I guess I believed everything he told me about you," said Finn. "The man was a formidable opponent."

Grace snorted. "If we ever need a lawyer, we're calling Lucius Roderick."

Chapter 44

Grace noticed the ship's name was *Endurance*, and commented that it was aptly named. The captain corrected her use of the word *ship*, which he said implied a larger vessel than this one.

"A ship has three masts, madam. We only have one."

"I'm sorry." Grace looked questioningly at Marguerite.

"Anthony's a stickler for nautical protocol," said Marguerite. "But I forgive him because today he's our champion."

"The correct term is sailboat or yacht," Anthony continued.

"Thank you, darling. Now when does this *yacht* sail?"

He pulled out his pocket watch. "At five bells."

"Oh, good grief, Tony! We're not sailors—what exactly does that mean?" Marguerite said exasperatedly.

He looked a bit sheepish. "Two-thirty. Stevens should be back by then."

"Thank you. I guess we have a little time to kill.

"Oh, before I forget…" Grace took off Marguerite's ring and handed it to her. "Thank you for loaning it to us."

"I was glad to help." She turned back to the captain. "What, pray tell, is Stevens doing?"

"Delivering a bag of mail if he can find someone at the Post Office. That's the only reason I was given permission to come across the bay. We're taking mail back with us, too. People are desperate to contact loved ones on both sides."

"The mail's already coming?" asked Grace.

"We brought the first bag,"

"I should've written a letter to my parents."

"You can write one in Houston—there's a place folks are gathering where they're posting names of the missing and deceased and where people are attempting to get word to their families and friends."

"Well, dear friend, thank you for getting word to me this morning." Marguerite turned and looked at the damaged wharf and backs of the buildings. "Our poor playground is broken. Did you know the Opera House collapsed? The bathhouses are gone. They may not even have a social season this year. Of the buildings and houses that survived, most every one of them suffered some kind of damage. And that unbearable smell, Anthony. It's bound to make people sick. At least the air's fresher here on the boat."

"We heard they cleared hundreds of bodies out from under the wharves, but we still saw quite a few in the bay on the way over this morning, along with every kind of animal carcass you could think of."

"Let's not talk about it, dear. But tell me, did you get a chance to check on my house? Was there any looting in the neighborhood?"

"Your house is fine other than some broken windows, and your trees lost some limbs. But Toby and Bertha have everything under control."

Finn jumped out of the boat onto the dock. "I'll be right back," he told Grace.

"Where you going?"

"You're not going home without a ring."

"You don't have to buy me..." she stopped when she saw his expression changing. "Do you know what size I wear?"

"No. Tell me."

"I don't know either."

He reached for her and pulled her out of the boat. "We'll be back in plenty of time, Marguerite. Come on—I saw a jewelry shop on the Strand."

"Do you think it's open?"

"If someone's there, they won't refuse my money."

"I can wait, Finn," said Grace.

He shook his head. "Since the boat ride isn't costing us anything, we can manage."

They found the narrow shop near the Hutchins Sealy Bank on the Strand. The door was open, but "for cleaning purposes only," the owner informed them.

"I have no jewelry out—we have to put new felt in the display cases."

"We only need a simple gold band, sir," said Finn. "We just got married, and I can't take her home to her parents without a ring. Please… do you have anything like that?"

The man sighed impatiently and set down his bucket and rag. "Follow me," he said, taking them through a locked door and up a narrow stairwell. He had them wait in a hall while he entered another locked door, and after a moment he brought a tray of gold bands of all widths and sizes. Grace picked up the lightest one, but Finn told her it would wear through in no time. He pointed to a thicker band, and she found one that fit her finger.

"How much?"

"Twenty."

"You're taking advantage of us—it doesn't even have a stone!"

"I'll do you a favor and let you have it for fifteen."

Finn looked at Grace. "Didn't we see another jeweler on the Strand?"

"All right, all right… ten dollars, and that's my final price."

"If we weren't in such a hurry…" Finn shook his head as he pulled out the ten dollars and paid him. "But we appreciate your time, though. Come on, Grace."

"Thank you, sir," she said over her shoulder.

They hurried down the stairs and through the store before Finn started grinning.

"Was that a good price?"

"I don't know—I just didn't plan to pay more than ten dollars for it."

Grace held out her hand as they walked outside. "Well, I think it's perfect. Thank you, Finn." She leaned over and kissed his cheek.

At the corner they stopped and watched a team of mules pulling a streetcar out of the mud.

"Is it in service?" Finn asked a man nearby.

"Nah—it washed off the tracks on 22nd Street. But I bet you they'll go back to mule-drawn trolleys temporarily before the electric lines are working again."

Across the street they noticed a comely woman had stopped to stare at the streetcar, too.

"Isn't that Pearl?" Grace said.

Finn nodded as he watched her. "Wonder what she's doing down here. I probably would've left the island if she hadn't convinced me otherwise."

"We owe her a debt of gratitude then. I wish she'd leave that lifestyle."

"She feels like she can't."

"Maybe she just needs some help."

Finn turned and looked at Grace. "What do you mean?"

"I'm not sure, but I know we're not the only ones who need rescuing around here. You know her better than I do. Go ask her to come with us."

Finn stepped off the boardwalk and walked across the street. Pearl's face lit up when she saw him and then she looked beyond him to see Grace. Her face broke out in an even bigger smile.

Grace smiled back and waved.

Finn stopped a few feet away, still standing in the street. "How you doing, Pearl?"

"I see you took my advice."

Finn nodded and smiled. "You were right—she wanted *me*, not Roderick. But I'd have been long gone if it wasn't for you."

"I'm happy for you, Cowboy. Where's your hat?"

"Probably at the bottom of the ocean by now."

"Rough night. What are you doing downtown?"

"I just bought my wife a wedding ring."

"You're already married?!" She looked up at Grace and pointed to her left hand and clapped.

Grace nodded and grinned.

"You sure didn't waste any time."

"It only took me six years," he said. "I'm glad you survived the storm, Pearl."

"There was a lot of wailing and praying and promises to the Almighty made under that roof Saturday. You'd have thought it was a church by the way we sounded. But then the sun came out the next morning and everything went back to normal, except for the damage. Are you available for hire? We sure could use you."

Finn shook his head. "Sorry, but we're leaving today."

Her face dropped. "You're leaving the island?"

"We're going home."

"Well, I wish you the best, Finn Samuel." She started down the steps to cross the street.

Finn offered her his hand and she let him assist her, but then he didn't let go.

"We want you to come with us."

She turned around to face him. "What?"

"You told me you wished somebody had come for you years ago. Well, we've come for you, Pearl."

She laughed ruefully. "Don't be ridiculous, boy. It's too late."

"I saw you watching that streetcar."

She swallowed. "That didn't mean anything." She looked up at Grace again. "Does she know what you're asking me?"

"She was the one who suggested it."

"And what in the world would you do with an ex-hooker?"

"I don't know—help you start over somewhere?"

"Do you know what I'm doing today? I withdrew my savings to buy out Mollie. The storm scared her so badly she wants to retire and get off the island."

"What about Kitty? What if she finds out her mother's a madam?"

"You told me you wouldn't tell!"

"And I won't, but your secret's bound to surface sometime. She favors you, too. She has your eyes."

Pearl's face softened for a moment, then she shook her head. "Well, Juju's her mother, and they'll be just fine. Lucius is negotiating to buy a mansion on Broadway for ten cents on the dollar. I just talked him into selling me his old house for fifteen cents on the dollar and to put it in Kitty and Juju's names."

"That's very generous of you. Have you thought about using your savings to start another business—a legitimate business somewhere else? Come with us, Pearl."

Grace walked up beside Finn. "The boat leaves at 2:30—it's right at the end of this road."

Pearl looked toward the wharf. Tears pooled in her eyes.

"What if I fail?"

"So you've thought about it?"

"Only a thousand times… but I don't know how to live in that world."

"With God's help, you can learn to," said Grace.

"How can God ever forgive a lifetime of sin? You know what I am."

"Did you know that there's a harlot in Jesus' lineage?" asked Grace.

Pearl's eyes narrowed like she didn't believe her.

"Her name was Rahab. My friend Marguerite told me about her just this week. I'd love for her to tell you the story—she's on the boat waiting for us."

Pearl looked wistfully toward the wharf.

"You haven't committed the unforgiveable sin, Pearl."

"We're starting over, too," said Finn. "You were the one who gave me the courage to face it with Grace at my side. Let us do that for you."

She looked back at them, but her eyes looked different this time. They looked… hopeful.

"Come with us, Pearl."

"You really think I can do this?"

"Yes, we do," said Grace.

"I don't have much, but I have a few things I'd like to bring with me. And I don't think I can face Mollie alone."

"Then go with her, Finn," said Grace. "I'll go back to the boat and let them know we'll have one more passenger."

Finn walked Grace a few steps away and kissed her. "We'll see you soon," he said and then whispered in her ear. "Did you just make that up about the harlot?"

"No—it's true," she whispered back. "Now go on," she nudged him. "Don't let her change her mind."

"Wait!" Pearl said as she walked over to Grace and Finn. The tears spilled freely from her eyes and she couldn't speak for a moment, trying to regain control.

Grace touched her arm. "It's all right, Pearl; take your time."

Pearl took a deep breath and finally spoke. "I need to tell you that from this moment on, my name is Katherine."

Chapter 45

Finn and Katherine were back on the Strand in a little over an hour.

"I don't know who was louder back there—Mollie yelling or Delilah wailing," said Finn.

"Mollie will never forgive me, but Delilah will come around eventually."

"What about the others?"

"They're probably relieved to see me go. I just need to make one more stop." She looked both ways before stepping down into the street.

Finn looked up at the building she was heading to. "Oh, crud," he said under his breath.

"I need to tell Roderick I'm leaving."

"He won't renege on your deal, will he?"

"No, and you don't have to go inside."

"I wasn't planning on it. You'd better hurry, though. We don't have much time."

"I won't be long." She walked on ahead of him.

Finn looked around the street, and noticed someone waving at him from the front of a store.

He couldn't help but smile at *La Longue Carabine*. He realized he needed a hat, too. Surely the little pistol sold something other than those fancy bowler hats. He headed back across the street.

The clerk grasped his hand and pumped it. "So glad you're still here, sir!"

"It's good to see you, Long Rifle."

The man laughed nervously and then cleared his throat. "Actually, it's Herbert." He lowered his voice. "But I noticed you must've found the place. Was that Miss Pearl with you?"

Finn nodded. "Long story, and I'm in a hurry. You wouldn't happen to have a hat similar to the one I had on when I saw you last, would you?"

"A Stetson? But it's woefully out of style. We have a few bowlers that didn't get soaked."

"I don't want a stylish hat; I want a hat to shade my head."

"You're impossible, but you're also the customer. Follow me." He turned around and walked inside the store. "We should have some cowboy hats back here somewhere."

Finn stepped around several people scrubbing the wood floors. "So you're not officially open yet?"

"We will be tomorrow, although some of the grocers were able to open today."

He carried a ladder to one of the shelves near the back and climbed up even with the highest two shelves. "Fortunately for you these weren't on display—they're some of the few items that didn't get wet. Black or gray?"

"Gray."

"What size?"

Finn ran his fingers through his hair. "7 and 1/4."

"You'd be surprised how many men don't know their hat size from one purchase to the next. They just come in and start trying on hats until they find one that fits well."

"My father's owns a dry goods store. I also know my neck size."

"I'm impressed. Try this one." He handed Finn a gray felt hat. "There's a mirror behind you."

Finn put the hat on his head and turned around and looked in the mirror.

"I can change the crown if you'd like. Just have to turn on the steamer."

"Don't have time." Finn turned his head one way and then the other. "You did good, Herbert. I like this one. What's your best price?"

"That's a Stetson… you know they don't come cheap."

"But they're woefully out of fashion on the island, remember? And you must not have been able to sell them, or they'd be down here drying out with the rest of this fashionable stuff."

Herbert frowned.

"How 'bout letting me have it at cost—at least you'll break even, and if folks ask me where I got this good-looking hat, I'll direct them to you."

"It does look handsome on you."

"Who knows… we may start a new fashion trend down here. You know what Pearl started calling me?"

"No… what?"

"Cowboy."

Herbert's eyes widened behind his glasses. "Give me five and we'll call it even… but don't forget to mention the store when people ask."

Finn paid him and wished him well.

He waited until he turned around before he grinned. He'd taken his second step out the door when something hit him hard in the gut, knocking the wind out of him. He fell to his knees.

"I knew it was you. Fancy meeting you here… Cowboy."

Hands grabbed him under his armpits and drug him around the corner of the building. He couldn't catch his breath.

"Nobody leaves my crew until I say so. And there's still plenty of work to be done around here."

Finn realized who the man was, but he couldn't seem to get enough air in his lungs to speak. "I… can't…"

"You can't what? See from under that big hat?" He knocked the hat off. "Is that better?"

Herbert came around the corner. "What's going on here, Jinks? That's a brand new hat."

"This isn't any of your business, Herbert. Go back inside."

Herbert disappeared.

Finn was on his hands and knees. "I can't go with you... I'm leaving town—they're waiting for me. I just got married—"

"Did you hear that Crete? He's leaving town, someone's waiting for him, and he just got married. I thought I'd heard every line in the book trying to get out of this duty the past few days, but you're the first to say you just got married. That's a good one," he said, laughing. Then he stopped. "You owe me two days of work... Cowboy."

"I don't owe you anything," Finn said, looking up. "What gives you the right—"

Jinks hit him in the mouth with the butt of his rifle, knocking Finn backwards.

"This here gun gives me the right. We're fixin' to go under martial law around here."

"Let him go, Jinks. He's telling you the truth."

Finn wiped the blood off his mouth and looked up to see Lucius standing on the boardwalk. Katherine and Herbert stood beside him. Other people had gathered behind them. Finn stood.

"The Sheriff said I could commandeer anybody at gunpoint or bayonet, if I needed to. He slipped away from me a couple of days ago—been avoiding his duty. Everybody's gotta help with the dead."

"He's not one of us, Jinks—he's just trying to get home."

The man looked at Finn. "You don't live here?"

Finn shook his head.

"Well, why didn't you say so?"

"I did."

"Well, what are you standing there for, Crete? Get him his hat!"

The man picked up his hat and handed it to him.

"I bought this fine hat at Herbert's store," Finn couldn't resist saying.

The man just stared at him like he was crazy, but Herbert stood there beaming.

"Sorry, Mr. Roderick," said Jinks. "We're having a hell of a time getting people to volunteer." He shook his head. "It's grisly— this job. It's the hardest thing we've ever done."

"I know, and we all appreciate what you're doing."

"Sorry," he mumbled to Finn before walking away.

"Nothing to see here folks," said Herbert, dispersing the people who had gathered.

Finn brushed off his hat and then looked at Lucius. "Seems like we've done this before, Roderick."

"But your face fared better than mine did."

Finn couldn't help but smile, then winced at stretching his busted lip. "I appreciate the help, though."

Lucius nodded. "Take care of her."

"I will."

Epilogue

Dalton, Texas… September 18th, 1900

Finn handed her the large envelope. Grace read the return address, which simply said, *H.C., Galveston, Texas.*

She looked up at Finn and smiled. "It's here!" she shouted in the house.

"What's here?" her mother asked, coming from the kitchen. Justin followed her holding a cup of coffee.

"Our marriage license—Daddy said he'd believe it when he saw it." She carefully tore open the end and pulled out the official-looking document covered in scroll work and calligraphy. "It's beautiful."

Allie reached for it. "Come out on the porch and let me read it to you, Justin. My eyes aren't what they used to be."

Grace and Finn followed her parents, each of them taking a seat on the porch off the dining room.

Finn looked around. "You know, this porch would make a good greenhouse for you, Mrs. Taylor. You wouldn't have to worry about your plants freezing in the winter."

"Momma, you should have seen the Greshams' house—she had a glass-covered conservatory on the east side, and it was right off their dining room, too! She grew all kinds of exotic plants year-round."

"Draw me some plans, Finn, and I'll consider it." Allie held the paper up to catch the sunlight and read, "State of Texas, County of

Galveston. To any Regularly Licensed or Ordained Minister of the Gospel, Jewish Rabbi, Judge of the District or Country Court, or any Justice of the Peace in and for Galveston County… Greeting: You are hereby Authorized to Solemnize the Rites of Matrimony Between Mr. Finn Samuel and Miss Grace Taylor and make due return to the Clerk of the County Court of said County within sixty days thereafter certifying your action under this license." Allie looked up. "Does that mean you have to go back?"

"Surely not," said Grace leaning over to read it.

"They'll have to hog tie me to go back there," said Finn.

Allie continued, "Witness my official signature and seal of office, at office in Galveston, the 9th day of September, 1900. And I can't decipher the clerk's signature, but I think I can read the preacher's name...."

Grace tried to grab for the certificate. Allie kept it away from her and swatted playfully at her hand.

"I can read it! Looks like… and I'm assuming the *R* in front stands for *Reverend* Henry Cohen. Oh, honey, I wished I'd been there. Did he do a good job?"

"Yes, Momma, he did. But you know you wouldn't have crossed that bay."

"You're probably right. And it took a tropical cyclone to get us off the ranch. We agonized until we found you in Houston, though. Your friend Marguerite sure had a pretty home. That was nice of her to invite all of us to stay with her. I think I could get used to having servants."

"Mother, that doesn't even sound like you!"

"Wait until you get old and tired, sweetie. And your other friend, Katherine—she had the most unusual-colored eyes. Now what kind of business was she in?"

Grace glanced at Finn. "Mostly charity work—she recently bought a house for a widow and her daughter in Galveston. And Marguerite asked her to accompany her around the state and country raising funds to help Galveston recover."

"Marguerite and Katherine. Who would be able to refuse those two beautiful women? What an exciting life they must lead."

Justin spoke up. "I bet you didn't expect to see Joseph and Jimmy in Houston either, did you, Finn."

"No, sir. That was a shock. I didn't even know they knew where I was—I assumed they thought I was down here in Dalton."

"Your family does check up on you every so often, Finn," said Allie. "Joseph sent a wire asking for you right after you left."

"That was the biggest shock—I hadn't even thought about Joseph selling the patents, but he was true to his word. He paid back every cent—course we don't own the rights to our inventions now, but maybe somebody else will be able to turn a profit with them." He looked at Grace. "It took almost losing Grace for me to realize that my worth and our security isn't in my bank account, but in God."

"That's right," said Allie. "We learned that the hard way, too. Have you decided what you're going to do with the money?"

Grace added, "We both need some new clothes, and Finn also needs to go back and get his things in Waco. But we're also thinking about using some of it to fix up the old adobe home place, if that's all right with you."

"So you're coming back to stay?" Allie looked hopeful.

Grace reached for Finn's hand. "We're coming home to stay. But if a cloud comes up, Momma, we're coming to the big house."

About the cover: The panoramic photo stretching from the back cover of the book to the front, courtesy of the Galveston Historical Foundation and Eloise Howell, was taken from the Walter Gresham House after the storm of 1900. The photographer faced east-southeast overlooking the ruins of Sacred Heart Catholic Church and the last remaining houses around 14th Street and Broadway, still many blocks away from the ocean. This photograph represents the phrase *swept clean* better than any other photo of the storm's aftermath the author found during her research. What used to be blocks upon blocks of houses leading up to the beaches in the background were completely swept clean by the hurricane's storm surge and devastating winds. When the photo is enlarged, the remaining pile of rubble of the destroyed Lucas Terrace Apartments can be seen in the background on 6th and Broadway Streets where Daisy Thorne and twenty-one others miraculously survived the storm. See more pictures, stories, and credits in the Author's Note.

The Last Key

Author's Note

What an exciting journey this story has taken me! I remember learning about Galveston's Great Storm of 1900 over twenty years ago during a short vacation to the island, and the story has fascinated me ever since. When I decided to use the storm as a backdrop in Grace and Finn's story, I read every book about Galveston I could get my hands on and discovered an even greater treasure when I learned about the history of this amazing city. I had no idea Galveston was the financial, cultural, social, and entrepreneurial capital of the South at the turn of the 20th Century. I've included a reference list of the books I read and continued to refer to while I was writing this story and hope this will spark some interest in further reading.

In *The Last Key*, I wanted to include as much true history as possible so I intertwined the fiction characters with real life events and people and their experiences. The names of actual people mentioned or used fictitiously in the story include Walter, Josephine, & Beulah Gresham, Walter Grover, Rabbi Henry Cohen, Daisy Thorne, Dr. Joe Gilbert, Rebecca Brown & daughters Bettie & Mathilda Sweeney, Betty Ballinger & cousin Hallie, Nicholas Clayton, Miss Russell, and Mollie Walters. Their true experiences were better than fiction, and I hope you'll want to learn more about them.

The three people I was most fascinated with were Rabbi Henry Cohen, Daisy Thorne, and Walter Grover. Based on what I read about them, I think I stayed true to their personalities in the fictionalized parts of their conversations.

Rabbi Cohen loved and helped people in general, no matter what their faith was or the type of life they lived. And two stories (of many recorded) that I used gave evidence to his character. He actually conducted a *Christian* graveside service for a prostitute, and in a separate incident he rescued a young girl that had been held against her will in the red-light district. I connected the two in this story, making Grace his initial link of involvement. You can read more about this amazing, but humble man in the book, *Kindler of Souls: Rabbi Henry Cohen of Texas*, University of Texas Press, Austin, 2007, written by his grandson and namesake, Rabbi Henry Cohen II.

Walter Grover sounded like such a down-to-earth individual who probably knew the island better than anyone else. And in spite of the horrific storm and the devastating aftermath, he loved Galveston Island and the Gulf of Mexico and continued to live out his days there.

I would love to have met Daisy Thorne Gilbert in real life. She sounded like such a beautiful, intelligent, and courageous woman. And the story of her romance with Dr. Joe Gilbert and his making his way to Galveston so quickly after the storm to find her could be a book in itself. Her survival during the hurricane was truly miraculous, so I wanted to share the before and after pictures of Lucas Terrace Apartments. The following photos include Daisy Thorne's actual notations (clockwise from the top): Our apartment, East front, sand hills here, Broadway [Street] at this side, South front.

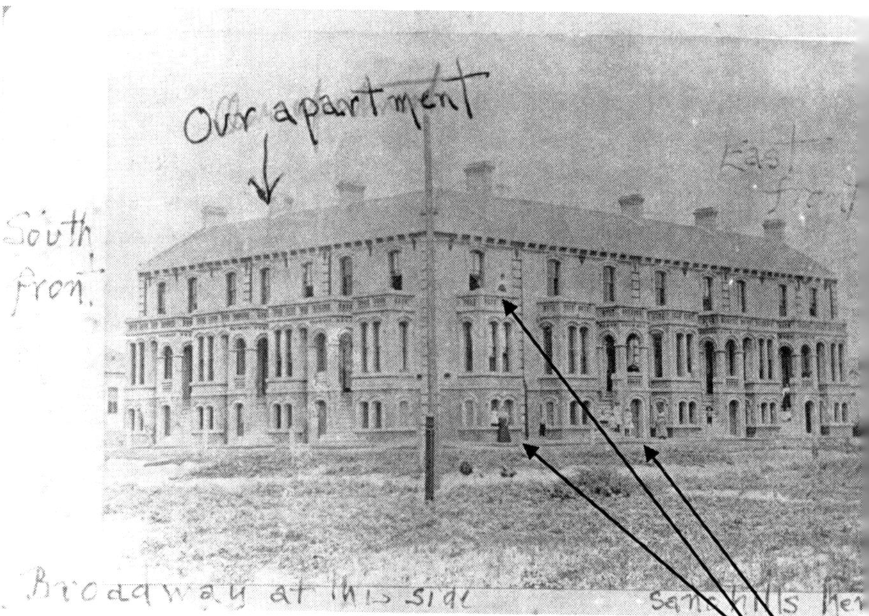

Courtesy of the Rosenberg Library, Galveston, Texas

You can see how large this brick building was when you see the size of the people posing in front.

The only part of the entire building that survived the storm was Daisy's second floor bedroom in the back of their apartment (see below). The photograph looks like it was taken from the backside of the apartment building facing south. A faded arrow at the lower right points to a sliver of the Gulf on the horizon, which used to be blocked from view by hundreds of houses, swept away by the storm.

Courtesy of the Rosenberg Library, Galveston, Texas

You can see some of Daisy Thorne's original notations and when they faded, she re-wrote them.

The photo below faces the front of what little was left of the Lucas Terrace Apartments where Daisy and twenty-one others survived the storm. God's hand of protection was on them that day.

Courtesy of Library of Congress, Prints & Photographs Division, LC-USZ62-123884

I broke my rule of minimal expository writing when it came to describing the Colonel Walter Gresham House on the following page, now known as the Bishop's Palace. This impressive structure has withstood every hurricane since its completion in 1893. Kudos to architect Nicholas Clayton!

Courtesy of Library of Congress, Prints & Photographs Division, HABS Tex, 84-GALV,26-1

If you ever get a chance to take the *Basement to Attic Tour* sponsored by the Galveston Historical Foundation, don't miss it. Photographs weren't allowed inside the house, but I took notes and made sketches throughout the two-hour tour. I felt like I'd stepped back in time, and the home's history is amazing. My favorite story the tour guide shared with us had to do with discovering which type of wood used in the house is considered the most expensive wood in today's market. I won't give it away, but I hope you'll visit this magnificent home and find out which one it is.

The following photo from the first landing shows the gorgeous hand-carved staircase and two of the three huge keyhole-shaped stained glass windows below the towering rotunda.

Courtesy of Library of Congress, Prints & Photographs Division, HABS Tex, 84-GALV,26-5

Galveston's Historical Foundation works diligently to preserve Galveston's history and its homes and buildings. Sadly, though, many of the structures I read about in researching the story are no longer there, whether by the hand of progress, subsequent storms, neglect, or even arsonists. But to see the community resurrect itself after suffering the worst natural disaster in our country's history is a testament to its citizens' strength and determination to survive and rebuild and even thrive again. The story of building the sea wall and substantially raising the elevation of over five hundred city blocks and the structures sitting atop them is a whole other story worth pursuing.

The following picture shows a small portion of the massive debris pile, in some places thirty feet high that stretched from one end of the island to the other after the storm. The camera faced west on Broadway Street, showing the front of the destroyed Sacred Heart Catholic Church and a block further, the Gresham mansion. The Greshams had a panoramic view of the storm's devastation from Josephine's art studio windows on the third floor turret just below the cone roof. The panoramic photo spanning the back and front of the cover of this book was probably taken from these windows.

Courtesy of the Rosenberg Library, Galveston, Texas

One of the benefits of writing is the process of learning about a particular subject, and in this case another exciting slice of Texas history. But what is even more satisfying in writing is what I learn about human nature, and especially about myself. One thought that really struck a chord with me is that too often we think that when life is going smoothly, that we must be in the center of God's will. But then how do we explain life's tragedies and heartaches, which come in varying degrees in all of our lives?

Last July my beautiful mother who lives with me was diagnosed with ALS or Lou Gehrig's disease. Last week I had to put down my seventeen-year-old dog. Next week I'll find out if my job as a school librarian has been cut next year since funding for education in Texas has tanked. But through it all I have the peace of God and assurance that my security & salvation is in Him.

Courtesy Rosenberg Library, Galveston, Texas

This photo was taken looking east at the intersection of Avenue L and 17th Street, the vicinity where the fictitious home of Lucius Roderick stood. This view is what Grace and Finn would actually have seen outside the door the morning after the storm.

Perseverance is one of the overriding themes throughout this book. In researching the word, I came across a quote by Jim Rohn*:

Don't wish it were easier; wish you were better.
Don't wish for less problems; wish for more skills.
Don't wish for less challenges; wish for more wisdom.

What a different perspective that is! And it made me realize that sometimes when we choose the easiest path, we've missed an opportunity to grow and are less prepared for hardships later. When we try to make things easier for our children now, we might have actually made it harder for them later.

What I've learned and am continuing to learn in life is that no matter what we're going through, God is with us giving us the strength to endure and even rise above our difficulties. I'm so grateful for His love and care. And I know this is preparing me not only for this brief life, but somehow for eternity beyond.

Thank you for continuing the journey of the Taylor Family Saga with me. Until the next one…

About the Author

The Last Key is Donna Van Cleve's fifth book in the Taylor Family Saga. She lives outside of Austin with her parents in an old-fashioned Victorian house with two porches, both of which are used regularly.

Reference List

Ashton Villa. Galveston Historical Foundation Web site. www.galvestonhistory.org. Accessed 5 August 2010.

Barnstone, Howard. *The Galveston That Was*. New York: Macmillan Co. 1966.

Bixel, Patricia Bellis and Elizabeth Hayes Turner. *Galveston and the 1900 Storm*. Austin: University of Texas Press. 2000.

Cohen, Rabbi Henry II. *Kindler of Souls: Rabbi Henry Cohen of Texas*. Austin: University of Texas Press. 2007.

Galveston & Texas History Center – Special Collections. Rosenberg Library. www.rosenberg-library.org/about/specialcoll.htm and www.gthcenter.org

Galveston Historical Foundation. *Bishop's Palace: Basement to Attic Tour*. Visited May 1, 2010. Tour Guide: Joseph Pellerin.

Galveston Historical Foundation & Eloise Howell. Panoramic photo taken from the Gresham's house. 1900.

Greene, Casey Edward. Head of Special Collections. Galveston & Texas History Center, Rosenberg Library, Galveston, Texas. Via email.

Greene, Casey Edward and Shelly Henley Kelly, ed. *Through a Night of Horrors: Voices from the 1900 Galveston Storm.* College Station: Texas A&M University Press. 2000.

Howell, Jay S. Assistant Director, Office of Institutional Effectiveness, The University of Texas Medical Branch, Galveston, Texas, for information found in the book, *The University of Texas Medical Branch at Galveston: A Seventy-five Year History by the Faculty and Students.* Austin: University of Texas Press. 1967.

Johnson, Frank W., et al. *A History of Texas and Texans Vol. 4.* Chicago: The American Historical Society. 1914. Google Books. http://books.google.com Accessed 21 Jul 2010.

Johnson, Jan. *Galveston in the Good Old Days: Infamous Postoffice Street.* www.twistedparrot.com/prostitutionpart2.htm Accessed Jul-Aug 2010.

Library of Congress Photographic Division. Historic American Buildings Survey Colonel Walter Gresham House. (HABS). www.loc.gov

Library of Congress Photographic Division. Galveston Disaster, Texas: house on Ave. N. http://www.loc.gov/pictures/item/2004680423/

Rohn, Jim. *Jim Rohn: America's Foremost Business Philosopher.* www.jimrohn.com.
*Quotes by Jim Rohn, America's Foremost Business Philosopher, reprinted with permission from Jim Rohn International c.2010. As a world-renowned author and success expert, Jim Rohn touched millions of lives during his 46-year career as a motivational speaker and messenger of positive life change. For more information on Jim and his popular personal achievement resources or to subscribe to the weekly Jim Rohn Newsletter, visit www.JimRohn.com.

Press Reference Library: Notables of the Southwest: Being the Portraits & Biographies of Progressive Men of the Southwest, Who Have Helped in the Development and History Making of This Wonderful Country. Los Angeles: Los Angeles Examiner. 1912. Google Books. http://books.google.com Accessed 21 Jul 2010.

Texas State Historical Association. *The Handbook of Texas Online.* www.tshaonline.org/handbook/online/search.html. Accessed December, 2009, June-July, 2010.

Weems, John Edward. *A Weekend in September.* New York: Holt. 1957. (Eleventh printing, 2008).

Wright-Gidley, Jodi and Jennifer Marines. *Galveston: A City on Stilts.* Charleston, SC: Arcadia Publishing. 2008.

LaVergne, TN USA
28 February 2011
218160LV00001B/5/P

9 781936 816019